_____Typhoon

ALSO BY JOHN GORDON DAVIS

Hold My Hand I'm Dying
Cape of Storms
Operation Rhino
Years of the Hungry Tiger
Taller Than Trees
Leviathan

Typhoon

A Novel by **John Gordon Davis**

E. P. DUTTON New York

to Max Lucas

_____**Part one**

In the summer in Hong Kong the sun beats down oily humid hot on the South China Sea and the harbor and the narrow teeming streets and the apartment blocks and the resettlement blocks and the tenements with cocklofts on the rooftops and the squatter shacks cut into the mountains and the factories and the godowns and the shops and the neon signs scrambling on top of each other, and the sweatshops and the fleshpots and the freighters from around the world and the junks junks junks and the bars bars bars. And the people; people everywhere, hurrying, crowding, working, money money money, and all the time the stamping of pile drivers and the roaring of the bulldozers chopping down the mountains to reclaim more land for the teeming people.

In the summer the great typhoons come across the China Sea, and the hot low sky turns black, and then come the winds with a dragon's roar, and the sea is thundering through the famous harbor and crashing down the waterfront streets, and the rain comes flying, hammering down thick as your finger, and the floods and landslides come roaring down the steep jungled mountains, and a lot of people die. There are too many people.

This hot day in May a big junk was tied up to the public pier in Central District of Hong Kong. She looked like any other of the thousands of junks in the harbor, but a large crowd was gathered round her, and a television crew was there.

A reporter was standing in front of the camera, and saying, "But this junk is something special. For she is not built of wood, or any other conventional boat-building material. She is built of . . *concrete*." He raised his eyebrows. "Ordinary builders' cement. And here is the *un*ordinary man who built her."

The camera rolled back to take in a tall, tanned man in shorts and several days' growth of beard.

"Mr. McAdam," the reporter said, "this may sound a silly question, but how does a boat made of concrete *float*?"

Jake McAdam replied, "It's the question most people ask. Particularly the Chinese fishermen, for whom I designed the junk. 'A boat of stone,' they say. And the answer is: it floats the same way as a boat made of steel floats."

"And you built her yourself?"

"Myself and my boatman, Mr. Wong." He indicated a short stocky Chinese with one squint eye: the camera swung onto him and Wong blushed furiously and turned away.

"And how on earth does one build a boat with concrete, Mr. McAdam?"

"That's exactly what my bank manager wants to know." The reporter grinned. "First you build a frame out of ordinary plumbers' piping. Over this frame you stretch several layers of chicken wire. Then you mix up a big mess of cement and sand. And then, in one day, you plaster the netting wire tightly with cement. And there's your hull. The deck is made the same way. And the fishing holds, and the engine room. All the bulkheads. Even the water and fuel tanks are made out of cement. And there you are."

"You've just come back to harbor from your sea trials. Are you pleased?"

"Delighted. I took her deep sea about three hundred miles. We met some big seas. She handled beautifully. And she's much faster than an ordinary junk."

"Why?"

"Because she's much lighter than a wooden junk, which has heavy ribs and beams. And lighter than steel. That's a most important feature. Fishermen with concrete junks will travel faster and use less fuel. I've also made the hull a little slimmer than usual, giving her a much better hull-speed. She's also stronger than a wooden boat, and much cheaper to maintain because there is no caulking to worry about, no wood to rot, no nails to rust. And, of course, she's much cheaper to build. Cement and chicken wire don't cost much. Timber costs a fortune these days. This same junk"—he pointed at his vessel—"built of timber, would cost the Chinese fisherman three times as much."

"Mr. McAdam, what is your purpose in publicizing this boat? For the last few days, I believe, you've been touring the fishing harbors showing her off?"

"Yes," McAdam said emphatically. "And I'm going to continue making a noise about her. Because every year a thousand new junks are built in Hong Kong. How many thousands of tons of timber is that? How many trees have to be cut down? How many *forests*?" He waved his hand earnestly, launching into his theme. "And

4

that's just for tiny Hong Kong. Think of China, the most populated nation in the world—how many forests must it cut down for the *hundreds* of thousands of new junks it builds every year? Then think of the rest of teeming Asia. In twenty-odd years' time the world population is going to almost double. How many fishing boats must there be to feed the billions? And how many forests must be cut down to build them? We've been spendthrift, gobbling up the world's resources as if the well would never run dry." He paused for emphasis. "The forests are vital to our environment. They make the oxygen we breathe. They're the home of a host of creatures. And they're beautiful. Ways *must* be found to protect the balance of nature, upon which our very lives depend. And building concrete boats is one of those ways."

The reporter said, "And are you now going to start manufacturing concrete boats on a large scale?"

"Yes, but I'm not so interested in the business side of it—I'm interested in selling people the *idea*. I built this boat on a remote piece of beach. Without electricity and without much fresh water. That's how easy it is. I'm now going to build a proper boatyard, yes. But what I really want to do is get the *idea* taking root." He pointed toward China. "I want to persuade the Communist Chinese to start. The Thais. The Vietnamese. The Koreans."

He could have gone on, but the reporter had enough footage. Soon the crowd began to disperse.

Jake McAdam lived in an apartment that looked down the steep mountain over the roofs of many other apartment blocks and old Chinese tenements with multicolored laundry hanging out of the windows on bamboo poles, and then the godowns along the wharves with the cargo junks tied up to each other and the harbor with the freighters from around the world and the ferries and the ocean liners and the American warships; then, across the harbor, the massive concrete jungle of Kowloon. At night the lights were a fairyland, shining on the water in deep stripes and sparkles of all colors, and the window lights were hazy glows. It was a magnificent, expensive view; the apartment block was called Dragon Court.

At four o'clock that afternoon McAdam left Wong in charge of the junk at the public pier and took a taxi back to his apartment. It was the first time he had been home in ten days.

In the corner of the living room was an iron spiral staircase. At the top was a door leading into the apartment above, which McAdam also owned. It was a womanless place. The windows were all closed; it was hot and stuffy. His footsteps sounded loud as he went opening windows. There were no ornaments. But on the wall was one large portrait of a very beautiful Chinese girl. He had painted it himself. And it was very good. But he did not paint any more these days. He had many other paintings, but they were locked away upstairs, in the apartment at the top of the spiral staircase.

He went into the kitchen, got a beer out of the refrigerator, snapped the cap off. He walked down the passage to his study to look for mail. The floor seemed to be heaving gently under his feet, because of his long time on the junk. The study floor was shining but the desk was a mess of papers and books, for the make-cleanee amah knew she should not touch papers. But there was a big neat pile of mail. He switched on the air conditioner and took a swig out of the beer bottle, then stood at the desk flicking through the letters.

There were several from his banks, which he did not care to open. Tomorrow. Then there was an invitation to a cocktail party for that very night. From "The Ladies of the American Mess," to meet Ms. Vanessa Storm Williams.

Jake McAdam smiled. He didn't know who Ms. Williams was, but the parties of the American Mess girls were always good. They lived in an adjacent apartment block, below and to the side, and from his windows he could see theirs. They usually did not bother to draw their curtains and from his desk in his office, without trying, he often saw them walking around in the nude, or in their underwear, which was always a pretty sight. They were good-looking girls. McAdam glanced down at their windows now, and he saw something he had never had the good fortune to see before: a girl on the living-room carpet, making love.

He could not see who the man was. She was on top of him, long legs astride him, and her blond hair swinging around. McAdam stared at them an astonished moment, then for another moment he wrestled with his conscience; then he sat down on the corner of his desk philosophically and watched them.

But it was almost over. After a moment she slowed her movements, and then she stopped; she crouched limply on top of him, then slowly toppled off. She rolled onto her back on the carpet with her arms and legs and hair outflung.

With a smile, McAdam picked up his telephone. He consulted a list. Then he dialed a number, and looked back at the window. A moment later he saw the girl get up off the carpet and disappear.

"Hello?" she said.

"Hello, is that Olga?"

"No, Olga's at work, can I give her a message?"

He could imagine her standing naked at the telephone, sweating.

"This is Jake McAdam—I've just found an invitation to a cocktail party tonight at the Mess, and I've phoned up to accept with thanks."

"Oh, good. I've heard about you, Mr. McAdam, I look forward to seeing you."

Not as much as I look forward to seeing you properly, madam.

"Is the party in honor of anybody's birthday?"

"No. It's my party, actually. To meet the important people of Hong Kong."

"And I qualify?"

"Oh, yes, you qualify."

"Well." He grinned. "Welcome to Hong Kong, Miss Williams."

2

Usually the American Mess parties were elegant humdingers. Theirs was a large old-fashioned, five-bedroomed apartment built in the Victorian days when apartments were like houses, with a long wide veranda and a big sunroof; often the girls sunbathed topless up there, and there was always a pretty array of scant female underwear drying on the lines. There were about ten semipermanent members of the Mess, but at any given time half of them were away living with boyfriends and there were always new faces. Hong Kong was a crossroads. Usually the American Mess parties flushed out the beautiful people of Hong Kong.

But this one was different. The front door was open and as he approached he heard only the muted sound of polite conversation. He walked in. There were only about thirty people, and most of them seemed to be men. He stood at the living-room door, looking for somebody to pay his respects to. He saw Derek Morrison, his bank manager, and thought, What the hell's Derek doing here? A Chinese waiter was passing with a tray of drinks and McAdam took a glass of beer. He saw Mervin Katz, of the Royal Hong Kong Observatory, and Kurt Marlowe, the American pilot who was going around with Olga at the moment. There was Jack Evans of the Fire Department, and his wife, Monica. Then a hand fell on his shoulder and he turned around. "Hello, Champion!"

"The seldom-seen man." Bernard Champion beamed. "I saw you on television."

"What qualifies you for this party? It's only for the important people."

"I'm a very important representative of the police. But tell me—how were the sea trials, really?"

"Beautiful. She handles like a yacht."

"Thank God."

"What kind of party is this? Who is this Vanessa Williams anyway?"

"Vanessa *Storm* Williams, please. Some kind of high-powered Yankee journalist come to sort out Hong Kong overnight."

There was Olga coming toward him. "I saw you on six o'clock television. Handsome brute, aren't you?"

"Hello, Olga."

"Come and meet your hostess." She took his elbow.

"I'll be back in a minute, Champ," he said.

"No, you won't," said Olga.

He saw her on the veranda, talking. She was tall and her blond hair was perfectly groomed up on top of her head and she wore a white low-cut dress that hung off her shoulders; she was laughing at something and her mouth was wide and sensual and her blue eyes were sparkling, and he thought she was beautiful.

"How do you do, Mr. McAdam! I've heard so much about you I know you already."

"Who actually do you write for?"

"I'm freelance. Until recently I wrote for the *New York Times*. Before that I worked for a group that owned a bunch of glossy women's magazines. I was one of those snotty ladies who wrote about 'Every Woman's Right to Have Multiple Orgasms.' And worried our readers sick about how a grown-up orgasm is vaginal, not clitoral, which is nonsense, by the way, in case it worried you."

"Orgasms are clitoral? That's definite now?"

"Oh, yes, the clitoris is back *in*." She added, "I believed it for a while because *I* have vaginal orgasms."

"You do?"

8

"But then I'm an unreliable case because I can have one in a dentist's chair if I put my mind to it."

He burst out laughing. He was going to ask her about the multiple orgasms, then he changed it in his mouth. "What aspects of Hong Kong do you want to write about?"

Her mood changed immediately.

"How about having lunch with me Friday next week?"

He was taken by surprise. "I was going to ask you to dinner."

"I can't until next week. Lunch, Friday? So we can talk quietly."

"Fine."

"About everything. What makes this place tick. But the thing I'm interested in most," she said, "are the Triad Societies."

He drew on his cigarette, nodded. "They'll be hard to investigate. They're secret, you know."

"I know."

"And deadly. But so secret we don't know much about them. Except they're into every type of organized crime. And their tentacles have spread around the world."

She said, "Are they more powerful than the Mafia?"

"In my opinion, yes. Much more. We know who the Mafia are. What they're into. The only trouble is proving it in a court of law. But with the Triads? We don't know who they are. They're in every walk of life. And the Triads are all over the world. Wherever there're Chinese communities. And that's everywhere."

She nodded. "The American police tell me their power is on the increase."

"Dramatically. They've moved into Europe in a big way with heroin and other narcotics. London and Amsterdam—"

"And in America."

"Indeed. They're muscling in on Mafia territory. And anybody who challenges the Mafia has to be extremely powerful. They've taken the London underworld by storm—and the police. The European police forces don't know what's hit them. They don't understand the Chinese. The Chinese mentality. The clannishness and secretiveness. And"—he shook his head—"their cleverness. You've got to be a Chinese to understand. Or an experienced Hong Kong policeman." He shrugged. "But I'm afraid you'll find our Anti-Triad Bureau not very helpful. They'll only speak in generalities. They know a lot, but they also know there's a helluva lot more they don't know. And most of what they do know they can't prove in a court of law under the laws of evidence."

9

She said, "You used to be a senior policeman, didn't you?"

At first he was surprised. Then he realized that Vanessa Storm Williams was the kind of journalist who would come to a party with enough notes on her guests to have them all eating out of the palm of her hand, and quickly.

"Yes. But I quit nearly nine years ago. At the grand old age of thirty-one."

"Why?"

"Personal reasons."

She let it go. "And now you're a successful businessman."

"Better say that quietly: my bank manager's here, and he'll burst into nervous hysterical laughter."

She grinned. "And a prominent conservationist. Do you belong to Friends of the Earth?"

"Yes. Do you?"

"Friends of the Earth and the Appalachian Trail Conference and some others."

He was astounded. She just didn't look the type. "Great! Have you done any walking in the Appalachians?"

"From Maine to Georgia." She added, "I'm tougher than your average blond broad with big tits."

"Christ." He was really impressed. "All two thousand miles?"

"All two thousand one hundred and fourteen. Have you?"

"I've only done about five hundred miles of it." It was hard to imagine her, reeking of sweat, slogging over those mountains in hiking boots with a fifty-pound backpack. "How long did it take you?"

"Six months. Five hundred miles is plenty. Six months is a long time to go without getting laid."

He threw back his head and laughed. Hell, he liked her. He felt for his cigarettes and offered her the pack. She took one. He held his lighter out to her and as she bent forward, he could see down the top of her dress. She was not wearing a brassiere and her breasts were big and firm and her nipples were brown against the white. Then she straightened up.

"Enjoy that, Mr. McAdam?"

"I'm sorry."

"Like hell you are." She pulled the top of her dress up a little. She gave him her dazzling smile. "Lunch on Friday, then?" And she left him standing there as she crossed the crowded room to join Bernard Champion. It was a few minutes before he realized that he still didn't know who had sent her to Hong Kong, or what she had come for.

Bernard Champion took a swallow of his whisky and breathed into his glass, and it made a weary sound.

"I'm the *only* person you should pay any attention to on the subject of corruption. Don't"—he jerked his head—"listen to McAdam." He shook his head anxiously at her, in difficulties where to begin for the uninitiated. "Listen . . . Hong Kong set up a branch of the police force called the Anti-Corruption Bureau. And all McAdam could say was, 'Putting the police in charge of anti-corruption is like putting a rabbit in charge of a lettuce.' *That* shows how prejudiced he is."

She said, "Is Jake antipolice?"

"On the contrary. He's just an idealist. In a less than perfect world." He groped for words. "Hong Kong is imperfect. But it's a perfect success story! It's unique. It's a capitalist bastion on the Red China coast, for heaven's sake. Such a contradiction is bound to have imperfections—but it *works.* Listen: here's an example. Print this story." He paused for effect, then went on, "There's a Chinese gentleman in Hong Kong called Herman Choi. He's a multimillionaire in any currency. He donates huge sums of money every year to charities. Many good works. Have you heard of him?"

Indeed she had. But she shook her head. She did not want to spoil his story. "Go on."

"It is not surprising, therefore," Champion went on, "that this philanthropic gentleman should be rewarded for his good works by getting a knighthood. And I have it on the grapevine that in the Queen's Birthday Honors that is what he is going to get. Homan Choi is about to become *Sir* Herman Choi."

She nodded encouragingly. She had been in Hong Kong five days and she had heard this, too.

"However," Champion said, "apart from his philanthropy, which he can well afford, Sir Herman Choi is also a big wheel in the 14K Triad Society. And he is one of the world's biggest traffickers in narcotics. Heroin."

She feigned surprise. "Christ!"

"Exactly," Champion said. "We can't prove it. And you can't quote me. But the police know it. The question is, Why do we knight this blackguard?"

He looked at her with brown earnest eyes. She said, "Go on. Why?"

"Part of the answer is that under the law a man is presumed innocent until proved guilty, and even more so if we can't even get him *into* court, let alone try him. The rest of the answer is—" He paused. "This crown colony exists for one reason only. Money! And the fact is that without the donations from the Mister Bigs of our Triad Societies most of our charities would go bang. The Triads relieve our finance secretary of a lot of bother with his budget every year. Every million dollars donated is another million that dear government hasn't got to contribute. Which helps our finance secretary get *his* knighthood in due course. And Ho-man Choi has let it be known that if he doesn't get his knighthood this year his donations will cease. So. Sir Herman it is to be. Print that. And," he looked hard at her, "consider what a poor flatfoot Chinese constable on the beat thinks about that. *Print* that," he said again, "because it's the only weapon we have against the bastard. There're no more drug traffickers in China, d'you know that? And opium was the downfall of China. Because Mao Tse-tung shot them all. That's the only way to stop the bastards. But we British? We give them knighthoods."

"That's a good quote."

"I'm telling you this so that when you investigate corruption in this colony you get things in perspective. If I can help you I'll be pleased to do so. Because you're writing about my home country, for practical purposes. And I'm bloody proud of it." He glared at her. "It's a roaring success story. For all its warts. It's got the highest standard of living in the whole of Asia. The factory worker, the coolie, the fisherman, they all work like hell and they're paid well. Trade increases twenty-five percent per year! Everybody prospers, from the lowest to the highest. This is a very conscientious government," he ended, "of a very difficult place."

"Conscientious for whom? For the ordinary people of Hong Kong? Or for the big taipans? Big business, the banks and the industrialists?"

Bernard Champion snapped, "The banks and taipans are the only reason for Hong Kong's existence. It's they who provide all the employment for the people."

"And the Triads? How does official corruption tie up with them?"

"It doesn't," he said. "The Triads are a phenomenon all of their own. There is no connection." His tone got hard. "Except this:

Triad power has increased enormously in recent years and has spread worldwide. And why? Because the Hong Kong police have been *emasculated*. The Hong Kong police have been made the scapegoat of so-called corruption purges! Experienced policemen have been hounded out of office, driven to retirement left, right and center. Their morale is low, their efficiency as a police force in this dog-eat-dog place is diminished! And crime has increased as a consequence—and the Triads . . ."

Vanessa nodded seriously, her eyes lowered as if she were trying to commit all this to memory. But behind her lashes, she was scanning the room, searching for McAdam.

There was a babble of voices, laughter, cigarette smoke. The invitation had read 7–9 P.M., but it was ten o'clock already and nobody seemed to have left.

"Do you," a voice said suddenly beside McAdam, "think I'm *eee*-vil?"

He looked down at Monica Evans. She had piercing green eyes, slanted upward, and big freckled breasts with a deep tight cleavage. "*That* little prick"—she pointed a long mauve fingernail across the room at her husband, Jack—"thinks I'm *eeee*-vil."

"Did he say why?"

She looked at him with her green eyes narrowed. "Say, Mc-Adam, why haven't I ever screwed you?"

"Because you never told me you cared."

"I don't care a damn. But *that* little prick"—she pointed her long fingernail again—"complains I've screwed *every*body. That I'm *eeee*-vil." She turned and looked up at him. "Why don't we put the record straight? And have a *mad* affair. And really give him something to complain about."

"I don't think so," McAdam said regretfully. "Jack-the-Fire" —he indicated with his head—"is a friend of mine."

She digested this. "You got to be the only bastard in the whole world who'd let that stop him. You know what, McAdam? You love 'em and leave 'em. But at least you don't bullshit them."

"Thanks, Monica."

"Don't mention it." She looked at him unsteadily. "Say, Mac, when are we all going to go swimming bare-arsed off your new boat I saw on television?"

"Any time you like."

"To-*night*!" she announced. "I feel like being *eeee*-vil!" She shot a finger at him. "Don't go away, McAdam—I'm going to organize a party."

Harry Howard was only fifty years old, but he looked about sixty, his face lined with the worries of thirty years of making a fortune in the cut-throat textile business and stock exchange, and coarsened with drinking too much to relieve the worry that he might lose it.

"What's good on the exchange, Harry?" McAdam said above the noise.

Harry Howard looked up at him. "What," he asked, "am I doing at this party? Never heard of the woman."

"Isn't she worth looking at, though?"

"Wants to know all about the problems of industry in this godforsaken place. Management. Import-export. Shipping problems. Personnel. Income tax. Employment of women. You name it, she wants to know about it. Got me taking her to lunch next week," he ended, mystified.

McAdam raised his eyebrows.

Harry Howard said, "Smart as a whip. What profit-sharing schemes do I have? Worker participation in management? Industrial conciliation? Export quotas? Overseas protective tariffs? Competition with China? The Common Market?" He waved his drink. "Had me nailed down in two minutes, promising her a breakdown on the whole fucking Far East economy." He shook his head. "What a powerhouse. Wouldn't like to be on the wrong side of her." He added, bemused, "What tits."

McAdam smiled widely. "What's good on the stock exchange, Harry?"

Harry turned and focused on him unsteadily. He took a gulp of his drink. Then his eyes bulged and he announced aggressively: "I'm going to get laid. Want to come along?"

"I think you should go home."

"I'm going to go to King Winky's an' get laid," Harry said. "Why don't you come?"

"Where're your car keys, Harry?" McAdam held out his hand.

Harry blinked at him. "Where'd I leave the car?"

McAdam patted Harry's jacket pocket. He slipped his hand inside and got the keys. "I'll get them back to you tomorrow."

Harry blinked at him. He took a gulp of his drink, then glared around. "All right, I'm going to King Winky's now."

"Okay, Harry."

Harry Howard looked at him. His bloodshot eyes looked almost sober again.

"The Lucky Man," he said.

"What?" McAdam said.

Harry Howard took a big breath.

"The Lucky Man Development Company. You asked me what's good on the exchange."

"Thanks, Harry."

He glowered. "Still a secret. Chinese outfit. Friends of mine. Into everything. Particularly real estate. Now they're turning themselves into a public company to raise capital." He looked at McAdam, steady for a moment. "The news won't break for a month. . . . When it does there'll be a queue a mile long all screaming to buy. Boss-man worked for me for years. Made a fucking fortune out of me. He owes me plenty of favors." He swayed. "I can get you a block of shares at par." He added, "Double your money in a year."

McAdam's mind was working fast, juggling overdrafts. "Thanks, Harry."

Harry swayed, looking at him; he started to add something, then he muttered, "Phone me when I'm sober." He added, "Shouldn't have told you at all. Trouble is I like you."

He knew Harry Howard wouldn't tell him anything when he was sober. "Tell me now, Harry."

"The boss-man knows a lot of people in the right places. . . . He's acquired a lot of valuable building sites. . . . And he's about to start building some very big apartment blocks. And that's all I'm going to tell you. Now I'm going to King Winky's."

McAdam handed him his keys.

It was a glorious night. The junk lay at anchor in the middle of Repulse Bay. There was a moon shining big and bright, the sea was silver and black and it was sultry hot. Two hundred yards away the long curved beach was silver in the moonlight, and the lights of the apartments twinkled through the dark palms and trees.

McAdam climbed up the swimming ladder onto the deck of his junk, dripping, naked. The cassette tape recorder was playing. There were clothes and glasses everywhere. There were the faraway noises of splashing and laughing from near the beach. He stood on the deck in the moonlight looking at the sparkling wedge of sea, the sky full of stars, the mountains brooding low and black and beautiful. And out there, the South China Sea. And his beautiful boat lying in the middle of it, perfect, strong, and ready to take him anywhere. Anywhere at all, to the Philippines, San Francisco, the Mediterranean. Oh, yes, soon he would do it. While the world was still beautiful. Before all the oceans were covered in oil, and the ocean beds killed by sewage and industrial waste, before all the skies were clouded with gasoline fumes and industrial smoke. He looked at his boat, with pleasure, in the moonlight; then he picked up a towel and draped it round his waist, went down the hatch and got a cold can of beer out of the refrigerator in the cabin. Then he lit a cigarette and went back up onto the wheel deck. A woman was coming up the swimming ladder, blond hair plastered wet against her head.

"Hello."

Vanessa Williams smiled. "Hi." She stood there in the moonlight, twisting the water out of her hair, the water running down her big breasts and over her belly, glistening in her pubic hair.

"Can I get you a drink?" There was splashing as some people dived off the swimming raft two hundred yards away.

"I've got one somewhere." She picked up a glass. Her legs were long and strong and perfectly shaped. He wondered if her knees were a little red from the carpet that afternoon.

He took a big swallow of his beer. He looked at her eyes, studiously avoiding her naked body. She lifted the glass to her mouth. He almost nerved himself into making a move at her. Then didn't. He cleared his throat.

"About these multiple orgasms you used to write about?"

She looked at him over the rim of her glass, taking a long slow sip, her eyes twinkling in the moonlight.

"That's a corny approach if ever I heard one, McAdam. Tell you what. Let's skip the preliminaries. And I'll show you."

He was taken aback for a moment. Then he smiled with nervous relief. He took her hand quickly. There were people swimming back toward the boat now. He hurried her down the hatch steps, into the saloon, toward his aft cabin, and opened the door. He led her in. He closed the door behind them, then locked it. They could hear splashing near the boat. He turned around and looked at her.

He took her in his arms, shaking, her breasts pressed against him, urgently feeling her body, fumbling, and her flesh was cool and wet and smooth and soft; she was still grinning as he kissed her hard, then her hand went to his loins and she took his hard penis and rubbed it against her wet pubic triangle, and all he wanted was to get her on the bunk and throw himself on top of her and push her firm thighs apart and thrust up into her warm wet body and he was trembling. He broke the kiss and began to push her urgently toward the bunk, and she was grinning as she said, "Easy, boy . . . lie down. On the deck."

He smiled shakily and got himself back under control. He lowered himself to the deck. Onto his back. She stood there over him, looking down at him, amused. "At sea a long time, were you?" Her long golden legs were astride, her hands on her hips, her belly and breasts towering over him, glistening with water in the moonlight shining in through the porthole. She stood there a long moment looking down at his body, then suddenly she got down on her knees. She knelt beside him, then lifted his penis in her cool hand. Then she leaned slowly, slowly toward it. He lay there watching her, breathing hard, trying to keep control; she leaned forward until her mouth was six inches from his penis, and he could feel her warm breath, then she stopped, her mouth poised, partly open, her eyes heavy, staring, her breathing hard; for a long moment more she knelt there in the moonlight, and he lay, watching her, desperately waiting: then she gave a moan and sank her mouth deep over his penis.

And later, on top of her, his arms straight, resting on the heels of his palms so he could look down at her body, thrusting hard in and out of her, her white breasts lolling heavy on her golden chest, her long legs wide open and straight and half up in the air, her eyes closed and her mouth half open, her arms flung wide on the deck, palms up, abandon all over her beautiful face, he thought it was the most exciting experience of his life. She was not making love to him, she was reveling, oblivious to everything but her lust.

A lot of other things happened that bright moonlit night. Twenty miles away five young Chinese males were swimming the fifteen miles across Mirs Bay from the shores of China toward the island of Hong Kong, mouths gasping, eyes fixed on the distant black silhouette of Kat O Chau Island. A snake-junk belonging to Vacations-in-Happiness-and-Tranquillity set sail from the muddy harbor of the Portuguese colony of Macao at the mouth of the River Pearl, bound for the archipelago of Hong Kong forty miles away, with forty-eight Chinese men and women packed down in her black fishing holds. A total of $17 million was lost and won at illegal gambling places at games of fan-tan, roulette and Mah-Jongg. The usual average of 3.1 people committed suicide. The parents of Mui Sai-sai, who was aged seven, sold her into concubinage to Mr. Chan Kit-ling for $1,000. A freighter from Singapore put into Hong Kong harbor carrying a substantial cargo of toothpaste and pickles and coffee, and contained invisibly in each sealed tube and jar were plastic capsules of pure heroin. One hundred and twenty-seven Hakka men and women stood sifting a total of seventeen tons of human excreta out of nineteen sewers to put on their paddy fields as fertilizer. A fishing junk from Thailand chugged through Hong Kong's black islands towing five tons of raw opium in big plastic bales behind her under the water. Lam Fat-li, who was doing very well as a clerk in the Hong Kong & Shanghai Bank, was robbed by three Chinese youths at knife point of his wristwatch and $5 while he was sitting on a bench cuddling with Miss Nancy Ho. Mr. Choi Ho-man, otherwise known as Herman Choi, O.B.E., held a dinner party for the leaders of the Boy Scouts and Girl Guides and the Society for the Blind and Physically Handicapped to discuss fund-raising measures. Man Lo-ling, a Communist fat cat who ran the Middle Kingdom Import-Export Agency, held a stag party for some of his business associates, serving stewed dog and monkey brains followed by a sex act by two American girls sent over by King Winky. A Royal Hong Kong Marine Police launch sighted the Thai trawler and decided to check it out, and the trawler crew cut the ropes dragging the bales of opium, noting exactly where they sank. In a tenement apartment Mr. Kwan was busy bleaching the print off one thousand American $1 bills while his friend Mr. Chan was happily working the little Itaglia printing press printing $100 on to each of them. Herman Choi received a coded telephone call at his bedside from a Chinese lady friend of his wife's canceling a dinner invitation for the next night, which meant that the Thai trawler had had to cut the ropes because of the Marine Police, and

Herman Choi replied that the dinner should be postponed until the night after tomorrow if that suited, which meant send the divers down the night after tomorrow if the coast is clear. Harry Howard went to King Winky's and got laid. Jake McAdam and Vanessa Williams made love.

Part two

Two thousand miles away, over the warm Pacific, a vast mass of warm, moist air was moving from all directions across the sea in a long, slow, clockwise curve with the rotation of the earth; and as the air moved it slowly sucked moisture up out of the warm sea. Where the masses of air came together they were rushing upward, because of their warmth, sucking up moisture all the way, and as the air rose it expanded in the lower atmospheric pressure, and as it did so it was cooled down a little; and as it cooled the moisture in the rising air began to condense and clouds began to form.

At first these clouds were only misty white and gray. Then, as they rose higher and expanded and cooled more, the moisture began to condense more and more, and now the clouds were turning darker, and now the moisture was condensing into tiny drops of water, and it began to fall. At first, for a long time, it fell only very finely, drifting down out of the darkening, rising clouds; then it began to fall more heavily, and more heavily still, down on the warm Pacific in the moonlight.

---4

At six o'clock every morning, before first light, her alarm clock rang and she was instantly awake, no matter how late she had gone to sleep. All the apartment blocks were in darkness, the harbor still; just the lights of the freighters at anchor and the neon lights of Kowloon silently shone in rainbows on the sea. She got up immediately.

First, naked, she did the ten basic exercises for women in the middle of the living room. Then she went to the bathroom and sponged herself off with her bucket of cold water, for there was a drought in Hong Kong and the water mains were turned on only every fourth day. Then she drank a pint of fresh California orange juice, ate a container of yogurt and one boiled egg and swallowed a vitamin pill. Then she left the American Mess in the sunrise and set off briskly down the steep winding roads of Mid-levels toward

Central, to the government Information Services Library, which was open twenty-four hours a day to members of the press. There she read old newspaper files. She sat in the library in the Chinese dawn and wrote in her Gregg shorthand:

"True that Hong Kong is governed by the Hong Kong & Shanghai Bank, Jardine-Matheson, the Jockey Club and His Excellency the Governor, in that order. But also true that Peking does not want Hong Kong governed any other way. Because Hong Kong is China's window on the world; China earns most of her foreign exchange through Hong Kong. Because China does much of her espionage through Hong Kong; it enables her to put the screws on Britain. Because Hong Kong *suits* China. Tomorrow China may change her mind, tomorrow there may be another power struggle in Peking. Tomorrow Peking could capture Hong Kong with a telephone call. Meantime, Hong Kong's Chinese know a bargain when they see it, and they make money while the sun shines. Hong Kong—Borrowed Place, Borrowed Time.

"Only Mao wanted to spoil it. They weren't enough, the Long March, the Great Thought Reform Campaigns, the Hundred Flowers Campaign and the Great Leap Forward. Finally he launched the Great Proletarian Cultural Revolution to remake man in his Communist image, to ensure there were worthy successors to his Communist Revolution. Put more crudely, the Cultural Revolution was a power struggle to get rid of his political enemies in the Chinese Communist Party.

"It spread to Hong Kong, too, and for six months the Communists rioted against the British in the streets. Then, his party purified, Mao at last let the Great Proletarian Cultural Revolution grind down, and let the pragmatists get back to the business of making China money.

"Mao released 800 million customers on the world, and Hong Kong got back to business as usual.

"And after Mao died, the Peking pragmatists really took over. Hong Kong booms now as it has never boomed before. The stock markets are wild. The investment money is flooding in from Europe and America, cashing in on the great Chinese money-mad mentality—work like hell and get rich quick. Coolies, amahs, stevedores, rickshaw boys, fishermen, sampan women and the great legions of Chinese white collars are hocking their life savings and their gold teeth to buy; every Tom, Dick and Harry is raising millions of dollars by issuing paper share certificates to the clamoring queues of Chinese. It's Shanghai, the Golden Mountain, the old China Coast all over again.

"While Hong Kong lasts. Borrowed place living on borrowed time. When China breathes, Hong Kong trembles.

"But what's all this got to do with us in America, the land of the free? The answer, ladies and gentlemen, is that at the boiling point of this international money-melting pot, at the center of this crossroads of East and West is the 'Hong Kong Connection'—the vicious heroin traffic that is poisoning America and Europe and the world. Hong Kong is the fertile field in which the conductors of this traffic operate—the Triad Societies, who are now outgunning the Mafia and the cops combined."

———————————————————— **5**

At the stock exchanges there was clamoring and gesticulating, and the clerks chalking up the prices and the jobbers shouting and the people crowding on the public floors; and in the scores of stockbrokers' offices across the town there was pandemonium, the clattering of the teleprinters and the clamoring of the telephones, the buying and the selling, people jostling to fill out buy-and-sell orders, and all the time the fever.

Every day the soaring stock exchange was front-page news. Every week in the newspapers there were editorials shaking heads about it. Prices were totally disproportionate to the shares values, they said. But the average Chinese investor could not read the editorials. All he understood was that you buy, then sell at a profit; it was like betting on a winner at the races at Happy Valley except that at the stock exchanges all the shares were winners. The people who could understand the editorials also understood the Chinese gambling fever and they gambled on the fever continuing to push the share prices up. The foreign money came pouring in and the share prices soared higher and the Chinese gambling fever got hotter. It was a dangerous spiraling circle, the editorials said, it was bound to crash. The smart investors would decide to take their huge profits and quit and it would be the mass of unsophisticated who would be left holding the baby. But they had been saying that for two years now. Every week the newspapers announced new companies offering their shares, every week there were long lines of queuing to buy, every new issue was oversubscribed many times. A lot of smalltime businessmen made a lot of money overnight by simply printing paper share certificates in their businesses and offering them to the public. Which is nice work if you can get it. And anybody could get it.

But Jacob Hogan McAdam would not.

It was a beautiful, bright Friday. It was a beautiful day to be taking a beautiful woman to lunch. But McAdam was in serious spirits. He was sitting in the assistant manager's office of the Hong Kong & Shanghai Bank, staring grimly out of the window. He had just heard his favorite moneylender, his good drinking friend and financial adviser, that very same Derek Morrison who had always lent him money for his other businesses, for his apartment purchases and the stock exchange, for air tickets and to pay his grocer —this very same bank manager had just refused to lend him half a million Hong Kong dollars to build his boatyard.

"I've never let you down."

Derek Morrison was grimly apologetic. "Not yet. But you still owe us a lot of money."

"But my assets are worth well over a million Hong Kong dollars."

"And you owe us over a million dollars, Jake. You've got no more security to offer us for this new loan, have you?"

"Yes. *Me.*"

Derek Morrison shook his head briefly.

"Jake. The only way for you to raise the money you need is to go public. Turn your proposed boatyard into a public company and sell 49 percent of the shares on the stock market."

McAdam stared out the window.

"No. It's dishonest."

"It's *not* dishonest," Derek Morrison said wearily. "It's the cornerstone of the capitalist theory."

"The Chinese public will buy anything at the moment. They don't know the risks involved."

"So you agree it's a risky project. Why do you expect us to lend you the money?"

"Because you know me! And you're professional moneylenders, for Chrissake!"

The banker sighed and sat forward. He said carefully, "Right,

Jake. We're professionals. And we know you. And . . . in all honesty and sincerity, we admire and respect you. Hard-working and as honest as they come. But, Jake? You're not a businessman."

McAdam turned and stared at him. "I beg your pardon?"

Derek Morrison smiled apologetically.

"You're not, Jake. Oh, sure—you've made money. You're imaginative and you work like hell. And you're as lucky as hell. But the fact is . . . you don't *care* enough about money. You don't *worry* enough about it. And it's our money, remember. You don't seem to go into these business ventures of yours because you want to make money. You go into them for some ulterior motive."

"My apartments are a sound investment."

"Sure. But they're mortgaged to us to the hilt. And now you want to go in for manufacturing boats," Derek Morrison said. "Concrete boats. Oh, sure, they'll float. But the hard fact is that this colony has hundreds of efficient boat builders and there's a public prejudice among the fishermen about boats built of concrete—"

"There was public prejudice a hundred years ago against boats made of steel."

"Indeed. But it's risky. And then I only have to probe a little into your motives and what do I find? Not a business motive. You don't want to corner the market; you want to teach your secret to all the boat builders of Asia so they can compete with you in mass-producing boats without cutting any trees down. Jake—" he shook his head at him—"we're not a philanthropic organization."

"Look." McAdam shifted around in his chair earnestly. "I've given you the wrong impression. This boatyard won't cost a lot of money. I'll build it with my own bloody hands!" He shook them in front of his face. "If I could build an entire junk on a bit of naked beach, I can build a big shed and slipway! And then it *would* be worth a lot of money—a permanent asset."

Derek Morrison said, "Jake, I'm not saying we'll never help you. But you'll have to raise some capital to show us. And after all the times you've gambled on the stock exchange, why do you adamantly refuse to raise the money for your project by going public? That's the answer to your capital problem."

McAdam sat back. "That's entirely different. I don't *gamble* on the stock exchange. I make my 10 percent and get out. Ten percent profit is enough for any man. But when I turn myself into a public company, I'm saying to the public, 'Invest in *me*.' I'm saying to the unsophisticated coolies and amahs, 'Trust me, put your hard-earned savings into my skills.' It's like asking a stranger for a loan—like borrowing ten bucks off a coolie."

Derek Morrison shook his head. "Your subtleties escape me."

"I'd feel a goddamn fraud," McAdam said.

The hot humid air hit him as he went through the doors of the air-conditioned bank, out into busy Queen's Road Central. All right, he thought. The Hong Kong & bloody Shanghai Bank had not shut the door on him entirely. He would raise some money somewhere, maybe on that new issue Harry Howard had told him about. And get things started. And then go back to them. And they weren't the only bloody bank in this town. It wasn't so bad.

And, by God, it was a beautiful day! The sun shone dazzlingly on the harbor, the junks, the ships, and the Mountains of Nine Dragons beyond were misty mauve in the heat haze. He slung his jacket over his shoulder. As he passed the bronze lions guarding the bank's doorway he gave them a stroke. The Chinese said that was supposed to bring luck.

He walked toward the foreshore and the Foreign Correspondents' Club, the best club in Hong Kong for atmosphere, company, news and the beautiful people. The China-watchers of the world hung out there, and it had a big elliptical bar so newspapermen could shout and argue with each other more easily. It had a fine view over Central District, the most expensive real estate in the world: the mighty Communist Bank of China with its big stone lions at revolutionary attention, the mighty Hong Kong & Shanghai Bank next door with its big bronze lions imperialistically recumbent, the Hong Kong Hilton, the Hong Kong Club, the Supreme Court.

He pulled a tie from his jacket pocket and slung it round his neck as he entered the club. He went straight through to the dining room to check out his table with the headwaiter. Then he glanced around the bar. She wasn't there.

Then he saw the elevator doors open, and Vanessa Williams entered the foyer. She walked confidently into the bar, her blue skirt swirling, bringing the sunshine with her.

He wanted to take her hand across the table as he said it, but instead he just stroked his finger once over the back of her wrist. "That was wonderful lovemaking the other night."

"That wasn't lovemaking, Hogan. That was just good fucking, and you know it."

He wondered if he had heard right. For an instant he was embarrassed. Then amused.

"Why do you call me Hogan? Jake's the name."

"It's your middle name, isn't it? I've done my homework. Besides, you *look* like a Hogan. Even if your surname was Hogan I'd call you Hogan."

"How does a Hogan look?"

"Like you. Nice. Rugged. Not too handsome."

He smiled. "Well. At least you agree the other night was good."

She smiled. "It was excellent, Hogan. You've been around long enough to know when you've done it well. And I'm paying for lunch."

"You are not."

"Yes, I am, I'm a visiting member." She snapped open her handbag and pulled out a notebook, flicked it open. Then she put a small pocket tape recorder on the table and switched it on. "I'm going to be picking your brains—and it all comes off expenses."

He sat back. He was amused, and impressed.

"Pick," he said. "We'll fight about the bill later."

She folded her knuckles under her chin and looked at him .and said, "I'm missing out somewhere. I've got a lot of facts. But I don't understand the *heart* of this place. I don't understand the Chinese. What makes them tick. Why are they so different?"

"I'll try to explain. It goes back a long time to the days when China was called Chung-kuo—meaning hub of the universe—and all the other peoples were outer barbarians, foreign devils. There was one high mandarin appointed by the emperor to trade with the barbarians on behalf of China, which was approximately the size of all Europe. The barbarians could come in to trade but they were confined during their stay to 'hongs,' which were their wharves on the banks of the River Pearl in Canton. The emperor ordered that a brick wall be constructed around the hongs so the foreign devils could not offend the citizens of his celestial kingdom."

He paused for a moment, watching her. He was impressed by the amount she could drink. And she obviously loved it. She drank the same way she smoked cigarettes: sensually, savoring the taste even as she concentrated on what he was saying.

"Anyway, that's what Hong Kong still is today: a hong where the barbarians can live and do business without contaminating the rest of China. But the Chinese who live here are not like the old celestial citizens. The Hong Kong Chinese are the ones who didn't want to be liberated by Mao, who fled to the crown colony when Mao marched into Shanghai—even though, at that time, the British colony was only a tiny tavern on the China Seas, a mere bazaar between the bars and brothels, without even enough water to drink.

"There were no houses, no schools, no work, no food. But these refugees made Hong Kong work, with their Shanghai know-how and their backyard sweatshops, making anything from shoes to ships and sealing wax, with nothing but sweat and muscle and sangfroid.

"That's the kind of people who made Hong Kong," he said. "And in spite of the Chinese gunboats they still keep coming, swimming Mirs Bay in dead of night, stowing away aboard the snake-junks from Macao, and creeping through the jungles past the People's Liberation Army guards to the tiny colony of Hong Kong."

The dining room was empty now, and the bar almost empty; he knew they should go. He had drunk far too much wine and then Irish coffee, and he had the taste for her now and he wanted to carry on drinking and then take this woman home to bed—but he had to get out there and raise half a million dollars.

She said quietly, "I'm gunning for Herman Choi."

He sat back.

"I see. . . . That will be very dangerous. Because he will gun for you. Literally."

"I'll take my chances on that."

"Why?"

"Because I want to crack the Triads. Starting at the top. I want to do what governments around the world have failed at.

In New York and Europe, and right here in Hong Kong, where the police are supposed to be on Triads."

"What makes you think you can?"

"What made Woodward and Bernstein think *they* could? Because a journalist doesn't have to conduct a legal investigation. The evidence I collect doesn't have to be admissible in court—it just can't be libelous. And believe me, I know how to write up what I find so it will slip between the slats of any libel law, even the Uinted Kingdom's."

"What's the U.K. got to do with you? I thought you were with the *New York Times*."

"*Was*, Hogan. I told you at the party, I'm freelancing now. Do you think I'd risk all this for a feature story in Sunday's paper? *Esquire* is backing me on this piece, but I've retained world rights. Once it's written, I can publish it in the biggest newspapers and magazines all over the world—*Der Stern*, *L'Europeo* in Italy, *The Observer* in London, *Cambio 16* in Spain, even the *Haagse Post* in the Netherlands and *Davar* in Israel—wherever there are Triads, which is almost everywhere."

McAdam leaned back, almost sober again. He said, "I see. Instant celebrity. You want to be the new Barbara Walters."

The corners of her full mouth tightened. "If you have to put it that way, Hogan. I prefer to say, the new Oriana Fallaci. Think of it—one hard-fact, international news story like this, one enormous scoop, and I'll be able to go anywhere in the world, cover any story."

"As long as you don't get thoroughly subdivided first by Herman Choi's cleaver."

She just smiled at him.

McAdam said, "I really must go now."

She looked at her watch. "Yes, me too. Can we talk again soon?"

"Of course."

She looked at her watch again. "Tell you what. I can postpone my appointment for an hour. Let's go back to your place and fuck."

He stared at her a moment, astonished. "No," he said.

She drew elegantly on her cigarette. "Do I shock you, Hogan?"

It was his instinct to say No, but he looked her in the eye, and said, "Yes."

"I believe in speaking the truth, Hogan. Not only is honesty the best policy, it's such fun."

He sat back, smiling. "Go on."

"Because most people are so unaccustomed to it that they're shocked. And why should the truth shock a civilized man?"

"Indeed."

"It gives one such a feeling of freedom. So tell me why you're shocked. Men often come right out and say they want to sleep with me."

"I believe it."

"Then why—" she smiled pleasantly—"should not women be permitted the same liberty in this day and age? When we fulfill equal roles. And fuck just as much."

He couldn't help feeling the shock every time she said the word.

She added: "When you have issued the same invitation, were the ladies shocked? Or do you only speak the truth when you feel on strong ground?"

"When inviting a woman to bed with me, yes. Otherwise, I use more conventional approaches."

"Whispering sweet nothings in her ear? Little kisses on her pretty neck? Pressing your cock against her pudendum. And finally a courageous pass at her tits? Ah, yes, all good wholesome stuff. Don't get me wrong, I enjoy the fumbling and bumbling of convention too from time to time. But when I'm horny I like to get straight to the point." She leaned her face in her hands and looked at him. "So, I am not on strong ground with you?"

"On the contrary."

"Now that's what puzzles me, Hogan. It seems you're being illogical. You see, I read you as a man of the world who's seen and done most things and who's unshockable. And who's fucked me once and presumably is looking forward to it again."

He lifted his glass and sipped. "It's not illogical—once I tell you how I read you."

She kept her eyes on his and nodded once.

"You are a thoroughly self-assured, thoroughly liberated young lady who knows exactly what she wants and makes no bones about getting it, be it your professional needs or your sexual." She inclined her head in elegant agreement. "And to those ends you will use people."

She cocked her eyebrow. "Don't we all?"

"And I have no objection to your using me, whether for my knowledge of Hong Kong or as a stud. I'll enjoy it. But if I'm to be used it will be on my terms."

She was listening attentively, enjoying it. "And your terms are that *you'll* do the soliciting—when *you* feel like it, not when I choose to grab your cock under the table."

He had to try hard to keep a straight face. "Right."

She rolled her tongue inside her mouth to smother her smile. "Where do we go from here?"

"You're beautiful."

"Thank you. You're a hunk yourself."

He said conversationally, "Tell you what. You've got an appointment and I've got to raise half a million dollars. Let's say to hell with both problems and go back to my place and fuck."

———————————————————————— **7**

Afterward she lay spread-eagled on his double bed, one long beautifully shaped leg bent, golden hair outflung, her breasts white against her tan. And her pubic hairs were fair. She watched him studying her.

"Yes, I'm a natural. Though I've been most other things. Just to test whether gentlemen really do prefer blondes."

He stretched out his hand and stroked slowly up her smooth thigh, up over her hip: it was the first time he had studied her naked, quietly; even her feet were sleek golden things, her toenails painted red; the texture of her, every line and curve and cleft of her was a sexual thing, to touch and look at and smell and taste, and where her thighs touched there was a secret olive line, and then the beautiful triangle of curly hair. She was the most naked woman in the world.

"What other colors has your hair been?"

"Flaming red. That was a real turn-on. It made me feel wanton."

"And before that?"

"Before that I was pitch black. And originally blonde."

"How do you feel now?"

"*Really* wanton. But would you like to try me red?"

He looked at her, surprised.

"I've got a terrific red wig. How'd you like red hair flamed out all over the pillow? And then black? Like having a brand-new woman every time."

He smiled. "You *are* a brand-new woman."

"But one needs variety, doesn't one?"

He looked at her, taken aback.

"You're shocked again, Hogan." She reached out and stroked his nipple. "Isn't variety the spice of life?"

"Possibly."

"Oh, definitely." She played with his nipple. "I can't understand sexual jealousy."

"But you must have been in love sometime."

"Oh, yes."

"And weren't you jealous of your lover then?"

She smiled her outrageous smile. "If he had any sexual energy left after I'd finished with him for the day, good luck to him!"

"Seriously."

"If he'd started falling for somebody else I'd have gotten uptight. Because I'd have thought I would lose him forever. But if he just screwed around and then came back to me, no way would I be jealous."

"Then I don't think you've been in love."

"Bullshit, Hogan!" she said pleasantly. She rolled onto her side and propped herself up on her elbow. "D'you think I've been around twenty-five years and don't know what love is? I've been very much in love. But even then, say, walking down the street, walking on air"—she twiddled her hands and fingers—"really singing inside, tra-la-la, and I happen to see a sexy man I've thought: *Hmmm, wouldn't mind screwing you!* Don't tell me men in love don't do the same. So why"—she gave his penis a playfully aggressive tug—"should we women be any different?"

He grinned.

She went on: "Screwing around on the side has nothing to do with being in love, Hogan. It's just satisfying a sexual appetite. Which in *my* case"—she blinked her eyes tizzily—"happens to be strong. It's no more significant than masturbation. Except"—she made her eyes sparkle—"it's much more fun."

He didn't believe she knew what she was talking about.

"You must've been in love, Hogan. Didn't you ever have a girl on the side from time to time?"

"As a matter of fact, I was the faithful kind."

She looked surprised. "That's so unnecessarily limited, though. And ungenerous, in fact. When you really love someone, you're

34

happy for them if they come home and say what a lovely day they had, what a lovely walk in the park. Sex should be the same. When someone you love has a fantastic sexual experience, you should be able to say, 'That's great, darling—tell me all about it.'"

He smiled at her. He wasn't sure if she was teasing him.

Her smile widened. "That way it's a real turn-on."

"Oh, yeah?"

"Oh, yes. Imagining your beautiful lover with a beautiful woman. Particularly the description of the details." She smiled at him. "Sex is such a—" she half closed her eyes—"wildly exciting business. The more one gets the better, not so? So . . . share your experiences." Her finger went out and stroked his nipple again. "Better still, to be there and actually share it with them."

He had been expecting it, but it was still a small shock. "Three in a bed?"

She half closed her eyes. "Super . . ." He smiled at her imitating the English. "Assuming, of course, that everybody turns everybody else on, all sexually attracted." She added, "I'm a little bisexual, you see."

He made himself shrug.

"Who isn't?" she said evenly. "Almost every girl I know who's honest admits she's a little interested. Even if she's scared of trying it. Some are afraid they'll like it and find out they're lesbian." She added, "Don't misunderstand, I'm not lesbian."

"No, I didn't think you were."

"I'm just a little kinky. I don't screw women alone. Oh, I've done it, sure, to try it out. But that's not my scene."

"What is your scene?"

"Bisexually? Three in a bed. Then it's all mixed up." She smiled at his disapproval. "I'm not hooked. It's just . . . fun. I'm only bisexual up to a nice wholesome point."

He believed her. And it was very erotic. She trailed her fingertip slowly down his chest and stomach toward his groin.

"I'd like to truly liberate you, Hogan. Introduce you to the truth about yourself. About all of us. Because underneath that straight guy that's lurking underneath that worldly guy"—she clasped her hand round his penis and shook it aggressively—"*there lurks a lovely animal!*"

He was laughing quietly.

"But we're luckier than animals, aren't we? Because we're the *naked* animal. We're the only animal"—she half closed her eyes again—"who's got the joy of nakedness. Of touching nakedness. Of looking at nakedness. Of being a voyeur! Of *sex for sex's sake*. . . ."

She let the words linger a moment. Then she said brightly, "I'm right, you know. Nature evolved us to be as horny as hell. That's why we're overpopulating the goddam earth."

He laughed.

"And so I've got to build concrete boats."

"Right. Shall I see if I can arrange it, Hogan? Three in a bed."

He shrugged. "Who do you have in mind?"

"Somebody beautiful. With lovely long legs."

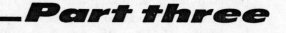
Part three

Wong Ting-tak, which means Wong Man-of-Great-Virtues, had fled to Hong Kong three times in the Year of the Hungry Tiger, before the borders were closed again. Altogether Wong Ting-tak was arrested, fed and deported three times by the Hong Kong police, and each time he crept back across the river and across the flattened fence and into the steep jungled foothills, running, scrambling, dodging, and each time he was arrested again and deported.

The third time the People's Liberation Army guards ordered him back to his native village. He marched in a long line of exhausted, hungry people, and there were guards all along the way. When darkness came Wong saw some young people leave the road and go creeping into the paddies toward Deep Bay, and he followed them. That night they heard the gunfire of the People's Liberation Army shooting the people again. It took them all night to creep down the valley, to the coast of Deep Bay. When the dawn came they threw themselves down between some big rocks, flat out on the sand, and slept.

When Wong woke up it was already sunset again, and the others had gone. He sat up, staring, then he scrambled up. He saw their footprints leading down into the sea. Wong stared. His heart was thudding; then he wanted to throw back his head and howl: "Come back! Wait for me!"

He threw himself back down on the sand. For five minutes he lay there, feeling full of fear, such as he had never known. It was the fear of death. Wong knew he was a strong man, and he could swim, but he did not know how far. The lights of the Hong Kong fishing village of Laufaushan were coming on across the bay now. It was fifteen miles away. He lay there a long time, then he got up on his knees, and prayed. Wong was not a religious man, and he had never prayed before to Tien Hau, goddess of the seas, but he prayed to her now, to keep him afloat. Then he prayed to the god of the east wind and also to Mister Rabbit, who lives on the moon, for the moon had something to do with the sea.

Then at last he took a long quivering breath and got to his feet. He flinched as his foot first touched the water. He waded as far as he could, until the sea lapped up over his chest. Then he gave a whimper and he screwed up his sweating face and kicked off the bottom.

Wong swam, his arms slapping the water, kicking his legs, out into the flat black sea and the night; he swam like that for maybe a thousand yards, and it seemed he must have swum a very long way; he was exhausted by the great hunger in his belly from the many days of walking, the running. He stopped swimming to rest, and to get the great ache out of his arms and shoulders and his legs. He looked about him and he could not make out the beach he had swum from, and he could not see the lights of Laufaushan above the black smacking sea. For maybe a minute Wong swallowed, desperately trying to gasp his breath back, then he started swimming again.

Thus Wong swam, thrashing and breast-stroking until he could swim no more, then rolling over onto his back, gasping and spitting, then rolling over and breast-stroking and dog-paddling again, sputtering, retching, blind, and all the time the agonizing ache in his arms and in his legs. For three hours Wong swam like that, and he felt such terror and exhaustion as he had never known.

The black current suddenly surged Wong sideways, and with the renewed strength of terror he thrashed and kicked, but he was finished, and the current took him. Wong could not fight it; the black silhouette of the faraway land slid past him, but Wong did not see it going. All he knew was that he must keep his reeling head up. For two hours the current swept him along, gasping, spluttering, terrified; then he hit the oyster raft.

The raft was made of bamboo and the oyster cages hung down into the sea. Wong was dragged a long way down the big old piece of bamboo, ripping his flesh, before he flung his arms over it and clung. And he was crying, with exhausted, desperate, clinging joy; he did not know what he was clinging to but he knew it was solid and that his head was above water. He clung and clung, and it was the best feeling in the world. He saw the first gray in the sky, then the land, the gray mountains not a mile away, and the oyster rafts all round. Wong clung there, whimpering for a long time; then he started to swim slowly through the rafts in the first light, and as he pulled himself along each one, the knowledge of them was the sweetest thing he had ever known.

8

It was humid, oily hot, even at sunrise. She was walking up Nathan Road, sweating already. Bernard Champion had offered to send a car for her any time she liked, but she had declined. It was good to walk and sweat.

She strode lightly, carrying only a light sackcloth shoulder bag. She was heading for the Man Ping resettlement estate and squatter area for the third time. Later on she was meeting Superintendent Champion for lunch. Her hair was piled up on top of her head, away from her neck, and a jeans skirt flapped just above her knees. Half her blouse buttons were undone to keep cool. She was not wearing panties. She seldom did; it gave her a feeling of freedom. And if ever a gust of wind let anybody see anything, good for them. She was in a happy mood. To write about something conscientiously you had to get out there and experience it and truly feel it. The more she saw of this place, the more she loved it.

Just half a mile up the golden mile of Nathan Road, cutting right across the middle of Kowloon, she came to Boundary Street. She pulled her little tape recorder out of her bag and said softly into it as she walked:

"In a way this street epitomizes Hong Kong. For Boundary Street is the official border between the British crown colony of Hong Kong, which was ceded to Britain forever by the old emperor of China, and the New Territories, which the British have only leased. In less than twenty years all the land on the other side of Boundary, all the factories, houses, apartments, tenements, and all the three hundred square miles of mountains and valleys and farms beyond, will revert to Communist China.

"About half of Hong Kong's teeming population lives and works on the wrong side of Boundary Street, and half of them are under twenty years of age. In twenty years' time Boundary Street is going to be a most heartbreaking street indeed. . . ."

An hour later she came to the resettlement estate. It was her third visit, but this time she did not have her interpreter with her. Now she almost knew the place. A whole mountain had been bulldozed flat, and on top the government had built the vast new resettlement estate: twenty massive concrete blocks each twelve stories high, concrete canyons reaching up, every apartment the same; masses of identical-looking laundry hanging out of the windows on bamboo poles, thousands of people all with the same black hair and brown slanted eyes, and all the time the noise: the singsong blare of Chinese radio, the screams of the thousands of children playing, the hammering and the jammering, the clattering of Mah-Jongg, the minibuses, bicycles, carts, wheelbarrows, hawkers.

She went to a cooked-food stall, sat down on a little stool and ordered green tea. She lit a cigarette and settled down to watch the world go by. She knew a lot of the people by sight already.

Chan Fat-ho was an illegal hawker. The government refused to license him because there were far too many hawkers already in Hong Kong's narrow streets. Chan Fat-ho lived in the squatter area immediately below the Man Ping resettlement estate. The rows between the shacks were narrow dirt paths that turned to mud in the rains. At every third row there was a water pump, and in every fifth row a latrine. And that was it. At the bottom of the squatter area were factories built like apartment houses, factories on top of factories, all the way down to the harbor.

Every morning at sunrise Chan Fat-ho left his shack and headed for the resettlement estate with his bamboo pole slung over his shoulder. From each end were suspended two tin cages, which contained his paraphernalia. Next to the estate began the massive blocks of factories, and there was a minibus terminal. It was a good area for hawking food, but it was illegal because of the congestion.

Chan Fat-ho set his pole down on the sidewalk. Then he hurried into the estate and filled his four-gallon tin with water. He put a big pot of rice on the stove to boil; on the other burners he put noodles and congee. He set the woks sizzling with gizzards. Immediately his first customers began to turn up. Chan Fat-ho hopped around on his bony haunches cooking, dishing out, chucking on more, taking money. All the time the people were hurrying along the narrow sidewalks into the minibuses and factories, and the cargo lorries were arriving and discharging and loading. All down the crowded street other hawkers were also doing good trade. There was a lot of competition, the food was good, and for one dollar Hong Kong, twenty-five U.S. cents, you got a gutful.

Vanessa finished her breakfast of fried noodles and gizzards and watched the street. She felt she knew Chan Fat-ho quite well now. They gave each other a smile each time and she had learned a few Chinese words. She knew his routine. He worked through the night, until the night shift at the factories had had its midnight break. Half a dozen times he had to run to the markets to buy more rice, vegetables, noodles, fish, meat. Finally Chan Fat-ho packed up for the day. That is what he did seven days a week every week of the year.

But twice a week Chan Fat-ho received a visitor who did not want rice or congee. Vanessa had seen this, too, and her interpreter had explained to her what was happening. On Mondays the visitor was the rent collector from the local branch of the 14K Triad Society. Every week their rent collector came to all the hawkers and collected $10 for use of their piece of sidewalk.

Chan Fat-ho's other visitor was an officer from the Hawker Control Force. Once a week the officer came and sat at one of the little tables outside a licensed stall. One by one the hawkers went up to the stall, ordered a cup of green tea and left a $10 note folded under the cup. Then the Hawker Control Force officer made his way to a teahouse in the next street and paid the rent collector of the 14K Triad Society 20 percent of what he had collected. If he did not, the 14K Triad Society would denounce him to the police as a corrupt officer.

Once every two weeks or so, Chan Fat-ho and the others were rounded up in a big green Urban Service truck and arrested for hawking without a license. At the local magistracy the hawkers were shepherded into the courtroom where each pleaded guilty and was fined $10. They shuffled out of the courtroom and down to the sheriff's office and paid. And that was that. Chan Fat-ho picked up his bamboo pole and went loping back through the teeming streets, back to the resettlement estate, set down his gear and started cooking again. Chan Fat-ho was satisfied. His customers were satisfied. The Hawker Control Force officer was satisfied. The 14K Triad Society was satisfied. Everybody was satisfied.

"Except us, of course," Bernard Champion said a little nervously. He had reserved a table for lunch at the Sheraton. She would much rather have had a bowl of noodles at a cooked-food stall but she did not have the heart to suggest it. He was so anxious to do everything well. And on the table was a vase of red roses. If ever a man wore his heart on his sleeve it was Bernard Champion. She knew that underneath that policeman's exterior he was in love with her. And that was a problem. Champion was a senior policeman, very knowledgeable, and he could help her a great deal. But he was not the kind you could love and leave.

So far, though, he was still being earnestly businesslike. She hoped she could keep the rest of the lunch that way. Thank God he had relaxed a little with a drink.

He said, "There're several others like Herman Choi, of course. But he is the biggest one. Yes, we know all about him. In a sense. In another sense we know nothing."

Her tape recorder was between them on the table.

"But he's only been into narcotics the last fifteen years or so. That's probably why he joined, to get the benefit of Triad secrecy. He's been a businessman all his life—a good one, too." He added: "Harry Howard's the man to talk to about Choi's earlier life. Choi used to work for Harry."

She nodded. He went on. "Choi doesn't physically handle any of the narcotics he deals in. He doesn't even see it. He provides the finance. The management. By remote control, through his flunkies. He buys raw opium from the Golden Triangle—that's the northern states of Burma, Thailand and Cambodia. From there the stuff is shipped to Hong Kong by a variety of methods, mostly by Thai fishing trawlers. It is taken to his factory here and processed by his chemists into heroin."

"And from the factory?"

"The refined heroin is packed. Some of it goes to retailers here in Hong Kong, but the bulk is shipped overseas. To Europe, via England and Holland, mostly. And also to America, more and more, lately." He smiled. "The Mafia are very worried about it."

"So is the American government. And how is it shipped to these places?"

He spread his hands. "Every way you can think of. Hidden in consignments of goods, very often. And by couriers. They agree to take a bag of it in their luggage for, say, two thousand dollars. Plus their air ticket. They're met at the airport of destination by the pick-up man. Of course, if customs find it, the pick-up man melts away.

"There are over half a million tourists a year to this tiny place. Thousands of hotels, bars, rooming houses. Over eighty thousand drug addicts, hundreds of peddlers. It's not hard to find couriers. But once the courier has agreed to the job, he won't see the man who propositioned him again. The stuff will be delivered to him by an addict, doing it in exchange for a free fix. Or even by an innocent hotel bellboy. If we catch the man delivering, that's all we've caught. He won't tell us who he got it from: he doesn't even know who it was, because it was another stranger." He looked at her soulfully. "We try, of course, but we never get back to the Herman Chois."

She thought. "If I could get a job as a courier . . ."

Champion looked alarmed. "What do you mean?"

She said, "If you could set that up, I could really get somewhere."

He stared at her. "You're not thinking of playing agent provocateur, are you?"

She looked at him, then shook her head. "No."

"Because if you are, Vanessa, don't count on me to help. My God, if anything happened to you . . . I couldn't possibly . . ."

He stopped. Apparently speech had failed him. She knew what was coming and tried to think how to head the subject off. God knew, she did not want to hurt him.

Suddenly, as if he had taken a deep breath to nerve himself, he leaned across the table and took her hand. He was hunched forward, his big hairy hand heavily on top of hers, his eyes wide in ardor, his mouth half open to speak. She blinked and collected her wits. She opened her mouth to say something, anything, and then Champion's throat croaked and she stopped. Then he stopped. They stared at each other for an agonizing moment, then she recovered. She put her other hand on top of his and squeezed it. "Jake," she said brightly, "Jake McAdam—why did he quit the

44

police force?" She removed her hands and took a cigarette. "Was he . . . in some kind of trouble?"

Champion sat back, still blushing, and fumbled for a cigarette. He lit hers hastily. His heart was still hammering.

"Have you asked him?"

"No. But the girls I share my apartment with say one minute he was headed for the top of the police, the youngest superintendent ever, and then one day he walked away."

Champion shook his head. "We never talked about it. It's seven or eight years ago now—not too long after his wife left him. Did you know that—that McAdam was married once? And had a child?"

She nodded. "Olga told me. She's known him since forever. She says his wife ran off with the little girl and he was uptight for a long time. Disappeared from the social scene or came to parties alone. Never with a girl. And meanwhile he's a big-wheel cop. Then suddenly he quits. *Then* the portrait of the Chinese woman appears in his apartment." She raised her eyebrows at him. "Who is she?"

Champion breathed nervously, wanting to ask why the interest in McAdam. He said, "I didn't even know he'd had a big relationship with a Chinese girl. Until after he left the force. Then I saw the painting one day."

She said persistently, "He was in Special Branch, wasn't he? The department that deals with espionage."

"Yes. They promoted him to superintendent at thirty. In those days that was genius. But Jake was a brilliant policeman, no doubt about it. And an intellectual—got a B.A. in political philosophy at Oxford. And a good service record, fighting the Communists in Malaya years before. Anyway, he was promoted at the time when we were having big Communist riots here during Mao's cultural revolution—you know about those riots?"

"Yes."

"Terrible. Lasted six months. Civil war. Running battles every day in the streets. And every day we expected Mao's Red Guards to swarm over the border." He shook his head. "Anyway, it eventually died down; then, about a year after the riots ended he suddenly resigned."

"And?"

"He just dropped out of sight. I saw him occasionally. He wouldn't talk about it. He looked like hell. He borrowed money and bought those two apartments one on top of the other. Prices were rock-bottom after the riots. Then he did something strange. I thought it was crazy. Instead of renting out the upper apartment, he joined the two with a spiral staircase. Then he knocked out most of the walls in the upper apartment and turned it into a massive artist's studio. And this is a very pricey apartment. And his reason is, he's going to devote his life to painting." He raised his bushy eyebrows. "And he did. Just painted, morning, noon and night. And he did quite well. The upper apartment was his gallery as well as his studio. He held lots of exhibitions. Sold a lot. Then . . ." he raised his eyebrows again. "One day he just quit painting."

She waited.

"Then he began to get back to normal. For him. He started taking out women again. And then going into business. Buying apartments. All on mortgage. And started speculating on the stock exchange. Borrowed all kinds of money. And now, as you probably know, it's concrete junks. Wants to build a boatyard and build more of them, but he's in debt up to his ears."

She nodded thoughtfully. He started to say something, then stopped. Then he said, "Jake knows a lot about this town. Is he . . . helping you much?"

She looked at him, then smiled her warm, dazzling smile. She said, "I think she was a spy. . . . You're being a great help, Bernard. Thank you."

Bernard Champion's heart turned over like a porpoise.

----------------------------------9

Bernard Champion sat bulkily on a sack of cement with a bottle of beer, watching McAdam and Wong laying bricks at the deserted piece of beach that McAdam had rented. Champion supported two Chinese children at the orphanage, whom he had brought along to swim. In the little bay the concrete junk was tied up to a new floating jetty which McAdam had built of oil drums and old timber.

"Why can't you use ordinary sea sand in the cement?"

"Because of the salt."

Champion said pensively, "I really am impressed. All this in two weeks."

The walls of the big boat shed were two feet high already.

"It won't fall down on you or anything? How do you know you're doing it right?"

"I bought a book."

Champion shook his head, then said tentatively, "Are you sure it's worth it? I mean, if the banks are all down on the idea, are you sure it's . . . right?"

"Oh, yes."

Champion looked unconvinced. But he didn't want to say anything discouraging. It was very hot. McAdam and Wong were both glistening with sweat. Champion watched Wong.

"He's good, too."

"He's a first-class chap. He'd work under water if I asked him to. But painfully shy."

"You've done so much . . ."

"The specter of bankruptcy. A great incentive." He slapped on mortar with his trowel and fitted a brick on top of it. "Just spent a fortune telephoning my banks in Switzerland and New York."

"No joy?"

He smacked the brick hard with the handle of his trowel. "You try convincing a Swiss banker on a long-distance telephone about concrete boats. Chap's probably never seen the sea." He scooped up mortar and slapped it onto the wall.

Champion smiled. "So how did you pay for all these building materials?"

"Credit. Thirty days. Oh, I've got enough money for this lot, he'll get paid. But that's about the end of it."

"Then what'll you do?"

"Starve."

"I'll grubstake you. I mean for groceries and that."

McAdam smiled as he emplaced a brick. "Thanks, Champ. Don't worry, the bank will grubstake me. They've got too much money invested, they need me alive. It's big money they're nervous about."

"But you haven't got enough materials here to finish, have you?"

"No. But if I can just get the roof on. That's a big step."

"And then?"

"Then go back to the bank. With something impressive to show them."

"And if they still won't lend you the money?"

McAdam snorted. Slapping mortar and a brick. "Then I'll just have to sell my apartment."

Champion shifted his bulk irritably. "And live where?"

"Right here. On the junk."

"Jesus. Why not sell the junk?"

"The junk won't fetch nearly enough. That's my whole argument, isn't it? It's a very cheap boat. I'm looking for something like a million Hong Kong dollars in all. Of course I'll sell it if I have to. But it's the only bit of advertising I have. Living proof for the fisherman."

"How can you live on a junk, for heaven's sake?"

"Just watch me."

"But you don't want to live like that for long. At your stage of life. It's a pretty Spartan thing."

"Tart her up a bit. No," he admitted, "I don't want to live like that. But when I get sick of it I can live right here." He pointed with his trowel at the old Chinese cottage.

"For heaven's sake, it's a ruin, almost. What a way to *live*, Jake. A bloody hermit. All because you want people to stop cutting down trees. Is it worth it?"

McAdam straightened, trowel in hand, sweating. He looked as if he was about to deliver an exasperated lecture. Then he abruptly scooped up more mortar.

"Yes. There's more to life than making money. Who needs the stuff anyway?"

"You do. And don't count on the apartment bringing you much. Both of them are mortgaged, I'm sure."

McAdam tapped a brick down firmly and did not answer.

"And it's not going to be an easy apartment to sell, I'm here to tell you. Not unless you put back all those walls you knocked down. You may be forced to sell it cheap. So cheap you *still* can't finish here. Leaving you with no boatyard *and* no apartment."

"Yes," McAdam said. He scooped up mortar.

"Well?"

"I said yes."

Champion watched him work. He thought for several moments, then he said, "A million dollars, huh? A quarter of a million U.S."

"To do it properly. But I can get by with much less. When I get the roof on this shed, I can start building boats. But it's uneconomic, I could only do one at a time. Unprofessional."

Champion smiled to hear McAdam talking about economics.

"Why not play the stock market a bit? It's easy money."

"What do I use for money?"

48

Champion made up his mind. "I'll lend you a couple of hundred thousand."

McAdam straightened again and stared at him. Champion added, "American dollars. But only to invest in the stock market. Not into this boatyard." He waved his hand at the wall. "This business is too dicey for my money. But what you do with your profit on the stock market is your affair."

McAdam stared at him. "How the hell have you got two hundred thousand U.S. dollars loose?"

"What the hell!" Champion said indignantly. "I'm a bachelor, I've got a good salary. And I've played the market all my life, you know that—and the horses. I've got nothing to spend my money on. Except gluttony."

"But—" McAdam shook his head. "Thanks very much for your kind offer. But how can you afford that, even if you've got two hundred thousand? Why isn't it sensibly invested?"

Champion said gruffly, "It *is* invested. But I can borrow a couple of hundred thousand against it, easily."

McAdam shook his head.

"There's good stuff on the market," Champion said. "And a few real good ones coming."

"Like Lucky Man?"

"I believe that's one of them. It's one of Herman Choi's deals, unfortunately, but a real gold mine."

McAdam said, "Choi, is it? How do you know?"

"Harry Howard told me. Besides, it's obvious. *Choi*—luck. *Ho*—good. *Man*—man. Anyway, I'd lend you any amount of money for an investment in that."

McAdam shook his head again. "Many thanks, Champ. But no, I just couldn't do it. I only borrow from the professionals. The banks—that's what they're there for. Not my friends."

Relief flickered across Champion's face. "Well, think about it," he said. "And think about *this* place."

They sat on the end of the jetty in the dusk, wet from a swim, feet hanging in the water, drinking beer from the bottles. The children were splashing. McAdam was completely taken aback: it was hard to believe what Champion was saying. Champion stared at the sea, half embarrassed.

"I've heard of it happening like this," he said. "A chap's about forty, bachelor, set in his ways. Thinks he'll never get married. Then one day he meets a girl, and—boom! He really falls in love.

49

And gets married. And I mean in love. . . . Not some infatuation."

McAdam looked at Champion's profile. Then Champion smiled sheepishly. McAdam wanted to put his arm around the guy and squeeze him. He started to say something sensible, then changed it. "And how does it feel?" he said carefully.

"Oh . . . it feels wonderful," he said lamely. *"She's* wonderful."

"That's great, Champ. But listen—"

"You listen to me." Champion held up his hand. "I've come all the way out here to tell you I'm in love, now don't go spoiling it." Then he gave his nervous panting laugh to cover his embarrassment. "A man's entitled to a little starry-eyed nonsense, isn't he?"

"Absolutely."

Champion hunched over the end of the jetty and stared at his feet. "What were you going to say?"

McAdam regretted it. "Nothing."

"Go on." He added gruffly, "I need to talk about it."

McAdam took a big wary breath.

"What I was going to say is . . . it may be . . . it's not uncommon, I believe, with people who've got profound scruples about"—he was going to say "screwing" and changed it—"going to bed with a girl before marriage—that when they do, they wake up with a disproportionate, unrealistic amount of feeling. Which is partly guilt and partly . . . sexual infatuation."

"Well, that's not the case. I'm not entirely inexperienced, you know."

"I'm sorry."

Champion glared at the sea a long minute. McAdam took a swig of his beer, waiting. Then Champion waved his big hand self-consciously and said to his beer, "Besides, I haven't . . . we haven't actually . . ." He shook his big head. "I'm not really talking about her body. It's *her.* She's highly intelligent. And so vivacious. She's got charm. And guts. And soul. . . ." He looked at McAdam and gave up.

McAdam decided he had to say it. "And she 's hard as nails," he said quietly.

Champion looked at him as if he had slapped him.

"She is *not!*" he said indignantly. "God, Jake! That's your trouble—you expect women to be nice docile creatures who'll look at you with big adoring eyes and let you run the world! So when you meet a woman who's as smart and get-ahead as you, a modern woman who's capable of doing a man's job, you say she's tough as nails!"

"I'm sorry—I shouldn't have said that. Look. She's a fascinating woman. She's a great girl. But, Jesus, Champ, does she even know what she wants—"

"And what's wrong with that?"

"Nothing—but she'll break your heart finding out! She'll love you and leave you. Because she's one of those modern women who don't want to be tied down. She doesn't *want* a permanent relationship. Especially in Hong Kong! She's a ship that passes in the night, for Chrissake. She wants to get her information, enjoy herself, and piss off back home to the land of the free."

Champion was glaring at him. "That can be changed. She won't be the first woman's libber to fall in love."

All right, McAdam thought. He'd said quite enough to make himself unpopular. He hoped Champion would drop the subject. If Champion wanted her he would never see the woman again.

Champion cleared his throat and said awkwardly, "You're seeing her soon, I believe?"

Here we go, McAdam thought. He said casually, "Yes, I'm taking her to dinner on Saturday night." He added, "She's got her knife out for Herman Choi."

Champion nodded, staring at the water. He took a deep breath, then said, "Have you been to bed with her?"

"Oh, Jesus!" McAdam glared at Champion. "It would be none of your damn business if I had." Champion shot him an agonized look, then dropped his eyes and hunched forward. McAdam's heart went out to him. "Look, Champ, I'm just helping her in her job, that's what she invited us all to her party for. But if you feel uptight about it I'll beg off dinner—I'm busy enough here."

"Don't be silly."

McAdam felt bad for having spoken so sharply. He put his hand on the man's shoulder and shook it.

"Come on, end of bullshit. You're not in love with anybody except San Miguel Breweries and the French wine industry."

Champion smiled sheepishly. "Sure."

It was like trying to eat soup with chopsticks.

She had vast sheaves of notes and transcriptions of tape recordings, she had facts running out of her ears, she probably knew more about Sir Herman Choi than anybody else alive, but she could not find a real chink in his armor. Plenty of scratches, even dents, which she could blow up into an embarrassing victory about the bastard, but it would not topple him. Kid stuff compared to the truth that somewhere in that pile of facts was a 489 of the 14K Triad Society and one of the world's biggest dealers in narcotics.

What she needed was a Deep Throat, somebody close to the throne who would meet her at dead of night and give her inside information. Bernie Champion had given her a lot of information generally, but on the subject of Choi he could only give her theory. McAdam the same. Harry Howard was the closest she'd got. Over a drunken lunch he'd told her a lot about the young Choi Ho-man. But when it came to Triads he could give her nothing solid.

The American Mess was empty but for her. The big dining room table was covered in her notes and tapes. Now she paced the living room, holding her tape recorder in one hand and notes in the other. She had been dictating for over an hour.

"By the following year," she said, "the political crisis in China was over, Hong Kong booming again. With the help of the bank manager and an impressive donation, Choi Ho-man was appointed to the board of the Society for the Blind and Physically Handicapped, and won respectability. Choi had been anxious to join this charity because on the board sat several taipans and legislative councilors. These people would be useful in expanding his business interests, and he would also get inside information about the stock market. And, he hoped, they would yield a lot of information about new government fiscal policies, sales of crown lands, introductions to many senior civil servants and to the corridors of power generally.

"Both hopes turned out to be correct, according to Harry. Through his fellow board members and a lot of intensive entertaining, Choi Ho-man doubled his personal fortune on the stock market with inside information. Friends of friends on the Trade Development Council could be persuaded, for a share of the profit, to direct business to his import-export, shipping and insurance enterprises. And when word came down that he would receive an O.B.E., he was offered a seat on the board of a local Chinese bank.

"There is enormous face in being a banker. Furthermore, as a director, he could arrange low-interest loans to his other companies—strictly illegal but, like so many other things in Hong Kong, done all the time. In his enthusiasm to accept, Choi did not consider this very point enough. At his first meeting of the board he learned that the bank was in deep financial trouble: one of the directors was bankrupt, and the official receiver, suspecting illegal loans, had called in the banking commissioner, whose auditors had discovered that almost all the other directors were up to the same thing. Indeed herein lay the bank's special interest in having Choi Ho-man on its board: his O.B.E. and his valuable contacts. He was outraged at these illegalities his co-directors had been perpetrating. He had been taken for a sucker for the first time in his life. But he recovered from his disappointment by delivering a homily and agreeing to use his influence on two conditions: one, the chairmanship of the board, and, two, all the bank's import-export, shipping and insurance business be channeled through his companies.

"Thereafter Mr. Choi approached the leading partner of the firm of auditors who had discovered the irregularities. This firm was international, headquarters in London, with an impeccable reputation. However, good old Mr. Choi was able to point a few things out to them. Firstly, they were auditors of the Society for the Blind and Physically Handicapped, and also of a number of banks, several of whom would be happy to take over this bank if it were left with its honor intact; and secondly, that he, Choi Ho-man, his export business, his insurance company, his shipping company, the Lucky Man Development Company, the bank and all the business of his co-directors would consider changing to this English firm of accountants. The leading partners were impressed by these arguments. They consulted urgently with their London headquarters who, while maintaining their impeccable standards, reluctantly agreed to cover up the irregularities.

"Choi Ho-man's donations to charities got more spectacular. His selfless devotion to various youth organizations, trying to give the young an alternative to the Triad gangs, became renowned.

In the normal course of events, a seat on the legislative council and later a knighthood were in the bag for our Mr. Choi. And, make no mistake about it, he let it be known that his donations to charity would cease unless those two things came to pass, in that order.

"And sure enough, next week, Mr. Choi Ho-man will become Sir Herman Choi. At the tender age of forty-six."

Jesus Christ. Disgusted, she picked up the tape recorder and microphone and stumped through to the bathroom. Depositing the recorder on the lid of the clothes hamper, she went to the tub and slammed on the cold tap. Today was water day in this neck of the woods.

She stepped into the cold bath, flinched despite her sweat, then lay down gingerly. Then she felt better, the cool water awash over her breasts. She picked up the microphone.

"But meanwhile, what about the Lucky Man Development Company?

"As a banker, Herman Choi was in a very strong position to raise capital. Hong Kong continued to boom, even during the recession years following the oil crisis. His Lucky Man Development Company quietly continued to buy choice underdeveloped properties and slum tenements which, through their contacts in the building office, they could have condemned as unsafe any time they chose. *Now* was the time to start developing.

"But not with his own money: with the public's. Lucky Man is to go on the stock exchange, with Sir Herman Choi retaining 51 percent. They are five-dollar shares being offered at ten dollars, and even at that price, Harry says, they are winners. They will open at fourteen or fifteen dollars. As soon as the slum tenements are demolished the shares will rise to twenty. . . ."

The bathroom window was open. From where she lay she could see the steep jungled mountainside behind McAdam's apartment. Five hundred yards up she could see bulldozers gouging a huge terrace out of the mountain for a massive new apartment block.

Jake spent the next two nights at the boatyard, laying bricks until midnight by lamplight. Then on Friday night he stayed up very late calculating over and over again the cost of building the boat shed—the best way first, then the cheapest way, then all the ways in between.

Before dawn he was suddenly wide awake, worrying. About money. He got straight up and started laying bricks again. At eleven o'clock he had to drive back to Kowloon for materials. At noon he had a meeting with his accountant. By twelve-thirty he had finally faced a few facts.

For the next twelve months he would be technically, legally, in a state of bankruptcy, his liabilities exceeding his assets. Which meant that if one single thing went wrong, if he failed to pay any one debt date and a court writ was taken out against him, he would lose everything. Lunchtime he spent pacing in the botanical gardens, the sun beating down, the sweat making his shirt stick to his back. At two o'clock he drove back to his apartment, where he telephoned four real-estate agents and put his apartment on the market.

Grimly he drove fast back through Hong Kong and through the Mountains of Nine Dragons, back to his boatyard on the remote beach of Tolo Sound. And stripped off his city clothes and started laying bricks again. Within two hours he had to throw down his trowel, shower, get back into his city clothes and then drive back to Hong Kong to take Vanessa Storm Williams to dinner. Which he dearly wished he did not have to do. He did not care that he was late.

She answered the door, and she was radiant.

"Forgive me for being late."

She leaned back against the door.

"You're tired. Should we just go to your place and have ham and eggs?"

"Oh, no!" He really wanted to take her out somewhere, now. He wasn't so tired anymore.

He decided to take her to Aberdeen, because that's what tourists usually liked to see, then to the floating restaurant. They took a walla-walla across the tiny harbor. The sun was getting low, the China Sea was flat, blue and golden, glassy smooth. The fishing junks were jam-packed, row after row of them, forests of masts, their great wood hulls gleaming browny-yellow, fishing nets and ropes everywhere. And in the middle of the teeming Chinese harbor were the two big gaudy barges, all lit up: the floating restaurants.

Any anxieties about the financial deep water he was heading for dissipated. He was entirely at home here, in the hustle and bustle. He loved it. And he was glad that he was part of it. Ashore, they picked their way through the boatyards, each carrying a bottle of cold beer. She could feel how he felt, the confidence of a man in his element.

He pointed at three Chinese chiseling at a single teak log, forty feet long, and he had to speak loudly. "That's the keel of a new boat. Those men are about to build a forty-foot deep-sea fishing junk without a single plan or even a drawing."

She looked at the log and shook her head. "No plans?"

"Just build her by eye. Same way they've been doing for two thousand years. Even the curved ribs, they'll just saw them into shaped sections by eye. Perfectly balanced. Deep-sea vessel. The builder won't even know the exact length the junk will be."

He took her elbow and led her to a teahouse where they sat at a wooden table and drank another cold beer. She looked about her. "If I could paint, this is the sort of place I'd do. But your concrete junks will change all the romance of it, Hogan."

"Partly, yes. But look at all this timber. And the enormous cost of it nowadays. Something must be done."

She looked at him, then said casually, "Why did you stop painting, Hogan?"

He was surprised she even knew he used to. "I burned myself out."

She studied her cigarette. She was about to say something, but he leaned back in his chair and said, "You've really done the trick with Bernard Champion."

"What do you mean?" She knew what he meant.

"He's in love. Try not to hurt him. He's a hell of a nice chap, and very serious."

"Yes, I've seen that. But there've been other women in his life, surely."

"Precious few." He leaned his elbows on the table and took a mouthful of beer. "You see, Bernie's really the marrying kind. He's had a few girlfriends, sure. But they've always been girls he thought he wanted to marry. And raise lots of kids with. But it's come to nothing every time." He added, "And they've all been the most beautiful girl in the room. Always falls for the beautiful ones, old Champ."

"And in between these girlfriends?"

"Bites the bullet. Sex is only for marriage. Confession and so forth."

She drew on her cigarette.

"Oh, God. You trying to tell me something, Hogan?"

"None of my business. But I presume you're going to be seeing a lot of him?"

She frowned. "Yes! He's a mine of information. And I'm going to Macao with him, to the bullfight."

"What I'm saying is, don't break that guy's heart."

"I don't want to break anybody's heart. Live and let live. I've only just come to town."

"Right. And you're off as soon as you're through."

They had a lovely time that night. He did not take her to the floating restaurant. She had been there and she thought it beautiful, expensive and a tourist trap. She wanted to go to McAdam's boatyard.

It was a beautiful night. The moon shone big and bright on Tolo Sound, a long, wide wedge of silver on the dark sea. The mountains were silver-mauve in the moonlight, and the village lights of Shatin and Tai-po were twinkling.

There was no road out to the boatyard, just two tracks worn by his car. His old station wagon bumped along the ridge of the mountain. Then he turned down toward the silvery sea. At the foot of the hill he stopped, and sat a moment with the headlights on. To the side were the rising walls of the big shed. But it was the old Chinese cottage that she was looking at.

"It's absolutely charming."

He unlocked the door and lit a candle. The two-room cottage

was made of stone and the roof was of old Chinese tiles. In the front room was a wooden bed, which he had knocked together himself, a table and two chairs. A bamboo cane stretched across one corner with clothes slung over it. In another corner was a small gas refrigerator and a stove. Piled everywhere were books and papers.

She smiled as she looked around. "And the other room?"

"My work room." It was dominated by a table covered with plans and geometrical equipment. Round the walls hung a large assortment of tools. Against one wall was a stout carpenter's bench. This room was tidy.

"Beer?"

"I thought you'd never ask. But let's take them with us while we look around outside. So far, I love it here."

He opened the refrigerator happily, then grabbed a flashlight and a big blue blanket and led her out into the moonlight. They walked between the trees toward the far side of the bay. There was a low stone wall. He shone his flashlight over; there was a startled grunt and a big pig clambered up, ears forward. And scrambling up groggily were a dozen pink piglets.

"Ah . . . why didn't you tell me you had pigs?"

"I wanted you to love me for myself. A guy with a good pig can't be too careful."

He took her hand. They tramped down to the beach and stretched out on the blanket McAdam had brought. Sometimes a small breeze wafted in off the sea, and the moon shone down on them big and bright as they made love, and swam in the bay, and talked, and then made love some more.

They lay on the blanket under the moon, water glistening on them, talking about anything but mostly about themselves. She looked at the boat shed, silhouetted a few yards away. It was the size of a tennis court; the walls about four feet high already.

"You're not just a pretty face, are you, Hogan?" she said lazily. "How many junks can you build in there at a time?"

"Three. All in different stages. Two curing while the third is being put together. Then while the last one is being cured, the carpentry is being done on the first one."

"Cured?"

"Letting the cement harden, settle down. We have to spray the cemented hull with water for three weeks, night and day. There'll be pipes everywhere." He added, "We use seawater, of course."

"How did you cure your junk, then?"

"I sank her."

"You *what-ed* her?"

"I just ran the hull down the slipway into the bay here. Opened all the cocks and she sank like a stone. Left her there for three weeks. Then hauled her up and put the engine and carpentry in."

She said, "How the hell did you refloat her?"

"Dozens of car inner tubes. Tied them to her hull, then pumped them up with an air compressor. Once you get her breaking surface, close all the cocks. Then pump her out."

"You and whose army?"

He smiled. "Wong and I. You should meet Wong," he added, "he'll interest you. He's a refugee. He swam fifteen miles to get to Hong Kong."

She said suddenly, "What happened to the Chinese girl, Hogan?"

"How do you know about a Chinese girl?"

"The painting. And the rumors."

He looked back at sea. "Don't pay attention to rumors, Vanessa."

"But the girl you painted . . . she was for real, wasn't she? You knew her well?"

He scooped up sand and let it run through his fingers.

"Yes. She was for real."

"What was her name? Or can't you tell me?"

"Her name was Ying," he said.

"Was she an artist, too?"

"She was a schoolteacher. And an artist, yes," he said unwillingly.

"Was she a good artist?"

He could answer that. "Yes."

She traced her finger in the sand. "Whatever happened to her?"

He breathed deep and looked at the sea. "I don't know," he said.

"Did she go away?"

"Yes."

"Where to? China?"

It was really the last question he was going to answer.

"Yes."

"And she's still there?"

"Yes."

59

She said, "Do you ever hear from her?"

He could answer that too. "No."

"Or of her?"

"No again."

She hesitated. Then asked, "Was she a Communist?"

He turned his head and looked at her. He smiled thinly. "Why the questions?"

She smiled. "You fascinate me, Hogan. I promise I won't write a story about it. Was she?" She added, "Most people who go to China are Communists."

"True."

"Or can't you tell me, because it's something to do with the Official Secrets Act?"

McAdam turned on his side and propped himself up on his elbow. He looked her in the eye as he took a sip of beer.

"Let's talk about you," he said.

She smiled. "Can I ask you one more question?"

"You can ask."

She said, "Do you still love her very much?"

They had had only a year together, living quietly, almost secretly—he working as a policeman, she as a teacher in a Communist school in Hong Kong. Slowly, gradually, he persuaded her to spend more and more time in his apartment. Finally she moved in. But it was never peaceful.

For she was a Communist—everything good and fine that an idealist can be—and she worried always that living with a European was changing her. She still taught in the school, but she had grown her hair long and straight because McAdam loved it that way. She let him buy her decadent clothes and underthings. She even kept bourgeois pets—a bird named Percy, a dog named Mad Dog, and a gluttonous mouse. And she worried for her father. He was an important man, a doctor up in the north, but still, if she got into political trouble, he would be in a great deal of danger. So when the message came, during the Year of the Hungry Tiger, at the height of the cultural revolution that was sweeping China and tearing Hong Kong apart, Ying went back to China.

She had been told it was an honor. That she had been chosen to represent her school at the May Day celebration in Peking. She was proud and happy, and he was terrified.

"This is no time for you to go to China, Ying! You know what's happening up there, anybody with the slightest hint of bourgeois about them is in big trouble. With us in our situation? The Red Guards would tear you apart."

She said, exasperated, "Jake, it's going to be *fascinating*. You yourself said you'd give your eyeteeth to see China now. It's history. And it's my country. And I've been chosen to represent my school. Six weeks off from school with all expenses paid."

That really impressed her, he thought bitterly. Scratch a Chinese and you find a capitalist.

"*And* I'll be seeing my father, whom I haven't seen in two years. I don't like leaving you, but of course I'm excited. Do you know what my principal said?"

Oh, Jesus, he thought. "What?"

"He said he had recommended me to go because I am the best teacher."

He held up his finger at her. "But *not* the best Communist! You'd be Red Guards' meat, Ying—"

"Darling," she appealed patiently, "only if they *knew* about us. If anybody knew, I would not have been chosen. When it was announced at assembly this morning, everybody applauded me. I am a People's hero!"

He refused to laugh at her joke.

"So how could a Red Guard know about us?"

Of course, they did know, had known almost from the beginning. When she came back, six weeks later, they laughed and hugged and cried and made love. But afterward, when they lay still and quiet, she took a big, trembling breath and said, without looking at him, "They want me to be a spy."

They had known all along, and only waited until McAdam was promoted to superintendent in Special Branch. While she slept, through that long first night, he drank and smoked and thought about what had to be done. And when he had thought and planned and thought again, it was all very clear. He faced the truth—that all was lost, and the only honorable, sensible goddamn thing to do was get out. Go to America, or the Caribbean, even Europe, and count on their forgetting about her father once she was no longer of possible use. He felt better then. No one would take her away from him. Not Mao Tse-tung and his seven hundred millions, nor all the queen's men.

As it turned out, it had only taken one man.

"Do you still love her?" she was asking again.

He looked at her. Then he said, "Let's talk about you, Vanessa."

"All right." She smiled. She half turned, and lay on her stomach on the blanket. "My mother was an actress. In the theater. And Dad's a politician."

"What kind of politician?"

"Senator. He was a Congressman for years. He was the youngest Congressman for a long time. Since the Boston Tea Party, to hear my mother tell it." She added: "She died rather young. Dad was only thirty then, his first term in Congress."

"How did she die?"

"Car crash. I was only small. But I remember how proud she was of Dad. They made a very dashing couple, I believe. The beautiful young actress on her way to stardom, and the handsome young Congressman." She smiled. "I think they both thought they were on the way to the White House. And maybe they were."

"I can believe it. And what happened then?"

She added, "She *was* extraordinarily beautiful."

She sighed cheerfully.

"I went to stay with my aunt, my mother's sister. Because Dad was always in Washington, sorting out the world. I was shunted off to a boarding school for rich little bitches whose mommies didn't want them underfoot. And then Dad went and married one of the mommies—a rich big bitch."

"And you didn't get on with her?"

"Hell, no! But I suppose I wasn't too easy to get along with myself. I wanted my own mommy. And my Daddy to myself." She shook her head.

"How do you get on with your stepmother now?"

"I still hardly ever see her. But she's an old rich bitch now. And I'm a young rich bitch."

"And your father?"

"He's still up in Washington, of course. Still too busy. I hardly see him. But we get along great. Still tries to spoil me when we see each other, to make up for having been such a rotten father. Seems to think I still like lollipops." McAdam smiled. "He's given up his designs on the White House. But he's very much the elder statesman. Frightfully proper. And very Boston Brahmin too, now, unfortunately."

She turned her head and gave him her brilliant smile.

"I must go soon, Hogan. But first I want to see the sun rise over China."

The gray began to turn to pink in the east, and then to a red and orange glow; they climbed the long grassy hill, hand in hand,

and stood on the top silhouetted against the dawn. All the islands were turning to mauve, and the early morning mist was drifting in below them, slowly billowing round the islands, creeping along the rocky shorelines; and now the east was turning red, fanning up into the sky, and then the sun came up. First just a crescent of flaming gold, then up it came before their eyes, slowly, then faster and faster, and now the whole horizon was on fire and the sea sparkled blinding gold and silver and the early morning mist was turning to shifting pink, and the grass on which they stood was golden sparkling green.

The following Wednesday Vanessa went out to McAdam's boatyard to get Wong's story. She came in the very early morning on a bus that was crowded with fishermen and Hakka peasants and ducks and geese; then from the main road she walked the four miles to McAdam's bay, swinging along, enjoying it. But there was nothing sociable about the visit.

She did the interview with Wong sitting in the shade under the banana trees, while McAdam carried on working. Getting the story out of Wong had been like drawing teeth; and all the time she had been very aware that McAdam was working. She was welcome to take his labor away for a couple of hours but he wasn't going to stop for her or anybody. Fine. She did think he might take time out for a cup of coffee with her, though. But by God, how he worked! In shorts, the sweat running off him, with studied concentrated swiftness. Like a Trojan, and the walls seemed to grow up in front of her eyes.

When the interview was over she firmly refused his polite offer to drive her back to the main road: working hours were clearly for working around here. She stood in front of him, very aware of the sweat glistening on him and the strong smell of man, and said in her formal way, "Many thanks again. Let me know when you're coming to town, I'd like to cook you dinner."

And she turned on her heel and started walking up the hill in the blazing China sun, her skirt swirling.

Which impressed him. Of course a journalist should go out and get her story, but it was a long, hot way back. It impressed him that she refused to disrupt him and considered a long, hot hike all in a day's work. He thought about her a good deal that day as he worked, sweating, laying bricks in the broiling sun. The image stayed with him, her walking over the hills, her long golden legs. And she wouldn't be wearing panties.

She was strong and she could take the heat of a Hong Kong roof-top. And she believed in doing her homework properly. But she could not take bullshit.

Right there in front of her binoculared eyes was a chunk of jungled mountainside spotted with plank-and-tin huts that she had been watching for almost three days with the police. In the last week she had watched the police raid drug dens on that piece of mountainside three times, and the following day they had been back in business.

Through her binoculars (her sweat on the eyepieces stung her eyes) she could see the addicts, skinny wretches making their way to the dens. She could spot eleven lookout boys dotted about, each in sight of the next, just sitting on the roadsides and on tops of the shacks.

Then, as she watched, a car drove brazenly up the mountain road. She saw a lookout boy wave. The car sped along the road between the huts, then it braked opposite the den and a bag was held out of the window, and an addict grabbed it. The car sped away and the addict walked toward the den. The radio of the inspector beside her rasped.

"Scramble. Black Hillman sedan number—"

She scrambled up with them and ran across the rooftop and clattered down the stairs. They burst out of the apartment building and ran flat out along the access road toward the den. Addicts were throwing themselves out of the doors and windows and crashing off into the bushes. The den door slammed in the first policeman's face. He kicked it open with a crash and burst in.

Ten minutes later it was all over. She stood inside the hut with the panting policemen and surveyed the haul: they had confiscated several bags of heroin (number 3, the reddish gray kind called Red Chicken) and had arrested the addict who took the bag. The inspector's radio rasped again, then he said to her excitedly, "Bloody marvelous! They've caught the Hillman! Had a shootout in Chai-wan. The driver was just an ordinary illegal taxi, he didn't know anything about it, but we've got the guy who was seen handling the bag."

"Great," she said.

She thought, *big deal*. What'll he tell you? He's a Triad man. If you can convince the jury that you saw him hand over the bag, he'll go to prison, where he'll be paid to keep quiet. In any case, there were plenty more where he came from.

She thanked the inspector and left the hut, followed by the faithful detective corporal whom Bernard Champion had assigned to her. When she reached the road she saw the fire engine had arrived. Jack-the-Fire was in charge, but he did not see her. They had come to burn the den and surrounding bush as soon as the police had finished collecting their evidence.

Big deal. A scorched-earth policy. Of a few huts. And two miles away the mansion of Sir Herman Choi stood resplendent, impervious. End of story.

End of bullshit. If the laws of evidence could not make the connection between Herman Choi and the ever-shifting heroin dens of Hong Kong, Byline Storm Williams certainly could. And would.

The next weekend there were bullfights in Macao, the tiny Portuguese colony forty miles away across the River Pearl. Bernard Champion had invited her to go with him.

Friday was the hottest day so far of that hot summer. The sun blazed down on the glaring South China Sea and on the narrow sweating concrete streets, and the sky was mercilessly blue. It was still sweltering hot at midnight when they boarded the S.S. *Fat Shan* for Macao. There were a lot of people crowding through Immigration and up the gangways; the bullfights were a big annual event.

Bernard Champion had used all his considerable influence to get the best of everything. Flowers and champagne in her first-class cabin, the best room in the Estoril Hotel in Macao, the best seats at the bullfight. And everything very proper; separate, though adjoining, cabins and hotel rooms. In case she thought him presumptuous. Now, as the ferry steamed down the fairway, they stood at the stern rail watching the beautiful harbor lights go by under the China stars.

Big Bernie Champion was nervous. He was in a new white tropical suit and tie, holding a glass of champagne, feeling very formal. He wished he could relax. He desperately hoped he could keep her to himself this weekend, and they wouldn't have to join crowds of friends. He was dreading having to take her down to the bar soon; they would be all over her, making jokes. And he would stand there, tongue-tied like an idiot.

"Isn't it beautiful?" she said.

"Oh, yes. It is."

She wished to God he would relax. And she was embarrassed by all the expense he had gone to for her. She had expected to spend the night against the bar like everybody else. But first-class cabins. Separate. She had expected to sleep with him when she accepted his invitation to Macao. But that had been some time ago. Now she knew Bernie better; she knew what an affair would do to him. And she knew McAdam. . . . Well, there were a lot of reasons, but in any case she hoped like hell that they could keep to their expensive separate accommodations.

Out of the corner of his eye Champion covertly looked at her golden neck and shoulders and the lovely cleft of her breasts and the full curve of her body. He found courage and awkwardly put an arm around her waist.

She stood close to him for just long enough, then gave him a warm smile. "How about letting *Esquire* buy *you* a drink, officer?"

As he had feared, it was jumping down in the big cocktail bar, jam-packed with people, most of whom he knew. The first person they saw was McAdam. With old Captain Neil O'Bryan and Harry Howard and Mervin Katz.

She was surprised. She had not seen McAdam for ten days, since she had interviewed Wong, and he had not contacted her. She had presumed (she damn well *hoped*) that he was simply too busy to come to town. And now here he was squandering a whole weekend.

"Hello, Champ! Hello, Vanessa!"

"You're looking fit, Hogan!"

He was. His face was deeply tanned and he must have lost ten pounds. "You're looking robust yourself," he said to Vanessa. He turned to Champion and nodded at his new white suit. "Are you in the ice-cream business?" He grinned.

McAdam was feeling fit, but dog-tired. He had intended working through the weekend, but at sunset he had suddenly thrown down his trowel and declared a holiday. He had given Wong $50 and driven home wearily, packed a bag and gone down to the docks and bought a ferry ticket from a scalper. He did not intend to see any bullfights. What he needed was people to drink and talk English with. He did not have a hotel room reserved in Macao. He didn't care where he slept, he didn't care about anything except getting a rest from that boatyard. And now here he was, confronted by Champion and Ms. Vanessa Storm Williams. Champ was introducing her to Captain O'Bryan.

"He's the captain of the *Fat Hong*—famous old ferryboat that used to do the China Coast run and River Pearl in the good old days. Ghost ship now. Eh, cap'n?" Champion beamed at him and gave a nervous laugh.

"Not given up the ghost yet," Captain O'Bryan said sharply. "She'll go plenty yet."

McAdam thought, *Poor old Champ.* The change in the guy since he fell for this one. Where was the big, burly, gut-laughing quick-witted Champ of last month?

Vanessa, he saw, had moved in on Harry Howard, picking his brain about the stock exchange. McAdam wanted to talk to Harry Howard himself about the Lucky Man Development Company, but now Vanessa was taking Harry aside. God, McAdam thought, doesn't she ever stop working? He knew who she was questioning him about: Herman Choi. He looked at the line of her body and had to make himself look away. Champion moved up to him and said with a bright forced smile, "How are you getting on—about selling the apartment?"

McAdam didn't even want to think about it. "No joy yet. Too big, the agents say. I'll probably have to rebuild the upper one first, as you said."

"Yes . . . Champion glanced covertly at Vanessa.

"For Chrissake!" McAdam put his hand on his friend's shoulder. "How can you be uptight about old Harry?"

"I'm not uptight," Champion whispered. He added, "I just hope this doesn't keep up all weekend. She's a glutton for work."

"Well," McAdam said significantly, "she hasn't got that long here."

Champion took a big gulp of his drink. "Maybe."

Oh, God, McAdam thought. "Show her around Macao, keep her away from the popular bars."

"Yes," Champion said. "She wants to find out about the refugees and all that."

"Good. Work on that."

The ship churned evenly across the South China Sea under the stars. In the bar there was hubbub, music, the air cloudy with smoke.

Mervin Katz, of the Royal Observatory, was with his girlfriend, Veronica, the Pan Am air hostess from the American Mess. Jack-the-Fire was there with his wife, Monica. McAdam saw the beautiful Kurt Marlowe, the pilot for the United States Navy Meteorological Department, making his way toward them through the people. He did not want Kurt Marlowe joining them; he could not stand the conceited ass. Kurt Marlowe came up behind Vanessa, slipped both arms around her waist and snuggled up against her bottom, grinning his perfect smile. "Hello, darlin'!"

"Oh, hello, Kurt, you're back again."

Her smile was less than warm, but Champion flinched inside. "Hello, everybody," Marlowe said.

McAdam leaned back against the bar. "What's the weather going to do next week, Dogs?" he said to Mervin Katz, ignoring Marlowe. "When are we going to be able to bathe again?"

"Speak for yourself." Marlowe smiled perfectly.

"There's not a typhoon within a thousand miles," said Katz.

Kurt Marlowe said, "Typhoon Rose is within fifteen hundred miles. I flew into her this morning. From the Philippines. Bad bitch."

"I'd love to visit your Royal Observatory some time, Dogs," said Vanessa.

"I thought you were investigating corruption?" Katz said. "Show me how I can make a buck on the side out of the weather and you'll be my pal for life."

They all laughed, except Kurt Marlowe, who said to Vanessa, "I'll fly you into a typhoon any time you like."

"Gee, thanks a million," Vanessa said dazzlingly, and McAdam smiled. Then Kurt Marlowe was dancing with Vanessa. She tried to lean well back in Marlowe's arms and talk brightly, but he would have none of that: he was holding her close, nuzzling her brow and cheek, and short of walking off the floor she had little option but to endure it. She could feel his erection pressing against her. That was par for the course, but it annoyed her. The guy presumed that it would turn her on. Almost all the girls in the

American Mess had been ga-ga about Kurt Marlowe at one time or another, and he was one of the best-looking men she had ever set eyes on, but he did nothing for her. In fact he irritated her. Because underneath that perfect smile and profile and prematurely gray hair there was massive conceit and calculating shrewdness.

Champion kept his back studiously to the floor, as if nothing was happening. He had hardly contributed anything all night, except his ready panting smile. McAdam's heart went out to him. He longed for Champion to stop suffering, but most of all he desperately wanted to get some sleep somewhere. "I must find a bench," he said.

Champion said, "You can have my cabin. We've got one each." He was about to refuse when Champion said, "Please take it. You'll be doing me a favor."

He pretended not to understand. The music ended. Champion glared at Marlowe: he was trying to keep her on the floor for the next dance; but she succeeded in leading him off.

"That's very kind of you, Champ," McAdam said.

Marlowe whispered in Vanessa's ear as they approached; then turned and walked away toward the toilet.

"Excuse me," McAdam said.

He found Kurt Marlowe in the toilet off the promenade deck, combing his hair at the mirror. McAdam leaned against the door and said quietly, "Please, Marlowe, do us all a favor. Lay off that woman."

Marlowe paused, comb poised, then turned to face him.

"Do *me* a favor, Jake. Mind your own business. Stop trying to spoil my fun. You've had your share, now it's my turn."

Afterward he did not know why he did it, and he was by no means proud of himself. But he lunged forward and in one movement grabbed Marlowe by the scruff of his neck and wrenched him off balance, flung open the toilet door and slung him out. Marlowe reeled across the deck, arms and legs flailing. He rolled over and over, then crashed to a stop against the rails.

Nobody saw it. McAdam straightened his collar with satisfaction. He had to resist dusting his hands. Then he turned and walked back into the bar.

He said goodnight and asked Champion to show him his cabin.

The next thing he knew, Champion was shaking him, smelling of toothpaste and aftershave lotion, and telling him they were docked in Macao, did he want to share their taxi?

McAdam shook his head.

"I've got a spare room at the hotel for you, if you need it."

McAdam shook his head. "Champ?"

"Yes?"

"I think I may be needing to borrow that two hundred thousand off you."

Champion flinched. "Sure," he said. "I told you, any time."

"Lucky Man Development. Harry Howard can get me a big block of shares at par, says they're a winner. Know anything about them?"

Champion said, "They're the one to go for, I hear. You're very lucky. But they're not coming on the market for another few weeks."

McAdam said, closing his eyes, "Thanks, Champ. I can last that long. I'll let you know. Maybe somebody'll buy the apartment."

"Sure," Champion said. He left.

Then the Chinese purser was shaking him, telling him the ship was about to sail back to Hong Kong. McAdam kept his eyes closed and said, "How much for this cabin back to Hong Kong?"

"Forty dollars extra," the purser said.

He burrowed his hand into his pocket without opening his eyes and pulled out a note and held it out.

He didn't want to see any bullfights, all he wanted to do was sleep. Most of all he didn't want to make things easy for Champion again.

_____***Part four***

It was the eighteenth of June, the official birthday of Queen Elizabeth the Second.

The room in San Francisco's Chinatown had a door at each point of the compass, representing the gates of the City of Willows, where the virtuous monks of the Shao Lin monastery founded the Triad Society hundreds of years ago to rid China of the foreign Manchu emperors and restore the Ming to the Dragon throne. On the altar was a large red wooden tub filled with rice to represent the countless thousands of Triad Society members. Next to the tub were the Red Club, symbolizing punishment, and the Sword of Loyalty and Righteousness. On the left sat the 489, the Master of the Society, and on the right sat the 438, the Incense Master. The other officials sat facing each other. The most powerful of these was the 426, the Red Rod, for he was the executioner.

At the eastern door stood two guards, armed with big swords. The group of recruits, who were called New Horses, came and gave the Triad handclasp, and the guard intoned: "Why do you come here?"

The New Horses replied: "We come to enlist and obtain rations."

The guard said, "The red rice of our army contains sand and stones. Can you eat stones?"

The New Horses replied: "We can eat stones."

Then the New Horses were allowed to pass the Mountain of Knives, crawling beneath the crossed swords of the guards, and the Incense Master lit five joss sticks and cried: "Tonight we pledge brotherhood in the Red Flower Pavilion. The brethren of Hung will live for myriads of years."

Three paper figures, bearing the names of traitors who had betrayed the society, were placed in a kneeling position, and the official known as the Vanguard smote off their heads. Then he intoned: "I bring you numberless fresh soldiers, iron-hearted and valiant, who wish to be admitted to the Heaven and Earth Society."

The New Horses approached the altar. They knelt and the Red Rod tapped the back of each with his sword and cried, "Which is harder, the sword or your neck?"

And the New Horses replied: "My neck."

Then the Red Rod official read the thirty-six oaths. And the New Horses repeated them.

The Vanguard intoned: "Loyally and faithfully we perpetuate the Hung family. The wicked and the treacherous will be broken into pieces in the same manner as this lotus flower." He smashed a lotus bowl with his sword. He picked up a live cockerel and chopped off its head, and held the flapping body over a bowl containing wine and ashes of the burned yellow paper, and added its blood.

The New Horses knelt before the altar, and held out their left hands. The Vanguard deeply pricked the middle finger of each man's hand, and intoned: "Do not reveal our secrets to others. If any secrets are disclosed, blood will shed from the five holes of the body."

The blood was added to the bowl. And each New Horse drank.

Now they were members of the Triad Society, sworn to a blood brotherhood from which only death could release them.

Choi Ho-man had once been a New Horse in exactly the same initiation ceremony in Hong Kong. Two years later, however, he had become the 489, the Master of the Hong Kong branch. Choi Ho-man was accustomed to buying what he wanted, but it was not his wealth alone that got him the rank of 489, it was sheer ability. He was a natural manipulator of people, and he had a genius for delegation of responsibility. He delegated so well that he did not even appear at meetings. Most ordinary members had never even seen him. But he knew everything that was going on, both in the Hong Kong lodges and overseas, and his orders went out very effectively.

Choi Ho-man had joined the 14K Triad Society in order to acquire his own private army, worldwide, with iron discipline and sworn by blood and fear to total secrecy and service. It gave him greater power than all the police forces of the world combined.

As the Triad initiation ceremony was being performed in San Francisco, Choi Ho-man was in a limousine, entering the guarded gates of Buckingham Palace, in London.

Twenty minutes later he was in a large, gilded hall, at the end of which, on a dais, stood the throne of England. Seated on the throne, crowned and in ermine, was Her Majesty the Queen, Elizabeth the Second.

Choi Ho-man was kneeling before the throne, and Her Majesty rose and in her hand she held a sword. She raised the sword, and then ceremoniously tapped Choi Ho-man once on each shoulder. He almost expected her to say, "Which is harder, the sword or your neck?" But Her Majesty said, "I dub thee Sir Herman . . ."

Then she lowered the sword and said graciously, "Arise, Sir Herman."

14

She had always thought female pride was a load of old bananas. It had seemed perfectly acceptable for her to drive out to McAdam's boatyard one fine day and say, "Okay, Hogan, if the mountain won't come to Mohammed, Mohammed's prepared to go to *it*. When am I going to cook you that dinner I owe you? American girls like to repay their debts."

But, all the same, she had had to rehearse it.

She opened the door of his apartment with one of the bunch of keys he'd given her, and put down a large bag of groceries. Then she walked through the apartment, opening the windows. The rooms were clean—his amah had obviously been there every day—but the place had an air of neglect and abandon about it.

She paused in his bedroom. She had an urge to go through his wardrobe. For a moment she resisted the urge, then she thought, What the hell. Did he *have* any decent clothes? If she knew what the guy looked like naked, and had every intention of getting him likewise again tonight, she was sure entitled to know what his clothes were like. She opened the big doors of his wardrobe.

As she had expected. Exactly two suits. A dark, conservative pin-stripe, well worn. And the other a black dinner jacket. She bet he hadn't worn that for a decade or two. Two police uniforms, one winter, one summer. Those really did go back almost a decade. The crowns of a senior superintendent on the shoulder tabs. There were his cap, gloves and swagger stick on a shelf. Sticking out from under the cap was a pistol. Not, she noted, a standard police revolver, but a civilian gun equipped with a silencer. She didn't touch it. On the floor a briefcase, a jumble of shoes, his old dress sword leaning in the corner. Jammed behind the sword were a number of scrolls. She pulled them out and unrolled one of them.

It was a university degree certificate. A Master of Arts, Political Philosophy, from Oxford University, England. She unrolled the next one. It had a big tea-cup stain on it. She read it. It was a citation awarding Assistant Inspector Jacob Hogan McAdam Her Majesty's Police Medal for Gallantry. Through the parchment, on the back of it, she could see a drawing. She turned the citation over. It was a child's crayon drawing of a princess with a big spiky crown on her head.

She smiled. She rolled up the scrolls and put them back. She closed the wardrobe doors and headed for the kitchen to start dinner. Then she passed the iron spiral staircase and she knew she could not resist. She didn't care. She had to know what was up there. She climbed up to the second floor and tried the door. It was locked. She searched through the small bunch of keys, selected the most likely-looking. It turned. She swung open the door.

It was an extraordinary sight, particularly because she knew what the apartment below looked like. All the walls except those of one bathroom and two closets had been removed, so the place was effectively converted into one huge many-cornered room with windows on all sides, flooding it with daylight. The kitchen appliances had been ripped out except the sinks, and shelves had been built all around them, holding tin after tin of paint. But the original bathtub, lavatory and bidet were still there, almost in the middle of the big studio, and over these he had built a wooden workbench: the washbasin and bidet were obviously used for cleaning painting equipment. Here and there still stood the white-washed structural pillars supporting the apartments above, and fixed on them were batteries of adjustable spotlights. Hanging on every wall and stacked at floor level were scores of big canvases on frames. But they were all facing the walls.

She stared. It was like entering a ghost house. There was dust, no footprints. A rocking chair. The windows all closed. Everything so still. It smelled of old paint and canvas. Complete silence. Just the sound of her breathing.

She walked slowly around the silent room, looking at the faceless canvases, the equipment. They had an air of waiting. She approached the painting hanging on the wall nearest the front door. The first painting one would see as one walked in, if this were a gallery. For a moment she hesitated. Then she turned the painting around.

It was the Chinese girl. The same girl as in the big portrait downstairs. The girl called Ying. And she was beautiful.

She stared at it. Ying. . . . She had a fine, handsome, squarish face. And big almond eyes, and thick eyelashes, and her pupils were large and black. And straight, jet-black hair. That was one of the differences from the portrait downstairs. The Ying downstairs had longer, softer hair, and she was smiling gently: this Ying was younger, and her hair was in two short tufty plaits that stuck out a little. Her face was sterner, and the look in her eyes was almost haughty. She had a blue denim shirt on and she looked hot, as if she were walking in the mountains. Adding to this impression was the background. It was a valley, below, mauve in misty heat under a mercilessly blue sky.

She turned the next painting round.

It was Ying again. This time her eyes were bright with anger. It was a remarkable painting of a beautiful, indignant young woman. You felt the girl had just been pointing, accusing. There was a story behind that accusation, she could feel it: it was an important moment in time, and he had enshrined it here. And she wanted to know what it was.

She moved slowly to the next painting and turned it.

She knew it would be the girl. But she was unprepared for the difference. Ying wore big cat's-eye spectacles that had once been stylish, and her big eyes were fixed in concentration. Her right hand was poised in front of her, almost reaching out of the canvas, and in it was an artist's paintbrush. Held up in her other hand, as if she had just taken it from her mouth, was a cigarette.

She stared at the beautiful, intense Chinese girl. In those concentrating eyes was a bright, almost serene, confidence; so different from the accusing Ying. Vanessa felt a twinge of unease.

God, the guy's good!

She went abruptly to the next painting. She almost did not want to turn it around.

Again she was surprised. And her journalist's mind said *Aha!* For here was the first bit of evidence. The girl *was* a Communist.

But oh, what a glorious one. In the background was a poster Vanessa had seen often around these parts, a marching column of joyous, healthy Chinese peasants carrying big sheaves of wheat into a Red Star sunrise over China. And in front of it stood Ying, her square face resolute and her big eyes glinting; her mouth was open, and you knew it was in song. You knew she was leading others in the singing, and you knew it was the Chinese national anthem, "The East Is Red."

She felt she did not want to look at any more paintings. But she could not stop now. She turned over the next.

And oh, yes. A Ying so beautiful Vanessa did not like standing beside her. She was naked, though only her head and breasts were painted, and in her big eyes was the complete happiness of a woman in love, who had just made love, and her hair was longer and tousled, and she looked breathless and maybe she was even sweating.

Vanessa breathed tensely, deeply. She began to go through the rest more quickly. Ying on a rooftop garden, watering flowers with a big red watering can. Ying poised in the middle of a graceful Tai Chi Chuan exercise, Ying swimming in the sea, her hair plastered wet to her laughing head, her black hair streaming behind her. Ying in glorious silhouette walking into the sunset with a dog at her side; Ying lying in a bathtub, reading a book. Ying . . . Ying . . . Ying. She had to find the end of the story. She was nearing the end of the hanging pictures now. Then she turned over the second to last one, and stared.

Ying's face was gaunt, pale, her big brown eyes staring, her full lips bloodless. And in those exhausted, staring eyes for the first time was irresolution. And grief. And yearning. And exhausted confusion. She wanted to say, "Tell me—tell me what happened." She could feel the grief in those eyes go straight to her heart.

She turned away from it. But she had to know now. She turned over the next picture and caught her breath.

Ying's eyes were full of tears, and she was cringing in fear. Her head was partly averted as if she had just been struck, and splatting from her nose and over her open mouth was rich blood. And on top of her head was a dunce cap.

Vanessa stared, sickened. She could feel the fear of the next shocking blow.

A dunce cap? Somehow that was more shocking and pathetic than the blood, than the cringing.

And the painting was unfinished. As if he could suddenly bear to paint no more, had suddenly thrown down his brushes. And had never picked them up again.

She locked the studio door behind her and walked slowly down the black spiral staircase. Her footsteps sounded loud in the empty apartment. She walked slowly to the kitchen, and began to unpack the big grocery bag. Through the open kitchen window she could hear the distant roar of the bulldozer working at the site four hundred yards up the mountain.

Everything was prepared, the roast ready to go into the oven, the vegetables ready for boiling. All she had to do was go back to the American Mess and shower and change, come back and switch the oven on. As she rinsed her hands at the sink, she noticed the huge construction site up the mountain above her again. For the first time she looked at it. She could read the big signboard: *Lucky Man Development Company Limited.* So this was one of Choi Ho-man's projects.

She stared at it, her hands poised at the tap. And a very lucrative project it would be. That was a very big bite those bull-dozers had taken out of the mountain; it was going to be one hell of a big apartment house in a desirable middle-class area, where rents were very high. Most apartment buildings in Mid-levels were tall and slim, because land was so expensive and hard to get; whereas this building was going to be tall and broad: a lot of apartments. Lucky Man was very lucky indeed: all the suitable land in Mid-levels had been snapped up long ago and what was left was so steep it was unsafe for construction. That building up there was going to be worth a fortune.

She looked at the building site a moment longer, then looked at her watch. She had enough time.

She walked up the long, winding road. She had not realized how steep it was. So steep that the road had been cut in two big hairpin loops. Between McAdam's apartment house and the Lucky Man site there were only two private houses, cut into the mountainside; the rest was virgin jungle. She walked up the hairpin bends, sweating, and at last she came to cars parked along the road opposite the site.

She stood, panting. A high wooden fence had been built around the site. She wondered why. She walked up to it and peered through one of the joints in the planking. There were workmen everywhere. Concrete-mixers were roaring. One pile driver was working already. The huge steel piston was hauled up mechanically to the top of the tall guillotine with a scream of steam, then it came crashing down on top of the big steel foundation pile, smashing it into the earth, like a huge hammer driving a huge nail, again and again.

She peered through other cracks. She was astonished at the size of the bulldozed area. It was about a hundred yards long and at least forty yards deep into the mountain. She looked at the mountain—the slope was forty-five degrees here at least, maybe fifty. The back end of the wedge towered high, a huge cliff of earth. Dozens of workmen were busy plastering the cliff face with cement, and building a retaining wall against it. The cliff was about one hundred feet high. And almost vertical. She could feel its menacing presence. She looked at the retaining wall of concrete bricks being built against it, and thought, *Thank God they're doing that quickly*.

Maybe it was the physical presence of that cliff, and the enormity of the wedge that had been cut out of the mountain; maybe it was the nerve-shattering scream and crash of the pile driver making the earth shake, but she wanted to get away from the place. All the same she made herself look around, trying to take in everything.

She turned around from the wooden fence and looked at the view the apartments would have. Directly below, way down there, was Dragon Court, the tall, narrow building where McAdam lived. It was a magnificent view. And nothing would ever be built in front of it because of the two private houses below the road, and the steepness. This was probably the best site in the whole of Mid-levels for an apartment house.

She walked along the edge of the construction site. Then she saw four Chinese men in suits emerge through a door in the fence, carrying briefcases, and she felt her pulse trip. One of the men was Sir Herman Choi.

She had seen him several times before in public, and she had seen many photographs of him. And every time it was hard to believe. Shortish, tubby but dapper, a pleasant face, a ready smile, twinkling eyes, a complete gentleman with a perfect Oxford accent. It was very hard to believe that once he had been a flunky in a small shirt factory. It was just as hard to believe he was a dealer in living death.

She watched him go. He was followed by his two male secretaries. The same two had always been with him, every time she had seen him. Chunky, heavy-faced, in impeccable suits, hair smoothly combed. They were his heavies, his bodyguards. She watched them go down into the road toward the big Silver Cloud Rolls-Royce. She had an urge to run after them and get him to talk, try to squeeze something, anything out of him. But no. She would have her interview with Herman Choi one day. And she would be completely prepared. She watched him drive off.

She turned and looked at the advertising board. It displayed an artist's impression of the huge apartment house to be built, and the legend read:

For sale: Twelve floors of luxury bachelor, two-bedroom and three-bedroom apartments. Children's playground and ample basement parking. Magnificent views.

She wondered why the bastards were going to sell them, instead of renting them. She looked at the views again.

Yes, they'd sell for a lot of money. And, yes, there was good *fung shui,* as far as she could tell. She had read a bit about the Chinese belief in the necessity of living in harmony with the elements: *fung shui,* literally wind and water. According to the Chinese your house or office or grave had to be in harmony with nature, facing the right things, and if it did not it had bad *fung shui,* bad luck, and you should certainly engage a geomancer to tell you how to reposition your furniture and doors and windows and tombstone to mitigate the bad *fung shui.* One of the two most important elements was water, and the other was dragons. Dragons slumber in the bodies of mountains and they are benevolent unless rudely disturbed, in which case they're a veritable bull in a China shop. And from here she could see at least two dragon mountains, one on Lantau Island and one on Lama Island, with the magnificent tranquil sea between them. She guessed it was excellent *fung shui*, and the Chinese would pay enormous prices for these apartments. About the only thing that could spoil it was if a dragon had been slumbering right here where they had gouged out the mountain, and the bulldozer had rudely disturbed him. She turned back to the barrier and peered through at the cliff face. And then she stared, surprised.

The earth of that cliff face was *reddish!* Not only had this piece of mountain been the abode of a dragon, but the bulldozers had actually wounded him. By the laws of *fung shui* that red color of the earth was the dragon's blood. Oh, brother, was this dragon going to be mad at Sir Herman Choi! The last time this happened, the government had been cutting a road and the redness of the earth proved they had cut smack through some poor dragon's spine—and the outraged dragon had kicked up a terrible plague of malaria and half a British regiment had died and the Chinese population had made the government put up a shrine to propitiate the dragon. Champion had shown it to her. And a Portuguese governor of Macao had had his head chopped off by the Chinese for doing the same thing!

Wouldn't that be fantastic? If a horde of outraged Chinese came and chopped Sir Herman's head off? She smiled bitterly. It was too much to hope, of course. But maybe she could make some capital out of it.

At first they felt strangely formal with each other, even nervous.

He had showered at the boatyard, but tonight was his water night and so when he got home he had showered and shaved again. He had even put on a tie. Maybe, he thought, it was the change in the apartment which made him nervous: it looked almost lived in. She had put flowers in the living room and dining room, and there were red mats, napkins and candles on the table. And coming from the kitchen was the home-smell of cooking.

She had just washed her hair and it shone soft and golden. She was wearing a full-length soft muslin skirt, flowing and gathered at her waist, and a white long-sleeved blouse of the same material, off her shoulders. He could glimpse the dark circles of her nipples through the fabric. She was beautifully, casually groomed, and he knew she had taken a great deal of trouble over herself. And he could tell she was nervous, too, under her flippancy.

Now the candles were half burned, they were drinking their second bottle of champagne, and they were more relaxed. His portable radio was softly playing, and down there were the lights of the magnificent harbor.

They did not talk about her work; she did not want to question him about Hong Kong. The only questions she wanted to ask were about himself, about that huge, strange studio up there: she wanted to say, "Do you still love her, Hogan? Tell me!" But she did not. They talked about a lot of other things and they began to laugh more. They did not talk about the boat to Macao, and how McAdam had slept in Bernard Champion's empty bed. Neither of them wanted to talk about that.

He did not want to talk about money, but once he found himself thinking how good his apartment was when it was lived in like this, he sighed and said, "I really don't want to sell this apartment."

"Do you really have to?"

"I suppose not. But it's academic anyway, because nobody wants to buy a monstrosity like this."

She said, "I think it's a lovely apartment."

"It is tonight. Because you make it lovely."

And the soft music playing; and the delicious knowledge of what they were going to do. He wanted to do it so much that he was worried he would not be able to. But first he wanted to dance with her: to turn slowly with her in his arms, with the harbor lights down below, not a soul to see them, to feel her golden skin and the soft touch of her hair and eyelashes, and the brush of her lips and the sweet warmth of her breath.

And later they did dance in the living room, by candlelight, close together, and he could feel her soft, strong body all the way down his, warm and tangible, her belly against him, her thighs softly moving, her breasts against his chest, the beautiful feel of her body through the thin muslin, and the soft woman smell of her.

And they kissed, long soft kisses, and their hands slid, feeling each other, then he gently pulled her blouse down over her breasts; and she unbuttoned his shirt so her breasts were against his chest, and they kissed more, and then he slowly peeled the blouse over her head. The candlelight flickered on her, and his hand went to the back of her skirt, and he unclipped it. It fell in a flimsy heap to the floor, and there she stood in only her high-heeled sandals, the candlelight flickering on her long legs; and she felt his hands tremble as he touched her.

Then he knelt slowly down in front of her and put his hands on her hips and kissed her flat belly, and then her thighs, and she felt his breath, then she put her hands down on his head and pulled his face gently against her. He kissed her soft intimate hair, and he felt bliss well up inside him and buried his tongue into her warm softness. And she tilted back her head and held him tight against her and parted her long golden legs for him.

_____**Part five**

Chiang Mei-ling lived with her parents in a low-cost housing estate and she worked at the beauty counter of a large department store in Mongkok. She was eighteen years old, and she was beautiful, and she was a virgin. She had a steady boyfriend, Mr. Ignatius Ng, who was a clerk in a bank, and one day they were going to marry, when they had saved enough. Mei-ling had to stay a virgin until her bridal night, the day after which Mr. Ng had to produce to his assembled family a bloodstained silk handkerchief to prove her virginity, whereafter she would have to kneel before her mother-in-law and serve her tea as a sign that she would always be a dutiful daughter. If she was not a virgin Mr. Ng would furiously reject her and her own father would throw her out of his house and her whole family would shun her forever.

That evening Chiang Mei-ling set off for home, walking to the bus terminal. Every evening she followed the same route. A lot of vice goes on in Mongkok, but Mei-ling felt safe; she knew many of the people by sight. She did not feel alarmed when a strange young man suddenly stepped out of an alley in front of her and offered to sell her a wristwatch. The next instant a hand pulled her into the alley and another slammed over her mouth. Mei-ling screamed into the hand and lashed out, but four men manhandled her down the dark alley and into a doorway.

Mei-ling was dragged, struggling, up two flights of stairs, then they pushed her into a dingy apartment. They threw her down on the bed and tied her struggling wrists together and rammed a gag in her mouth. She lay there heaving, wild-eyed, her heart pounding with terror. The four men stood round her, grinning lecherously. The leader said, "We are the 14K. You can choose which one of us is going to fuck you and he will be your protector afterward. If you do not choose, we will all fuck you. Who do you choose?"

Mei-ling screamed and thrashed on the bed and beat her legs, and her screams were strangled in the gag. The four young men of the 14K Triad Society stood round and grinned and they knew they had made a good selection: once she was ruined she would be too ashamed to run away.

One young man wrenched her dress up over her stomach, and hooked his fingers under her panties and jerked them down. With a practiced flash he pulled out his flick knife; then he lowered it, and touched her breast with it. Then he swept it on high with a shout, and suddenly plunged it into the mattress between her legs.

He slashed the panties off her thighs. He grabbed her skirt

and slashed it off in one wrench, then he slashed her blouse off. And then he began to tear off his own clothes, shouting: "*So now we will all stab you!*"

And he leaped between her writhing thighs and ground his penis into her and thrust with all his might into her body.

In all Chiang Mei-ling was raped nine times that night. Afterward they made her wash the blood and semen off her thighs and private parts, while they all watched. For three days they kept her in the room. Mei-ling did not resist them any more, she just lay down numbly on the bed when ordered and opened her legs. They brought her food, and they brought her clothes.

On the third day the 14K Triad member responsible for the protection of the Yellow Lotus apartment house arrived to take her away. He was jolly, and he fussed over her, and she was so grateful she wept on his shoulder. They took her down into the street to a taxi. They guarded her carefully, but they knew she would not run away. She would never run home, for the unspeakable shame that had befallen her.

16

Jake McAdam telephoned Superintendent Bernard Champion. They arranged to rendezvous in a girlie-bar in Kowloon. McAdam wanted a quieter place for such solemn business, but Champion insisted on the bar.

It was a short meeting. Bernard Champion pulled out his checkbook as soon as he walked in and, without talking any more about it, did a hurried calculation on the back converting American to Hong Kong currency. Then he wrote out the check for the equivalent of $200,000.

"Many thanks, Champ," McAdam said sincerely.

Champion said gruffly, "That's what friends are for."

"What about a receipt?"

"You'll give it back to me. It won't be for long anyway. You can't lose on those shares."

"Listen," McAdam said, "I'm not that far away from the bankruptcy court. You better have something to show."

"You won't be bankrupt now. Fifty percent profit, standing on your head. But if you want, I'll tell my solicitor to post you something. Just sign it and bang it back to him."

"Okay."

McAdam looked at him. He knew why Champion was being so abrupt. Champion gulped his beer like a man who didn't know what to say and who wanted to get this over with. McAdam made himself say it.

"Champ? I'm sorry. About you and Vanessa."

Champion shot him an embarrassed look, then he looked away. "It's not your doing. It's got nothing to do with the loan. A promise is a promise and I give it gladly. I knew it wouldn't work. She's too . . . good for me. I'm just a fool."

"Champ? She's leaving soon, anyway."

"Right."

Champion glared at the bar, then took a swallow of his beer. Then he took a sharp breath.

"Are you in love with her?"

McAdam was taken aback. Then he shook his head.

"Champ, that question doesn't arise. She's going in a month."

"Well, it should arise." He shot McAdam a hard look to cover his feeling. "You've got to forget the past. Because Vanessa's not forgettable."

Then he banged his glass down. "All right. I've got to go now." And he turned and walked hurriedly out of the bar.

They saw each other often, that long hot month of July.

Sometimes he planned ahead and telephoned or sent her a telegram from Tai-po village to make a date to take her out to dinner, and sometimes she rented a car and drove out to the boatyard uninvited when she had finished her work or when she had easy dictating or transcriptions to do. She bought a big orange beach umbrella and a folding table ("You can have them when I go, Hogan"), and she set them up on the sand near the water. Sometimes she sunbathed while she worked, lying on the floating jetty. Every time they met they spent the night together, either at the boatyard or at McAdam's apartment. But they did not get much sleep.

"Why don't you ever ask me what I do on my free nights, Hogan?"

"Because I want your orange beach umbrella when you go."

She smiled. She stroked his eyebrow with her fingertip. "Oh, Hogan."

"What *do* you do on your free nights?"

"I don't have any. When I'm free I come to you."

"Ah, I get it. Silly me."

She smiled. "Hogan? I'm not screwing anybody else."

He kissed her nose.

She said quietly, "Why don't you build your crazy concrete boats in New York?"

"Maybe I will one day." He added, "I'll just rent that bit of beach next to the World Trade Center. Good spot."

She sighed. "Oh, Hogan, beautiful Hogan . . . I'm a New Yorker. Through and through. The big bright apple and all that jazz. And you build concrete junks on the China coast. To keep the natives from chopping down trees." She turned her head and looked at him. "This isn't a very realistic discussion, is it?"

"No, it isn't."

"Let's forget it took place," she said.

They walked along the coast from Deep Bay in the west almost to Shataukok on Mirs Bay in the east, through the fishing villages with their oyster rafts that once upon a time had saved Wong, and up through the fish farms and duck farms built out into the tidal flats, and then up into the mountains at Lokmachau overlooking China. They walked through the jungle along the stout British chain-mesh fence, built to keep the China refugees out, and they looked down from there into China, where the peasants worked the paddy fields under big red banners, and the People's Liberation Army soldiers stood guard in their concrete pillboxes. Once upon a time he had been the police inspector in charge of this border, and he told her something about those days, the Year of the Hungry Tiger, the year of the great famine, and the people swarming over this river and this fence.

They sat and looked down from there into China, and watched as the sun went down over one-quarter of mankind, and the mountains and the plain turned to mauve. He was staring at it silently and she said quietly, "She's somewhere over there in that vastness, Hogan."

He was brought back to reality. He did not say anything.

"Do you still love her?"

"It's a long time ago, now," he said.

"Why did you quit the police force, Hogan?"

"That's a long story."

"In a nutshell?"

He shook his head. "It won't go into a nutshell."

"Were you in trouble with the Communists?"

He smiled bitterly. "In a manner of speaking." Then he shook his head. "They were also in trouble with me."

Ying had thought they were simply going off to spend the weekend on the junk. She was too worried—sleepless and exhausted—to look forward to it much, but she knew McAdam needed to relax, and Mad Dog loved going out on the water. McAdam had asked her to trust him, but still she wondered what they were going to do.

In the weeks since Ying's return, McAdam had quietly spent time and money preparing his deep-sea junk for a long voyage. They would set off as for a weekend on the boat, but once out of the bay he would sail and sail until they reached Manila.

He knew Ying would never agree. Would never leave her father, no matter how carefully he explained that her father would not be alarmed once she was away from Hong Kong. Would never leave her beloved China. So Ying would be asleep. After dinner that night McAdam fixed her a mug of hot milk and into it he put two sleeping pills. And when she had gone off, yawning and drowsy, to bed, he raised the anchor and set off for the international lane between China and Hong Kong.

They were in the international lane when Chester Wu found them. First McAdam saw the lights, flashing two miles off, signaling him *Stop your vessel.* When he ignored the Morse code, next came the big thud of their cannon.

"All right," he bellowed. "All fucking right!"

Then they were boarding, bringing Ying up from below, arresting them for entering China waters illegally.

"*Bullshit!!*" McAdam shouted. "I am in the international lane!"

The Chinese officer said again, "You are under arrest. Put your hands on your head, and give me your gun."

They towed the junk in and took McAdam and Ying in a vehicle through the quiet streets, and McAdam knew that they were on the China side of Shataukok, and that they would be brought to the Public Security Bureau offices. There he was put into a cell, without Ying, but after twenty minutes they took him to an office.

91

As he was brought in, blinking in the light, he saw the man rising behind the desk, his hand outstretched.

"Hello, Jake," he said, in his perfect Oxford English.

It was Chester Wu.

Wu said quietly, "We were watching for you."

McAdam knew that all the bluffing and all the arguing would do no good. They had seen him preparing the junk; they knew he had been planning an escape, not a pleasant off-island weekend. And when all the bluffing was over, Chester Wu had them bring in Ying.

Her hands were handcuffed together and they had put a big white dunce cap on her head. She stared ashenly at McAdam, and Chester Wu only had to hit her once. As she cringed, nose streaming blood, waiting for the second blow, McAdam bellowed, "Yes! Yes, you fucking barbarian!"

And the bargain was made. McAdam would return to Hong Kong, to take up his new job as Superintendent of Special Branch. He would feed information regularly to Chester Wu. If all went well, Ying might be returned to him—to marry him and be his hostess, to help him spy on the British in Hong Kong. When that might be, Chester Wu couldn't say. That depended on how good a job McAdam did.

They said goodbye in Chester Wu's office, with the guards waiting outside to return McAdam to his ship. The weekend was over.

"At least we'll be seeing the same sun," she whispered against him, holding him tight. Then the guards came and gripped him on each side. She turned away, and he could see only her long black hair as she bowed her head, and hear only the sound of her sobs.

The Old Man and Dermot Wilcox had listened to McAdam's story. This was their chance to feed Chester Wu a great deal of valuable disinformation, and they took it.

For eight months he met Chester Wu out on the water between China and Hong Kong. For eight months he lived as a double agent, hating what he had to do but always hoping Chester would keep his word and send Ying back to him.

Then Dermot Wilcox got word that she was gone from Kwantung Province, that she had been sent up north to her father's hospital. McAdam knew then that he was dreaming, that she would never be returned to him. He also knew that Chester Wu

92

had to trust her, or she would never have been allowed to travel so far and be with her family. That was the day McAdam quit the police.

She had always loved the Chinese national anthem, "The East Is Red." For a long time, as he painted in his gallery, he never saw the sunrise without thinking of that song, and of her. He knew she was living the life of a good Communist, and that he would never see her again. What he didn't know, couldn't know, was what she thought of when she saw the morning sun.

━━━━━━━━━━━━━━━━━━━━━━━━━━━━━**17**

A lot of other things happened those days, those weeks. Every day about one hundred illegal refugees from China got into Hong Kong, by swimming Mirs or Deep Bay, or packed down in the holds of the snake-junks from Macao. A total of twenty-nine tons of raw opium from the Golden Triangle was smuggled in by junks, ships and planes and converted into three tons of heroin in a total of twelve laboratories, for export to America and Europe. Vanessa Storm Williams tried to get an appointment with Sir Herman Choi and was told that Sir Herman was very busy for the next fortnight. Jack-the-Fire rescued a would-be suicide from a rooftop by tying a rope around his own waist and diving at him out of a helicopter. The four stock exchanges in the colony hit an all-time high and the newspapers again warned of another crash. A Triad battle was fought in Shamshuipo between the 14K and the Wo Hop Wo, with axes, knives and bicycle chains, and six youths were killed. An average of two buyers a day expressed interest in Jake McAdam's apartments, then declared them either far too big or far too expensive to remodel.

The walls of the boatyard's big shed were almost finished, but McAdam was beginning to run out of materials and he had not yet bought the roofing and windows. The pylon foundations on the Lucky Man apartment block were finished and the walls were growing up at a phenomenal rate with two shifts of builders working twenty-four hours a day. The company published a two-page prospectus in the *South China Morning Post* of its assets and liabilities, giving legal notice that it was to turn itself into a public company, inviting the public to subscribe for shares.

Chiang Mei-ling was persuaded by a kind young man to run away from the Yellow Lotus apartment house, which was a brothel protected by the 14K Triad Society, to the Oriental International apartment house, which was a brothel protected by the Wo Hop Wo Triad Society.

In New York City, San Francisco, Los Angeles and Chicago eighteen Mafia hitmen walked into six Chinese restaurants and shot the owners at point-blank range. The next day the prefect of the Paris police received an anonymous telephone call from a man speaking French with an Indo-Chinese accent, advising him that, contrary to official belief, heroin refineries in Marseilles were still functioning, and providing him with the address of a big one. Within an hour the Marseilles police had a shootout in a suburban villa with a number of Sicilians and seized a large quantity of heroin, worth $4 million on the streets of New York. The next day the United States Coast Guard received anonymous information as a result of which a Mexican fishing vessel was boarded as it hove to off San Diego and one ton of raw opium was found cemented under the concrete ballast in its bilges.

These were record hauls and they made international headlines; the police were jubilant and claimed that they had broken the spine of the Mafia supply route. It shook the Mafia to its family foundations. Their own traditional method of war had backfired on them. How had the Chinese known their system and their plans? And who had given the orders? It indicated an organizational cohesion they had never suspected. As a result there was going to be a shortage of heroin on the streets of New York and San Francisco. A gap the Chinese Triads aimed to fill.

That week a fishing trawler set sail from Bangkok and in her holds were many bales of black raw opium, bound for the heroin refineries of Hong Kong. It was a massive consignment of twenty tons, which would become two tons of pure heroin, worth many millions of dollars on the streets of America. Choi Ho-man was going to hit the Mafia's distribution network like a typhoon, and make a killing.

That same day the subscription lists for the shares in the Lucky Man Development Company officially opened. The application forms, accompanied by checks, were to be submitted to Sir Herman Choi's bank, and from early morning and right through the day there were queues of people all the way down the street, waiting to hand in their applications.

Sir Herman Choi threw a charity luncheon at the Hilton Hotel to benefit the Society for the Blind and Physically Handicapped, and Vanessa Storm Williams wangled a press invitation out of one of her friends at the Foreign Correspondents' Club. As she was introduced to Sir Herman she presented him with a gift-wrapped parcel, with her most dazzling smile, and by her prearrangement a press photographer's bulb flashed. Inside the gift-wrapping was a birdcage and inside the cage was a carrier-pigeon and a letter which read:

Dear Sir Herman,

I have been trying for weeks to arrange an interview with you for my American readers but I can't get past your secretary. Please place a note in the pigeon's ring saying when you will see me, and release it from the nearest window.

Everybody guffawed, including Sir Herman Choi, and then and there he scribbled a note granting Miss Williams an appointment for the following week, and he released the pigeon out of the Hilton's window, to more roars of applause, and the flashbulbs went again.

That day a meeting was held in a Chinese restaurant between a heavily guarded representative of the 14K Triad Society and a heavily guarded representative of the Wo Hop Wo Triad Society, to discuss the matter of Chiang Mei-ling. They were not very important members of their respective Triad Societies; all except the two negotiators were only muscle men, and the business they were discussing, namely one Chinese prostitute who had fled from the protection of one society to that of the other, was of no great economic importance to either, for there were plenty more where she came from. Sir Herman Choi did not even know about the meeting and would not have been much interested if he had. But what was important was the principle, and both negotiators had the full authority of their respective Red Rods: the 14K had lost face when Chiang Mei-ling was stolen from them, and they were demanding $36,000 in compensation, a sum which would have made the Wo Hop Wo lose face. The representative of the Wo Hop Wo refused to pay and the meeting broke up ominously, and both sides knew that meant war.

And a thousand miles away over the South China Sea, the typhoon called Rose was roaring round and about herself.

Part six

First there was the vast mass of moist air over the warm Pacific
Ocean. Because warm air is lighter it rose and formed an area of
low pressure, and because of this more warm moist air moved over
the sea to take its place. This air rose also, and thus the winds
spiraled inward and formed a rotating eye. As the warm moist air
rose, the water vapor condensed and heavy rain fell: tremendous
amounts of latent heat were released into the eye and heated the
air, which rose faster and harder, and more warm wind rushed
in to take its place. Now the bands of wind were a roaring wall
around the eye, black with rain, and the whole mass was five
hundred miles wide, moving across the Pacific, feeding off the sea,
and the winds were over one hundred knots.

Mervin Katz passed Vanessa a photograph of it.

"The weather satellite sends us three photographs a day—
that's the third."

It was taken from space, and it showed a mass of black cloud
spiraling counterclockwise inward round the eye, like water circling
into a drain. The black clouds were streaked with gray; the whole
mass was beautiful and violent.

"It looks so magnificently ominous."

"Ominous," Katz said, "and omnipresent. A typhoon can form
over the Pacific at any time of the year, because it's warm. But
now, July, August, September, they're the real bad months. And
it's my job," he added, "to forecast the bastards."

It seemed like the first time she had smiled in days. He went
on, "I get help, of course. Information from land stations all over
Southeast Asia, as well as ships and balloons. And satellites. We
also get information from the U.S. Navy reconnaissance planes
that fly into the typhoons in our general area." He added, "That's
a terrible job, even worse than mine. You know Kurt Marlowe, the
American pilot, don't you? He does that."

She said, "How far away is Rose now?"

"Nine hundred miles. But that doesn't mean much. Here, look
at the latest map." It showed the South China coast, Taiwan, the
Philippines, Vietnam. Laid over it was a heavy dotted line, studded
at intervals with twirls. "That's her course to date. Look at it. . . ."
The dotted line veered and looped, swung from north to south and
doubled back on itself. "She's been looping around like that for a
month."

"Is that unusual?"

"No. Typhoons march like Genghis Khan's army. They can

stop, curve, loop, swoop. All without warning. But this bitch? I've never seen one skip around this much. Ever."

"Can't you just rely on your radar? It shows up on radar, doesn't it?"

"Sure. But the radar only reaches two hundred and forty miles. We can see the typhoon beautifully once it gets within range. But by *that* time the damn thing's almost on top of us."

She said, "Do you think she's going to hit us?"

Mervin Katz breathed out through his hairy nostrils.

"As a meteorologist? Anything can happen. But if you want to know what I feel in my water?"

"Yes?"

He looked at her. "She's coming," he said. "I got the feeling in my water. Suddenly, one day soon, she's going to veer northwest. And then keep coming."

18

McAdam had arranged to take her out to dinner that night, and uncharacteristically he had even reserved a table. But when he got to his apartment after dark to shower and dress he found a meal prepared in the kitchen and a flippant note telling him not to touch the oven, she had gone back to the Mess, and would be back when she was clean.

Her bright mood was still to the fore when she came in, looking lovely, but he could see behind it. She kissed him and breezed into the kitchen. He followed her in and poured two beers but she busily examined her pots and the oven. He leaned against the sink and said, "What's wrong, Vanessa?"

"Nothing." She shot him a smile over her shoulder and went back to the pots.

"Is anything wrong at work?"

"No."

He looked at her back. All right, he thought. He had lived long enough to know that he would find out soon enough.

She said without looking round, "Everything's going swimmingly, as you would say. Like swimming against the tide. Any advice from an old China hand about how I handle Sir Herman Choi at the interview?"

He felt sorry for her. She had worked so hard on that bastard. And she had put together an excellent, polished article; she had let him read it. It would embarrass Choi, it would make excellent scandal reading. But it wouldn't make her famous. If all the queen's horses and all the queen's men and Interpol and the FBI couldn't crack Sir Herman Choi's armor, he didn't think much of her chances in one interview in his mansion surrounded by his unseen bodyguards. But there was no stopping her; she had the bit between her teeth and he admired that.

"What are you going to throw at him?"

She said, "Play it cool. And charming. And then start in on him. Provoke him to anger. Finally accuse him directly. Then"—she turned around and folded her arms grimly—"I can at least publish his angry denials. 'No, I am not a Triad member. No, I am not a heroin trafficker! No, all the rumors about me are vicious gossip!' A clever journalist like me can do it."

He smiled, proud of her, sorry that his own work had kept him from being more of a practical and moral help to her. He said quietly, "You're great, Vanessa."

For the first time ever he saw embarrassment flicker across her face. "Thanks, Hogan." She turned back to the stove and stirred a pot unnecessarily.

It was a restrained dinner, although she tried to be normal. She talked as if he were an old acquaintance whom she had not seen for some time. McAdam sat there, waiting for it. He wanted to put down his knife and fork and take her hand and say, "All right, Vanessa. What is it?" But he waited.

She said, "This story isn't going to make it in the U.S. Not big enough—unless my interview with Herman holds some real surprises. But I'm still going to do my best to damage Sir Herman Choi."

"Good for you. How?"

She played with her wineglass. "Something new I've found. It probably doesn't add up to much. On the other hand, it's a nice bit of local color. It could be a good way to begin the story. *Or end it.* And with a bit of luck," she said, "it may adversely affect the value of his goddamn Lucky Man shares. Particularly if the story appears in a big local newspaper like the *South China Morning Post* on the first day the shares hit the stock exchange."

McAdam's fork stopped in front of his mouth. "What?" he said.

She smiled wanly. "*Fung shui,*" she said.

He stared at her, then felt relief flood over him. "Oh? What about it?"

She said, "My subhead will be '*Un*-Lucky, Man, *real* unlucky!' That may frighten off the Chinese share-buyers." She pointed at the wall. "That huge apartment block that he's building just up there? Bad *fung shui,* man."

He smiled. "I'd have thought it had excellent *fung shui.*"

She shook her head. "Oh, yes. It overlooks the water and two mountains with dragons. On the face of it, excellent. But," she held up her finger, "they had to bulldoze out the mountainside. And that cut slapbang through some poor dragon's spine!"

McAdam tilted back his head and laughed. "Who told you that?"

She smiled. "Don't laugh at me, Hogan. It makes a good little story. And it could help, which God knows I need. Nobody told me. I went up to the site, and I saw it."

"What did you see?"

"There's a huge cliff face where they've cut a massive terrace in the mountainside. And that cliff face, Hogan," she said, "is *red.* And as any Chinese will tell you, that's the poor dragon's *blood.*"

McAdam felt the smile freeze on his face. He stared at her. "Red what?"

"Clay. And soil, of course."

"Clay? And soil? Not rock?"

"No. A few bits, sure. A dragon can't be too choosy where it sleeps, you know. But mostly clay. And *red,* sir."

Trying to wipe the consternation off his face, he picked up the wine bottle and sloshed some more into both glasses. He smiled hastily at her joke, but his mind was racing. *That cliff face was made up of clay and soil? Not solid rock?* Jesus. In a mountainside that steep? He knew enough about building to know that that should never be allowed, particularly in Mid-levels with its bad record for landslides. A terrace that big would cut all the natural support out of that piece of mountainside and the whole building could collapse if it wasn't on solid rock. And he knew enough about building law to know that a cut that big into ordinary soil would not have been allowed officially—some silver must have changed hands. He tried to say it casually.

"How steep is that cliff face?"

"Vertical. Almost literally."

Jesus. She didn't know it yet, but she had found a big fat crack in Sir Herman Choi. She had found the story that would really land the bastard in trouble, a prosecution for corruption, public fraud. God knows what. But, Christ, he had just invested two hundred thousand borrowed dollars in Lucky Man, and he didn't want her beautiful little story breaking until he had sold his shares. On the very first day. Nine o'clock next Thursday morning. He put his knife and fork together casually and said, "Are you sure it was *red* clay, Vanessa? And soil?

"Saw it with my own eyes."

"Well, I'll go up tomorrow morning and have a look at it."

"Too late, Hogan, the bastard's too smart for that. He used to have a wooden fence around it—I looked through a crack—but now the wall is brick. Why? Don't you believe this reporter?"

He smiled. Thank God for that brick wall. "Of course. But I think you'll find he's employed a geomancer. To appease the dragon. Government often has to do that, to keep the Chinese happy, with all the mountains we bulldoze down for resettlement blocks."

"And *does* that satisfy the Chinese?"

"Yes. Costs government a fortune."

"So you don't think I'll get anywhere with that story?"

"No," he said. "I don't."

She twirled her wineglass.

"Well, I'm going to publish it anyway."

He said, "When?"

"Next Thursday morning. The day his shares hit the market."

"Have you told the editor of the *South China Morning Post* about the *fung shui?*"

"No, I'm keeping that as a punch line."

"Is he definitely going to publish it?"

He lit a cigarette. He had to work on it to keep his hand from shaking.

"He hasn't seen the story yet. But he's interested."

He inhaled his cigarette deeply.

"I think you're underrating the story. You should at least try it out on *Esquire* before you give it away to a local paper here."

She was shaking her head. "No, no way. There's no U.S. link-up. They'll have to write it off."

"So what if they do? Try the London *Times* or the *Observer*. Herman Choi was knighted by Elizabeth's own hand; there's a local tie-in for you. You can't just give up, Vanessa. You've worked on this too hard. If London and New York both turn it down, you can still get Choi in plenty of trouble here in Hong Kong. But don't do yourself in, too."

He was trying so hard that he believed himself. And, by God, he was right. She *could* still hang Choi—only, please God, not until after Thursday.

She smiled at him. "Thanks, Hogan. You're a lovely man."

There were tears in her eyes, and suddenly he realized that her remoteness all evening had not been because of the story.

"Hogan?" He looked across the table. "Please don't interrupt me. Let me say what I must."

He nodded.

"Hogan? This is the last night I'll see you. Because . . . I'm going home one of these fine days, and I must control my feelings." She took a big breath. "I'm still in control and I'm going to keep it that way. But if I saw any more of you it would become very difficult."

She lit a cigarette and puffed out smoke hastily.

"Nothing can come of us. You live in Hong Kong. And I live in New York. And neither of us wants to change. And in those circumstances I certainly don't want to be in love with you, ten thousand miles away."

She paused.

"And I certainly do not want to get married." She looked at him. "Please believe me. This is not some kind of female ploy. I think one day I will get married. If I want to have children. But certainly not now."

She puffed hard on her cigarette, then blew out smoke.

"And please don't think that I imagine that you want to marry me, either. I don't believe you do. Possibly for several reasons. But the most important is that you're still involved with the past. You're still in love with Ying."

He didn't say anything.

"And that's your business, Hogan. I'm not making any demands upon you; in fact the opposite—I'm leaving you. For my own reasons."

She looked at him.

"She's very lucky to have your love. Wherever she may be or whatever she's doing, she's got that with her and that's a gift beyond price." She looked down at the table. "But the most important thing I want to say is this. You may be trying to forget her, but you're not out of the woods yet. And you must get out of them—now, Jake. Because there's a whole beautiful world out there in the open, and you deserve the best of it. And you're not really like me in at least one respect. You *do* want a deep, permanent relationship with one person."

She glanced up at him. He was staring at the center of the table.

"But . . . few women could live with you while Ying is still in your heart."

They were silent for fully a minute. She stared at nothing, her cigarette burning away. McAdam stared at the center of the table, thinking, unable to think. He had been expecting it, and hoping it wouldn't come. He didn't know what he was going to say, what he wanted to say.

She said, "Please, Jake. If you love me the slightest, don't say anything. My mind is made up. Please don't even try to delay the evil hour."

She stood up and looked down at him.

"Goodbye, darling Hogan."

He stared at her. Then she gave him her dazzling smile, but her eyes were moist. She turned on her heel and walked out of the apartment.

He sat where he was, stunned. He listened to her footsteps ringing down the corridor to the front door.

For an hour he sat at the table. Then he slowly got up. He picked up his keys and walked slowly out of the apartment. He rode down in the elevator to the basement garage. Then he got into his car and drove through the night, back to the boatyard. He did not sleep that night. At three o'clock in the morning he got off his bed and lit a pressure-lamp, went out to the shed, mixed up concrete and began to work, the sweat running off him in the moonlight. And Sunday dawned.

That Sunday was bad. It was completely quiet, the sun beating down, reflecting back at him off the hot hard China earth, hazy, shimmering, all the way to the horizon, and the sea was oily blue and flat. There was not a sound but the lonely noise of his trowel slapping mortar and bricks. He did not have a hangover,

105

but his body was sick for sleep and the whole world seemed bad. At four o'clock that Sunday afternoon he could take no more, and he threw down his trowel and flung himself on his bed. But he could not sleep. He did not fall asleep until midnight, and he was suddenly wide awake with the dawn of Monday. And there was nothing else to do but get up and start working again.

At five o'clock that Monday afternoon he knew what he had to do. He walked solemnly to the end of the jetty and dived in. Then he waded ashore and pulled on some clothes. He swallowed half a glass of whisky, got into his car and drove back to Hong Kong.

The amah answered the door. As he walked toward the living room he heard a man's voice, and then he heard her laugh. The living room was empty. Through the French doors he saw Kurt Marlowe sprawled on a wicker chair on the big veranda. Then he saw her, half hidden by a potted palm. There was a bottle of whisky on the cane table beneath them. If it had been anybody other than Marlowe, he would have gone away and waited until tomorrow. McAdam stood in the French door.

"Good evening."

She looked around at him, surprised. Then he could see she was a little drunk. She was wearing a flowing Japanese kimono. "Hello," she said.

Marlowe said nothing, just looked at him with one eyebrow cocked. McAdam looked back.

"Do you mind leaving us alone for a while?"

Marlowe stared at him indignantly.

"Yes," he said. "Yes, I do."

McAdam looked at Vanessa. She blinked and slowly turned her head to Marlowe.

"Better go, Kurt. I'm sorry."

Marlowe sat poised. Then he put down his glass. He stood up theatrically, bent over her chair and kissed her forehead.

"See you soon."

"*Hasta la vista,*" she said.

Marlowe turned and strode past McAdam into the living room. He closed the front door with a slight bang behind him.

"Well, Jake?"

"I'm sorry about that."

"Like hell you are." She sloshed whisky into a glass for him. "Cheers."

"Did you have a date with him?"

She laughed. "It's happened! I never thought I'd see the day when Jake McAdam asks me what I'm up to. No. He just blew in with the typhoon. Dropped by to see if he could get into my pants."

McAdam sat down. He took a big sip of whisky.

"I said I didn't want to see you again, Jake. You're not being very fair."

He said: "Why don't you call me Hogan?"

"I don't want to call you Hogan any more. Quit stalling. Why did you come? Not for the same fluffy little thing as the beautiful Kurt Marlowe, I hope."

McAdam took a firm breath. He said, "I don't accept what you said last time."

She looked at him.

"It's not for you to accept or not accept. I'm going. As surely as the sun will rise in the east. And you live here. And ne'er the twain shall meet."

"Don't go."

She said with quiet exasperation, "Hogan. Stay and do what? I'm an American, through and through. My career's there. My whole life."

He said, "And live with me." He held out his finger. "Last time I heard you out without interruption. Now you give me a hearing, please."

She sat back.

"Live with me, Vanessa. You said yourself that you wanted more than anything to go international, to break out of New York. Well, this is your chance. Even if the *Esquire* piece doesn't turn the trick, you can send home good articles from here. You can become an expert on China. On the whole Far East. With your talent for work and getting to know people."

She was listening. He went on.

"And *live* with me, Vanessa. We could give ourselves a chance. Three months. Six months. A year. . . . We've got a great relationship, Vanessa. Don't throw that away lightly. We're very compatible. We could have a great life. We can take off on the junk and sail the world. It's within our power. We can get out there and do things that other people only dream about. We're both the kind that *do* go down to the sea in ships."

He stopped and looked at her. "Don't go, Vanessa."

She said quietly, "And what happens after our trial period? What happens if it's a failure?"

"I don't believe it will be."

She said, "I go back to the States and start all over again. With a broken heart."

"For God's sake, take the risk!"

"And if the trial period is a success? What do we do—apart from going down to the sea in ships?"

"We'll get married."

She nodded slowly. "And what about the lady upstairs?"

He didn't understand her for a moment. "What lady?"

"Upstairs in your gallery," she said quietly. "Ying."

He stared at her. "Have you been up there?"

She nodded, slowly. "Yes."

For a moment he was angry. Then he controlled it. "Then you'll have noticed that the paintings are all turned to the wall."

"But they're still up there, Hogan. And in the living room she's not turned to the wall. I'm not telling you to take her down. I'm just telling you that it's significant. Of your emotional condition."

"My emotional condition is well under my own control now, Vanessa."

She smiled wryly. "I don't doubt it. Controlled. I've seen plenty of evidence of that. But in your controlled way you still love her."

"There's an important difference in practical life between always loving somebody from a long time ago, and being *in* love."

"I understand that, too. But what I don't understand is how do you feel about me?"

"I'm in love with you, Vanessa."

She stared a long time at her drink, then said quietly, "Thank you. I mean that." Then her blue eyes flashed. "And I mean this too. *Bullshit*, Hogan! Oh, I admire your honesty! That you admit you still love her. That you come to me tonight with a solid proposition of a trial period. And all that jazz. Fair enough! It's what you want. But don't"—she jabbed her finger between her breasts— "expect me to go overboard about it! You finally manage to admit that you're *in* love with me. But getting you to say it was like pulling a goddamn tooth out of you! Which is also fair enough—because it's how you truly feel. And believe me, I want the truth. And the truth is you *don't* love me! If you did you'd have burst straight out with it. 'Listen, I love you! I'm not letting you go!' But no, you come here with a well-thought-out proposition and the final thing you mention, under cross-examination, is that you're in love with me. I don't believe it's true. You're still in love with her."

"It *is* true," he said quietly.

"And that's not the only thing I don't believe, Hogan. Listen. I've given this whole thing a hell of a lot more thought than you have. Because *I'm* the one who's going to get hurt, and *I'm* the one who's got to give up her life back home. And I'm a bit drunk now and I've been a bit drunk for two days. And this is what I think: we're *not* compatible. For a whole lot of reasons. And one of them is that I'm not half as big and bold as I act! Much as I hate to admit it. Everything I've made in life I've got the hard way by working twice as hard as others. And I want to keep what I've got. I've never done anything adventurous that wasn't under the protection of my employment. But you don't give a damn about security. About money. I'm *envious* of you. How's that for compatibility? Sure, I'll go down to the sea in ships. But only if you make me. And I'll be shit-scared."

"Bullshit."

She snorted and ignored the comment.

"But that's not the half of it. The other half is far worse. And that is this." She looked at him unsteadily. "You're a straight guy, sexually, Jake. You're a great fuck, you're a wonderful lover. But straight. And I'm as kinky as hell. I'm a fantasist, McAdam. Believe that. Gang-bangs and threesomes and foursomes and moresomes! And I want to share them with you, to tell them to you, to turn you on to the same thing—and I can't. It wouldn't turn you on, it would shock you to the marrow. And it would haunt you, and finally you'd want out."

He said, "Try me."

"You couldn't handle such thoughts—you wouldn't tolerate it. Let alone do it."

He said, "I don't think you would either, when it came to the crunch."

"'But I *want* to be able to! Don't you see? When the honeymoon's over between me and you and we get down to day-to-day living, I'll revert to type. You're a straight, loyal guy. And I'm not—not naturally. Not until you came along. By nature I'm a whore."

"You're not!"

She cried, "Not a paid one—just a willing one! Do it for free. For kicks. And I'm bisexual—"

"You are not."

"I am! Do you think I don't know what I want? Christ, you don't even believe I'm telling you truth; that's how far apart we really are."

109

He said, "I'm getting tired of this, Vanessa."

She slapped her forehead.

"My God! 'Tired of this,' the man says. The arrogance of it! The sheer *ignorance* of it! You're so goddamn ignorant of how women can feel—of how *I* feel—so unimaginative about sex, that you don't believe it. Well, I'll tell you what, McAdam, take me to a whorehouse right now and I'll prove it to you!"

Insulted, he rose to the challenge. "All right, I will."

"Okay!" She slapped the table. "Let's go!" She stood up and picked up her whisky and gulped it down. "Then see if you believe me! And *then* see if you can live with it!"

19

They drove in grim silence. She stared straight ahead. So did he.

"You're really going to go through with this nonsense?"

"Yes."

But he was sure that when they got there she would chicken out. He pulled into the basement garage of Nanking Mansions, in Causeway Bay.

Almost all the space available in Nanking Mansions had been sold. The ground and first floor were vast shopping arcades; above were offices and sewing shops and apartment-factories that made plastic flowers and dolls and transistor radios. And above that were ten floors of apartment-hotels with names like the Cherry Blossom and the World of Suzie Wong and the U.S.A., and they were all whorehouses. On the sixteenth floor was the Oriental International apartment house.

The elevator opened straight into the whorehouse foyer. There was a big mahogany desk with reception *foki* sitting behind it with an abacus, and the lamplight was dim red, and there was a strong smell of incense. Beside the main door were two little godshelf altars, with offerings of mandarin oranges and joss sticks burning: one was to the god of brothels, the other to the goddess of fornication. The clerk stared at them an instant, then professional inscrutability returned.

McAdam said, "Can we see the Mama-san, please?"

Vanessa said loudly, "And a drink, please?" She looked around the foyer and sniffed. "Sex, McAdam—the joint reeks gloriously of sex."

The Mama-san came into the room. She knew McAdam but her eyes gave away nothing. "Good evening."

"Mama," McAdam said, "this lady is my brand-new wife and she wants to see how I spent my money before I met her."

The Mama-san's face broke into a smile.

"Long time no see!" She turned to Vanessa. "Mister Mac not very good customer, you know—" and she burst out laughing nervously.

They followed her through the reception room. There was a long mahogany bar and cane bar stools. Around the room sat a dozen girls watching television. They came out of their boredom when they saw Vanessa. They stared as she crossed the room. She flashed them a smile. One of them was Chiang Mei-ling, in a red dress.

Vanessa sat down on a bar stool and crossed her legs seductively. McAdam leaned against the bar. "Two double whiskies, please. Well, here we are." He jerked his thumb over his shoulder. "Which one do you fancy?"

She retorted, "All of them. Which do you fancy? You're going to fuck her too."

"Oh, am I? Good."

She turned around to the Mama-san. "How many rooms do you have?"

"Twelve," the Mama-san said. "Very good. You like see?"

"In a minute. And are these all the girls?"

"Two working now."

"Is tonight a quiet night?"

"Not busy," the Mama-san said. "Monday."

"And how much are the girls?"

The Mama-san looked at her. "You want girl?"

Vanessa laughed. McAdam smiled grimly. "But how much are they?" she repeated.

"One hundred," the Mama-san said. "About twenty U.S."

"That's cheap: a good hooker in New York costs fifty. And how long does she stay?"

"Until you're finished with her," McAdam snapped.

She turned around to him conversationally. "That tall girl in the red dress—she's beautiful, isn't she?"

"She is."

She turned to the Mama-san. "Can we see the rooms now?"

They followed her out of the room, down the corridor. The lights were soft pink under ornate Chinese shades. The Mama-san stopped at the first mahogany door. "Venice Room." She opened the door.

And there was Venice on the wallpaper all about them, the Piazza San Marco, and in the middle of the room was a double bed built into a gondola.

"Fantastic!" She walked into the room. She sat down experimentally on the bed and the Mama-san flicked a switch. The lights went out and stars appeared in the ceiling. The gondola bed began to sway gently, and from somewhere came the voice of a gondolier singing in Italian.

He followed down the corridor. He didn't know whether she was stalling or not. The next was the Tokyo Room. The floor was tatami matting and in the middle was the futon, the mattress; the walls were sliding Japanese paper screens and there was the tiny dressing table one had to kneel before, and in the other corner the sunken bath. The Mama-san slid back one of the paper screens. On the wall behind it was a lifesize photograph of a Japanese garden full of cherry blossoms, and a bird began to sing.

"Oh, wow."

The next was the Bangkok Room. "Occupied," the Mama-san said. Then followed the Taj Mahal Room and the Manhattan Room —"Occupied"—and the London Room and the Paris Room. All the walls were papered with blown-up photographs of the cities they were named after. Then they came to the Heavenly Pacific Room.

It was circular. The ceiling was domed, and the big double mattress was set in a bulbous mass of inflated white vinyl that looked like a cloud. "Get on bed." The Mama-san beamed.

Vanessa piled over the cloud-mass onto the mattress and lay on her back, arms outflung. The Mama-san switched out the lights. And suddenly the domed ceiling was a starlit sky and in one corner there was a brilliant sunset going on, sinking below a horizon of silhouetted palm trees, the glow flaming up as the sun inched down, and on the opposite side a silver moon was rising. Then the Mama-san flicked another switch and the cloud-bed began to rise. It rose up gently toward the ceiling on a hydraulic jack, and out of the silhouetted palm tree came the fluted strains of Hawaiian music. Vanessa lay there on the cloud-bed laughing as it came down.

She slid off the bed and stood up. She looked at him.

"This one."

"Very well," he said tersely.

Vanessa Storm Williams lay spread-eagled on the cloud-bed, naked, waiting. Her tape recorder was on the chair. The door opened and McAdam came back in.

"Two minutes," he said. "None of these girls will do it: they're getting an expert down from King Winky's upstairs."

He sat down on the edge of the cloud-bed and folded his arms. She said, "Get undressed, Hogan."

"Like hell I am."

"Get undressed. You defied me and brought me here. Now I'm going to prove I was telling the truth."

He glared at her.

"Very well."

He took a big mouthful of whisky to try to get some drunkenness back, then stood up and started to undress. His fingers were shaking. She was so damn beautiful. Lying there, her big white breasts lolling magnificently, her belly flat, long legs: she was the incarnation of sensuality. But he still expected her to back out. What she proposed was in principle one of the most sensually exciting things he could imagine, every man's fantasy. But he felt sick in his guts. She was watching him undress, her eyes slow with liquor, her wide smile mocking.

"What're you uptight about, Hogan? You don't think I'll do it?"

He said nothing. He didn't want to provoke more bravado.

"McAdam—this is supposed to be fun. Most men would think so."

"It is. I can't stop laughing."

She tossed her head and burst out laughing. Then she almost held out her arms to him. "Oh, Hogan."

The door opened and a woman came in. "Hello," she said.

They stared at her. She was about twenty-eight and European. She was tall, poised, with black hair swept up on top of her head, and she was good-looking and pale and aloof.

"Hello," Vanessa said languidly.

"Okay," the girl said, and they caught the slight American accent. "Just relax, I understand what's wanted. If there's anything special, tell me."

She began to get undressed. She slid her dress off her shoulders and it fell to her feet. She had long legs, in black stockings with a

113

red suspender belt and brief white frilly panties, and her breasts bulged out of her brassiere. She bent her arms behind her back and unclipped it and her breasts were free. Vanessa was looking at her appraisingly. McAdam tried not to stare. He could just make out faint stretch marks of childbirth on her belly. He wanted to ask her who she was. The girl sat down on the chair next to the tape recorder and peeled one stocking off. Then her panties and the suspender. "All right," she said. She came to the cloud-bed and smiled down at Vanessa professionally.

"You're very beautiful," she said.

"So are you."

"Sorry about the tan, don't get much sun in this job."

The girl put one knee up on the bed and said, "Who takes charge?"

McAdam muttered, "I think you'd better."

Vanessa shifted over on the bed. The girl lay down beside her. Then she got up onto her elbow and smiled down at Vanessa.

"Your first time? With a lady?"

Vanessa shook her head.

The girl smiled disbelievingly. "Don't be nervous."

She bent and slowly kissed her on the mouth. Vanessa lay there rigid a moment, then her arm went uncertainly round the girl's neck. McAdam stared at them kissing. He could not believe it. The glorious woman he thought he was in love with making love to another woman. It was like a dream, and it did nothing for him. He was in a sort of half-angry daze. The girl uncoiled an arm and felt for his, then pulled him down. He resisted, then he came down onto his elbow beside them, looking at them. Vanessa moved her mouth away from the girl's and looked at him defiantly.

"Well, Hogan?"

He said thickly, "Well, what?"

She started to say something else, then said, "How do you feel?"

"Fine."

"Enjoying it?"

"Sure. What man wouldn't? Unless he was arrogant, ignorant and unimaginative."

She looked at him. "Kiss her then." She added, "But kiss me first."

He shook his head.

"Goddamnit, McAdam," she whispered, "this is meant to be fun!"

She gave him a fierce smile and then she suddenly slid down

the girl's body to her breasts and began to suck her nipple hard. McAdam looked at her, his woman's mass of golden hair on the girl's breasts, and the girl lay there with her eyes closed and her lips apart. Then Vanessa writhed down, fiercely kissing the other other woman's stomach and hips and loins, and her mass of golden hair dragged down the girl's belly, and the girl sighed and her legs woman's stomach and hips and loins, and her mass of golden head was between the girl's legs, and the girl's hips were writhing and her hand was buried in Vanessa's golden hair, gripping it; and then one hand snaked up the girl's body and found her nipple and began to twist and pinch it and her other hand slid over and found his loins, and suddenly McAdam's dazedness snapped. It snapped in a rush of lust and angry hurt, and nothing else mattered and he was going to fuck these two women, and his hand hit the hydraulic switch.

The lights went out, the Pacific night flicked on, Hawaiian music flooded the room. The cloud-bed rose through the Pacific night with the whore writhing in the middle of it, McAdam on top of her and Vanessa watching him from the back, and he thrust deep inside her and now Vanessa had her arms around his chest and she was fiercely kissing his back and it was the most wildly erotic feeling in the world, a woman beneath him and a woman on top of him and their wet writhing warmth; and he thrust and thrust and thrust—then suddenly agony shot through him as Vanessa sank her teeth deep into his hip and crunched. He yelled and Vanessa hung on fiercely, then let go and lunged at the switch, and the Pacific night disappeared.

Disappeared with a snap in mid-Hawaiian lovesong, and the overhead lights came on bright, and the cloud-bed slid back down toward the floor with a thump. Vanessa leaped off it and ran into the bathroom and slammed the door.

McAdam stared at the door, shocked, feeling the pain in his hip, then a smile broke over his face.

"Vanessa! Come back!"

She yelled from within, "Go ahead and fuck her!"

Then he heard the bloodcurdling yells down the corridor and the crash of axes and the screams.

20

The gang of 14K Triad burst out of the elevator into the Oriental International foyer to avenge the stealing of Chiang Mei-ling, yelling and swinging their axes and cleavers and bicycle chains on high. The clerk ran backward, arms flung up, and they bounded after him, swiping and slashing; an ax smashed his shoulder. They smashed their axes into the big mahogany desk and the chairs and then the door leading into the corridor, bellowing above the girls' shrieking, and the Mama-san was screaming into the telephone to the police, and the door smashed open on its shattered hinges and the Triad men burst through.

The girls scrambled screaming down the corridor for the fire escape, as the five Triad men erupted into the bar, where the Mama-san was screaming into the telephone. One swiped her with a club and another sliced the telephone in half with an ax and the others were smashing up the bar. Swinging their axes, bellowing and yelling, they smashed the mirrors and bar stools and the sofas and chairs and the television set. Down the corridor the axes were smashing up the Venice Room and the Taj Mahal Room and the Tokyo Room and the Manhattan Room and the London Room, hacking the beds and the windows and the wallpaper and the lights and the bathrooms. McAdam had flung himself at the door of the Pacific Room to lock it, then he heard the first girl fling herself against it screaming and wrenching the handle. He looked wildly for something to arm himself with, grabbed a chair and pulled open the door, and the girl reeled in. Three more were screaming past the door toward the fire escape, but it was locked, and the girls were frenziedly shaking it. McAdam wrenched the last girl into the room, then flung the chair up in front of him and lunged out into the corridor to cover the other girls, and the axman crashed into him.

The axman swung at him and the ax crashed off the chair back into McAdam's forearm, and he rammed the chair with all his might into the man's chest and crushed him against the wall. The man tried to swing the ax up again and McAdam rammed the chair with all his fury into his face, and his shriek was cut off and the ax dropped to the floor. McAdam swung his fist far behind and hit him with all his might in the guts, and the man doubled over and crashed to the floor. McAdam reeled, the blood running from his arm. He grabbed the ax and looked wildly once up the corridor, and then a man bellowed something and the Triad men were scrambling out of the rooms and rushing back toward the elevator. And there was a shattering of a window behind him, and then the scream.

It was a scream of absolute terror and it came from the girl called Chiang Mei-ling as she fell from the sixteenth-story window. Mei-ling fell through the air, arms and legs outflung, her hair streaming behind her and her eyes and mouth wide in terror, and the wind tearing the scream from her mouth: she hurtled through the night down toward the street lights and she screamed all the way till she hit the pavement.

McAdam lurched up the corridor, panting, his right hand clutching the wound on his left forearm. Suddenly there was just the hysterical sobbing of women. He looked into the ruined bar. The Mama-san was sitting in the corner, sobbing, clutching herself; he looked at the *foki* lying in his blood in the shattered foyer, then knelt down and felt his pulse. He was alive. He walked shakily back down the corridor to the Pacific Room.

"Vanessa!"

The door opened immediately. She was dressed, wild-eyed, shocked; she closed her eyes and clutched him tight.

Then the elevator doors opened again. The police had arrived, led by Superintendent Bernard Champion.

He heard Champion speaking loudly and fast in Cantonese, giving orders, asking questions. There were other male voices; he could hear policemen checking the other rooms. McAdam leaned against the wall of the Pacific Room while Vanessa feverishly wrapped a towel round his arm; then he shouted, "Champion! Bernie!"

He heard Champion striding down the corridor, then he stood in the doorway in his uniform and riot helmet, big and hairy and astonished. "Jesus Christ! What're you doing here?"

"Just visiting. I think I'd recognize one of them."

"And *you?*" Champion glared at Vanessa.

Vanessa glanced at him, then continued binding up McAdam's arm. "I asked Hogan to show me what a Hong Kong brothel was like."

Champion looked at the other girl in amazement. Then he snapped, "With a naked prostitute! *Jesus Christ, what are you doing to this woman?*"

McAdam snapped, "Mind your own business, Bernard! I said I'd recognize one of them."

"It is my goddamn business! Jesus Christ . . ." He stood there, outraged. Then he turned on the prostitutes and jerked his thumb. "Out!" he shouted in Cantonese. "Go and wait in the foyer—and you." He strode and picked up the dress and threw it at the American girl.

They hurried out of the Pacific Room, sobbing and sniffing. McAdam was pulling on his shirt impatiently. Champion closed the door with a slam, then turned back on them furiously. He held out his finger, and it shook: "Of all the . . . *twisted* things to do."

"Dry your eyes, Champ," McAdam muttered. He started tying his shoelaces, with difficulty.

Vanessa snapped, "Please just tell us what happens now. Hogan's got to get to a hospital—"

Champion stared at her, quivering. "What do you think happens now, Vanessa? Do you realize what you've got yourself into? Do you realize that a girl lies dead in the street out there and you're slap-bang in the middle of it as witnesses? That you're going to have to stand up in court and tell them what the hell you were doing in a whorehouse? What's your newspaper going to say about that? How're you going to look? Like a goddamn whore yourself. Which you are!"

"Shut up, Champion!" McAdam snapped.

"I don't mind giving evidence, Bernard—it's my duty to do so," said Vanessa.

"Don't you, indeed? But that's only half the story, Vanessa Storm Williams. This is a Triad murder—a Triad Society gang war between the 14K and the Wo Hop Wo over a prostitute that one stole from the other. Do you think they'd think twice about killing off any witnesses?"

McAdam said, "She saw nothing, and even if she had there'd be no reason for her to give evidence."

Champion turned on him furiously. "Right, because now you expect me somehow to keep your names out of the case because

of the scandal and because you're my friends—or used to be!"
There was a sharp rap on the door and he barked, "Come in!"

McAdam finished tying his shoelaces. He looked up and saw
an angry middle-aged Chinese man in the doorway. Bernard
Champion turned to him. The man said in Cantonese, "Can anybody identify them?"

"I don't know yet."

The man snapped in Cantonese, "Then find out! I pay you
enough! I want every one of them hanged, otherwise it's war!" And
he turned on his heel and strode down the corridor.

McAdam froze over his shoelace. He had understood the
Cantonese.

Champion growled, "Do you want to be taken to the hospital
for that arm?"

"No. I can get there myself."

"Then get out of here fast. I'll telephone you tomorrow." And
he turned and strode angrily down the corridor.

The dawn was just breaking. They walked slowly down the steps
of Queen Mary Hospital. The harbor lights were still on, the whole
world quiet. His arm was numb from the anesthetic. They walked
silently across the dark, deserted parking lot toward his car. They
were both wide-awake exhausted: the night seemed unreal. They
reached the car; and she stopped and turned to him.

"Hogan? I want to say something."

He looked at her in the dark and waited.

"I'm sorry. For what I put you through. That . . . sexual
ordeal. For what I put *us* through. It wasn't very mature."

He said quietly: "On the contrary. Adult to adult, you set out
to prove by deeds what words could not prove."

"And failed. But what happened tonight has nothing to do
with my going home. Or with Ying." She looked at him in the

dark. "I don't want to do it again, what we did tonight. I lied to you, Hogan. I was just trying to tease you before . . . to get your wave-length. To see if it turned you on. Because, to be honest, the idea *did* turn me on. But not"—she shook her head wearily—"not now that my emotions are involved."

She looked at him earnestly.

"Okay? What I'm saying is that I am in love with you. I love you. Do you understand?"

She stood there, leaning against the car in the dawn.

"Oh, Christ, Hogan—*hold* me."

He sat silently at the kitchen table in the apartment while she cooked them steak and eggs, feeling the throbbing come back into his arm. She was quiet. He did not want to think about it, he did not know what to think. And he kept turning something else over and over in his head. And did not want to think about that either, what he had heard in the whorehouse. He *must* have heard wrong. Not Champion. Not big lovely Bernardo. He must have misheard: maybe his Cantonese was not good enough. But he knew it was. He suddenly thought of something.

"Was your tape recorder running all the time?"

She suddenly remembered it. "Yes."

"Where is it?"

"In my bag." She went to her bag on the table and pulled it out. "What do you want to hear?"

"Just the end. Just from when that man knocked on the door and spoke to Champion."

She pressed the rewind switch, then listened. Suddenly Champion's angry voice was saying, "But that's only half the story, Vanessa Storm Williams."

"Okay, give it to me . . ."

He bent his head and listened intently. He heard the rap on the door and Champion shouting "Come in" quite clearly. Then he heard the Chinese male speak rapidly in Cantonese in the corridor. It was very indistinct. He switched the machine off.

"Can you turn off the frying pan?"

"They're nearly ready, they'll spoil."

He heaved himself up out of the chair and started for the door.

"What are you listening for?"

"Hang on."

120

He sat down on the sofa in the living room. His body ached. He held the machine close to his ear and played it again and listened. He could barely hear the Chinese man say in Cantonese, "Can anybody identify them?"

Champion said, more distinctly, "I don't know yet."

The Chinese man replied, "Then find out! *I pay you enough.*"

He rewound the tape and listened again. That time he did not catch it. He snapped it back to rewind, then listened again. And he heard it again: "*I pay you enough.*" Vanessa came into the room.

"What is it?"

"Nothing."

"I'm not a fool, Hogan."

He looked at her grimly. "I think Champion's on the take."

"You've got to be joking."

"If he is, it's in the nicest possible way. Just part of the general rake-off his staff sergeant collects, on his own Chinese initiative— it's almost traditional. Or was until the prevention of bribery purges. Oh, Christ"—he shook his head wearily—"I shouldn't have said anything. Until I can confirm it."

She waved her hand at the tape recorder. "But haven't you just confirmed it? What's this about the Chinese man who came in right at the end?"

"He's the owner of the whorehouse. And he's obviously protected by the Wo Hop Wo Triad Society. I heard him say to Champion, 'I pay you enough. I want every one of them hanged, otherwise it's war.' And it's on the tape. In Cantonese."

She was staring at him aghast. "My God!"

He held out his finger. "Now listen . . . if you think you're going to use this in a story, you're mistaken! Because this is a very serious allegation."

"You're damn right it is! And what do you mean, 'In the nicest possible way—it's almost traditional?' It sounds as if you condone it!"

"Of course I don't. I'm saying it's an easy trap for a young copper to fall into and he's stuck with it the rest of his life—"

"Is that why you quit the force, Jake?"

"Oh, Christ . . ." he said contemptuously.

"Okay, I'm sorry! But I'm not having you cover up for any crooked cop! I've heard enough excuses for corruption in this rotten town, from Herman Choi down! If it's on that tape I'm publishing it."

"Like hell you are! *I* won't have it. It's got to be properly handled."

She cried, "*You* won't have it? You mean you won't let it be known because Bernard Champion's your friend."

"Certainly he's my friend! And he's got the right to explain himself first."

"You mean give him time to cover his tracks! Are you going to go to the Anti-Corruption Bureau with this story? No! You're going to go to Champion. And he'll explain it away and your conscience will be salved and we'll never hear anything more about it!"

His nerves were gone and he wanted to shout, but he controlled himself and said softly, "Do you want to take it to the Anti-Corruption Bureau? Hell no, because then it'll be sub judice and you can't print that bloody story. You want to publish your sensational story, *then* turn him over to the courts—*after* you've already judged him guilty!"

She snapped, "He lent you money for your boatyard!"

"So what?"

"It's ill-gotten money—and you don't want to admit it to yourself!"

"Oh, bullshit. I didn't know, did I? And anyway I'm repaying him on Thursday. The only point is the guy's got the right to clear himself before you blow the whistle on him!"

"I don't believe you. How can you repay him all that money on Thursday?"

"Because," he said wearily, "he didn't lend it to me for the boatyard, he lent it to me to invest in the stock market."

"And you're selling on Thursday?"

"Right."

She stared at him. "Why not tomorrow? Why not Wednesday? Have *you* bought Lucky Man shares, Jake? They go on the market next Thursday."

"Yes. So what, again? Lucky Man published a perfectly accurate prospectus in the papers as the law requires, certified by perfectly good accountants, and they're legitimate shares. I'm quite sure Choi has also got shares in San Miguel Breweries, Hong Kong Telephone and the Hong Kong & Shanghai Bank—should I sell my shares in those because of him too?"

She cried, "Christ! Russian and Japanese goods you boycott because they still hunt whales! But you borrow Champion's bribery money to buy shares in Herman Choi's company! And you're the guy who thinks my exposé on him is too good to waste on the locals! Well, I tell you, you better sell those shares pretty damn quick because that Lucky Man story is being published if I've got to shout it around like a town crier!"

She snatched up her tape recorder, stormed into the kitchen and grabbed her handbag. "Goodbye!"

She slammed the front door behind her.

_____**Part seven**

It was Tuesday afternoon. It was fiercely, humid hot, the haze hung over the sparkling harbor, the sea was flat and the Mountains of Nine Dragons were hazy purple and brown. She knew she should sleep but she was wide-awake, her brain clear: she had been drinking ever since she had left McAdam early that morning, drinking while she furiously typed her story about Bernard Champion, but she was not drunk. She had taken the story to the offices of the *South China Morning Post,* then headed back to her apartment, walking dully through the busy streets, a tall, beautiful woman whose face was gaunt with tiredness and the determination to get drunk enough to pass out. Now she was in bed, eyes shut. When she woke she was going to wrap up her business and get the hell out of this place.

22

The desk of Superintendent Bernard Champion, Queen's Police Medal, Colonial Police Medal for Gallantry, was always piled high with the investigation files of his junior officers, for he insisted on knowing everything they were doing and ensuring they did it fast and perfectly. He was scrawling a caustic directive on the investigation diary of a file when he looked up to see Jake McAdam standing in his office door.

"For Chrissake!" he said angrily. "Couldn't you have got yourself announced?"

"No. Because you've been avoiding me. Why haven't you returned my calls?"

"What do you want?"

McAdam closed the door firmly behind him.

"Is this office safe to talk in?"

"What d'you think we are, the CIA? What the hell do you want to talk about? I'm very busy."

"Unbusy yourself. I've come about a very serious matter that concerns you."

Champion leaned forward. "I am furious with you. More than that—disgusted! That's the only word."

"I didn't come here for any homilies. My private life is my affair."

"Then keep your perversions to yourself! Don't corrupt others! Good God." He sat back furiously. "Isn't she enough for you?"

McAdam snapped, "Who was the Chinese who came to the bedroom door in the whorehouse?"

Champion was taken aback. "I've no idea who you're talking about. Probably one of my plainclothesmen."

"Bullshit. No staff of yours would speak to you like that! He was the owner of the whorehouse, wasn't he?"

"Oh, *him*." He shrugged. "Bill Lu. Everybody knows Bill Lu. He owns one of the best whorehouses in Hong Kong, doesn't he? What about him?"

McAdam said, "That was a rival Triad raid; you told us so yourself. The raiders were 14K. That makes Bill Lu a Wo Hop Wo, or he pays protection to them."

"Brilliant. You really shouldn't have left the cops. I don't know how we've muddled along without you all these years."

"I heard him say to you in Cantonese, 'I pay you enough.' "

"What," said Champion slowly, "are you implying?"

"I'm implying that you are in his pay. That directly or indi-rectly you are receiving a rake-off from him and all the other brothel owners in your district."

Champion's face was pale. "I beg your bloody pardon?"

"You heard me."

Champion slammed his big hand down on his desk. "I should throw you out!"

"You'd better deal with me rather than somebody else. I heard it distinctly. My Cantonese is plenty good enough."

"What do you think you heard him say?"

"He said to you, 'Can anybody be identified?' You answered, 'I don't know yet.' He said, 'Then find out! *I pay you enough. I want every one of them hanged, otherwise it's war!*' "

"I've absolutely no recollection of it! Come on! Repeat that in Cantonese!"

McAdam looked him in the eye. He repeated it in faultless Cantonese.

Champion said shakily, "I do not remember any such thing being said. You are mistaken! In all that hullabaloo how could you have heard anything clearly?"

McAdam wanted to believe him. "Champion, I've got it on tape. Vanessa happened to have her tape recorder running."

Bernard Champion stared. "I want to hear that tape."

"You'll have to get hold of Vanessa. We aren't seeing each other any more."

Champion slumped back in his chair. "If this happened—which I don't remember—but if it did, he probably said, 'We pay you enough,' meaning we, the public, pay you, plural, enough."

McAdam dearly wanted that to be true.

"It was very clear. And he went on to say that if you didn't catch them it meant war. That was a Triad man throwing his weight around with a policeman he knows."

Champion snapped, "He's not a Triad man as far as we know. He just pays protection. . . . For Chrissake, Jake. You know me. Do you believe I'm corrupt?"

"I don't want to, but on the evidence I see . . ."

Champion's eyes were hard and hurt.

"I've heard you out, McAdam, only because it's the right thing to do between friends. But can't you see what's happened? We all know that the brothel owners try to pay off the police staff sergeants. And some of them take it. We can't prove it. We all know it's wrong but we also all know it's the system, and it enables the staff sergeants to lean on the underworld. I'm not debating the rights and wrongs of it, but it works. And Bill Lu assumes that because he pays off my staff sergeant that I'm in on the business. And I was so preoccupied with you that it sailed right over my head! I was *stunned*. Can't you appreciate that? You can take that or leave it, Jake. But it's the truth!"

"I'm sorry," McAdam said.

Champion said stiffly, "You were quite right to mention it."

"And I'm sorry about her. About hurting you."

Champion kept his mouth grimly closed.

McAdam waited. Then he stood up.

"Come on," he said. "I'll buy you a drink."

Champion remained seated. "No, thanks."

McAdam looked at him with exasperation.

"All right. Just one more thing. Don't keep our names out of the case for our sakes. In fact, I insist on giving all the relevant evidence needed."

"Don't tell me my job."

McAdam gave him a last look.

"So long, Champ," he said. "See you around." He added, "You'll have your money back soon. I'm selling as soon as they open on the market."

He double-parked his car outside the first public telephone box. It was fiercely hot inside. He dialed the American Mess. It rang and rang and rang.

He got back in the car and drove to the nearest telegraph office, where he wrote out a wire to Vanessa which read: *I am absolutely satisfied the man is innocent stop please repeat please do not publish differently love Jake McAdam*

Then he crossed out the word "absolutely."

He drove back into the New Territories, and resolutely put the subject of Champion out of his mind. He had plenty else to think about.

He detoured to the Shatin Heights Hotel. He sat on the veranda and chain-smoked and drank three beers, staring out over the valley and the hazy sea.

Then, finally, he got up and went slowly to the public telephone.

It seemed unreal. His hand was shaking a little. He dialed his old boss, the Commissioner of Police, on his private line.

"Jake, my boy!" the Old Man said.

"I'd like to claim a favor, sir," he said. "I'd like a meeting with you. With the Director of Special Branch present." He added shakily, "A political favor, sir."

23

She received both McAdam's telegram and a telephone message from Bernard Champion when she got back to the American Mess late that afternoon. She crumpled up the telegram and threw it away. Her pulse had tripped when she had seen the name at the end, then had come anger. He had done exactly as she had said he would. McAdam had confronted Champion, just as she'd predicted; Champion had convinced him and now was calling to try to convince her, too. Well, she wasn't going to oblige. It was for this very reason that she had decided against confronting the charming roly-poly bastard herself. He would huff and puff and look at her with his big brown soulful eyes and give some story that could be neither proved nor disproved. No way. She crumpled up the telephone message and was about to toss it into the basket, too, when she stopped.

She stood there a full minute, thinking. She only had five days left. She needed more patience. Leave no stone unturned.

She smoothed out the note.

Jake McAdam's footsteps sounded loud to him as he was escorted down the long, familiar corridor of police headquarters by the commissioner's fresh-faced aide-de-camp. It was almost nine years since he had been here, but the place smelled and felt and sounded the same. He was not remembering those far-off days when he was the blue-eyed boy of this police force; what he was numbly remembering now were the bad, haunted, nerve-screaming days. The aide-de-camp led him through the outer offices, and then there was the Old Man, standing up from behind his desk, his gray devil's eyebrows up encouragingly. "Jake! A long, long time no see."

"Hello, sir." Through the unreality of it he was surprised that the Old Man looked so much older. From an armchair in the corner the Director of Special Branch rose lankily, his hand languidly ready.

"Hello, Jake. "

"Hello, Dermot." He shook hands with him shortly, without warmth. Dermot Wilcox returned to his armchair.

"Sit down," the Old Man said. "Can I get you a drink?"

"No, thanks." He did not want to sit either. He would much rather just stand there and tell them what he wanted and get out. But he sat.

"How've you been keeping, Jake?"

"Pretty well."

"How're your concrete boats getting on? Most impressive, I thought, when I saw it on television."

"Fine." He shifted in his chair, then looked at the older man squarely.

"I want to see Chester Wu," he said, and it sounded loud in his ears. "Very urgently."

Dermot Wilcox murmured, "I thought so."

"I take it he's still up there as head of the Public Security Bureau in Kwantung Province?"

Dermot nodded.

McAdam went on shakily, "I'd also be grateful for certain information, if you can give it to me, but even if you can't, I still want to see Chester. But, please, gentlemen, no deals. I won't do anything for you in exchange. You owe me a favor."

The Old Man started to speak and Dermot cut in quietly, "It might be argued that you owe *us* a favor, Jake. After all, you're still alive. And after all, you only did your duty, as a policeman. And we had trained you in espionage—at considerable public expense, I might add."

McAdam let it go. He said grimly, "I could arrange a meeting with Chester myself by going to the Bank of China. Or the New China News Agency: they'd get hold of him. But it's urgent, and I'm sure you could do it for me immediately through your network. As long as Chester does not know that you're arranging it. He must think I'm acting alone."

Dermot said mildly, "When do you hope to see him?"

"Tomorrow night. Or as soon thereafter as possible."

"And where?"

"The same place. On my junk. Or anywhere in China waters. Mirs Bay is best." He added, "Same identification signals."

"And what makes you think he'll come?"

"He'll come. If he thinks I've got something to tell him. In the same way as you gentlemen agreed to see me."

Dermot drawled, "We thought you just might want to rejoin the club."

"So might Chester."

The Old Man shifted in his chair. "*Are* you interested, Jake?"

Dermot said, " We can give you a new cover. Put you in KGB section. One favor deserves another."

McAdam shook his head. "I can go to the New China News Agency if you won't help me. It'll just take longer."

The Old Man said, "Why the urgency? There's a typhoon coming."

Dermot Wilcox drawled, "Because his girlfriend's leaving soon. Oh, yes, I know about her and you. Just routine information."

The Old Man sighed. "And what exactly do you want to ask Chester Wu, Jake?"

McAdam took a *big* breath. It seemed unreal.

"I want," he said, "to ask about Ying." He took a deep breath. "Where she is. What she's doing."

The Old Man was staring at the center of his desk. Then he looked inquiringly at the Director of Special Branch. Dermot Wilcox shook his head moodily.

"I wish we knew. The last we heard she was in the People's Liberation Army. Intelligence corps. On the Russian border, I think," he said.

The Old Man looked back at his hands on the desk. "Is Dermot right, Jake? This is because your girlfriend's leaving? And you've got to make a decision?"

McAdam nodded, "I *want* to make a decision," he said.

Dermot laced his hands together on top of his head.

"We'll help you," he said. "We'll arrange it for Friday, tomorrow's too soon. But on one condition. We want to hear everything Chester says. About anything. Including Ying. Is it a deal?"

"Yes. But that's all I'll do."

"I'm glad for your sake you're doing this, Jake," said the Old Man. "Chester Wu will probably tell you nothing. *He* doesn't owe you any favors, particularly after all the misinformation you fed him. But at least you may lay a ghost. . . ." He looked at him. "You must forget the past."

Thursday dawned riotously red into a cloudless sky. That morning McAdam listened to the seven o'clock weather report on his portable radio at the boatyard. It was predicted that it would probably be the hottest day in the history of the colony of Hong Kong.

"Typhoon Rose is centered approximately six hundred and fifty miles southeast of Hong Kong and is continuing on her northwest course at a forward speed of about ten knots. If she maintains this speed and course she is expected to come within the four-hundred-mile radius of the colony about this time tomorrow, Friday, whereupon the Number One Typhoon signal will be raised. If she continues thereafter she may be expected to pass near the colony sometime on Saturday. This is an advance precautionary warning only, as no typhoon signal has yet been raised, but boat owners and building constructors are advised to prepare themselves for the task of securing their vessels and scaffolding, and farmers should prepare themselves to secure their standing crops and live-stock . . ."

He switched off the radio. Tomorrow night. It was cutting it fine, with the typhoon. But he would goddamn make the meeting. Then he stripped off his shirt and went grimly to work, until he could go and telephone his stockbroker.

At nine o'clock the stock exchanges opened. They were all crowded and clamorous as usual, the telephones ringing and the jobbers scurrying and signaling and the tickertapes clattering and share prices changing on the boards. Almost everything was up on yesterday's prices. But the most important share to be listed was Lucky Man Development Company.

At half-past nine McAdam stood sweating in the public call box of Tai-po village. He had a crumpled copy of the *South China Morning Post* in his hand. He had scanned it feverishly from cover to cover. Then he telephoned his broker.

"Okay, Mac," the broker barked. "I've sold them. At fourteen dollars a throw."

McAdam heaved a sigh of relief. "Thanks," he said.

"I still think you're a fool. They'll be up to fifteen by tomorrow. Okay, I got to go now, it's like a madhouse."

McAdam hung up. He stood there, mouth dry, the sweat running off him. Examining how he felt.

Forty percent profit on $200,000—he had just made $80,000. He was rich again. His money worries were all but over. With $80,000 he could keep his apartments and put the boatyard in business.

And how did he feel?

Not a thing. Not a jot of elation. He had not earned it. He had been lucky. With his friends. And with Herman Choi's reputation as a brilliant businessman.

He felt like a fraud.

Then he went to the telegraph office. He sent a telegram to Vanessa at the American Mess. He did not want to telephone, and hear her voice. It read: *In your own interests do not publish your Lucky Man story until you've seen me at Foreign Correspondents' Club on Saturday love Hogan.*

24

Captain Kurt Marlowe, United States Navy Meteorological Department, was a very handsome man, and he knew it. He was tall and gray-haired with just the right amount of lines around his blue-gray eyes, square-jawed and deeply tanned, and his teeth were white, even and perfect. Kurt Marlowe had had almost every woman he fancied, except Vanessa Storm Williams. She thought him beautiful. She also thought he was a conceited pain in the ass, and anyway until recently he had been screwing her friend Olga, and Olga had been crazy about the man. But Vanessa had to admit that on the closer acquaintance afforded by a lunch date at the Mandarin Hotel, he could be absolutely charming.

Kurt Marlowe was playing it very cool with her today, and not—unless she was badly mistaken—out of any contrition for his past brashness: Kurt Marlowe, with a wealth of experience, was working on the principle that the conquistadorial instinct of beautiful women is best aroused by a display of male indifference. Furthermore, he knew full well that she wanted a favor from him, after having been pretty damn offhand with him in the past. So Kurt Marlowe was playing it charmingly cool. And she just wished that, with the miserable way she was feeling, she did not have to go through this bullshit.

She said, "Do you develop a sixth sense about these phenomena?"

He played with his wineglass.

"Yes, one does. And she's a bad one. I've never seen a typhoon hang around so much. Roving round and round. She's like a recurring bad dream. Winds of over two hundred knots. Black as ink. And rain like I've never seen."

"How do you fly into something like that?"

He loved answering that question. Casually.

"Fly in low. About a hundred feet above sea level. *With* the wind, not against it. The winds are always going in a counterclockwise direction, in toward the eye. So you edge into them"—he swept his hand in a slow circle—"keeping the winds on your port tail." He tapped the heel of his thumb. "And in you go—and crash bang!" His hand dived and jumped and rolled. "You're thrown all over the airplane, black and blue. And the wings are trying to tear off and the plane's trying to hurl itself into the sea." He shook his head and gave her his charming grin. "Hell of a way to earn a living."

"And then?"

"Have to keep going like that. Trying to force your plane toward the eye. Can't see a thing, of course; you're flying by instruments."

"How long does that last?"

"Depends on the typhoon. Gets worse all the time because the strongest winds are round the wall of the eye. When you get to the hard wall of the eye all hell's breaking loose. The wings are really tearing off and the plane's flooded with water. Then suddenly"— he burst both his hands open—"you are sort of *hurled* out of the wall into the eye . . . and it's dead calm."

She was fascinated, despite herself. "And what's it like in the eye?"

"Superb." He held his hands above his head. "Great wall of whirling clouds, miles high. Like being in a huge spinning well. A huge stadium of clouds, spinning round and round you. And you're in a dead calm. And it's hot. And you can see the sea down there now, because it's usually clear sunshine in the eye. Though it's a sort of hellish glow. And the sea is like a boiling pot. Big waves crashing together and sucked upward."

"How close down to the sea do you go?"

"Right down. Twenty feet. Zoom across the top of the waves. To test the air pressure and the temperature down there. And the wind speeds."

"And then?"

"When we get to the opposite wall"—he tilted his hand upward—"climb up. Circling up and up. Testing wind speeds and temperatures and air pressures and density. Up, up, up toward the sun. It's magnificent."

She was considering the best way of doing it. The best was doubtless to use her charms, but she hated to with this conceited man.

"Could you take me with you on one of those flights?" Then she gave him a forced seductive smile.

He had been expecting it.

"I could swing it."

"I'd be terribly grateful. What does it depend on?"

He said, "No trouble getting you aboard here—I'm the senior officer. The difficulty would be if we have to land in the Philippines."

"Why would we have to do that?"

"If the typhoon keeps heading toward Hong Kong I have to put down in Manila tomorrow night. Standing orders. And she *is* heading this way. We'd have to smuggle you off the plane. And," he added casually, "we would be stranded in a hotel for a couple of nights."

She noted the "we."

"That would be all right." What the hell, she thought, it would serve McAdam right. "I'd hate you to get into trouble."

He looked at her and his blue-gray eyes twinkled.

"Oh, I'm prepared to risk it, if you're game."

She felt her anger flare but she controlled it. "Game for what?" she said sweetly.

"That depends."

"On what?"

"On you."

You brash prick, she thought. "I don't understand . . ."

Kurt Marlowe was also no fool. "On whether you're game for a very rough flight." He smiled evenly.

Staff Sergeant Pang Man-kit was big and fat and tough, and he was a first-rate policeman. He knew Hong Kong in general and his own district in particular like the back of his hand. He knew every crook and their spheres of operations and influence, and those whom he could not get convicted under British law he could more or less control by other means. He was hard on those who crossed him, generous to those who helped him, and he kept his bargains. Staff Sergeant Pang understood very well that a crook who owed you a favor was more useful than one who owed you nothing. Throughout his district he was respected, feared and even liked. No major reported crime had ever gone unsolved in his district during his tenure of office.

Staff Sergeant Pang was furious about the raid on the Oriental International whorehouse. He was not particularly angry that the 14K Triad Society had abducted a woman into prostitution, nor about their subsequent raid itself, for both events were to be expected from time to time. He had been angry because his information network had failed to tip him off so that he could forestall the raid by leaning on the right people, and now he was even more furious that though he had cracked the whip his network had still not come up with any information. He and his men had interrogated hundreds of people, scoured for clues, leaned on the underworld for help, but nothing had been forthcoming. It was loss of face. Staff Sergeant Pang was slipping, losing control of his district. It was a sign of the times. Police authority had been undermined, their prestige sapped by the purges under the Prevention of Bribery Ordinance, and the Triads were stepping into the power vacuum left behind them.

"I must increase the reward, sir," Staff Sergeant Pang said.

Superintendent Bernard Champion glared at the file. In the old days Staff Sergeant Pang would have set the reward without consulting him. The official scale of rewards to be offered by the police for information in this type of offense was set at one thousand Hong Kong dollars (about two hundred U.S. dollars) from his own pocket without batting an eye to make sure his network supplied the information. The trouble nowadays was that such a reward would indicate that Staff Sergeant Pang had assets beyond his policeman's salary, which in itself was an offense under the Prevention of Bribery Ordinance..

"How much?" Champion said grimly.

"Two hundred thousand, sir," Staff Sergeant Pang said. "This is a murder."

"Jesus Christ! You'll have Anti-Corruption Bureau round here in five minutes."

"They are testing me, sir. If I don't show the Triads that I still have the power, things will get worse."

"We haven't used any muscle yet. We could knock over some whorehouses to prove our power."

But Champion knew that was stupid as soon as he said it. That would only do more damage to the information network: brothel operators were an excellent source of information. A blitzkrieg on the whorehouses to prove who was boss should be kept as a last resort. He snapped, "You can raise the reward to fifty thousand. That's over ten thousand U.S. dollars, for Chrissake."

Staff Sergeant Pang stood there solidly. "Not enough, sir. I lose face."

"If Anti-Corruption hears about it you'll lose your job! And your freedom. Fifty thousand is a great deal of money! And," he held out his finger to him, "not a trace, do you hear! If this ever comes out I'll deny this conversation ever took place!"

That night Vanessa looked across Bernard Champion's living room and said quietly, "I am not going to argue with you, Bernard. If I were sitting on a jury I might, just *might*, give you the benefit of the doubt. But I am not on a jury. And I do not believe you."

Bernard Champion sat slumped in the armchair. His face was gray. He did not know what to say. He had had secret hopes that he would convince her at this meeting of more than his innocence. He had known from the moment he saw her again that he was still hopelessly in love.

"And will you also publish how you came to be in the whorehouse in the first place?"

"Oh, yes, Bernard. The best way to get through this life is to have nothing to hide. I'll simply write what happened. If I stick my nose into politics here, I expect to get it bloodied."

"Politics?"

"That's a figure of speech, but of course it's politics! Money is politics and politics is money. How to get more wealth. Corruption is against the law but the law is disregarded because by so doing the whole place runs smoothly and law and order is maintained." She banged her hand on the armrest. "That's what everybody's doing in this place! Even Hogan—even McAdam, who's so honest he won't turn his company public until he's proved its worth! But what does he do instead to raise his money? He buys shares in Herman Choi's company. One of the biggest traffickers in human misery in the world, one of the biggest villains unhung! And whose money does he borrow? Yours."

Champion opened his mouth, but she cut in, "And the government's the same! For years the Hong Kong government knew its civil service was corrupt. But did it crack down? No! Because that *system* worked! So everybody turned a blind eye—and they find it politic to award Herman Choi a knighthood! Because he donates a fraction of his profits to charity."

She looked at him witheringly. "I thought you were a man of integrity when I first met you. But by your own admission you permit your staff to abuse the law. And where does this graft come from? It's almost *clean* graft, you say, because the law banning prostitution and gambling is stupid. Well, *bullshit*, Bernard! Because that graft comes from narcotics, too."

Champion whispered, "It does not!"

"Crap, Champion!" she cried angrily. "Where do you think heroin comes from these days? Not Turkey and Marseilles any more. Not the French connection any more. No, the Hong Kong connection!" She jabbed a finger at him. "*Your* connection! Your district! Your beat, Bernard! And that's what you're permitting your staff to share in. And you're *worse* because you have the authority to stop them."

Champion was staring at her, white-faced. He said huskily, "But not the practical power. If I did, the information network would break down, our whole leverage over the underworld—"

"Then destroy the underworld, Bernard! Come down with a crack of thunder and knock the living shit out of them. And start a new information system! Be a damn *policeman!*" Suddenly her eyes were brimming with tears. She too had compromised. She had held off sending in her story on Sir Herman Choi and the bad *fung shui* for fear of affecting the shares and landing McAdam in bankruptcy. It was a small thing, sure, especially compared to Bernard's behavior of a lifetime, but suddenly she felt a little less pure. Tomorrow was her interview with Choi. Fiercely she hoped to learn something that would justify her having put McAdam above her principles.

She got McAdam's telegram when she got back to the American Mess late that night. She read it, then threw it away.

She hardly slept that night. Before dawn on Friday she got up and sponged herself down. She did not eat anything because Kurt Marlowe had warned her not to. Then she left in the sweating sunrise and set off for the government Information Services offices. She sat in their library, fiercely trying to concentrate on their files on Sir Herman Choi and her own copious notes before the interview.

At eleven o'clock, she could stand the tension no longer. She went to the Hilton coffee shop and had a bottle of beer and a hot roast beef on rye to steady her nerves. Then she went to the ladies' room, tucked her mini-tape recorder into her panties, led the microphone wire up against her skin and fixed the tip of it into a buttonhole on her blouse. She covered the buttonhole with a brooch. Then she set off into the blazing midday sun to the mansion of Sir Herman Choi.

It was hard to believe.

"Miss Williams, how nice to see you! But where are your pigeons? Aha-ha-ha!" She had laughed too. He was so charming, his English so English (he *must* have taken elocution lessons), his house so elegantly, tastefully Victorian, his manner so gentlemanly, it was hard to believe that she was in the presence of a major criminal. At least with the Mafia types, those she had met, you *felt* their ruthlessness as you feel the catness of a cat, and even their clothes seemed to give them away. But not Sir Herman Choi. Even the electronically operated iron front gate had been casually ajar. No guard dogs, no heavies, just a cat sitting in the sun on the path grooming itself. A beaming amah who had answered her knock on the front door. And the young men she had seen at the building site turned out to be so quietly, self-effacingly courteous, so immaculately groomed in dark suits, that it had been almost impossible to believe they were bullet-proof-vested bodyguards. And here she was now sitting in the registered offices of the Society for the Blind and Physically Handicapped (there had been a big brass plaque on the front gate), while the two bodyguards in the general office studiously typed and worked away at the society's philanthropic business. She had concentrated on keeping her mind mean.

He was saying, "We're trying to extend our activities from the physically handicapped to the youth as well. We'd like to be involved in things like Outward Bound, because it seems to us that in this cut-throat society the youth are in as much need of vocational guidance as the physically handicapped—probably more so, because of our peculiar social problems of congestion and the limited future of the colony. And there's a big difference between what these youngsters want and what they're likely to get. We Chinese *all* aspire to being white-collar workers, Miss Williams, whereas the colony's *raison d'être* is industry. They *need* our help."

Beautiful, she thought. She said earnestly, "Is it true, Sir Herman, that dope peddlers are actually selling drugs to school children outside the very school gates?"

Sir Herman Choi crossed his elegant legs and sighed.

"Unfortunately it is. Which"—he spread his hands—"is another reason for the youth needing our help. The devil finds work for idle hands, the saying goes. And what have these youngsters got once the school bell rings? Where are their playing fields? I feel it's up to privileged people, and organizations like mine, to help them."

Good. She knew exactly how she was going to write her story now. She was longing to slip the knife into him. But she had to provoke him, goad him into saying something indiscreet.

"Can't your organization help protect the youth from the predations of the Triad Societies?"

He spread his hands again.

"Alas, Miss Williams, even the police seem unable to protect them from the Triads. All my organization can do is offer youth some kind of alternative to Triad membership."

"Moral leadership?" she said sweetly.

"Exactly." He looked at her, then glanced regretfully at his watch.

She said quickly, "Just a couple more questions, Sir Herman, please . . ." She gave him her dazzling smile, and he smiled charmingly in return.

"First, are you a religious person, Sir Herman?"

He looked mildly amused.

"I am a baptized Christian. We Chinese are not generally renowned for our piety. We are really a rather pragmatic race, who believe traditionally in many gods. And our code of conduct is still very Confucian. Should we say I am a Christo-Confucian?"

"Combining the best of both worlds?"

"I try to," Sir Herman Choi said modestly.

Good quote. She said, "Can you tell me a bit about your chairmanship of the board of directors of Lucky Man Development Company, which has just gone public?"

Sir Herman Choi looked mildly surprised. "It is only one of many companies in which I am involved, Miss Williams."

She said, "Yes, but it's your latest baby, isn't it? The one you've been slowly building up for years, ever since you were a young man starting with nothing. It's such a success story in itself, it sums up your whole life—it's almost the American dream." She looked at him brightly. "Oh, I know all about you, Sir Herman, I've done my homework!"

He looked amused and flattered. "Ask away, Miss Williams."

"First of all, do you believe in *fung shui*, Sir Herman?"

He looked surprised, then laughed.

"Show me the Chinese who doesn't, Miss Williams! In his heart of hearts, no matter how cynically modern he is. Once a Chinese, always a Chinese; you can't expect too much of us. I'll even bet old Mao Tse-tung believed in *fung shui*. Why?"

"Well," she said briskly, "I've read up a bit about *fung shui*, and it seems to me that where your company is building that massive new apartment block in Mid-levels, it has excellent *fung shui*."

Sir Herman Choi smiled. "Oh, yes, so they say. It should be a good spot to live." He added, "We bought that site years ago, before Mid-levels was so congested."

"You've got the magnificent view of the water, bounded by those two islands with mountains containing sleeping dragons. And equally important, the road up to the site is hairpin bends, which is excellent because evil can only travel in straight lines?"

He smiled. "So they say, true."

She smiled, then said, "Isn't it rather a shame that with all that excellent *fung shui*, you had to go and ruin it all by breaking a dragon's back when your bulldozers gouged out that huge terrace?"

He put amused puzzlement on his face.

"I don't follow you, Miss Williams."

She was surprised but delighted with his reaction. "I notice that you've built that high brick wall around the site so nobody can see in. But I peeped in one day when the wooden barrier was still up, and saw that the cliff face was *red* clay. Anybody who knows anything about *fung shui* will tell you that when you cut a mountain and find red clay or soil, it means that you have cut a dragon's back. And I wondered if you had built that wall around the site to conceal the red soil of the cliff from prospective purchasers who would be frightened by the bad *fung shui*."

"Miss Williams, you're not thinking of publishing such a ridiculous story, are you?"

It did sound rather ridiculous. "Why not, Sir Herman, if it's true?"

He said quietly, "Because it is *not* true, Miss Williams." He waved his hand. "Not just the *fung shui*—the whole story's ridiculous. Because that terrace is cut into solid rock."

She opened her mouth to protest, then she stared at him. As the truth dawned on her.

"I see . . ."

And she wanted to slap herself on the forehead and jump for joy. *She had found it!* The chink in Sir Herman Choi's armor had been staring her in the face!

"I see. Solid rock. Of course, it would have to be, wouldn't it? Silly me."

Sir Herman Choi smiled frostily. "I'm afraid so." He watched her.

She put on a straight, earnest face. "Because it's common knowledge that Mid-levels is an area that has a lot of landslides." She added hastily, "I'm only quoting what I've read in newspapers, of course. But apparently the mountain slope is made up of jumbled soil and granite, and when the heavy rains come the weight of the buildings is sometimes too much for the mountain slope and the landslides occur."

Sir Herman Choi nodded warily. "Correct."

"Now . . . I take it you've investigated this?"

He looked at her hard. "Miss Williams, I am not an architect, I'm only a businessman. But I can assure you that this danger *has* been investigated, goodness gracious me!"

"But as chairman of the board, have you *personally* satisfied yourself there is no such danger?"

"Of course I have! Miss Williams, I sincerely hope that you aren't thinking of publishing an alarmist theory like that, which would be highly libelous and enormously injurious to the company."

She pretended to be embarrassed by the rebuke, then went on, "Have you inspected the site, Sir Herman, and seen the solid rock?"

Sir Herman Choi knew now that she was definitely a wolf in sheep's clothing but he kept his cool.

"Miss Williams"—he smiled with dignity—"I accept the certificates of my professional advisers in such matters. I have seen the site. Seen it, yes—inspected it, no."

"And how much solid rock did you see, Sir Herman?"

He looked theatrically at his watch.

"Miss Williams, I resent your manner. But to answer your question: I don't recall, for the simple reason that the cliff face was already concreted over. And now"—he stood up—"I'm afraid I must ask you to leave."

She said icily, "Sir Herman, you visited the site three Tuesdays ago—and the cliff face had only been partly concreted over. And the cliff was clearly not solid rock—it was red soil! I know because I saw it and I also saw *you* there."

He said slowly, furiously, "Miss Williams, I repeat, I am not a construction engineer. I believe the word of my architects and not the wild allegations of an insolent young foreign journalist! Now will you kindly leave?"

She sat on. "In short, that is why Lucky Man is going to *sell* those apartments instead of *renting* them—to pass the risks on to the innocent purchasers! And that is why you put that wall around the side, and concreted the cliff face so hastily!"

He clenched his fists at his side and his voice shook. "If you print one word of these spurious allegations—"

She cut in calmly, determined to shatter his cool, even at her own risk. "I know very well what you are, Herman Choi. You're one of the world's biggest traffickers in narcotics—you're one of the world's biggest dealers in human misery and death! You're also one of the leaders of the 14K Triad Society!"

"*Get out of my house!*"

"Which specializes in international narcotics traffic and prostitution and gambling! London, Amsterdam, Los Angeles, New York—you *are* the Hong Kong connection!"

"*Get out!*" he shouted.

She smiled brightly. "I hope for an answer first, Sir Herman."

"I *deny* it.

"Knight of the. realm. All his charitable works—the Christo-Confucian who wants to help the youth."

"*If you don't get out I'll throw you out.*"

"I'll print that, too," she said sweetly. "And your denial, of course!" She picked up her bag and stood up.

Sir Herman Choi got himself back under control. He hissed, "You print one word of those libelous allegations and you'll regret it!"

"What'll you do, Sir Herman? Sue my publisher? We will have a lovely time proving my allegations are *true*. And proving beyond all doubt that that Lucky Man apartment block is *not* built on solid rock! Because that wall would be very easy to chip away;"

She saw the fear flash across his face and she felt a thrill.

"Good day, Sir Herman!" She turned on her heel theatrically. He did not move.

"Suing you in court is not the only course of action open to me, Miss Williams."

She felt her pulse pause in fear for the first time. She stopped. But she could not show she was afraid, she had to goad him—goad him into saying something incriminating. She turned slowly.

"I beg your pardon?"

"There are more ways of killing a cat than stuffing its throat with libel writs."

"Please be more specific."

Sir Herman Choi suddenly strode to the wall and jabbed a button. Instantly the door opened. One of the Chinese men stepped into the room. He looked at her with hooded eyes.

"Ah, the heavies. I was wondering where they were."

"Drive Miss Williams back to her apartment."

"You're not serious!" She walked past the Chinese man and out the door of the office. She was shaking; she had to control herself. She heard Sir Herman Choi snap something in Chinese, then the footsteps coming behind her, and she broke into a run. She ran, panic-stricken, high heels clattering, through the general office and down the wide marble corridor for the front door. She looked wildly over her shoulder, and the man was after her with Sir Herman Choi behind him. She flung herself at the door, wrenched the bolt back and pulled at the door, and it jerked on the chain. She cried out and grabbed at the chain, and Sir Herman Choi and his man were standing right there, smiling at her.

She stared at them, wild-eyed, panting. Sir Herman Choi smiled. "Our conversation never took place, Miss Williams."

Her fingers shakily pulled the chain off its latch. She swung the door against her hip. Outside was the short flight of steps to the big ornate iron gate. Sir Herman Choi stared at her a long moment, then he said quietly in Cantonese to the man, "Later."

The man stood there with his arms hanging loosely at his sides, looking at her through narrowed eyes. Gradually she realized that he would not stop her. She fumbled the door open and rushed through the doorway and down the steps out into the sunshine. Down the path to the open gate. She ran flat out, hair flying, without looking back, until she reached the intersection at the bottom of the street and saw a taxi. She ran, waving her hand, yelling, and it stopped.

She clattered to a halt against it, and looked back over her shoulder. The man was not there. She swept her hair off her face and flung open the door. She sprawled across the seat and panted: "Airport!"

She lay there, sprawled, gasping. Then her hand went down to her stomach and she felt the little tape recorder.

She heaved herself up and looked through the rear window. She could not tell if any of the cars behind were following her.

_____***Part eight***

The sunshine was blinding, hazy, hot; but way over there beyond the horizon the sky was black for hundreds of miles, and the black winds were roaring at two hundred knots, and the sea was howling, great waves crashing and flying in galloping canyons. And beneath the great spiraling eye of typhoon, the sea was sucked upward into a seething dome, a hundred and fifty miles wide, billions of tons of crashing waves. And from way, way up, high above the earth in the brilliant sunshine where the weather satellite was orbiting, taking photographs, the typhoon called Rose was a silent, gigantic, slowly moving, writhing whirlpool, making its way across the curvature of the earth.

For over thirty days that picture had been coming through on the recording equipment of observatories round the world: Manila, Saigon, Hong Kong, Peking, Taipei, Tokyo, Guam. For thirty days they watched her at the Royal Hong Kong Observatory, digesting and collating data about her from satellites, ships, aircraft, and from the American reconnaissance aircraft which flew into the middle of her almost every day. For twenty-seven of those days she had moved erratically, twisting, turning, looping, northwest, southwest, southeast, doubling back, massively, slowly; but for the last five days she had been turned toward Hong Kong.

27

From five thousand feet up and a hundred miles away she did not look like the satellite photograph. Vanessa sat behind Kurt Marlowe in the cockpit of the United States Navy aircraft, and said into her tape recorder above the roar of the engines:

"Just a vast blackness that blots out the whole sky ahead, the whole horizon. You cannot see where it begins and ends . . . awe-inspiring. And ominous."

She was not sure how much the tape recorder was picking up. She was wearing a flying helmet, with earphones and mouthpiece that enabled everybody to speak to and hear each other, but she had switched hers off to make the note.

She was wearing a flying suit, with a lifejacket on top. She was strapped tight into her seat around her waist, with another set of straps across her shoulders and breast. Next to Kurt Marlowe sat the co-pilot, who had the unlikely name of Fairweather. Next to her, across the flight-deck aisle, sat the radio operator, and behind him the navigator. Aft, seated at portholes just behind each wing, sat the two observers, watching the engines. They had taken her aback. God, if you need a guy to tell you your engines are knocked out. . . .

The crew looked young and all-American-boy naïve, with the exception of big-wheel Kurt Marlowe. She had to admit that he did look exceedingly dashing. At this moment he was the most important man in her life, because he was the one who was going to get her out of this machine alive, and that gave him an importance that was almost sexual.

She stared through the windshield at the vast black violence ahead, and at the sea down there, blue-black in the afternoon sun, white caps flying off the swells; she tried to notice everything and to live every moment of it. She had to concentrate hard to bring her mind back from her encounter with Sir Herman Choi—and from a small bay in Tolo Sound. The radio operator spoke over the intercom, "Latest report from Hong Kong. She's slowed right down, forward speed about one knot."

Kurt Marlowe said over the intercom, "Descending to five hundred feet."

The nose began to turn downward, and she felt herself straining against it. She forced herself to relax and leaned forward to look. The sea was looming up at them, nearer and nearer. The sun was left behind, the light was turning gray. The aircraft nosed down, lower and lower, and now she could make out the height of the swells. And now the lashing sea was coming up, up, up to meet them, then the nose leveled out, and Kurt Marlowe's casual drawl came over.

"Five hundred feet. Our speed one hundred and fifty knots, wind speed eight-eight knots on our port tail. Height of the swells fifty-odd feet at present."

Ahead was only dense black through the gray light. He half turned his head and said to Vanessa over the intercom, "We'll be cutting back our speed soon. We'll keep the winds on our portside tail and we'll be curving in toward the eye with them. Counterclockwise."

She said, leaning forward, "How long before we get into that black stuff ahead?"

"Not long. These winds here are just the outside edge; they're getting stronger every minute. She's a bad one. Are you scared?"

152

"Are you?"

He grinned. "Not yet."

She looked around at the rest of the crew. They were all grinning at her. But they looked pale and nervous behind their smiles. "What do you mean, 'Not yet'?"

"I'm shit-scared every time. I really should have joined the infantry."

She did not like hearing him talk like that, but for the first time she almost liked him.

Fifteen minutes later she felt the winds really hit them hard. Outside it was dark gray and the sea down there was flying black and white. The winds hit the aircraft on her portside tail and the machine lurched sideways and down toward the black sea, and Kurt Marlowe pulled on the controls and the whole cabin strained about Vanessa and the straps wrenched at her guts and her head was flung sideways. The aircraft lurched and dived, and then roared up again, and then blackness out there plunged in front of her eyes, and through the shock of it she heard Kurt Marlowe say, "Getting into it now."

The aircraft roared into the blackness. The howling walls of winds and hammering rain hurtled the aircraft along, engines screaming, the big wings leaping and bucking. It staggered and shook and fell, and she wrenched about in her seat; her head jolted and jerked, her stomach heaved. The aircraft staggered and fell again and screamed upward again, and the whole crew were thrown against their safety straps, clutching at their instruments. The rain smashed against the glass and came spurting into the cabin at the joints, the instrument panel was leaping in front of her eyes, her stomach was heaving against her ribs and Kurt Marlowe was rasping into his mouthpiece, "Wind speeds one hundred and ninety knots—thick driving rain—visibility nil—estimated radial distance from the eye forty-five miles—"

She grabbed for the plastic bag and tried to get it up to her mouth and her hands shot one way and her head flew the other, and she threw her head toward the bag and out it came, her roast beef on rye and San Miguel beer in a big choking eruption.

28

In Hong Kong it was bright, blazing hot, and the air was motionless. From high places in the colony the Number One signal showed, the big black letter T and the three bright lights, the standby alert. It was broadcast across the colony by government and commercial radio and television in English and Cantonese.

"Attention! Attention! The Number One Typhoon Signal has been raised by the Royal Hong Kong Observatory. Typhoon Rose is situated approximately three hundred and ninety miles southeast of Hong Kong. She is following a due northwesterly track at a forward speed of ten knots per hour. Wind speeds near the eye are in excess of two hundred knots. If she maintains her present course and speed she will enter the colony's waters at about noon tomorrow, Saturday."

But out in the harbor, packed with ships and junks and ferries and cargo lighters and sampans, and down in those narrow teeming streets of shops and banks and godowns and money changers and bars and tenements and resettlement blocks and squatter shacks cut into the steep jungled mountainsides—down there that Friday afternoon it was business as usual.

In number three court of Causeway Bay Magistracy the magistrate was conducting the committal proceedings in the case of *Regina* vs. *Ong Man-kit* and three others, charged in respect of the raid on the Oriental International apartment house. Superintendent Bernard Champion sat next to the police inspector who was the prosecutor. At the back of the court sat Staff Sergeant Pang. On other seats sat the other witnesses: the Mama-san, some of the prostitutes, and Bill Lu, the owner. They had all given their evidence. Beside them sat various members of the 14K Triad Society, listening. Committal proceedings are only a preparatory examination of the evidence of the witnesses, at the end of which the charge is put to the accused, whereupon the magistrate decides whether or not to send them to the Supreme Court for trial.

The prosecuting inspector said, "I close the case for the crown, your worship. May charges of manslaughter be put to the accused."

He handed the prepared typed charges to the orderly, who handed one up to the magistrate and one copy to each accused. The interpreter began to translate the charge aloud to each of them. Then he turned to the magistrate and said, "Each defendant understands the charge, your worship."

The magistrate sat forward. "Well, there's something *I* don't understand, Mr. Prosecutor," he said.

"Yes, your worship?" The prosecutor stood up.

"I don't understand why on earth you are only charging the accused with manslaughter," the magistrate said. "My view of the facts and the law is that the charge should be murder."

Superintendent Bernard Champion felt his stomach contract. The prosecutor stood there, looking helpless.

"I am only following instructions, your worship," he said. Then he added, "None of the accused struck the deceased. None of them pushed her out of the window. She jumped by herself."

The magistrate snapped, "She did not jump by herself—of her own volition! She was forced to do so to escape the accused gang who were brandishing murderous weapons and who looked as if they were going to murder her! For the purposes of the law she was forced to jump—*by the accused.*"

The prosecutor mumbled, "As your worship pleases . . ." Bernard Champion sat white-faced. Staff Sergeant Pang glanced across the gallery at the 14K man. The man glared at him, then narrowed his eyes. The four accused in the dock had not understood the English.

The magistrate was writing on the charge. Then he looked up and said, "Mr. Interpreter, tell the accused that I am amending the charge to murder. It now reads as follows: 'That they did, upon the same date, and at or near the Oriental International apartment house in Hong Kong, wrongfully and unlawfully and maliciously kill and murder Chiang Mei-ling, contrary to common law.' Then formally read that charge to each one of them again."

The interpreter said, "As your worship pleases."

He started to read the new charges to the accused. Bernard Champion sat waiting for the reaction. As the interpreter read, incredulity came into the faces of the four. Then the first one's face contorted in outrage.

"Protest!" he shouted in Cantonese.

The magistrate looked up.

"Behave yourself, young man!" he said in the same language.

The accused pointed at the staff sergeant and shouted desperately at the magistrate. "He made a deal with the 14K! He paid two hundred thousand dollars for us to be arrested if we pleaded guilty to manslaughter only! He promised not murder! Now he breaks his deal!"

The magistrate stared at the accused, astonished, then he picked up his pen and said quietly, "Say all that again slowly. . . ."

Fifteen miles away, the other side of the Mountains of Nine Dragons, Jake McAdam was ready to board the junk. He had already stocked it with beer and water and hard rations. Now he picked up a bottle of whisky and the portable radio and said to Wong, "I'll be back early tomorrow morning, at sunrise; be sure to be here. Then you will have to take the boat to the typhoon shelter."

He turned and walked down to the jetty and climbed aboard the junk. He pulled away from the jetty and went chugging up Tolo Sound toward the open sea. He had quite a long way to go before night through the many islands, before he came to Kat O Chau Island, and the China waters of Mirs Bay beyond.

The vast horizon was hazy blue and the wind blowing on his sweating chest was warm. On the horizon he could see many junks, coming in toward Hong Kong already running from the typhoon. He and Wong had worked feverishly that day, securing the last sheets of abestos on the roof of the new boat shed and installing the sliding entrance doors. But in his heart he did not believe that anything of his boatyard that he had built with his own muscle and sweat and desperation would be standing when he got back. And as he headed slowly for Mirs Bay and Chester Wu, he knew he didn't care.

Ten miles away, over the Mountains of Nine Dragons, the Red Rod of the 14K Triad Society received certain instructions from Sir Herman Choi. The instructions needed no discussion. The only question was how the orders should be carried out, and that was his decision alone, for the Red Rod was the expert in matters of murder.

Certain aspects of the job were immediately apparent: there was a typhoon coming, and if the killing could be made to look like the typhoon's work, so much the better. Drowning was the obvious possibility. Being hit on the head by a heavy flying object was another. Or falling from a big height, as from a veranda, or down a stairwell. Strangling, knifing or shooting should not be used, for such a death could not be attributed to a typhoon.

But it was urgent. His instructions were that the woman would most likely be found either at an apartment known as the American Mess in Hillside Road of Mid-levels district, or at the apartment of one McAdam, an ex-policeman, in Dragon Court.

The other part of the instructions which the Red Rod of the 14K Triad Society received was much simpler to execute. It was that nothing was to be published in the English language press about Sir Herman Choi or the Lucky Man Development Company until further notice.

That was easy to arrange. The 14K had Triad members among the typesetters of both the *South China Morning Post* and the *China Mail*. Men who exercised control over the printers' union and could call a strike on some pretext or other.

29

For another hour the aircraft flew around the outside of the eye, fighting farther and farther inward; for another hour the plane roared and screamed and bucked and plunged, with the winds getting fiercer and fiercer; for one more hour Vanessa clutched her seat and did not hear the things the crew were shouting to each other, and she did not care, all she wanted was to die; then suddenly, when the black winds were at their maniacal fiercest, the aircraft burst brokenly through the roaring wall of wind, and suddenly the blackness was gone and the cockpit was flooded with eerie sunshine and the aircraft subsided into smoothness.

"We're there," she heard Kurt Marlowe rasp.

In the eye.

She sat slumped in her seat, held up by the straps, the sweat running off her in a sheen, her lipstick smudged, and the taste of vomit in her mouth. She stared at the splendor in front of her—the magnificence, the great walled arena of black clouds, fifty miles in diameter, bathed in sunshine. The black cloud-banks spiraled up, up, like vast tiers of seats, and they looked stationary in the sudden deafening tranquillity. The light was golden-gray and silver. The engines were a lilting celestial drone. Then Kurt Marlowe was rasping over the intercom, "Report wind speeds round the eye of over two hundred knots. Barometric pressure in the eye still falling . . ."

She looked dazedly around at the rest of the crew. The radio officer's eyes were red from vomiting and he had a big bruise over his eye. His right hand was strapped to his instrument desk. The navigator grinned at her ruefully. Kurt Marlowe said, "You all right, darlin'?"

She was so relieved she could have kissed him.

"Fine." She breathed deep and quivered. "What's the significance of the barometric pressure still falling?"

"The typhoon is still intensifying."

Then he nosed the aircraft downward, and she saw the sea again, just five hundred feet below. It was a vast caldron, gray spray and froth flying off the crests, and the troughs were seething from all directions and clashing together. Marlowe took the aircraft low so he could take meteorological readings, while the radio officer was sending the information back to Hong Kong. They flew all the way around the circumference of the eye, the winds like a black wall at the portside wingtip. Then they began to climb.

Round and round and upward and upward, a tiny battered flying machine against the roaring walls of wind: way up to the very top it flew, and now the eye of the typhoon was a vast black well below them.

Kurt Marlowe said over the intercom, "Give me a bearing for Manila."

Vanessa sat, strapped in her seat, her hair sticking to her temples and neck, her empty stomach squirming, dreading the moment when they would fly out again. She did not care that she had to spend the night in the bed of Kurt Marlowe in Manila; all she cared about in the whole world was living through the next two hours.

A professional assassin always sticks to his preferred method of killing. The strangler will not use a knife, the knife artist will not shoot, the gunman will not bludgeon to death. But the trick killer is versatile. He studies his victim's circumstances, then uses any effective tactic permitted by his instructions. The Triad man who was sent to murder Vanessa Storm Williams was a very good trick killer, one who specialized in making the death look like a misadventure.

As the sun was going down that Friday evening, the killer

entered a public telephone box at the bottom of Hillside Road. He was short and lean and very strong, and his eyes were flat and cold. But he was wearing a business suit and at a glance he looked like any Chinese white-collar worker returning home. He put some coins in the slot and dialed the number of the American Mess. It rang a few moments, then the amah answered.

"Wei?"

"Is Miss Williams there, please?"

"Nobody here."

"What time are you expecting her home?"

"Hah?"

"What time she come back?"

"All missies come back different time."

"Do you know where she is?"

"Tonight Friday, always party, you phone F.C.C."

"Where?"

"I give you number."

The amah consulted a list on the wall and then slowly read him the telephone number of the Foreign Correspondents' Club.

"Thank you," the man said.

Then he dialed McAdam's apartment in Dragon Court. The telephone rang and rang in the empty apartment.

Then he telephoned a third number. It was answered promptly. This time he spoke in Cantonese.

"My face is pale, but my hands will be red."

Then he hung up.

He walked up Hillside Road toward Dragon Court in the early darkness. Another man came up a ladder street, and nodded to him casually.

The second man went on into the gathering darkness. He made his way to the old-fashioned apartment house in which was located the American Mess. He climbed the stairs to the third floor, inspected the lock on the front door, then the back door. Both were simple. Then he investigated the steps leading up to the roof. From the corner of the steps he had an excellent, concealed view of both the front and back doors. He walked over the dark roof and looked down onto the big open veranda below. A long drop, but easy enough to climb back up. He marked down the corner of the rooftop steps as the place where he would settle down and wait.

The first man walked casually into the foyer of Dragon Court and summoned the elevator. He got out at the sixth floor.

The sixth-floor foyer was empty. He tried the door. It was locked. Then he dropped to one knee and took an instrument out of his pocket, inserted it into the keyhole and delicately turned it, listening carefully. The lock slid open. He stood up, wiped the door handle with a handkerchief, pulled on gloves, entered the apartment and closed the door behind him.

He went quickly, silently through the dark apartment, checking it out and looking for the best place to hide. Then he saw the spiral staircase.

He climbed it cautiously. He tried the door. He listened intently. Then he picked the lock.

The door swung open. He stared inside. A thin smile crossed his face. It was an absolutely ideal place to wait. It even had its own front door, opening onto the seventh-floor foyer.

The sun was going down over Hong Kong, riotously red.

All across the horizon there were the navigation lights of junks coming in, to get to the typhoon shelters ahead of the rush. In the harbor big ships were getting ready to move to typhoon buoys, and those that could not get them were getting ready to put out to deep sea ahead of the typhoon to ride out the storm. They would be loading and unloading cargo all night, the lighters clustered around them. Shopkeepers were beginning to board up their windows. But in the bars and restaurants and clubs and brothels it was still business as usual.

As the last of the sun went down, Jake McAdam's junk chugged into the tranquillity of Double Haven. It was a beautiful stretch of deserted water, surrounded by steep green islands. About two miles ahead, around the point, was the village of Shataukok. Down the middle of Shataukok ran a road called Chung-Ying Street, which means China-England Street, and on one side stood the Union Jack and on the other the red flag of China with the five gold stars. It was the official border between the British crown colony of Hong Kong and the People's Republic of China, and this was the only place where no fence separated the two countries.

About a mile ahead was the steep ridged island of Kat O Chau. McAdam's face was gaunt as he looked at the island in the sunset. Once upon a time, a long time ago, he had come here with her, and they had planted two pine trees up on top of that ridge.

He looked at his watch, then cut his engines, and just drifted. It was suddenly very quiet, magnificently still in the hot sunset.

He had an hour and a half to wait before he had to sail round that island and out into China waters.

It was unreal, being here again. And hauntingly real. But now he was here he did not want to think about her, to remember and find out, which was the very thing he had come for. And he did not want to look for those two pine trees against the sunset.

He uncorked the bottle of whisky, and took a big swallow. The liquor burned down inside him.

All right, he thought.

And he picked up his binoculars. He swung them up to the ridge of the island in the sunset, and he looked for them, and his eyes were burning. Then he found them.

There they stood, side by side in silhouette against the sunset. As if they were on fire, black against the vast glowing red. Side by side, and their outstretched branches were just touching.

Six hundred miles away, Vanessa walked unsteadily through Manila International Airport toward the ladies' room. She could still hear the roaring of the engines in her ears and the marble floor was heaving up and down. She was pale, and she knew she looked like death, and apart from the fact that she knew she looked terrible, she felt marvelous. She did not care what she looked like, nor even that she had peed in her pants and that it showed loud and clear—she didn't care about a goddamn thing except that she was out of that typhoon. She tottered into the toilet. It was empty, but she did not expect that to last too long, and she did not care about that either. She went to the corner and ran water in two basins. Then she started to undress. There was only one way to handle the mess she had gotten herself into.

She kicked off her shoes, stripped off her blouse, undid her skirt, then peeled off her panties. She shoved everything into one basin of water. She squeezed two handfuls of liquid soap out of the dispenser and then swished it vigorously into the soaking garments. She sank the top of her head into the other basin, and sighed as the cool hit her scalp; then she tossed her wet hair over her neck and splashed her face with cold water. Then, stark naked, she lifted one long leg up onto the basin and proceeded to sponge off her body, vigorously and entirely.

Ten minutes later it was all over. A dozen people had interrupted her and she had ignored each one cheerfully. She had dried herself off, wrung out her clothes and pulled them on wet, combed her wet hair and put on her face. She took one last look at herself in the mirror.

Then she picked up her handbag jauntily and walked out. She crossed the big marble concourse with her wet clothes sticking to her and headed for the bar to meet Kurt Marlowe.

She gulped her first brandy down in one go, slapped $10 on the bar and said, flushed, "Another round."

Kurt Marlowe grinned at her and put his hand in his pocket.

"No," Vanessa said, "let me buy you a drink for that ride." She held up her new brandy at him. "You flew that machine magnificently."

"Thanks." He smiled modestly. He glanced appreciatively at her nipples, showing through her wet blouse.

She took a gulp of brandy. "It'll all be in my story next month. 'Those magnificent men in their flying machines.'" She added, "Let me buy you lunch when you get back to Hong Kong."

He looked at her, quizzically. "When *I* get back? You'll be flying back with me."

"No more typhoons for me, darling! I'm flying back by good old scheduled airline and that's only if there isn't a train." She finished off her brandy in a gulp and then smiled at him and put her hand on his shoulder: "Thanks very much for taking me into that holocaust—and even more for getting me out! It was very kind of you. And now I have to rush. . . ."

He stared at her. "Where the hell to?"

"There's a Philippine Air Lines for Hong Kong in forty minutes —probably their last flight until the typhoon's over."

Kurt stared at her indignantly. "Hey, we've got a deal!"

"A deal? I don't understand. . . ."

"Don't pull the coy and girlish bit with me, baby! You know very well that we made a deal at lunch—a tacit one, but clearly understood!"

She wagged a finger at him. "Now, now, Kurt, don't spoil your image!" She bent forward and gave him a big kiss on his cheek. "I really must dash. Fly carefully!"

She twiddled her fingers at him and turned on her heel and hurried away. She looked back once and blew him a bright kiss and twiddled her fingers again. His lips mouthed, *"Bitch!"* She did feel a bit like a shit, but her heart was singing.

Jake McAdam's junk plowed slowly past the point of the island of Kat O Chau. The engines were going *doem—doem—doem* in the silence of the black sea. On his portside, the lights of Shatau-kok twinkled slowly past. Ahead was Mirs Bay, and China waters.

There were no lights on other vessels within miles. Far away, up there across the black sea, twinkled the lights of a commune. He swung his binoculars slowly across the black horizon. Far away he could just make out a string of navigation lights. That would be a fishing junk fleet putting back to China ahead of the typhoon.

He rubbed his fingers across his brow, and he felt them tremble. He did not want to remember. He did not want to remember the heartbreak, the dread he had felt all the many times he had been here long ago, the dread of what they might tell him, and the hopes. Oh, God. The hope, every minute of every day, that at the next meeting Chester would say, "Okay, Jake, old man, it's all worked very well and we're moving on to phase two now. We're letting Ying go back to Hong Kong and you two can get nice and respectably married and you can move up to the top of the Hong Kong Police Force—and keep spying for us, of course."

He did not want to remember. And the raw solid fear that any time Chester might have said, "Jake, old chap, you've been feeding us disinformation all this time, haven't you? Her Majesty's been using you as a double agent all this time, hasn't she? And here you are in China waters! I'm sorry, old man, but I've got to arrest you as a spy. There'll be a trial, of course, but I'm afraid we're going to shoot you. *And* her, of course. . . ." One day, any day it could have happened, it was bound to happen. But she had saved him from that, although she did not know it. She had thought she was only saving his honor.

That was the last time, and Chester had brought her with him, the hostage, and she had blurted out defiantly at both of them, "I do not love you any more, Jake! I despise you! I will have nothing more to do with this disgraceful business! I love China but I despise you for spying on your own country and I refuse to be used any more! If I ever come here again it will only be if they drag me in handcuffs! And I shall stand mute!" And she had turned her back to them, shaking, and she had stood silent from that moment on. And there had been no way he could tell her what he was really doing.

He looked behind him at the silhouette of Kat O Chau; then at the lights of Shataukok, trying to calculate his position in the dark. Then he cut his engines. He was about inside China waters. He left the wheel and made his way up to the bows. He threw the anchor over.

Then he went back to the wheel. He sat in the silent dark, waiting, and trying not to think.

It was after ten o'clock. The typhoon was still more than twelve hours away. Hong Kong's Kai Tak Airport was still in business, but not as usual.

A jet airliner can land, discharge passengers, refuel, take on passengers, turn around and take off again in forty-five minutes if it has to. Aircraft were still arriving and leaving, but only those whose schedules provided for a quick turn-around: planes that normally had a long stopover in Hong Kong were being diverted to airports in Taiwan and the Philippines with their passengers. All the hotels were jam-packed, with tourists arriving and tourists trying to leave ahead of the typhoon, luggage everywhere, people crowding in the foyers, the lounges, the passageways, the bars, round the reception desks, people asleep on the lobby chairs, the reception clerks hustling, bustling, answering the same questions over and over, the telephones shrilling.

Vanessa was the first off the Philippine Air Lines jet, the first through Immigration. She did not have any luggage to wait for, so she dashed through customs. She hurried across the huge clamorous marble concourse, dodging people, making for the public telephones. She grabbed the only empty one, deposited fifty cents, dialed.

Across the harbor, the telephone suddenly rang in McAdam's dark, silent apartment. Upstairs in the gallery the killer stiffened, his eyes alert. The telephone rang and rang.

She waited, excited, nervous. She could imagine the apartment, empty, dark, the sound of the telephone.

Then she hung up impatiently.

She got her coins back, redeposited them, fingers shaking. She dialed the American Mess. Maybe there was a typhoon party on there, maybe somebody there would know where he was.

It rang shrilly in the big, old-fashioned apartment.

Outside on the dark stairs that led up to the roof, the second Chinese man heard it ringing. In the servants' quarters, beyond the kitchen, the old amah, Ah Li, stirred in her sleep. She lay there, hoping the ringing would stop, then she got creakily out of bed and shuffled down the long wooden corridor, her long pigtail hanging down behind her. All the missies' bedroom doors were open, which meant that none of them had come home yet. On the other hand, they all *might* come home soon, with *all* their boyfriends. As she shuffled up to the telephone it stopped ringing. The old woman swore in Cantonese, turned round and went back down the corridor, mumbling.

Vanessa banged down the telephone and recovered her coins. Then she redeposited them and dialed the Foreign Correspondents' Club.

"Hell*oo* . . ." a cheerful voice said. In the background she could hear laughter and singing.

"Is Jake McAdam there, please?"

"Haven't seen him. Hang on . . . nope."

She sighed, impatiently, as she hung up. Then she felt her heart singing again. She knew where he was. With a typhoon coming, where else would he be?

She drove as fast as she could over the rough tracks, her headlights bouncing ahead of her, the rented car jolting, her eyes looking far away. She slammed to a stop at the top of the hill and looked down into the boatyard's cove.

His car was down there! But there was not a light shining, even a crack. She slammed her hand on the horn and waited, her heart hammering. Then she shoved the car into gear and ground down the hill.

She wrenched on the handbrake, slung open the door.

"Ho—*gan!*"

She went round the side of the cottage, to the front. No light. "Hogan!" She tried the door. Locked. She rattled the door hard, and shouted his name again. He *must* be in there, his car was here.

Then she noticed the junk was not at the jetty.

Of course! He had taken the junk to the typhoon shelter at Tai-po.

She gave a frustrated sigh.

Damn. He was just a few miles away down Tolo Sound. But she would never find his boat in the dark among all those hundreds of junks that were crowding in the typhoon shelter. And ten to one he was asleep already down below, he would never hear her shout.

Oh, Hogan, beautiful Hogan. Don't tell me you're going to spend the typhoon on that junk when we could be in bed making beautiful love!

But, no, he wouldn't stay on the junk. Wong would be there to look after it, and anyway he had sent her a telegram to meet him at the Foreign Correspondents' Club tomorrow. He would leave the junk to Wong as soon as it got light and come back here for his car. Maybe any time now, maybe even now he was walking across the hills in the dark.

Well, she would wait for him right here. Here where his car was. She didn't want to go anywhere else. She just wished she could get into that cottage and lie on his bed and wait for him and smell his body on the sheets.

She went to his car, opened it and slowly got in. She ran her fingers over the steering wheel, to feel close to him. It was completely quiet.

Maybe she should go home and have something to eat, and sleep until daybreak.

Or go to his apartment; she still had a front-door key, though she'd given the key ring back to him. And have a lovely long bath with a long glass of beer. And then get into his bed.

He saw the navigation lights of the junk long before he could hear it, just the small red and green pinpricks. He stared at the lights. They were a long way off yet. He had about fifteen minutes to get himself under control.

The lights blinked off once and then came on again. He got up, went to his control panel, flicked a switch and blinked his navigation lights off, then on again.

The silhouette approached in the dark, the engine quietly thudding in the silence. Then a flashlight swept the junk and blinded him. He shielded his eyes.

"All right," he snapped, "switch that damn thing off."

"Are you alone, old man?" Chester's voice said, in his perfect Oxford accent.

"No, I'm bristling with marines. And I've got a submarine shadowing you."

"Mind if we check, old chap?"

"Go ahead."

The junk hove to against his and half a dozen men came aboard with submachine guns. They went clattering below. A tubby silhouette stepped aboard.

"Jake," Chester Wu said. "How nice to see you again."

"Hello, Chester. Sit down."

"I'd rather you came aboard my old tub. New boat, huh? Concrete, I hear. That's pretty wild. Stand up, old man. Hands above your head."

McAdam stood up with a sigh and raised his hands. Chester Wu frisked him.

"Okay, you're clean."

"Of course I'm clean. I don't want trouble."

"Come on, then. Up to the bows? It's cooler."

McAdam picked up the whisky bottle and his cigarettes. He stepped off his junk onto Chester's and they sat down on the bows. Chester smiled at him in the dark.

"What makes you think I won't arrest you, old man? As a spy. For all that horrid disinformation you fed me."

McAdam took a small swig of whisky, then passed Chester the bottle. "Got any glasses?"

"The bottle's all right. Well?"

"Because if you were going to liquidate me you could have done so easily enough in the last eight years. Because I'm more useful to you alive than dead. Or rotting in a People's prison."

"And how can you be useful to me now?"

He steeled himself to keep his voice level.

"I can be useful, all right. But first you've got to be useful to me." He added, "Please."

"Oh? How?"

He took a deep breath. His voice sounded loud.

"How's Ying?" he said.

Chester said carefully, "Why should I tell you how she is?"

McAdam's voice almost trembled. "For two reasons. First, as a man. For compassion's sake. . . . You're a decent human being at heart, Chester!"

Chester smiled. "That's true. What is the second reason?"

"I'm rejoining the club."

Chester stared at him in the dark.

"You don't say!"

"All right—don't believe me."

"Which end of it?"

"Not the China end, obviously. Not directly."

"Okay. We'll check your story out."

"*If* you can."

"But what's your price?"

"How's Ying," he said again.

Chester Wu looked at him.

"She's fine . . . " he said.

"And?"

"And what?"

"Where is she?"

"She's in Canton. Just up there," he added.

"Doing what?"

"Teaching school."

You fucking liar, McAdam thought. You want to keep the carrot on the same old string.

"What's happened to her? Has she married? Has she got a baby? A boyfriend?"

Chester said hastily, "No." Then his tone changed. "I'm not impressed by all this drama, Jake. I know very well that you've got a new girl now. An American blonde called Vanessa Storm Williams. Quite taken Hong Kong by storm I hear, a-ha-ha. I know all about it." He added casually, "Just routine tabs we keep on you."

McAdam made himself smile.

"You don't say?" He breathed deeply. "And what about Ying's private life? If she's allowed one in the People's paradise."

Chester said airily, "I don't know about any boyfriend."

"And how does she feel about me?" It wasn't as hard to say as he had thought it would be. He added, "Surely your thought police know."

Chester smiled indulgently at the little joke. "That's for you to find out, Jake . . . through me. In due course. In return for information. I don't pay in advance."

McAdam felt his anger flare. It was just as it had been before. They had all the cards. And he had invited it. Wanting to be free, he had put himself back in the same chains. He couldn't leave her, in his mind, unless she had already left him.

Then, suddenly, he knew what he was going to do, what the

real truth of this meeting was. Because he knew Ying. He stood up and picked up the whisky bottle.

"Okay. It's no deal."

He turned toward his junk.

"Just a moment, old man!"

"It's no deal, Chester! Because you're lying about her! And you're lying because she still won't cooperate with you. You've known about this meeting for forty-eight hours, don't tell me you haven't asked her. If she were cooperative you'd have her here right now to show me. But it's no good dragging her here in hand-cuffs, is it?"

Chester said, "She still loves you, Jake."

"Then why didn't she come here with you?"

"She still feels the same."

McAdam jabbed a finger at him: "You see, you admit she's still a handcuff case! You've shown your cards, Chester! And that's not all you've lied about. Because she's not just up there in Canton, she's in Manchuria! And she's not teaching school, she's in the People's Liberation Army intelligence. You can't order the army to do a damn thing, can you? They'd tell you to stick your handcuffs up your arse if they wanted to. And that's not all of it! She's probably married since she's been rehabilitated and thought-reformed. To some nice colonel. She's probably got a family. She's got her own life now. She's gone, Chester! From you and me!"

He turned and stepped across onto his junk angrily.

"You're wrong, Jake."

"Okay, I'm wrong! Tell your guys to get off, I'd hate to do them the favor of taking them to Hong Kong."

"You presume too much."

"Yeah, okay, anything you say!"

Chester Wu stood on the gunwale of the junk. "What makes you think I'll let you go, just like that, after all the trouble you've caused me?"

McAdam pushed in the decompressor and turned the ignition. The engine ground over, then took, *doem—doem—doem.* He was so sickened that it was easy to lie.

"Because I'm rejoining the club, Chester. I'm much more use-ful to you alive and back in business than dead. And any informa-tion you could squeeze out of me now is eight years old."

He left the wheel angrily and went up to the bows and hauled in his anchor. Then he untied the rope holding the two boats to-gether. Chester watched him.

"You'll be back, Jake."

McAdam was back at the wheel. He looked at him squarely.

"Yes," he lied. He added, "Don't call me, I'll call you."

Chester looked at him. "Any messages for Ying?"

He felt a rush of bitterness, that the bastard was still trying to use her.

"Yes! The message she didn't send me. Give her my love."

He rammed the gear lever into forward and opened the throttle.

As the junk swung round back toward Kat O Chau he looked up at the ridge. He could just make out the two pine trees against the night sky.

"Goodbye," he whispered. "Goodbye, Ying."

And he rammed the throttle up to full.

_____*Part nine*

At three o'clock that Saturday morning the first winds came. The typhoon was still many hours away: these were just the peripheral winds. They came out of the dark sky, gusting over the black sea, a short erratic burst, then still again, then another, jerking the trees and bushes, ruffling the sea, then gone again. Then another one, harder, so the windows slammed and curtains billowed and the sea slapped, then gone again into the darkness.

Most of Hong Kong was battened down. And out there, the black sea was studded with the red and green lights of junks coming in from deep sea at full throttle, making for the typhoon shelters.

32

The first gusts of wind whipped through the banana trees at Mc-Adam's cove and beat against his car, and she woke up. She sat up, startled. She looked at her watch. Almost three. She was muzzy with tiredness. She squeezed her eyes with her fingertips and then looked at herself in the rear-view mirror.

She was hot, her wrung-out clothes creased and sweaty. *I look awful.* She sucked her lips as she ferreted in her bag for lipstick. Then she pouted in front of the little mirror, put the stuff on. She looked at herself in the mirror. Bared her teeth. Not even a tooth-brush.

There was only one thing for a smart woman to do. Leave a note on the steering wheel, go and have a real sleep, fix herself up. And *then* come back.

In many places in Hong Kong the typhoon parties were in

swing, the parties that kept everybody captive for twenty-four hours at least and where everybody ending up sharing beds and carpets and sofas. At the Foreign Correspondents' Club it would go on all weekend. Vanessa had heard about them. As she pulled up in her rented car outside her apartment block at four o'clock that Saturday morning she knew by the unusual number of cars parked close together up on the sidewalk, some of which she recognized, that there was a party going on upstairs at the American Mess.

She sighed behind the wheel. She wanted to be alone with her thoughts, she could not bear the noise and the laughter and the bullshit. She wouldn't get a bath with everybody in and out of the john. And probably somebody was screwing in her bed. She put the car into gear, and drove the extra fifty yards to McAdam's apartment block. She swung the car down the concrete drive, down into the basement garage.

It was dark. She drove the car into McAdam's parking space, cut the engine and switched off the lights. The slam of her car door resounded in the cavernous garage. Then she started walking for the elevator, her footsteps ringing on the concrete. She pressed the elevator button, and waited. Just then another gust of wind came whipping in off the sea and up the mountainside, and between the apartment blocks and she heard the creak of trees outside the garage entrance. Suddenly the elevator door opened. She got in.

She was not feeling sleepy any more. She just wanted daylight to come, so she could get back out to the boatyard looking beautiful and find Hogan before the typhoon cut them off from each other. And she needed something in her stomach.

The elevator doors slid open on the sixth floor. She stepped out.

Her footsteps were loud in the silent foyer. She stood at the door, rummaging in her bag for McAdam's key. She found it, and unlocked the door. She shut it behind her. It was dark, but some light came in from the stars. She walked slowly into the living room and sighed happily. She felt she had come home. And she wanted to *smell* the place. She walked slowly to the big French windows and looked out at the harbor.

The sea was studded with lights of the junks coming in, running from the typhoon. There was a big freighter putting out to sea. All the buoys had big ships tied up to them, all lit up, all facing the same way, swinging with the tide. She looked down and sideways at the American Mess. Without opening the windows she could see the veranda, people on it.

Thank God she was here.

She turned and walked briskly down the corridor to the main bedroom, unbuttoning her blouse as she went. She snapped on the light and went into the bathroom. She spun the taps and water gushed into the tub.

At the top of the spiral staircase the door silently opened a crack. The killer listened to the sound of running water, then smiled faintly.

In the bathroom she pulled off her blouse and slung it on the floor. Then the telephone rang.

She turned off the taps and dashed out of the bathroom, across the bedroom, down the corridor. She flung herself into McAdam's study and snatched up the telephone in the dark.

"Hello!"

There was a moment's surprised silence. Then, "Is Jake there?"

She recognized the voice. Disappointment swept over her.

"For God's sake, Bernard, it's four o'clock in the morning!"

She heard him breathe deeply.

"I'm sorry, but I've got to talk to him." He added, "I've been awake all night."

"He's not here, Bernie. I think he's at Tai-po typhoon shelter. I'm going there at daybreak to look for him. What message can I give him?"

She heard him sigh again. He sounded a little drunk.

"Can I come with you?"

She closed her eyes. No no no . . .

"Look, I'll tell him to phone you." She added, "I haven't seen him myself for some time, you see."

Silence.

"Yes, I see . . ."

"What is it, Bernie?"

"Vanessa? Are you up?"

"Right this red-hot moment I'm up at the telephone."

"Can I come and see you?" He added, "Please . . . I've had a sleepless night. I've got to talk to somebody."

She closed her eyes in the dark and suppressed a sigh.

"Okay. But I must leave here before daybreak. And I have to take a bath. How long will it take you to get here?"

"Five minutes."

"Five minutes," she said. "Okay, Bernie."

Through the crack of the door at the top of the spiral staircase the killer was listening.

He silently closed the door. He needed more than five minutes.

She put down the telephone. She went through to the kitchen and switched on the electric kettle.

He had big dark rings under his eyes. He stood at the window, staring at the harbor, while she read the letter he had thrust at her.

Dear Sir,

In terms of the Prevention of Bribery Ordinance, I hereby require you to account, within seven clear days of today's date, for all your assets, of whatever kind in all parts of the world, and the means whereby you acquired them. Failure to comply with this requirement constitutes a criminal offense.

You are further advised that failure to account satisfactorily for all your assets raises a legal presumption against you in a court of law that you acquired the assets by corrupt methods.

The wind buffeted the window.

"Have you *got* a lot of assets?"

"More than are good for me."

"But"—she waved her hand—"you're a bachelor. You're a senior policeman on a good salary. You play the stock market. Can't you account satisfactorily?"

Champion snorted, turned to the bottle and poured another large whisky.

"No."

She stared at him. Her reporter's mind was working. "How did this arise?"

He said bitterly, "That bloody whorehouse raid that you were involved in. My staff sergeant paid a massive reward for information. We made a deal with the accused. Manslaughter instead of murder. The bloody magistrate changed it back to murder. The accused squealed and blew the whole story. This was yesterday morning. By last night that letter was served on me. I've been with my lawyer most of the night."

He sounded near to breaking.

"What did your lawyer say?" she demanded.

"That I'm in trouble . . ." He added, "He also told me how to get out of it."

"How?"

He turned and walked across the room, his face gray.

"Run away. To England. Or America."

"*England?* I would have thought that was the worst place. Hong Kong's a British colony."

He sighed. "The safest place. Because our extradition treaty only applies to Hong Kong crimes which are *also* crimes in England." He turned wearily without looking at her. "There is no such crime in England as failing to account for your assets. Or in America."

"I see. Have you still got your passport?"

"Yes. That's a loophole in the law. I'm not on any kind of bail, either. I haven't been accused of any crime yet, until I fail to provide the explanation. They could physically stop me leaving if they caught me trying, but that's all. That's all I've got to do. Just get through that airport without them spotting me."

She said sharply, "What do you want me to do? And Hogan?"

He turned and his eyes were suddenly full of tears.

"Nothing! Just sit there! Just be my friend!" He looked out of the window. "Run away?" He shook his head. "You can't run away from yourself, Vanessa."

She knew that too, now.

"You've got to be able to look yourself in the eye. And say . . ." Then he whispered: "Oh, dear God . . ." He half turned and looked at her, haggard. "What's important in life, Vanessa? Honor?" he appealed.

He waited. Then he cried, "Help me! I'm asking you! What good is honor going to do in prison? What good is it going to do to say I owned up?"

"What do you want to hear?"

He smashed his fist down on the back of the chair.

"What do you think! You're a woman of the world! You know how this town works!"

She took a big breath. "Bernard, listen to me. No, I do not want to see you in prison! But, Jesus Christ, I cannot and will not make up your mind for you!"

"I'm not asking you to make up my mind! I'm asking you to tell me about honor! In this dishonorable town!"

He stopped, glaring at her.

"Yes, Bernard. Honor is absolute."

There was a long silence.

Then she said quietly, "What are you going to do?"

177

"I don't know," he said.

Outside the windows the winds came in gusts. The very first light was coming into the sky. She said softly, "I must go now."

He said dully, "You haven't had your bath."

"Yes, I must have it. And go."

He sat there, staring at nothing. Then he said, thickly, "Can I stay here till you go?"

Her heart went out to him.

"Yes," she said.

At the top of the spiral staircase, the Chinese man had listened to everything.

He turned and silently crossed the gallery. He opened the front door, and stepped outside.

He would have to wait until later in the day.

33

All over the sea, from all directions, the junks were converging on Hong Kong for shelter, even junks of the People's Republic of China. By dawn all the typhoon shelters were almost full: junks, fishing trawlers, sampans, pleasure craft, lashed to each other, forests of masts, sail tightly furled and lashed down.

With the first light McAdam was throttling down Tolo Sound. He was wide-awake—exhausted. He did not think he had ever seen so many junks. Every few minutes the short gusts of wind lashed down the sound. His portable radio was tuned in to the government's Cantonese broadcasts, which gave hourly reports on the situation at the various typhoon shelters. And it sounded as if Taipo was one of the worst.

"Your attention. The Royal Hong Kong Observatory has raised the Number Eight Typhoon signal. Gale-force winds, perhaps exceeding one hundred and fifty knots, should be expected in the next ten hours.

"The following precautions should be taken by everybody. . ."

Twenty minutes later McAdam rounded the point of his boatyard bay, and there was Wong waiting on the jetty.

He edged up against the jetty and Wong swung aboard; Mc-

Adam shoved the gear lever astern, and put back out into the sound.

He did not even think about his car.

He gave the wheel to Wong. He went to the main mast with the binoculars, climbed up the foot rungs and looked at Tai-po with the binoculars in the sunrise.

The mouth of the typhoon shelter was dense with junks, crowded tight as an armada; blue clouds of diesel fumes were rising and hanging. He could smell the urgency of *tai-fung,* the typhoon, in the air.

Twenty minutes later he steamed up to the edge of the crowded boats. For three hundred yards ahead of him the mouth was jammed with acres of masts. Somewhere in that mass was a channel with junks maneuvering down it to find a place to tie up to another junk. McAdams was dog-tired now.

"Did you sleep last night, Elder Brother?" he asked Wong. "Yes, First Born."

McAdam dragged his hands down his face. "We will wait two hours," he said. "Then if it does not look as if we will get in, we will go elsewhere."

"Where?"

"Down there." He pointed down the foot of the L-shaped sound toward the village of Shatin. "It is quite well protected by the mountains there."

He took off his wristwatch and gave it to Wong. "Wake me in two hours."

He turned and walked slowly down the hatch into the cabin. He threw himself on his back on the bunk and pressed his fingers to his eyes.

The sun was up by the time Vanessa was jolting along the hilltop track toward the boatyard. The gusts of wind were harder up here in exposed places: they buffeted the car, and flattened the grass and bushes. She came to the hilltop overlooking the boatyard and stopped.

His car was still there. She rammed hers into low gear and ground down the steep track. As she got near the bottom she stuck her head out of the window and bellowed: "Ho-oh-gan."

She slammed to a stop beside his car and climbed out. A gust of wind whipped through the banana trees, whipping up her dress, and she clutched at it.

"Hogan!"

Then she saw her note, still on his steering wheel. She snatched it up and turned it over to see if he had written anything on the reverse. *Nothing.*

She hurried round to the front of the cottage. She shook the door for confirmation. Then she walked disconsolately back to the cars. She got into his with a sigh and sat there, staring at the sound. Junks were thudding past out there.

Well, she would just have to wait.

Another burst of wind came and the banana trees bent. She peered up through the windshield. The whole sky was hazy now. And over there toward the south it was gray. The sweat was running off her again. And she still had not had anything to eat.

She would wait a couple of hours. If he wasn't back by then it would mean he was stuck on his goddamn junk.

In the typhoon. . . . She closed her eyes. For the first time in her life she was afraid for somebody else.

By eleven o'clock that morning the sky was getting dark. The gusts of wind were coming harder and more often now, and out there the South China Sea was swelling and breaking higher. Tolo Sound was protected from the winds and the open sea by the Mountains of Nine Dragons, but swells were seething under the gusts and the waves were breaking along the rocky shoreline.

At eleven o'clock McAdam's junk was steaming down Tolo Sound. He had given up trying to get into the shelter. A lot of other junks were doing the same, and some of the bigger ones were putting back out to deep sea, to try to ride out the typhoon far away from rocks.

The sun was almost gone behind the haze, and the sea ahead was nearly black. Al the way down the long jagged sound, on both sides, were other junks, anchored far apart. All the anchored junks had their bows pointed south.

He had to give himself plenty of space. When he was approaching the end of the sound, he swung the junk around and went steaming back up the channel again. He chose his place and swung the wheel to starboard. He put the engines astern, then into neutral. Wong scrambled up to the bows. He grunted as he picked up the big anchor. He slung it overboard with all his might.

McAdam heard it splash. He waited, sweating, for the junk to drift and take up the slack in the anchor rope. Then he went up the bows himself to look.

The anchor rope was tight, stretched out. He paid out a bit

more, until he estimated that he had the correct drag, maximum resistance to the weight of the boat. Then he untied the smaller Sanforth anchor. He stood up, heaved the anchor above his head, and hurled it with all his might.

He pulled in the slack. Then he tested the main anchor, pulling on the rope firmly. It held. He pulled it once more a little harder, and it came loose out of the sandy mud.

He cursed and then hauled the anchor in with all his might, hand over hand. He heaved it up out of the black water, onto the deck, then stood there, heart thudding. The smaller anchor still held the big junk.

"Bring the dinghy."

Wong lowered the rubber dinghy into the chopping sea. He rowed it round to the bows, then stood up and hung on to the gunwale. McAdam heaved the big fifty-pound anchor over the edge and lowered it down into the little boat.

"Out there!" He pointed.

Wong rowed the dinghy through the slapping water.

"There."

Wong left the oars and scrambled up, and heaved the anchor over the side with a big splash.

McAdam waited, then pulled in the slack.

"Hold fast, you bitch!"

He tested it. It held. He looked around at the shoreline, at the nearest junk. At the sky. A gust of wind swept over the Mountains of Nine Dragons and funneled down the sound.

There was nothing more they could do. Except wait.

At noon that Saturday morning Vanessa was driving her rented car down the tarmac road back to Hong Kong. She had left another note for McAdam on his steering wheel.

She had stopped at Tai-po and tried to see his junk among the masses, but it had been impossible. Now, as she drove through the gusts of wind down the edge of Tolo Sound, she was not looking for his boat, but was glancing at the profusion of junks at anchor. Then suddenly she thought she saw it, and slammed on her brakes.

It was the yellow rubber dinghy that she spotted, half a mile away across the sound. She peered across the water at it. Yes—she was sure!

She gave a long blast of her horn, then a burst of short ones, then scrambled out of the car. The wind flapped at her as she ran stumbling round the car to the edge of the road, where the stone embankment dropped straight into the slapping sea.

"*Hogan!*" she bellowed, waving frantically.

She shouted and shouted, dashed back to the car and blasted the horn some more. The wind snatched her shouts away to nothing, and the spray hit her. For ten minutes she tried.

For another ten minutes she sat in the car, watching the junk, the wind buffeting. A few times she could just make out a figure moving about.

Then she sighed, started her car again, and drove slowly back to Hong Kong.

Her note said that she would wait for him at his apartment. That was where she wanted to be. But she could not bear to go there yet, with nothing to do but wait.

Part ten

The radar screen of the Royal Observatory was a little bigger than a television set. Mervin Katz stood beside it, with an air of morbid proprietorship. Vanessa stared at the machine. The rotating radar beam showed up in the screen as a thin white line going slowly round. And in that rotating beam showed Typhoon Rose.

With each sweep the typhoon glowed, spiraling blackly and brightly inward to the eye.

Her nerves were going. She had had only three hours' sleep last night in the car, and she was sick with worry for McAdam on the junk. That terrifying mass on the radar screen, that same whirlpool she had flown into yesterday—it was going to hit him, on the sea, on a junk. She tried to force herself to concentrate.

Katz pointed to the black eye.

"The eye's still two hundred and fifty miles due south of us. But the nearest big winds are only about fifty miles away at this moment."

"How long before they hit us?"

"About four, five hours. But the first big gusts will hit us in half that time. You should get home soon."

"I wish to God McAdam had got into a typhoon shelter."

"Don't worry. McAdam's the luckiest guy I know." Then he went on tactlessly, "Can't rely on typhoon shelters anyway. If Typhoon Rose arrives on schedule she'll coincide with normal high tide."

"Oh, my God, Katz . . . what happens?"

"Okay, forget it."

"Tell me!"

"Well, in 1932 a typhoon coincided with high tide and caused a bejezus big wave that knocked out all the typhoon shelters. Eleven thousand people died." He said apologetically, "You know about the typhoon and the water?"

"No."

"Well, a typhoon causes a dome of sea to rise up. By a kind of suction. And that moves with the typhoon. And if that dome of sea arrives at the same time as normal high tide it can be very bad." He added, "Look, don't worry—"

"Don't worry! Do you think I can get a boat to go out and get him off? Or a marine police launch?"

He smiled and put his big hand on her shoulder.

"Listen. Jake's on his precious boat for one reason—he refuses to leave it. Wild horses wouldn't get him off. And he also wouldn't leave that boat boy to his fate. Thousands of other junk people will be out there on their boats. He'll be all right."

She stared at him, then turned away and paced across the floor.

The China sun beat down through the haze that hung over the sea and the islands. It was muggy hot between the hard gusts of wind. The streets were almost deserted, all the shop windows boarded up.

There were still a few taxis running, a few trams. There was one Star ferry shuttling back and forth across the harbor but it was almost empty. Some junks were still coming in. The big typhoon buoys were all full of ships, the "B" buoys all empty because they were not heavy enough to hold a ship during a typhoon.

The radio repeated at half-hourly intervals in English and Cantonese and Chiu Chau and Tanka:

"Here is a special announcement: The Royal Hong Kong Observatory has raised the Number Nine Signal . . . All precautions should already have been completed . . ."

All precautions were being taken; in the police, the fire department, the public works department, marine department, the army, navy, air force, the volunteer services, government information center. All policemen were on emergency standby. The Special Operations Room next to the 999 Room was opened up, with the big maps hanging on the walls, the flags and lights marking positions, the hot-line telephones connected up to all other stations, to special mobile units, the public works department, the government information center, H.Q. In the public works department the emergency officers and their equipment were ready, from bulldozers to drainage maps.

In the fire department daily routine had been done in full dress, from hitting the pole to fire drill, climbing drill, rescue drill; hoses, ladders, pumps and engines had been tested, fire engines were revving and roaring. Now in all the fire stations round the colony the firemen were lying on their dormitory beds, boots on, ready to hit the pole within sixty seconds of the alarm bell ringing for fires, floods, jammed elevators, landslides, house-collapse. The army was on standby for manpower duties and engineering jobs, the air force for helicopter rescue operations, the navy for sea rescue operations. Government information staff and certain trained volunteer servicemen were on duty all the time: camp beds, coffee percolators, sandwich boxes were everywhere, telephones and teleprinters were tingling with anticipation.

As the first high wind came, Vanessa swung her rented car down into McAdam's basement garage. The wind howled through the cavern. She clutched her dress about her and bent her head and ran back up the drive-in, into dark Hillside Road. She battled her way down to her own apartment block and dashed into the entrance.

She took the back service staircase, let herself quietly in at the kitchen door, and was hit by the typhoon party.

Music, laughter, loud talking. The kitchen was a mess of bottles, glasses, food, wrappings. She tiptoed hurriedly down the corridor to her bedroom. She opened the door quietly and was confronted by a large pair of spread female buttocks on top of male thighs.

"Oops—sorry."

The girl slid off the man hastily and clutched the bedspread up to her breasts. The man lay there, drunkenly unsurprised, his erection unabated. She didn't know either of them. "Come and join us!"

"Do you mind if I take a raincheck?"

She hurried to the wardrobe and grabbed a few things. Then to the dressing table, and snatched up a few cosmetics.

"Bye—have fun."

She didn't mind. If her bed had been empty she would have collapsed into it, and then regretted it when she was woken by a drunken reveler. Oh, no, all she wanted was his apartment, his things about her. She hurried to the bathroom and got her toothbrush, hair conditioner and bath salts. Yes—it was still bath day, lucky her. And two sleeping pills.

If she wasn't beautiful when he came out of this goddamn typhoon it wouldn't be for want of trying.

Then she tiptoed back to the kitchen, and sneaked out of the door. The wind coming up the stairs billowed her skirt up above her hips.

Upstairs in the gallery, the Chinese killer heard the front door open in McAdam's apartment below. He sat dead still in the rocking chair behind the closed door at the top of the spiral staircase, and listened.

She came in panting because she had climbed the six flights of stairs. She knew better than to trust an elevator during a typhoon. She locked the front door behind her. Then she flung herself onto the sofa.

She lay there a full minute in the near darkness, eyes closed, getting her breath back. Then the wind beat against the windows and she opened her eyes in a sudden realization: the windows had not been fortified with tape to hold flying glass.

She sighed. She was dead tired. Then she heaved herself up off the sofa.

It was almost like night outside, though she knew that somewhere behind that blackness the sunset was still going on. It was an unearthly darkness, full of foreboding. She could hardly see the sea, but the lights of the apartments and ships were burning. She walked to the French windows that led onto the veranda, and opened them. There was no wind at that moment. She stepped out into the hot darkness.

Then another burst of wind came.

Hard and sudden, and the trees below bent in the darkness. She clutched the veranda rail, and her hair blew and her skirt flapped and the curtains billowed into the living room. She clung there, feeling the strength of the wind, and she wanted to stand out here and feel the winds that would blow McAdam, and share them with him.

At the top of the spiral staircase the door opened a crack. The killer stood there a moment, looking down. Then he opened the door.

He started down the iron steps, silently. Carefully. Below him, in the dark, were the open French windows. Outside on the veranda, she stood holding the rail, eyes closed, waiting for the next burst of wind, concentrating on McAdam, trying to communicate with him by thought. And behind her in the dark living room the man came silently down the spiral staircase to kill her.

One smart blow on the back of her shoulders and one grab at her knees to tilt her up, and over she would go. A wild scream, clutching at the air, arms and legs outflung as she plunged six floors to a sudden sharp death on the dark concrete below. Nobody would see her go in the dark, and nobody would hear her, with all windows closed.

Then the big gust of wind struck. She jerked back and opened her eyes. Behind her the French door banged against itself, and she turned. She strode into the dark living room, and slammed the window closed behind her. Six feet from her the killer froze on the spiral stairs.

He stood absolutely still in the dark as she bolted the French windows. Then she turned her back on the spiral staircase, snapped on the air conditioner, switched on a reading lamp, and walked out of the room to look for insulation tape to secure the windows.

The killer retreated silently up the staircase.

She found a big roll of adhesive tape in his office, and a pair of scissors. She spread the tape across the glass, from corner to corner and side to side, like a spider's web. She went methodically from window to window, room to room. She was very tired. But it was better to be working, doing something.

It was night by the time she finished with the windows in the bedroom. And outside the wind was coming harder now, beating against the glass almost all the time. She threw the roll of tape onto the chair, walked into the bathroom and spun the taps. She threw in a big dash of bubble suds. She sat down on the edge, eyes closed, waiting for the tub to fill.

Then she suddenly remembered the gallery upstairs. She had to tape those windows as well.

Well, she'd better do it now, before she zonked out.

She heaved herself up, went to the bedroom, picked up the tape and scissors, and walked down the corridor into the living room. She crossed to the spiral staircase and began to mount it.

She plodded slowly up, round and round. She got halfway. Then she remembered. She didn't have the key. It was on McAdam's key ring. She stood there, wearily, considering what to do. It was serious. If those windows went . . .

There was nothing she could do. But she'd better try the door anyway. Maybe by some chance he had left it unlocked.

She sighed and pulled herself forward on the handrail and started on up the stairs again. She came to the second last turn.

Then she remembered the bath. The taps were still running. She could hear them.

"Damn!"

She hesitated wearily, turned and clattered back down the staircase.

She hurried across the living room, down the corridor, into the bathroom. The bath was full, the bubbles frothing up to the rim, the room full of steam. She spun the taps closed. Then she went and felt the water.

It was good and hot. She hesitated again.

Well, even if that door to the gallery was open, it would take her an hour to tape all those windows. And by then this lovely bath would be cold. She wasn't going to waste that.

She would check the gallery afterward, before she went to bed.

She began to unbutton her blouse.

At the top of the spiral staircase, the door quietly opened. The killer listened, then began to come down the stairs.

Outside in the blackness the wind beat the windows and howled up the stairs, but it was quiet in the apartment. She sat naked on the toilet seat, eyes closed.

The killer heard the tinkling, the most defenseless sound in the world. He stopped at the beginning of the corridor. Absolutely still. He wanted her *in* the bath. He did not want to leave bruises or splashes or other signs of struggle. He stepped silently backward into the living room, and waited.

Then he heard the sound of flushing.

She piled her hair up on top of her head, pinned it; then she climbed carefully into the bubble bath. It was very hot. She stood a moment, adjusting to the heat; then she slowly lowered herself

190

into it, and eased herself down the bath, so the suds slid up over her breasts. Just her head and neck were exposed.

She sighed and lay there, eyes closed.

Bliss.

Down the corridor, in the living room, the killer did not hear her getting into the bath because she had done it so slowly. He waited, alert, listening.

She lay silently in the bath for a full minute, just feeling the heat soak into her tired limbs. Then she felt the beads of sweat forming on her face. She slowly opened her eyes.

What she wanted was a long cold beer and a cigarette. She lay there half a minute considering it. Then heaved herself up out of the water.

The killer heard the splash of the water, and he thought she was now bathing. He came on tiptoe down the corridor.

Vanessa came naked, soapy, through the bathroom door, heading for the kitchen, when she saw him. All she registered was the terrifying dark shape of a man coming at her down the corridor, and she screamed.

She stumbled backward into the bedroom, and the killer lunged down the corridor. She grabbed wildly at the door to slam it as he threw himself at it. She flung herself against the door with all her might, her wet feet skidding on the floor, and she shoved and shoved, screaming and heaving, and the door flew open.

She reeled back wild-eyed down the side of the bed and the killer burst into the room. She scrambled, terrified, up onto the bed, threw herself at the open wardrobe and grabbed wildly for McAdam's gun. She snatched it out, and as he lunged at her she jerked the trigger. There was a sharp popping noise, and the silenced gun leapt in her hand. The bullet smashed into the wall and the killer threw himself sideways against the wardrobe.

She scrambled back up onto the bed, holding the gun in front of her with both hands, her breath coming in juddering gasps. The killer shoved himself off the wardrobe and lunged at her. She screamed in terror and pulled the trigger again and again, and the gun jerked in her hands and the bullets smashed into the wall. She leapt off the bed and fired again with both hands, and the bullet hit his chest just below his shoulder.

He crashed onto the floor, blood welling out of the side of his chest; she stood shuddering, her face contorted in horror, mouth open, the gun shaking in her hands. For a long instant the killer lay sprawled on the floor, his face creased up in agony; then he looked up at her, and began to get up. She gave a strangled cry of terror, leveled the gun at him blindly and fired again.

The last bullet in the gun smashed through the other side of the killer's chest and knocked him back to the floor. The blood was now spreading out from under him.

She crouched by the wardrobe, whimpering, the gun still pointed at him in both trembling hands. She pulled the trigger again, and the gun went click.

His chest covered in blood, his hands and face smeared with it, his face screwed up in murderous fury, he got to his knees. He stretched out both his bloody hands toward her, and staggered up to his feet. She threw down the gun and lunged into the wardrobe to grab McAdam's sword.

She wrenched off the scabbard and thrust the sword desperately in front of her, gripping it with both hands. The killer's eyes glinted. For a long terrible moment he stood there, the blood pumping out of him, then he bared his teeth in a horrible grin, and lurched at her. She swung the sword wildly up over her shoulder like a club and ran toward the bathroom door, swinging the sword on high, and the killer came at her and she screamed and swiped at him. The sword slashed the air in front of him, and she threw herself hysterically through the bathroom door, reeled round and slammed it. The killer rammed against the door and she screamed and heaved against it with her naked shoulder.

Suddenly the door burst open and she lurched backward. Her legs hit the edge of the bath and buckled, and the killer grasped for her.

She crashed backward into the water, legs upflung, the sword in one hand, and the killer grabbed her foot. She screamed and wrenched and kicked and swung the sword, and he grabbed her wrist. She twisted and thrashed, and then thrust, with all her might. The point of the sword stabbed into his breast, and he staggered back against the wall.

She scrambled up out of the bath, gasping. The man slumped against the wall, the blood spurting out of his chest, then he lurched toward her again. Holding the sword in front of her like a bayonet, eyes screwed up in horror, she rammed it with all her terrified strength into his stomach.

The killer doubled over, clutching the sword in both bloody hands, and hung on to it. She wrenched it out of his grasp, then rammed it again with all her might into his guts. The point hit the wall behind him. The blood was pouring out of him, and her screams of horror were just hysterical gasps.

The blood welled up and out of his contorted mouth, and he looked at her once, then slumped and slid down the wall. She looked in horrified disbelief at the bloody man, then staggered across the bathroom and flung herself through the door, naked, sobbing.

She wrenched open the front door. The wind howled up the stairs about her as she almost fell down them. Face contorted in terror, she escaped into Hillside Road and the howling night, and the wind got her, and she fell on hands and knees. She scrambled up, and lurched into a staggering run toward the American Mess.

_____*Part eleven*

At about ten o'clock that night the first big wind came from the north, rushing in a black curve across the South China Sea, roaring like an express train. The wind lashed the waves up before it to send them crashing up onto the waterfronts and across the streets, and leaping up high over the rocks and the big concrete break-waters of the typhoon shelters, and the packed junks rolled, timbers grinding, gunwale to gunwale. The big ships in the harbor suddenly heaved against their buoys. And with the end of the first big wind came the first rain.

The rain swept across the islands in great black furls like curtains, and through the streets and up the steep mountains, lashing the jungle and the squatter shacks. And the water came rushing down the steep mountainsides, cascading down onto the roads and ladder streets between the apartment blocks and tenements, frothing, rushing down onto the foreshore.

But Typhoon Rose was still a hundred miles away and her winds were very much stronger than this.

35

The firemen were sprawled on their bunks, exhausted, dirty, dazed. They were in full firefighting gear, dripping water and ashes and blood, the sweat pouring off them, smoking their first cigarettes in hours, their feet up for the first time in seven hours, but with their fireproof boots still on, because when the alarm next went they had to hit the pole within sixty seconds.

Always with our fucking boots right on, Jack-the-Fire thought. He sprawled on his back on his office floor, eyes closed, face streaked with black, hair matted. He had been wearing his boots for a hundred years. He was clearly going to die with his boots on, because he was going to die any fucking moment. The mere sound of the next alarm bell would kill him by itself.

The two-way radio was rasping all the time next door; he was trying not to listen to it. Fires, landslides, collapsed houses, collapsed roads, floods—firemen and fire engines and fireboats being ordered here, there and everywhere at once. There were twenty-one fires on both sides of the habor and in two typhoon shelters.

"Fire alarm at Nanking Mansions—"

"Jesus," Jack-the-Fire muttered, eyes closed.

Then the alarm was shrilling and they were leaping off their bunks and running for the pole and hurling down it to the red fire engines below, and Jack-the-Fire was yelling: "Come on!"

In exactly fifty seconds the last man was clinging to the fire engine and the big red machines roared out of the doors into the typhoon. The fire engines lurched in the wind and the men clung fiercely on, heads down. At the corner a big drain had burst and water gushed out like an oil well and the winds lashed it away. A car was overturned. Ahead was a wide road rushing like a river in the headlights. The fire engine roared across the rushing street, wheels spinning, and then a big neon sign came hurtling down the concrete canyon, and it would have gone flying over the fire engine, but at that moment fireman Chan lifted his head, and it hit him on the back of his helmet at a hundred miles an hour. The mass of flying steel sliced off the top of Chan's skull as if it were a boiled egg, and took his body with it, hurtling into blackness. Nobody saw him go.

The fire engines stood axle-deep in rushing water, arc lights beaming up, fire hoses jetting. The fourth to the tenth floors of Nanking Mansions were ablaze, the winds driving the fire upward. The fire had started in an illegal plastic-goods factory on the fourth floor. The people below the fourth floor had fled downward and were already safe. But many people above the fourth floor had fled upward, scrambling, trampling each other, whores, pimps, sailors, screaming, shoving, coughing. And firemen were fighting up the flooding stairways.

Big Cheri was lying on the bed in King Winky's penthouse brothel, admiring her magnificent breasts in the mirror and humming untunefully, and Harry Howard was getting dressed, when suddenly the bedroom door shook and there was a roar of wind in the corridor, and then black smoke gushed under the door. Harry stared at it a long uncomprehending moment, then Big Cheri sat up so her bit tits bounced. "Gosh," she squeaked. "Fire!"

"Fire?" Harry Howard croaked. "How can there be fire with all this rain?"

"Don't just stand there, Harry," Big Cheri squeaked. "Go put it out!"

"Oh, my God," Harry gargled. "Oh, my God—water—water—"

He went scrambling into the bathroom looking for something to pour water into, and there was nothing except the two toothbrush glasses, and he bellowed at Big Cheri, who was still clutching her breasts, "Call room service for a bucket!" and turned the taps on full blast.

At that moment the front doors of King Winky's whorehouse exploded open under the force of the black wind roaring up the stairwells, and with the wind came the screams of the people struggling up the stairs. The wind roared through King Winky's whorehouse and smashed the windows at the end of the corridor and the long carpet went sucking out, and the wind hit Harry Howard's door and blasted it open.

The door sent him flying backward on top of Big Cheri. He scrambled up, clutching his bloody nose, and screamed, *"Get out!"* He grabbed Big Cheri's arm and heaved her up and lunged, choking, into the teeth of the blast, dragging her after him, and the first of the fleeing mob came stampeding up the corridor. Harry and Big Cheri were crushed up the stairs that led to the roof, up against the iron door. Harry beat on the door, feeling wildly for the bolts, and rammed them back, and the iron door suddenly disappeared, whipped into the howling blackness by Typhoon Rose, and it took him and Big Cheri with it. They were flung out on the rooftop and over the concrete, on their faces in the lashing wind and rain, and the mob came fighting after them.

Thirty minutes later there were still a hundred people trying to fight their way along King Winky's corridors and up onto the roof, but the ones at the end would not make it. There were over three hundred and fifty people packed onto the rooftop between the water tanks and the elevator housings, on top of each other, and there was no more room to scramble to. The rooftop heaved and surged with bodies trampling each other in the blackness, trying to get away from the terror of the fire that was now leaping red and yellow through the black smoke of the doorway. Fifty people lay roasting in King Winky's corridors. The rooftop was getting hotter from the flames below. For the moment the lashing rain cooled the concrete and the winds tore away the smoke and the intense heat. But when the eye of Typhoon Rose passed over, the winds and the rain would stop, and it would be deathly still.

36

Captain Neil O'Bryan in the *Fat Hong* knew from the screeching radio that there were thirty-one ships dragging anchor at this moment but he could only glimpse flashes of lights through the lashing spray. He could not see how close to the rocks of Lantau Island he was. He could not even see the waves, he could only judge them by their massive pounding on his hull, and great sprays flying over the bridge. The bows crashed down into the troughs so the whole ship shook and the waves resounded like cannon.

Captain Neil O'Bryan clung to the bridge-wing, lashed, sodden, eyes screwed up, his skinny legs braced. The *Fat Hong* was dragging both her anchors, but he had his engines grinding ahead to diminish the drag. "Hail Mary, full of grace," he croaked fiercely over and over into the lashing rain, "Hallowed be Thy name . . ." And he could not even hear himself.

](no)

200

Suddenly he saw bridge lights through the storm. He lurched frantically toward the wheelhouse.

"Do you see them—lights?"

The helmsman could see nothing through the rain-lashed glass. "Up anchors!" Neil O'Bryan bellowed at the bridgeman, and he reeled at the telegraph and rammed it up to half ahead. "Starboard forty-five degrees!" Then he shouted into the radio transmitter: "Ahoy there! *Fat Hong* calling unknown ship bearing down on her off Lantau. Heave over, for the love of God! *Fat Hong* turning east on her starboard. Do you read me, for the love of Jesus!"

The Chinese seaman was fighting his way over the foredeck. He threw himself at the port anchor winch and began to heave in the anchor. Then through the rain the blurred bridge lights on the U.S.S. *Dreadnought* could suddenly be seen, heaving upward, fifty yards ahead, big and terrible, then they were gone again. The next wave smashed him away from the starboard anchor winch before he could turn the handle, sucked him over the rail, and he was gone.

The *Fat Hong* was heaving to starboard, her old engines pounding, but one dragging anchor was still holding her. She was broadside on to the big galloping troughs now, and she heaved over under each impact in a massive roll, then rolled back again in the bottom of the trough, then the next wave hit her and she rolled again, and Captain O'Bryan was hurled into the corner of the bridge-wing. He lay stunned, then he started to scramble up, and then he saw the awful lights again.

"For the love of Jesus and Mary!"

Twenty yards off his portside bridge-wing, looming blurred and terrible way up above him as his ship rolled the *Dreadnought* was broadside onto him, crashing and rolling with the waves; for a long instant he saw her, then she rolled to port as the *Fat Hong* rolled to starboard, and she was gone in the spray and rain. Captain O'Bryan bellowed into the gale, *"Starboard hard!"* and flung himself into the wheelhouse and rammed the telegraph to full ahead. He grabbed the megaphone and clawed his way out onto the port bridge-wing. The *Fat Hong* rolled to port as the *Dreadnought* rolled to starboard. The bridge-wing came rolling toward him, and he yelled into the megaphone: *"Get out of the way, for the love of Christ!"*

The wave broke over him and *Dreadnought*'s bridge missed him by two yards. He clung to the bridge-wing, gasping as it swooped upward and away from the *Dreadnought* like a ferris wheel with her starboard roll, then she began to roll back. *Fat Hong* crashed into her portside roll and Captain O'Bryan saw the *Dreadnought* bridge-wing coming swooping down toward him, the big wing of steel looming huge, and he screamed into the wind and reeled backward to get out of the way of the mass of steel, and the *Dreadnought*'s bridge-wing crashed down onto his.

The *Fat Hong*'s port bridge-wing was torn off the wheelhouse with a terrible cracking under the crashing spray, and O'Bryan went with it, headlong into the sea below. He fell between the two mangled ships as they tore apart and rolled in opposite directions again, but he did not fight the sea because he could not any more. The two ships started rolling back toward each other, and O'Bryan was crushed between the two steel sides as they cannoned against each other.

Again and again the two ships rolled and crashed against each other in the blackness, and already they had made gaping holes in each other, and the *Fat Hong* was taking water fast when she capsized and sank.

It was almost daybreak.

The rain had stopped, and with daybreak McAdam could see the lights of junks plowing up Tolo Sound as he was, taking the troughs head-on.

He clung to the main mast, lashed to it by his waist with a lifeline, one hand trying to shield his eyes from the seas and wind. The bows reared up again into the running swell, then swooped down the other side, and the sea hit him full blast, and the lifeline wrenched at his guts. The winds were fiercer than ever. But he hardly felt them—all he felt was the sudden exhausted elation that the horror of being blind was almost over. He could just see the shorelines on both sides now, and he could see something on the sea, and it was marvelous to know that there was nothing ahead. He clung tight to the mast as he feverishly untied the bowline around his waist, then he staggered back to the wheelhouse.

"Daybreak, Elder Brother! And the rain has stopped!"

Wong clung to the wheel, sodden and exhausted. "But the typhoon is not over."

"But it will not be like last night again! By tonight it will be gone!"

The junk shook as it crashed down into the trough, and the spray lashed the wheelhouse in a sheet. He could not even hear the pounding of the diesel engine just beneath his feet.

"Just hold her there! There is nothing ahead."

McAdam lurched across the wheelhouse and down the hatch into the cabin. He pulled open the drawer and his hand found the whisky bottle. He staggered back into the wheelhouse and braced himself. He felt marvelous. His concrete boat had performed perfectly. He passed the bottle unsteadily to Wong.

"Drink! It will be good for you!"

Wong took a swallow, choked and suppressed a retch.

"Again!"

Wong clung to the wheel, head down, shuddering. McAdam clapped him on the shoulder.

"Be joyful, Elder Brother! It is nearly daylight! And our ship of stone has survived!"

Suddenly, when they were at their blackest and fiercest the winds vanished.

Suddenly the sky could be seen again, a circle of blue, with the great amphitheater of black walls rising up to it, and the light was eerie. It was humid sweating hot. Suddenly the jungle stopped thrashing and hung there, sodden, broken. Suddenly there was no more roaring, only the noise of the water cascading down off the mountains and rushing down the streets. It was like a silent battlefield, just the water swirling, the broken cars and the neon signs scattered up the streets. And the waves were no longer battering the waterfronts, just big swells seething, confused. Out on the rocky coastlines of the islands eleven big ships lay wrecked, but ships which had been dragging anchors suddenly held; Hong Kong was inside the eye of the typhoon.

The broadcast went out again and again:

"We repeat, this is only a temporary lull. The eye of the typhoon is passing over Hong Kong. We are on the inside edge of the eye. It will pass in approximately sixty minutes, whereupon the winds will return at the same velocity, but from the opposite direction. All people should remain indoors. All vessels should prepare to receive the wind from the opposite quadrant. Shipping is warned that the return of the winds will coincide with high tide and bigger waves can be expected. . . ."

At the Royal Air Force strip the helicopter was being rolled out of the hangar.

"In," Jack-the-Fire shouted to his firemen. "In!"

The helicopter flew flat out, roaring low over the rooftops. They could see the smoke from Nanking Mansions. He looked at his Chinese firemen. They were wet, dirty, tired, like him. But the shine on Jack's face was not water, it was sweat. Good cold fear. Even in big airliners Jack never flew quite sober; he was terrified in a helicopter. "How long?" he said to the pilot.

"Half a minute less than the last time you asked. About one minute more."

"How much time have you got to get this flying machine back before the shit hits the fan again?"

"Forty minutes."

"What'll you do if the typhoon comes back before you've made it back to base?"

"File a complaint."

The helicopter went chopping into a big circle, approaching the Nanking Mansions roof. The smoke belched up in a dense black cloud. The flames leapt through the windows, orange and yellow and red and black. They could not see the people on the roof through the smoke. On the next roof, across the yawning chasm of the street and fifty feet lower, there were firemen waiting. "What do you want me to do?" the pilot shouted.

Jack was leaning out of the door, clinging on tight, trying to see the rooftop through the smoke, some point to drop onto without falling seventeen floors down to the street. The helicopter lurched in the rising heat, the smoke whirling away from the propeller blast. And down there on the rooftop the piled bodies were writhing, clawing, gasping, suffocating, dying; people were hanging over the wall, trying to scramble away from the roasting concrete. Jack spoke into the intercom:

"Hover over the center. About twenty feet. We'll bail out by ladder. Then keep hovering there to blow the smoke clear while we rig the slide."

The helicopter came chopping back over the concrete canyons. Way down there were the fire engines and ambulances. Jack did not look. The propellers were blasting the smoke off the roof and he could see the gesticulating people clearly now. "Hover!" Jack rasped. "Away the ladders!"

The rope ladders unrolled, and the first man was already scrambling down, the helicopter rocking under the shift in weight. Jack swung down the ladder in the propeller blast. The first two firemen were trying to sort out the dead and injured.

Jack dropped down onto the concrete and began to shove his way toward the steel door, pushing people aside, shouting into his gas mask, "Make way!" He saw a naked woman with magnificent breasts and a mass of blond hair, and she was cradling the bloody head of a man saying, "There, there, Harry, there, there . . ." The last fireman in the helicopter was throwing the equipment down. Jack lowered his helmet and disappeared through the black smoke of the doorway.

He could see the flames leaping, and feel the heat beating on his asbestos suit, roaring up the corridor toward the open steel door like a chimney. And below this floor there were half a dozen more ablaze, roasting that rooftop, without the wind and rain to cool it. He scrambled back up to the roof. Seven firemen were shoving through the people toward him lugging fire extinguishers. They scrambled through the door, gas masks on under their visors, and disappeared into the smoke.

Jack-the-Fire struggled across the rooftop to the water reservoirs. A nylon rope had been fired across the chasm from the roof to the next apartment block, and the cable had been dragged across.

Jack's men were rigging their end of the slide, lashed around a water reservoir; now they were pulling across the chair on the running tackle. Jack pulled off his visor and gas mask, grabbed the nearest woman by the arm and bellowed, "Women first! Into the chair!"

The firemen swung the chair underneath her buttocks. "Hold tight!" Then she saw the yawning chasm beneath her feet and screamed. "Away!" Jack bellowed, and away she went, screaming out into thin air, eyes screwed up, hair flying, through space down toward the firemen on the rooftop below. Now the people were heaving and clutching to be the next to go. Jack was back underneath the roaring helicopter at the rope ladders.

"Come on!" he roared. "Up! Up!"

He grabbed a woman and she started scrambling wildly. Now they were mobbing around the rope ladder. *"One at a time!"* he bellowed. *"No grabbing!"*

Three minutes later the helicopter was full. It went rocking up, into the sky, then it banked away, chopping over the concrete jungle toward the Police Sports Club where the ambulances were waiting.

A second helicopter was coming toward the rooftop. Jack was growling into his radio, "We need another helicopter! Heat intense, these people can't take much more. Also oxygen-starvation. The only chance is to blow the water reservoirs and then follow it with men—so get another fucking helicopter and stuff it full of firemen and get its arse up here because I'm going to blow them reservoirs before these people roast alive!"

The circle of blue sky was almost gone over the Mountains of Nine Dragons. The black wall was coming back over the sea. There were thirty people left on the rooftop. The smoke was billowing out of the door again, black and choking; people were hanging over the wall, coughing, gasping. Jack knelt at the base of the water reservoir, placing a plastic explosive charge. He slid the detonator in, then scrambled backward, trailing the electric wire. Another man in the chair went hurtling off over the canyon. Then the third helicopter came overhead and the propeller began to blast the smoke away.

Jack waved it down, it hovered and the two rope ladders unfurled. "Up!" Jack roared. They started clawing frantically up, people surging, shoving to be the next to go. "Last one!" He grabbed Big Cheri by the arm. "Up, lady!"

Big Cheri squeaked at him, "Excuse me, Mr. Fireman, but I think my friend should go and I'll go on the slidy thing—"

All Jack saw was the big smudged mouth moving through the mass of flying hair, and the magnificent breasts. He shoved her regretfully. "Get up there, lady!'

"But Mr. Fireman, sir!"

A man shouldered her aside and swung onto the ladder, and Big Cheri staggered backward, and then another man grabbed the ladder and started clawing up it. Jack yelled at the pilot: *"Get out of here before they pull you down!"*

The helicopter rose, lurching, straining, with the two ladders full of widely clinging people; it rose two feet, three, four, six, and the ladder laden with people was swinging across the rooftop. Harry Howard lunged blindly as it swung past him in the roaring blast of the propellers, and grabbed it with two hands and clung on for dear life, and he was swept kicking off his feet in the roaring blast, and the helicopter keeled under its swinging weight as it roared across the rooftop. The wall was sweeping toward him with the terrible nothingness yawning below, and everybody was shouting at him to let go.

"Come back, Harry, you'll fall!" Big Cheri screamed, and she lumbered after him as he was swept across the rooftop and her clawing fingers just got him by the pants and she clung on as she was dragged on her knees screaming, "Let go, Harry!" Jack-the-Fire was bounding after her bellowing, "Leggo, for Chrissakes!" and Big Cheri hit the wall and let go. As she was about to crash over the wall, Jack-the-Fire hit her from behind in a sort of wild rugby tackle, both arms flung around her waist and his face

206

squashed against the side of her ample buttocks, and the helicopter keeled out over the chasm. It roared down with the two ladders swinging wildly, the pilot wrestling to get her back under control. The helicopter fell twenty feet, sideways, then she came back under control, lurching and staggering. The pilot gave her full throttle to drive her up out of the chasm; and she began to lift. She lifted slowly, shuddering, and she was going to make it; she was gaining altitude slowly but surely, juddering, and now her screaming propellers were almost level with the rooftop again, and Jack bellowed, *"Mind the wire!"* and as he yelled, the propellers hit the chair cable stretched across the concrete canyon, and the blade smashed and went spinning off into the air. For a long moment the helicopter paused at the top of the concrete canyon, then it lurched sideways and fell.

A roar went up from the street below and inside the helicopter there were screams of terror; it went down fifty feet, then it hit the side of the blazing building at the tenth floor and went skidding straight down the blazing wall, then it burst into flames—great orange flames that billowed into a ball around it. Then it bounced off the wall and went tumbling down through the air for the last sixty feet, and crashed in a splat of flying flames onto the street below.

37

McAdam sat slumped over the wheel, sodden, his head in one hand, his other holding the whisky bottle. Wong lay stretched out on the wheelhouse deck, fast asleep. McAdam yearned to lie down but he knew that if he did he would pass out.

It was steamy hot. Directly overhead the sky was blue, but just beyond the mountain it was black again, the walls of winds silently coming closer and closer. He sat, waiting for them. They had taken a new anchorage, in good water, the bows pointing southeast now, whence the backlash of the winds would come. The sea seethed in the eye of the typhoon, heaving and slapping against the hull, as if it did not know where to go.

He got up stiffly.

"Wong!"

Wong did not stir.

"Wong. Elder Brother!" He crouched down wearily and shook him.

Wong's eyes opened and he sat bolt upright, staring.

"The winds are coming back. And it is nearly high tide. The waves will be even bigger."

Wong creaked to his feet. McAdam hefted his lifejacket on.

"I go on the mast?"

"No. We should be able to see enough with the daylight."

He put the whisky bottle away and lit a cigarette.

Then the howling winds came back with a dragon's roar.

The tidal wave that got McAdam and Wong came from way out in the South China Sea. It came rolling toward the South China coast and it hit the outlying islands and went crashing and leaping up and around them; and it went rolling through Hong Kong harbor, thundering against the big ships and over the junks, leaping over the waterfront and sweeping cars down the streets and piling them up on top of each other; it smashed down storefronts and swirled into the doorways of the tenements and up the stairs. The great wave heaved up the freighter *Gonzalez* and carried it over the waterfront and down onto the street.

When the wave was about five hundred yards away McAdam saw it, through the rain and the flying spray lashing his face and eyeballs. The junk had dragged its anchors again and they were in the middle of the sound, Wong at the wheel, McAdam lashed to the mast. It was the biggest wave he had ever seen, a great wall of water coming galloping down toward him. "Watch out!" he roared to Wong, and it was a roar of terror and fury and hate and the knowledge that he was going to die. Through the fury he knew also that he somehow had to make his beloved concrete junk take this terrible wave head-on, try to plunge it up and over and down the other side. McAdam bellowed to Wong into the wind and he untied himself from the mast and clawed his way forward to heave in the dragging anchor.

Wong could not see the wave through the rain-lashed glass but he could see McAdam heaving in the anchor and trying to bellow something to him above the bedlam of the wind and sea. It was not until the wave was one hundred yards off that Wong saw the wall of water looming; for a moment he stared at it, not comprehending, clinging to the wheel, then suddenly he understood what McAdam was bellowing at him—"*Head straight into it!*"—and he gave a strangled shout of terror and exhaustion, and rammed the throttle full ahead, clutching the wheel tight. McAdam fought his way back to the mainmast, and started desperately to undo the knot of his lifeline so he could get back to the wheelhouse. He bellowed *"Hold her into the wave!"* and wrenched at the knot with one hand. He wrenched and wrenched and he could not do it with one hand and he bellowed a terrified curse and let go of the mast and wrenched with both hands and he fell. A wave crashed over him and he toppled onto his knees and grabbed for his knife and he could not find it. He bellowed again in fury and looked wildly into the lashing spray, and he knew he was not going to make it. The wave was fifty yards off now, rearing up and coming as fast as a man can run, and McAdam knew the only thing he could do. He flung his arms around the mast fiercely and yelled over his shoulder to Wong. *"Hold fast!"*

Wong held the junk fast head-on. He could see almost nothing through the rain-lashed glass except McAdam at the mast: Wong clung to the wheel, legs apart, braced for the terrible wave he knew was coming and that was surely going to kill him.

When it was thirty yards away he saw it again through the sudden clarity of the glass, the approaching wall of brown sea, the spray lashing off it and the waves driven before it, and Wong knew that the junk could never get up and over that wall of sea, it would smash right over him and drag the boat to the bottom. He gave one long howl of terror, and swung the helm hard to starboard.

The bows came round and McAdam saw the wave suddenly swinging crazily aside and he bellowed: *"No! No! Back!"*

Wong held the wheel hard over and the bows came right round. McAdam looked back and saw the terrifying crest coming curling over behind him, then he felt the stern of his boat riding up up up the slope of the killer wave.

Then it hit the stern like thunder and crashed over the wheelhouse, and the wave picked the boat up and carried it. Like a giant surfboard, the boat was hurtled down the sound toward Shatin village. The wave carried the boat down the sound for six hundred yards, then it hit the beach with a crack like cannon and exploded over it, and the junk rolled over onto her side and went with the wave over the beach and over the road and into the paddy fields beyond.

McAdam was flung with it by the rope round his waist, upside down and head over heels, trying to thrash his way to the air; then the mast broke and his lifeline was gone. He fought wildly to get back to the air, then his head broke surface and he too was carried over the road into the paddy field.

Five hundred yards down the beach, the wave exploded over the Shatin village seawall, and went marauding right through the village carrying all before it, junks and sampans and carts and people, across the road and into the paddy fields and over the railway line; the wave went a thousand yards up the Shatin valley before it began to draw back toward the sea.

For thirteen hours Typhoon Rose raged across the colony, and the winds reached 190 miles an hour. Ten walls collapsed at a low-cost housing estate. Three aircraft were destroyed when their hangar blew down. Five hundred army, navy and air force catering staff worked round the clock feeding 62,000 homeless people. Thousands of tourists were trapped in their hotels. Over one thousand junks were wrecked and over two hundred boat people drowned. A groom at the Shatin riding stables saw the tidal wave coming and managed to turn ten of the horses loose to fend for themselves, and they swam wildly against the waves, but the rest were drowned, kicking and whinnying in their stables. One hundred tons of boats were lying in the middle of Kai Tak Airport runway. A rock as big as a tram crashed down the mountain, buried eleven squatter shacks, and cut a swath through the Chinese cemetery below, leaving tombstones and coffins and bones everywhere. Four men were swept off rooftops trying to save their cocklofts. Big Cheri Fontaine flew naked through the typhoon on the slide to safety, clutching her magnificent bosom. Twenty-seven typhoon parties were a roaring success. The anchor of an American freighter dragged up the cross-harbor telephone cable and Hong Kong and Kowloon could not contact each other except by radio. Twenty-seven thousand other telephones were knocked out. The fire department rescued over 5,000 people from being burned, suffocated, drowned, and crushed. Over 4,000 cars were destroyed, flooded, overturned. Altogether thirty-seven big ships were wrecked on the rocks.

Typhoon Rose was heading northward into China. Gradually, the winds began to get slower. And slowly it was getting lighter now, the sky no longer so black; there were moving banks of gray, and you could see the harbor again through the rain, the water rushing down off the mountains, great yellow muddy torrents pouring down the streets, and the new piles of landslides, and the cracks in the roads and the crumbled cars, and the rocks and the debris.

Then the typhoon was gone, and the great rains came.

_____**Part twelve**

The rain came down out of the vast dark mass of clouds moving like molasses across the China Sea in the wake of Typhoon Rose. It came down first in furls and curtains with the last of the winds, sweeping across the roofs and hammering down the streets, on the wreckage and devastation and the stretchers and the ambulances. Then the wind was completely gone, and down it came, straight. Gray and hard and thick as fingers, and the harbor was invisible again. More water came rushing down off sodden mountains, cascading down over the embankments and swirling down the steep winding roads, carrying rocks and branches and debris. The rain came hammering down as it had never done before.

38

The rain drummed on the hood of Vanessa's rented car as she
came out of Lion Rock tunnel above the Shatin valley. In the
car with her were two policemen. The valley was misty gray in
the rain, but she could see the junks lying wrecked in the paddies,
the sheen of water over the whole valley. She hunched close to the
windshield as she drove fast, her tires roaring on the wet tarmac,
the windshield wipers sloshing. But she could not see the sea
through the rain. She took the final bend down in the valley.

Ahead the road disappeared under a sheet of water.

The Chinese inspector beside her said, "I think it is too deep,
madam, better we go back through Sekong."

"No, damn it! That'll take hours."

She rolled her front wheels into the water, then declutched
down to low gear and accelerated. The seawater curved up off her

wheels. She could not see the road. It was like driving into a lake. But she was not going to give up. She drove through the water, hunched over the wheel. The inspector sat beside her peering anxiously.

"Is the road straight here?"

"I don't remember, madam."

She did not care a damn about the car—that was Mr. Hertz's problem. She saw a dead horse on the left. She glimpsed some junks, lying on their sides, up there in the valley. She drove another two hundred yards, then she could just make out the first buildings of Shann village ahead through the rain; she was sure the road was straight the rest of the way. She roared her engine and slammed up to second gear, and suddenly the front of the car plowed nose first off the road and jolted into a ditch.

"Oh, *shit!*"

She sat behind the wheel, furious with herself. She slammed the car into reverse and roared the engine. The rear wheels screamed in the water and the car did not move.

"Oh, *fuck!*"

She flung open her door without hesitating and grabbed her umbrella. "Sorry, gentlemen. Come on!" She sank up to her shins in water, slammed the car door. The water was only just below the top of her rubber boots. The policemen came plodding stoically after her in their regulation boots. The inspector was speaking into his two-way radio in Cantonese, telling headquarters what had happened. They would bring the American woman back eventually, he said. But before she would sit still for a prolonged interrogation about the man she had killed, she insisted they help her find an Englishman.

She came splashing up the sunken road into the outskirts of the village, the policemen splashing beside her. There were dead chickens and dogs and cats everywhere, and some dead water buffaloes and more horses. The rain teemed down. Ahead she could see the red fire engines and the big blue police trucks and the ambulances, and the people milling. She saw the collapsed walls, the roofs smashed off. There was a junk crashed on its side right on top of a building. People were loading the dead into sampans and rafts. She looked desperately around. There were firemen and policemen everywhere but they were all working. She saw a fire officer standing by a Land Rover, talking into a radio transmitter. She hurried over to him.

He was saying, "Dead, one hundred and seventeen so far. Over and out." He looked at her wearily, the rain splashing off his helmet.

"I'm sorry to trouble you, but I'm trying to get to Tai-po; are there any vehicles going through?"

"No, madam. Road's washed away. So is the railway line. Only way is via Sekong, the long way."

She waved her hand behind her. "My car's gone off the road down there."

"Sorry, can't spare any vehicles to tow you out yet."

"No, of course. I'm looking for a man called Jake McAdam, do you know him?"

"I know *of* Mr. McAdam. Was he in Shatin at the time of the wave?"

"He was on his boat around here."

The officer looked at her. "If he was on a boat . . ." He took a weary breath. "Come with me, please."

He led her between the vehicles and people, up toward high ground. Her policemen hurried after her. They both had their hands on their gun holsters now, eyes darting everywhere. They came upon a big mass of people. The officer parted them. Then she blanched. There was a long row of dead people laid out, over a hundred yards long. Chinese were crowding past and bending over them, weeping and sobbing.

"There're a few Europeans. Would you care to look?"

She stared at the row of dead, muddy faces. "Oh, my God, Hogan . . ." She walked down the rows of bodies, heart pounding. They were all lying on their backs, face up. There were many children. She felt sick, stunned. She could not feel proper compassion, only dread. That she was going to see his dead face lying there. She could not look at the faces of the children.

She walked slowly, dazedly, down the long, dreadful line, glancing at each battered face. A woman was bending over a baby, examining its head; she looked up, stricken, and then laughed hysterically. She came to the first dead European, she did not look twice, and her heart thudded faster. It was an elderly priest. Then the next. Out of the corner of her eye she saw two ambulance men stagger up with another body.

She hurried on. She could see one more European body ahead, and it was young and with brown sodden hair.

She stood in the teeming rain, aghast, staring at the body and shaking her head, then she plunged her hands into her face and gasped, *"It's not him!"*

And she reeled around, sobbing and laughing hysterically into her hands. "It's not Hogan!"

She looked about joyfully for the fire officer to tell him so he could rejoice with her. He was coming toward her through the rain.

"Is Mr. McAdam the man with the concrete junk?"

"Yes!"

He pointed back at the valley.

"I've made some inquiries. They tell me the concrete junk's down there."

She ran through the rain, splashing down the flooded road, half sobbing, the policemen running beside her. She fell onto her hands and knees, scrambled up and ran splashing on. Then she saw the first junk lying on its side in the gray paddy and she yelled, *"Hogan!"*

She ran on, panting, her hair plastered to her head. The junk was too small for McAdam's. She could dimly make out more junks farther ahead.

"Ho-gan!"

The rain deadened the shout. She ran on, stumbling, splashing, gasping, until she was opposite the junks. They were two hundred yards off; she tried to shield her eyes from the rain. And her heart lurched. She was sure the farthest junk was Hogan's. It was the right size.

She jumped off the edge of the road and landed with a splash on the edge of the paddy, on her hands and knees. She picked herself up, and her boots sank up to her shins in mud, the water up to her thighs. She pulled herself forward, plodding fiercely. The policemen followed her. She waded, her feet sucked into the mud. When she had gone fifty yards she had to stop. Her breath was coming in painful gasps, her legs trembling. She stood, shielding her eyes, trying to see through the rain. The inspector panted, "You stay here . . . I will go . . . to look . . ."

"No. Thank you." The junks had disappeared again in a heavier curtain of rain.

When she was a hundred yards off she saw the junk more clearly in a gap in the rain. *It was Hogan's!* She saw six water buffaloes up to their bellies in front of the junk. Four men were heaving on the junk and the water buffaloes were straining.

"Ho-o-gann!"

She ran, splashing, sobbing, clawing the water.

"Please, God . . ."

She staggered on, blindly, splashing, and she could not see the junk any more, and she was crying now. When she was fifty yards from the junk she saw it again through the rain and she cried out, "Ho-gann!" and she fell again. She picked herself up, muddy, crying, and then she saw him.

He was splashing through the water toward her, his hair plastered to his head. She cried out and staggered, and she fell in his arms. And he clutched her tight against him and she kissed him fiercely, crying and laughing.

39

The rest of that day was confused. And exhausting and shocking. And happy.

All the bloodstains had been outlined in chalk, the photographs taken, the exhibits taken into custody, the statements recorded; then the apartment had been cleaned up. The bullet marks on the walls and the splintered wardrobe were the only evidence that remained. The Superintendent of the Criminal Investigation Department was showing him a pile of glossy photographs. The officer said, "He crawled down the stairs to the second floor before he died."

"Good God." McAdam still could not believe it. He looked at the photograph of the dreadful body sprawled, head downward, on the stairs, the blood smeared all the way down behind him, blood trickling down the stairs ahead of him out of his mouth. Then he looked at the photograph of the body in the morgue. The killer eyes still staring. Vanessa sat beside him on the sofa, but she could not look at the photographs.

"You took his fingerprints."

"Yes, sir. And traced him through records. He's a suspected 14K member, but we can't prove it. He's got a few convictions for wounding and affray, and he's suspected of being one of the 14K hit men, but there's absolutely no way we can prove his connection with Herman Choi, I'm afraid."

"Jesus . . ." He heaved himself up off the sofa and paced, exhausted. "And what did Choi have to say about Vanessa's story?"

"His lawyer said it for him. Flat denial. Seething with righteous indignation. Miss Williams rudely made these scurrilous allegations and he told her to leave."

"And what are you going to do about her story? That that cutting up there is not into solid rock."

Vanessa said grimly, "They're going to examine the architectural plans in the building ordinance office when they reopen tomorrow."

He said to the superintendent, "But are you going to open up that retaining wall he's built against the cliff face, to see if there *is* solid rock?"

"Yes, sir. But we'll have to get a court order for that. And it would have to be supervised by experts. We can't just go and do it off our own bat. We've only got Miss Williams's word for it, and with all due respect to her, she's not a trained observer in those matters."

McAdam cursed. "A court order will take weeks!"

"Well, a week, anyway."

She said angrily, "Well, I'm going to go ahead and publish my story."

"Certainly," the superintendent said. He added bleakly, "Just give me a chance to sell my Lucky Man shares tomorrow. If the stock market isn't under water."

She smiled wearily.

McAdam said, "I think we'd better get out of this apartment, in the circumstances. Go to a hotel."

The superintendent sighed. "I can't stop you going anywhere, sir. But it will be much harder providing police protection at a hotel. And I must emphasize that Miss Williams needs the best protection we can provide."

Vanessa shook her head. "I don't want to go to a hotel, Hogan. Shut up in a room, a cop at the door. Here we're at home, everything we need. . . . I'm not scared of this apartment, with you here."

The superintendent said, "Here it's easy, sir. We'll just billet a couple of men upstairs in your gallery. And one guarding the front and back doors; you won't even know they're there."

"How long's this going to go on for?"

"At least until Miss Williams has given evidence at the inquest." He added, "And if your theory's right, Miss Williams may need even more protection after she's published her story. And

Lucky Man goes bang. And Herman Choi up for public fraud. She would be a vital witness."

McAdam dragged his hands down his face.

"We must go away," he said. "A holiday. And come back for the inquest and the trial."

"If the theory's right, that the Triads are after Miss Williams, especially if she's going to be a witness at any trial of Choi—"

"There'll be a trial, all right," McAdam promised.

"—then going away where we can't protect you isn't very wise, sir. The Triads are everywhere these days."

McAdam stared out of the gray window at the rain. Then he sighed and said, "Fly, fly away . . . somewhere where it's clean, and sunny. And safe. To Africa . . ."

Later, when he was to try to do so, he could not remember the details of what happened the rest of that day, and the next. All he remembered were feelings, and the rain coming down. Feeling exhausted, feeling outrage, feeling happy, feeling strong; feeling drunk, feeling sensuous, feeling lust, feeling love. Even feeling safe. But the strongest of these was the love. Only these feelings would he remember, no matter how hard he tried to break them down and say: Now when did that happen? How did that come about? But this he would know loud and clear, and forever; that he was glad with all his heart about these feelings. In his dreams he would remember and relive them, be happy again, wonderfully happy and alive, and she, too, tall and strong and smiling and laughing and in love. What he remembered he would be glad with.

They hardly slept that night. They made wild, exhausted love on the big double bed, drank champagne, and then made love again. Her long legs wrapped around him, her arms lashed around him and her hips and breasts grinding up at him and her mouth locked on his, sucking and biting. "*Oh, fuck me, fuck me, fuck me,*" she cried. And the joyous bliss of her body in his arms again, strong, soft, smooth, locked writhing into him and around him and under him, and her hair outflung on the pillow, and the glorious smell and taste of her, and the slipperiness of their sweat and the warm wet depth of her.

And they lay beside each other, panting, sweating, happy, exhausted. Neither of them wanted to sleep. He would remember she said softly. "For weeks I've been talking to you in my head, Hogan. Why should I sleep now?"

And he leaned over and looked down into her eyes, and said, "I love you."

And she looked at him and then kissed him.

"I love you too, Hogan," she said.

He said, "Then why didn't you come back?"

"Why didn't you? Why didn't you send me flowers and all that stuff?"

"Because you wouldn't have come back if I had."

"No, I probably wouldn't have. But what're the other reasons?"

"Because I was in love with you. And who wants to be in love with somebody who has every intention of taking off to the wide blue yonder?"

"That's why I wouldn't have come back if you'd sent flowers. Why does a girl like me have to fall in love with somebody who doesn't want me taking off for the wide blue yonder?"

And she lay there, on her side, her golden head propped on her hand, and she looked at him, smiled softly and said, "I'm back . . ." And she kissed him. And kissed him and kissed him again. "I'm back," she whispered.

And the rain came back.

She said quietly, "Every time I saw anything beautiful I thought, I must tell this to Hogan. Every time I read something interesting I thought, I must discuss this with Hogan. Every time I got steamed up about something I wanted you to get steamed up with me. Every time I got excited about something. Every time I got angry. Every time I heard a joke I wanted to tell it to you to laugh with me. . . . I didn't want to fall in love, Hogan. I wanted to be free." She spread her arms. "I didn't want to have to gear my life around anybody else. I wanted to come and go as I liked. The power of that kind of freedom. Nobody can hurt you, nobody can tell you what to do."

"Except it doesn't work forever."

"It works fine, until your emotions become involved. Then other laws take over. And you're just like everyone else who's ever been in love."

She lay back on the pillow, then flung her arms wide.

"Except, of course, nobody has ever, ever been as in love as I am."

They had a bath together, then. There was plenty of water again in Hong Kong's reservoirs. She stood in front of the steamy mirror piling her hair on top of her head, the steam rising up, her breasts moving as she pinned her hair.

They lay deep in the hot bath drinking cold wine, and they were completely happy.

She said, "What are we going to do about your junk?"

"I'm going to leave her right where she is in the middle of the paddy field for a month. And I'll rig a spotlight on her. She's a wonderful advertisement like that. The concrete junk that crashed five hundred yards inland and did not spring a single leak. Not a *crack*! And I'll get the television people out there when I tow her out. With a team of water buffaloes and thirty men. And we'll push her straight back into the sea. And she'll float like a bloody cork!"

She threw back her head and laughed in the steamy bubble bath.

"McAdam—the only guy who can make a gimmick of his disaster. You better come to America, they'll pay a fortune for you on Madison Avenue."

They lay in the bath, feeling the hot balm of it on their exhausted bodies, and they talked about some of the wonderful things they were going to do, and see, and feel.

And the rain came down.

40

It rained without ceasing.

It beat down on the steep jungled mountains, came cascading into the basements of the apartment blocks, and the big drains choked and burst; it soaked down through the sodden slippery clay of the mountains and down through the jumbled soil and granite, and the landslides came. That night there were more than twenty, and more than fifty people were caught in them. The army and the police and the firemen were everywhere digging for the bodies and dragging out the survivors, and all the time the rain hammered down.

He woke up late that Monday morning. She was standing at the window, looking at the rain. She was wearing his silk kimono and the gray light from the window made it transparent.

"Come and look at the rain."

They stood at the window side by side. Somehow it felt good and earthy and exciting: they were together, and they were rested, and they were safe, and there was nothing in the world they could do about the rain except stand there and wonder at it.

They had a lovely morning. She had been up early finishing her story on his typewriter and she was going to deliver it today to the editor of the *South China Morning Post.* And then McAdam was going to take her out to lunch, the best damn lunch in town, bodyguards and all. They had plenty to celebrate. They went through to the kitchen together to make breakfast. They had to put the lights on. She opened the refrigerator, and there was nothing in it but beer and three bottles of champagne and some cheese and olives.

"There's nothing to eat—not even milk for coffee."

"Then we'll just have to have champagne."

But they did not get dressed yet. They took a cold bottle of champagne into the living room and sat cross-legged on the carpet, drinking it. He would remember the first cold sips, going down good and clean and sparkling. The police had delivered a newspaper but neither of them wanted to read it. It was full of photographs and headlines of the typhoon damage, and now more about the rain damage. When the bottle was nearly finished, she got up to get cheese and biscuits and olives and she brought back another bottle of champagne with her. After this bottle they were definitely, but *definitely*, going to get dressed to go out for lunch. He opened the bottle and the cork hit the ceiling with a pop and champagne spewed up frothing and they grabbed for the glasses. They were both laughing.

It seemed an excellent idea, more champagne.

And the rain soaked down through the clay and jumbled granite of the mountain and the massive weight of the jungle pressed down. The water rushed down over the vertical man-made cliff behind the Lucky Man apartment building; it poured down onto the foundations and soaked down to the deep concrete piles; and gradually, slowly, sucking, widening, the man-made cliff that was not solid rock began to part from its mother mountain, under the massive weight of the apartment block. Then suddenly it gave way in a great wrenching chunk, three hundred yards wide and fifty feet deep, with a great roar above the hammering of the rain, and it began to slide.

It slid uncertainly at first, a chunk of mountain slowly tearing itself out, and the apartment block heaved and teetered, tottering on its foundations, still erect, then the moving chunk of mountain hit the road below, and the apartment block keeled slowly over. It hit the steep mountainside below with a crash like an explosion, and the mountain shook, and then the whole mass of building and mountainside came crashing down the steep slope.

"What's that?" She frowned.

He listened, then got up and went to the back window.

"Good God . . ."

She was already beside him. Together they saw it.

At first they did not understand. They saw the great scar of earth three hundred yards wide way up there through the teeming rain where the Lucky Man apartment block had stood. "What's that up there?" Then they saw the whole of the mountain moving, and they still did not understand. Mountains should not move. Then they heard it above the hammering of the rain, the distant rushing roaring, like a faraway train. And then they saw it come.

They saw the great mass of jungle and mud and concrete come sliding down the mountain, and behind it the mountainside itself lumbering down toward them, tearing itself up and getting bigger and bigger, like a wave; and then they could see whole floors and walls and pillars tumbling in the terrible mass, and they understood; then they saw it hit the first hairpin bend of Mountain Road.

The huge mass smashed down onto the road and the road disappeared, swallowed up; and the great avalanche did not falter, it just kept on coming, huge chunks of road tumbling with it, plowing up the jungle in front of it. They stood there, staring. This was a phenomenon, something happening far away. Not yet fear, just astonishment, at the mass of mountain carrying all before it. But of course it would stop. For ten long astonished seconds they stared at it, seeing it come crashing down through the rain toward them; now it was fifty yards away, now forty, now thirty, and now they could hear the roar of it, like the roar of an express train. And it was not going to stop.

"God, Hogan!"

He grabbed at her and shouted, "Jesus!"

And it hit Hillside Road behind Dragon Court. The avalanche hit Dragon Court at the second floor; one hundred thousand tons of landslide hit the wall at thirty miles an hour, and the whole building shook under the tremendous impact, then the concrete caved inward, and the building broke. She screamed as the floor staggered beneath them, and he shouted *"Vanessa!"* and clutched at her wildly, to drag her away from the terrible thing that was happening. He reached for her as the room caved sideways and she was wildly trying to scramble up, her face shocked and terrified, one arm desperately outstretched to him; for a long terrible moment the building seemed to waver, trying to recover its balance, then it began to fall over, and Vanessa slid. She slid screaming on her hip across the floor with her hand outstretched, and he lunged after her, the floor giving beneath him, to throw himself on top of her to protect her from the terrible weight that was going to crash down on her.

The tall apartment building went over slowly, smashed in two, fourteen floors of apartments leaning over like a giant felled tree, slowly at first, then more quickly. McAdam flung himself at her across the floor, bellowing above the crashing of furniture, desperately trying to get to her; then the whole world exploded in smashing blackness. Fourteen floors of apartment building crashed down on top of itself; and he heard only the deafening explosion and her screaming in his ears.

― 41

It was completely black.

He came to, with the instant realization of what had happened, the horror of where they were. He jerked his head up and bellowed.

"Vanessa!"

And his forehead hit concrete. He tried to pull his legs up, and they were held, crushed under concrete. He tried to fight himself free and he smashed his face again on concrete six inches above and fell back, stunned. Warm blood in his eyes and mouth.

"Vanessa—answer me!"

He tried to lunge sideways, but his right hand was held, crushed. But his left arm was free. He swept it sideways and his knuckles scraped concrete. "Vanessa!" he roared. He lunged his hand again and swept it in an arc as far as it would go, and he wrenched and wrenched at his right hand to get it out from under the concrete, and shouted:

"Vanessa! Vanessa!"

In his frenzy he did not feel the blood and the agony of the wrenching, all he knew was the desperate fear for her. Vanessa lying here somewhere in the blackness under tons of concrete. He would fight through all the concrete in the world to get to her. He lunged and wrenched and kicked and roared her name a long time.

Then he heard her whisper. "Hogan—"

"Yes! Vanessa! Where are you?"

And he wrenched again, then fell back, gasping, to listen, and all he could hear was his heart and his own rasping, and all he knew was that she was lying somewhere near in the darkness, under tons of concrete but *alive alive alive*, and he felt strong enough to tear the stuff off her hunk by hunk and drag her out of there by sheer force.

He shouted again. "Vanessa! Where are you? Keep calling!" He tried to wrench the right hand free again.

"Vanessa! Is my voice coming from your right or your left?"

And she answered in a whisper: "My right . . ."

"Then stretch out your right hand!"

And he flung out his left hand as far as it would go. It seemed the most desperately important thing in the whole world that they could just touch hands. "*Stretch*, Vanessa!" he cried, and he felt the flesh tear on his right hand, but all he cared about was throwing his left arm as far out as possible, and suddenly skin and nails tore off his right hand and it came free from under the concrete and he could lunge sideways farther, and then his fingers touched hers in the blackness.

Just her stiff, quivering fingers, and he cried, "Oh, Vanessa, I'm sorry . . ."

Oh, God, when you love somebody, and she lies dying, her flesh lying there in the terrible blackness, her life being slowly crushed out of her. . . . McAdam swelled his chest and roared and heaved to throw the concrete off him to get to her and drag her out before she died. But he could not shift the terrible weight, he only beat and smashed himself against the concrete six inches above his bloody face. He wrenched and heaved, but all he could do was touch his love's fingertips.

225

After a short time he got himself back under control.

He lay there, shuddering, his eyes screwed up, trying desperately to think.

The living-room carpet was underneath him. But not under her hand. She was a little higher than him, on his left. His head was higher than his feet. To his right, the broken floor rose, then dipped away. This was the living-room ceiling, just six inches above him. How exactly was he held? By his thighs. He could feel nothing pressing on his knees. His feet—he could just move them. He felt with his fingers, and he could feel the beam across his thighs. He stretched his feet as far as he could, and he thought he could feel the carpet bunched up. Somewhere over there on his left would be the remnants of the iron spiral staircase. He reached his left hand up behind him, groping for the ceiling, and he felt it slope away upward sharply. There would be space to crawl there.

He clenched his teeth and tried to push with his heels and ease his body upward, out from under the concrete beam. He felt the flesh of his thighs pull, unbearably hard. He slumped again, then took a breath and tried again. Then he tried sideways, trying to shift his body and legs left under the beam. No . . . to the right? He tried, holding his breath: the beam held him firm, his flesh pulled unbearably. He slumped back. He was feeling the searing pain in his raw right hand now.

Then he remembered the policemen in the gallery. They would be just a few feet above him.

"Police!" he bellowed.

He waited, listening. No reply.

"Police!"

Nothing. Only the distant roar of the rain.

He lay still, trying to think. It was no good shouting for help above that roar. Save your strength until help is near. He tried to hold her hand, and all he could do was press her fingertips.

"Vanessa! Are you in pain?"

He waited for her answer, heart pounding, heart breaking.

"*Vanessa! Are you in pain?*"

"No . . ."

Then he heard her sob out loud once.

"*I can't feel my legs, Hogan . . .*"

Oh, God . . .

"Your legs are all right—it's only because your nerves are pinched."

226

She didn't say anything.

"Vanessa, do you hear me?"

"Yes . . ."

He took a big shuddering breath and he was so desperate for her he wanted to shout, Your legs are all right! Believe me!

"Vanessa, how are you lying?"

She whispered, "On my back."

Thank God. "Is your head higher than your feet?"

"Yes."

"Where is the concrete pressing?"

"On my stomach . . ."

"Can you breathe all right?"

"Yes . . ."

"Good. Don't talk, just listen. Save your breath. If you want to say yes, press my fingers once. If you want to say no, press them twice. All right?"

She pressed his fingers once.

"Vanessa . . . don't struggle. Save your strength until they come. Just try to rest. Do you hear me?"

She pressed his fingers once.

"The fire department will come soon. They will."

She just lay there.

"They must be here already. It doesn't take them long to get onto a disaster like this." She did not do anything. "They're here already, Vanessa, working to get us out."

She pressed his fingertips. He took a shuddering breath. Desperately trying to think what was happening. What to say to her, to help her. Trapped, impotent under tons of concrete and not knowing what was happening to her body. Where the fire department was. How long it would take. And, oh, God, how many tons of concrete were lying on top of them and how do they move it without crushing her!

He screwed his eyes tight in the blackness.

"They're experts at this. They know how to do it. We can *breathe*. We can last a long time like this. For days. For *weeks*. They'll get us out, I promise you!"

She whispered, "Are you cold, Hogan . . . ?"

He was not cold. He had not yet thought about cold. But now he knew she was cold! Tons of concrete crushing down on her guts and she was cold! All he could do was press her fingertips.

"No. Are you?"

"No," she lied. "I'm just exhausted, I guess."

He tried to think whether she should sleep or whether she should fight to stay awake. Maybe she would choke in her sleep. Maybe her body would not fight the cold if she was asleep. "Don't fall asleep. They'll be here soon, Vanessa, save your strength but don't fall asleep, can you do that?"

She pressed his fingertips.

He tried to listen for the sound of rescuers, and all he could hear was the rain.

And the rain came down. Running down through the mass of concrete in thousands of little waterfalls, gurgling, rushing. He tried to listen above it for sounds of people. Eyes closed, trying to hold the panic down.

How long have we been here?

Suddenly he remembered his watch. He worked his left hand over his chest. He got it up to his chin and peered through the blackness. No luminous dial. He jabbed his wrist against his chin to feel for it. Nothing. *Wasn't he wearing his watch at the time?* He twisted his head and peered at his right arm in the blackness. Nothing.

He twisted to look for the glow of the dial, he crashed his forehead against the concrete above him, he twisted his head furiously again, and he saw it—the tiny glow of the dial. And he gasped out *"Thank God"* and lunged his raw right hand out toward it. He could not reach. He worked his head and shoulders sideways, then stretched again. He still could not reach. He breathed furiously and stretched again, his raw bleeding fingers quivering, his forehead pressed up against the concrete, and the tip of his middle finger just touched it. And he gasped out, fiercely, and tried to stretch one inch more, feeling the new desperate fear of not knowing the time, of infinite blackness going on and on, not knowing what day it was, how long pain, how long thirst, how long hunger, how long help, how long life, the terrible blackness stretching on and on for ever! He ground his forehead against the concrete, stretching and he wanted to bellow, *For Chrissake help me, just one inch*—and then he collapsed.

He lay still, breathing long and slow, trying to get his strength and control back, trying to think.

How long have we been here? One hour? Two? *They must be here now!* Firemen, police, ambulances, digging.

Why can't I hear them? *Why can't I hear them?*

228

All he could hear was the water. No bangs, no shouts, no machinery. And no light. Just blackness.

"Vanessa, can you hear me?"

She pressed his fingertips once.

He took a long slow breath.

"We're in pretty good shape. They're working on getting us out right now. . . . Just listen to me. There's plenty of air getting through. There's no water getting to us, we won't drown. No broken bones. We're not even really in pain. All we've got to do is wait, Vanessa. It will only be hours. Just rest. . . . Have you heard me?"

She said, louder, "Won't the concrete crash . . . when they try to move it?"

"No! They're experts! Just for Chrissake don't think about it!"

He did not say any more about it. To stop her thinking about it.

Try your body again, he told himself.

He moved his feet. They moved. Stiff, cold, constricted, but they moved. He tried to tighten his leg muscles; he could just feel them move, numbly, under the weight.

He slid his hands down the side of his hip, and he felt the tip of something metal, and he knew it was his transistor radio.

He pulled it up his side, heart thudding in anticipation. He dragged it up to his chest. The switch clicked and he waited. Nothing happened. Then he remembered the volume. His fingers found it, and suddenly the blackness was filled with song:

"Will you still need me
When I'm sixty-four—?"

He snapped the radio off.

"Vanessa! You hear that?"

She did not answer. He felt his stomach lurch in panic.

"Vanessa! Answer me!"

"Yes?"

Relief flooded over him.

"Were you asleep?"

"There's a radio playing . . ."

"Yes—listen to it, try to stay awake. Do you hear me?"

"Yes."

"Vanessa—tell me what's happening to you. Are you in pain?"

He waited, heart thudding.

"I can't feel anything. . . . Just let me rest . . . I've had a busy weekend. . . ."

229

Oh, God, yes, just let her rest and feel nothing!

"Save your strength for when they come . . ."

She whispered, "I thought you were going to take me out to lunch, Hogan?"

His eyes burned. "Oh, I will. The best bloody lunch in town . . ."

She whispered, "So he got me after all, Hogan—that bastard."

"He hasn't got us, Vanessa! We're getting out!"

Then she whispered softly, "There goes my story, Hogan. Everybody will know it now, no Oriana Fallaci for me . . ."

"Oh, Vanessa, what a thing to worry about now!"

She snorted. "Once a journalist, always a journalist. You can't expect too much of us, Hogan . . ."

And he thought his heart would burst for wanting to fight and save her.

He switched the radio on again. Suddenly he was shivering. At first he thought it was the shock. Then, suddenly, he was deep down-to-the-bones cold. And with the cold came the numbness, his back and shoulders numb where they pressed to the floor. And the terrifying unfeeling in his legs.

High above the black masses of clouds the airliners circled, banked up, waiting for air traffic control's permission to land. It was brilliant sunset up there. Then, one by one, they came down into it, the black suddenly hurtling past the windows, the rain beating against them. They came screaming in over the rooftops, flying entirely on instruments, and only at the last moment could the pilot see the blurred lights, then the runway lights through the rain.

Kai Tak Airport was mobbed with people. Tourists held back by the typhoon were trying to get out, airlines had laid on extra flights, incoming traffic which had been delayed by the typhoon was arriving as fast as air traffic control could let them in. The marble floors were messy with rainwater, the vast concourses smelt of damp clothes and umbrellas.

Bernard Champion stood tensely in the queue for the Pan American flight to Los Angeles and Mexico City. He was wearing his police uniform under his civilian raincoat. On the pocket of his tunic, concealed now by the raincoat, was his airport police security identification pass. His face was haggard. But he did not look about him. The security pass was what he relied on. With that he would not have to go through Immigration control, he could simply walk through, as a policeman. Immigration control was where they would be watching for him.

But maybe the airlines had been told to watch out for him, too. The check-in counter in front of him was his first hurdle. He was sweating. If only he had thought ahead he could have bought a forged passport in another name in Macao. But it was too late to regret that. The man in front of him was at the counter now. The airline girl looked tired. Thank God for that. The man moved on. Champion picked up his suitcase and put it on the scale. "Good evening."

He passed her his ticket. His hand was shaking.

"Mr. Champion?"

She had her head down, scanning her list.

He waited, heart pounding.

"Passport, please.'

He handed it across the counter, his hand trembling.

She opened it to the photograph. She looked up at him. He felt his stomach lurch. Then she lowered her head.

"Champion . . ."

Out of the corner of his eye he saw two figures in khaki approaching. He glanced sideways furtively. Two Chinese constables were walking toward him. He looked hastily away, heart thudding. But they were strolling. He fumbled for his cigarettes, to light one to shield his face. The airline girl was talking to her supervisor now. He felt himself go white. "Mr. Champion?"

"Yes?"

The supervisor looked at him.

"When did you book?"

"Yesterday. Through a travel agent."

"We don't have you on our list."

"But I was in the office when the agent telephoned. I heard it confirmed!" He had to get on this plane. "Is the plane fully booked?"

"Completely. Except first class."

He closed his eyes.

"I'll go first class."

He wrote out the travelers' checks, hand shaking.

He had closed himself up in his apartment for three days. He could not bear to see anybody, nor to be seen. He had wanted to hide, to turn his face away from the world. He had hardly eaten. He had sat through the typhoon, slumped in his armchair, drinking, and unable to get drunk, listening to the typhoon without caring. Then the rain. He had not listened to the radio. He had not looked at the newspapers that had been pushed under his door. He had not wanted to know. To know, feel, even see, in any way to be involved in the place that was no longer his home.

He walked through the airport crowds, sweating, dry-mouthed. This was finally it, the end of a lie. The end of twenty-two years' service as a policeman. This time tomorrow policemen would be looking for him.

He was in an emotional state. Even his nervousness at the weigh-in counter seemed a long time ago. Ahead was the Immigration barrier. As he walked he unbuckled his raincoat. He pulled it off, slung it over his arm. There were long lines of people waiting. He walked past them, toward the nearest Immigration officer sitting in the glass kiosk.

He walked to the top of the queue, stepped around the woman being processed. The Chinese Immigration officer looked up at him. Champion pointed to his security pass on his tunic. The officer nodded. And Champion walked through. It was as easy as that.

Bernard Champion walked numbly into the departure lounge. It was full of passengers. He headed for the lavatories.

He locked himself into a cubicle, and opened his handgrip. He pulled out a shirt, sports coat and slacks, and hung them on the peg. Then he took off his tunic and shorts, and put on the shirt and slacks. He stuffed his uniform into the grip. Then he left the cubicle and went to the washbasin. He stared at himself in the mirror.

This was what his life had come to. Shedding his police uniform, his career, in a public lavatory. Everything he knew, all the law, all the tricks, all the expertise, all the people; he would never use them or know them again.

He was a criminal. On the run.

He stared at his white, gaunt face.

He did not care who saw him. He walked through the crowded departure lounge. He was not going to the bar, he was not looking for a seat; he was just walking. He had intended to stay hidden in the lavatory until his flight was called but he had to get out, to move. To try to contain his welling grief. If one person, any person, had given him sympathy he would have broken down.

He heard the television say soberly:

". . . at the Dragon Court disaster in Mid-levels. So far the death toll is seventeen . . ."

He stopped. The television was mounted on the pillar right in front of him. He stared at it.

It took him a long confused moment to register what he was seeing. A huge black and white pile of rubble. Misty in the continuous rain. Firemen and policemen and soldiers toiling. Then the picture vanished and the newscaster reappeared, talking about something else.

Bernard Champion turned abruptly. He strode dazedly back toward the lavatories. He locked himself into a cubicle, unzipped his grip and pulled out his tunic. His fingers were shaking almost uncontrollably. Then he ripped off his shirt.

Requests. "Lemon Tree." "Yellow Submarine." There was a little red light on the radio's dial; he lay shivering, staring at it, singing under his breath. There was a time check and all he caught was "twenty-three," and he lurched up and hit his forehead on the concrete. It was after that that he passed out the first time. Then he heard the American accent saying cheerfully:

"Now for some more bad news! Latest reports from our frantic friends at the Royal Observatory are that it will continue to rain cats and doggies tomorrow!—bringing the rainfall up to its highest since the founding of the colony. But every cloud has a silver lining, and it's for you lucky people who thought you had to go to school tomorrow. Yes, you've guessed it! Our lovely friend the director of education has announced . . . wait for it! *No* school tomorrow! How about *that* for a silver lining! So just stay tuned to your favorite Far East Rayyy-di-oh! And here we go with that mind-blowing deee-eep brown voice of Lee-ee Marvin, singing that all-time smash hit—yes, you've got it . . . !"

Lee Marvin's voice filled the blackness, singing *A Wandering Star.*

He lay still in the blackness, eyes tight closed, trying to concentrate on the music and not feel the cold and the numbness. The announcer's voice was saying:

"—another report on the Hillside Road disaster, and we have

233

our man Kevin Gray reporting from the area. Come in, Kevin!"

"Thank you, Mike! And a real disastrous-looking scene it is in the glaring arc lights and pouring rain. Dragon Court lies in a heap of rubble and jungle and mud and broken furniture. Firemen and the police and army are here in force. The whole area has been cordoned off, to hold back the crowds of friends and relatives of the poor people trapped in the debris. Hundreds of willing people are helping. Over three hundred people, men, women and children, are lying dead and alive in that horrific mess. It is a desperate race against time. Already twenty-five people have been unearthed but nineteen of them were dead.

"I am told by the fire officer in charge, Jack Evans, that one of the major dangers is of further landslides. And that the weight of the men working to move the debris will cause the mass of concrete to shift and crush the people still alive. Wooden barricades are being built to try to stop further slides. What more can they do except work and pray?"

The tears were running down his face and he wanted to shout and laugh and cry.

"Vanessa—they're here! They're digging for us!"

He flung out his hand to hers.

"Vanessa! Wake up! They're digging. Everything is all right—"

She was asleep. He lay back, panting, the happiness and relief choking up his throat. He had to restrain himself from bellowing to them. And he wanted to clutch her tight in his arms and laugh and hug her.

Ten minutes later he felt the water. Suddenly water was trickling through the crack in the ceiling above him, onto his chest. Then he felt the water on the back of his head and under his shoulders and he put his hand up to feel, and he felt the mud.

Then he smelled the gas.

The rain poured down, silver in the arc lights. Jack-the-Fire rasped into the two-way radio in his command tent:

"Priority, priority. Strong smell of gas coming out of upper levels of disaster site. Instruct gas company to cut it off at source, repeat gas company to cut off gas supplies for this whole area immediately—do you read, over."

The voice came crackling back from headquarters. "Affirmative, over."

"And send gas company to scene immediately. Use of oxyacetylene cutters has been stopped until gas is cleared—and we desperately need to use them. Also send K12 cutting equipment urgently. Also an extra lighting unit and generator. Over."

"Two numbers K12 already en route to yours. Two army mechanical shovels also en route, over."

"I don't think we can use mechanical shovels yet, due to tenderness. Or we could bring the whole lot down on top of us and victims. We have to go by hand at this stage, using great care to avoid dislodging debris. We're still attempting to extricate the four people reported in my last message. Can now confirm that they are a family all from one apartment, the man confirms that he lived on the twelfth floor and he thinks the thirteenth floor was empty. We'll have them out in about ten minutes and can then probe down to eleventh floor better. A good access into the tenth has been found, two men are in there now searching as far as light permits. Calling into the debris is producing some response from victims but we badly need those additional lighting units. We've only got one petrol generator going near the lower level at the moment. We've moved it well away from the gas and I don't think it's any danger at the moment but we can't rely on it. Message ends. Over."

"Roger, can confirm that additional lighting units are en route. Can also now confirm that gas company will have cut off gas at source within a few minutes but they say that it will take some time for gas in pipes to dissipate. Also the electricity company is leading an extra power line in, the engineer will report to you for your disposition when connected. Over."

"Roger. Since this message began can now report arrival of fifty troops of Welsh Regiment with additional porto-power and lighting. We should be all right for lighting and manpower for the time being. Over and out."

Jack-the-Fire rammed his helmet back on his head. He turned to Bernard Champion and the building ordinance officer. "Figured out anything?"

Champion looked at him, plastered wet. "He thinks the sixth floor—McAdam's—has taken the brunt of it. The building probably broke about the seventh floor. Floors seven to fourteen probably came down like a concertina, all on top of six." Then he turned furiously on the building ordinance officer. "Why the hell did the goddamn Lucky Man block come down? Which idiot in your office approved the plans?"

"He's retired now."

"Well, he's bloody well coming out of retirement! Where is he now?"

The building officer pulled a wry face. "Not far. He now works for Lucky Man Development."

"Oh, yes! Lovely!" said Jack Evans. "All right, Bernie. Jake is my friend too, don't forget. But you've got to do as you're told. Try to be a hero and you may lose more lives than you save."

He turned and plunged out of the tent into the rain. Champion stared at the building ordinance officer. Then he grabbed him by the shoulder and pulled him out of the tent. He pointed furiously at the disaster site in the dazzling arc light. "Whereabouts is the sixth floor?"

43

First there was just a faint whiff of it.

McAdam lay still, eyes staring wide in the blackness. *Gas.* His instinct was to scramble away from the killer smell, to writhe and shout out to her. He lay rigid, holding his breath: then he had to breathe out. Then he began to breathe in lightly. Immediately he smelled it again. He cut the breath off.

Stronger.

He lay there, mind trying to race. She was out, asleep. He breathed in slowly, and it stank all the way.

His hands were at his shirt. He clenched his teeth against the agony in his raw right-hand fingers, then sank both hands into bunches in the fabric, and ripped. He felt the cloth tear.

His broken fingernails caught in the fabric. The pain screamed through his hand. He ripped again, the nail tore off his finger. He lay there rigid, gasping, his fists bunched at the agony.

Then he thrust the strip of shirt out into the blackness, feeling for the water coming through the ceiling. He soaked the cloth, then he groped fiercely for her.

"Vanessa! Wake up!" He found her hand. "Vanessa! Put this over your face!"

"Hogan—"

"Put it over your face!"

And then he was coughing and choking and his hand groped for his face, trying to filter the terrible gas through his clawing

236

fingers. He sucked in a big lungful and tried frantically to spit it out and grab some clean black air; then his head was swimming and he fell back.

Where Bernard Champion was working, the rubble was forty feet high, the highest part of the disaster. Somewhere in there was the sixth floor. The upper floors, as the building officer had said, had crashed down onto the sixth. Champion was working with a gang of soldiers under the leadership of a Chinese fireman. They stood in a phalanx, the front row heaving the chunks off, hefting them over to the row behind.

Champion worked like an ox, mud up to his knees, the rain beating down on his back. His heart was pounding from the exertion. There was a strong smell of gas still, although the gas company had cut it off. He seized a chunk of concrete.

"Here's one . . ."

Just an arm was sticking out. They grabbed the next slab of concrete and slung it to the side. Underneath it was another slab. They heaved it up, grunting, slipping underfoot. And there lay a Chinese girl of about twelve.

"She's alive!"

Her eyes were closed and her face was pulpy with blood but her chest was moving. "*Stretcher!*" the soldier bellowed. Champion and the firemen were throwing the concrete off her legs. "Broken leg . . ."

The fireman pulled out his walkie-talkie radio. "Stretcher needed at position F. One Chinese girl, broken leg." Champion knelt beside her and said in Cantonese, "You're all right now. What was your apartment number?"

The girl mouthed: "Nine . . . B . . ."

"Who else was with you when it happened? Just shake or nod your head. Your mother and father?"

The girl stared at him dazedly, then nodded.

"Brothers and sisters? Two? One?" The girl nodded. He rasped to the fireman in charge. "Family of four."

The ambulance men came sloshing through the mud. Champion got out of the way, his mind racing. If that was 9B, where the hell was 6A? The rubble was thirty feet high above the girl. Then sloped off down the hill, past G, H, and I sections, down to where Jack was working. Farther uphill toward Hillside Road, past positions E, D, C, B, the rubble was not as high but it was smothered in mud. Was 6A farther uphill or deeper into that pile in front of him—or at the very bottom of it? The ambulance men started lugging the girl away. She was crying hysterically now. What the hell should he do? The soldiers were back into the rubble. "Another one!" somebody shouted. Then the firemen bellowed, *"Watch out—"*

There was a loud grating above the hammering of the rain, and everybody looked up and saw it move, a big slab of concrete beginning to slide off the top of the pile: it slid slowly six feet, sending tons of small rubble before it, and everybody was scrambling backward in the mud, then it came in a rush. The soldiers scattered backward, and as the fireman scrambled backward he fell. He flung one arm over his head and tried to get to his feet, and the concrete slab hit him across his right thigh and he fell back with a shout and the whole slab crashed down on top of him. He lay half buried in the mud. Champion went over to him.

"My leg—"

Champion unclipped the fireman's walkie-talkie.

"Position F calling command post—we need a cutter or a pneumatic drill—we'll need a stretcher, too—over."

The fireman gasped: *"Saw a foot sticking out—over there."*

The smell of gas was much stronger, flooding out through the dislodged debris. And the rain drummed down.

44

The arc lights glared up the steep mountainside above Hillside Road, onto the huge swath of collapsed earth, three hundred yards wide and four hundred yards long. The army engineers were erecting barricades across the vast raw wounds in the earth, to try to hold further landslides.

At Hillside Road the army engineers had laid steel plates to replace the collapsed road and the barricade there was nearly finished, big walls of timbers and steel struts. Water came rushing down the great raw swath of the collapsed mountain in tumbling streams, carrying mud and rocks and branches. It hit the barricade and leapt up over it, gushing down onto the collapsed apartment block below. Scores of soldiers were feverishly digging ditches to try to lead the water away. The director of fire services said into his radio: "Colonel Tompkins of the engineers considers there's a fifty-fifty chance of another landslide and his barricades will only hold a small one. We need more lights and barricades higher up. I want a geologist's survey of the area—try the building ordinance office, they should have one; if not, try the university. I have ordered lookouts to be posted on the tops of surrounding buildings to watch for further slides."

Just below collapsed Hillside Road, the army engineers were erecting the steel and concrete base of the heavy-duty crane that would be able to swing over the mass of debris and lift off the concrete slabs. At B and C sections, three good tunnels had been found through the piles of jumbled concrete. Firemen were crawling, squirming through like chimney sweeps. They had found seven people, but five of them were already dead. The two survivors were trapped by concrete.

The fire officer in charge said into his walkie-talkie, "The smell of gas has almost gone up here and I consider it safe to use the K12 cutters. But now we've got water problems. It was draining away well but now something must have blocked the exits. We're rigging a pump to go down with the cutters, over."

Down at the bottom of the disaster site Jack replied, "Are you sending down an air line as well? Are the victims in danger of drowning? Over."

"We're getting the air compressor set up now. One victim is in distinct danger of drowning, the water is already up to his chin, but Mr. Johnson is down there with him and he's got a piece of tubing to breathe through if it goes over his nose. Over."

"Well, get those cutters going and report as soon as possible. I daren't use the mechanical shovels down here until your guys are out of those tunnels. Out. Command Post—send this message back to H.Q. control: Strong smell of gas persists down in lower and middle sections, so we still can't use the cutters. Nor can we use the army's mechanical shovels because of tunnel work on upper sections. However, we are doing very well by hand down here and with the army engineers' heavy-duty winches, which are doing a great job. We have uncovered another six persons, four alive but in bad condition. We have found two access tunnels, and are penetrating them now. We believe we've reached the tenth floor. However, until the gas clears and we can use the cutters, it's getting

239

slow. My boys are exhausted, we need some temporary relief. Haven't they got any more C.A.S. personnel on standby? Also get six more crowbars. Christ knows what's happened to them all. Also get another pneumatic drill from somewhere. Over."

The voice came back from the command post tent:

"Roger, can confirm another twenty-odd Civil Aid Services have reported for duty and are being sent already. Also Queen's Gurkha Rifles en route from border area, don't know how many yet, over."

"Roger, and tell H.Q. we need something to eat and drink—water, water, everywhere and not a drop to fucking drink. Over and out."

Down there in the blackness the gas was still percolating through the honeycombs, locked in pockets between the slabs of concrete. And the water ran through the debris, damming up here and leaking away there. And the rain came down.

Dreams ended and mind-wandering began.

He knew they were trying to kill him and he roared and thrashed and fought, and they ran away. But he knew they would come back and he lay there hiding, cunningly quiet, waiting for them.

And he was by a stream and the water ran sparkling clean over the smooth stones and little rapids and he walked along the banks casting into the pools and eddies so the trout would not see him and he knew this stream from a long time ago, every pool and rapid, and he went down it fishing every place expertly, fleetingly; then he came round a bend and there was the lemon tree, and she climbed up out of the stream and her legs were golden, smooth and strong and he kissed her lovely thighs as she stood on the bank and they were cool and soft against his face and she looked down at him smiling and she touched him with just her fingertips and they were icy and she whispered, smiling, "Will you still love me when they cut my legs off? Tomorrow they're going to cut my legs off, you know—"

And he shouted, *"Over my dead body"*—and he was fighting up the bank and it was made of black concrete and he was crashing his head again it, roaring, *"Over my dead body!"*

And the blood was thick in his eyes and he could taste the salt of it and his head was pounding. "Vanessa!" he roared, "Vanessa—"

And he lashed out into the blackness for her hand, and he found it. He collapsed back, crying for joy because it was only a dream. And the gas was gone.

When he woke up again the thirst had set in. And he could not open his eyes.

His fingers scrabbled frantically on his blood-caked eyelids and he forced them open, blinking and shaking his head, and the scabs got in his eyes, rough and sandy, and he lurched and rubbed his eyes frantically, and the scabs scratched across his eyeballs and he wanted to roar and shake his head. Then he forced himself to lie back, to control himself.

And the dry, raging thirst. *Water*. His left hand felt out blindly in the blackness for water. Nothing. The leaking through the roof had stopped. And he could hear water everywhere, water gurgling, the rain roaring down.

"Vanessa?" His tongue was caked, stiff.

"Vanessa!" he rasped, and his hand groped desperately for hers. And he found it, feeling for his.

"Are you . . . thirsty . . . ?"

He waited. Then she pressed his fingers weakly once.

"Feel for water. Both hands . . ."

Her hand moved away. *Oh, God, let her find water*. He lay there, eyes screwed up against the agonizing scratching. He felt her hand come back, feeling for his.

She pressed his fingers twice.

He clenched his teeth to control the fury.

"Were you asleep?"

A long pause. The rain. She pressed his fingers once.

"Go to sleep," he whispered.

He lay, eyes screwed up, trying to breathe through his nose. He gripped one eyelid and pulled it down to make it weep and wash the scabs out of his eye. Then he took his other eyelid, too, with his raw right-hand fingertips. And slowly, slowly, the blood scabs began to melt away across his sticky eyeballs. He blinked, and tried to open his eyes, and there was grating pain again and he could not tell in the blackness if he was seeing anything.

Saliva. He clamped his mouth shut and tried to breathe through his nose. But he could not. *Saliva*. He held his breath and tried to suck the saliva up out of the roots of his jaws. His tongue stuck dry to the roof of his mouth.

Then he felt the cold again. The bone-chilling cold. But many times worse was the horror of the numbness from the crushing concrete he could only half feel; and a thousand times worse was the knowledge of her flesh crushed and torn and bruised, bloody, senseless also. He groped in the blackness for her hand.

Part thirteen

The rain glinted on the oilskins and bare skin and the khaki.

Men toiling everywhere, clambering, lugging, digging, man-handling the big chunks of concrete aside, chunk by chunk, the pneumatic drills were roaring, the electric cutters screaming, breaking up the beams and the big slabs of concrete, winches and ropes and steel cables, and the stretcher-bearers plodding up steep muddy slopes to the ambulances. Kevin Gray's voice came over McAdam's radio in the blackness:

"You can hardly hear yourself above the rain, and it's hard to see. And with the water coming down the mountain, it has turned the whole disaster area into a tremendous bog, further hampering the efforts of the rescuers.

"There have been several other minor landslides in the night which threatened to crash down on the rescuers. But makeshift barricades have held most of it back. Soldiers are digging channels frantically to divert the water but a lot is getting through and it is feared that it may either drown trapped survivors or cause the massive pile of wreckage to shift and crush them.

"It is difficult, tragic work indeed. Nonetheless, a great deal of progress has been made through the night, with reserves replacing men who wear out. It is a scene of heroic activity against tremendous odds to save the victims trapped underneath the wreckage.

"But why did the disaster happen in the first place? Why in this modern age of building construction was the disaster not foreseen and prevented? The answers to these questions are not yet known, but one remembers a similar disaster in Kotewall Road in 1972. Inquiries are being made at the building ordinance office as to how the Lucky Man Development Company obtained clearance for its Mid-levels development plan. It has just been discovered that the building officer who actually approved the plans now works for Lucky Man, and an editorial in the *South China Morning Post* calls for an investigation into what it terms 'the possibility of a monstrous public fraud.' "

He went on: "So far forty-seven people have been rescued alive, and the bodies of forty-nine other people have been recovered. Most of the living are suffering from serious injuries, and all are suffering from shock. . . ."

The disc jockey's voice came back brightly. "And we say au revoir for a moment to our man Kevin Gray for a few words from our *sponsor* . . . !" and the strident jingle of the advertisement for Dab Aftershave Lotion came over.

244

Somewhere in the blackness something shifted and through the cracks and crevices it came, the mud.

First he felt it on the back of his shoulders, and he reached his hand back and felt the cold stickiness. He put his fingers into his mouth and felt the grit. He spat it out. *Mud.*

He lay still. If mud was coming through now, so must water. He rasped: "Vanessa—wake up! Feel for water . . ."

He waited. "Mud . . . ? Or water . . . ?"

She whispered, "Mud."

"Water will come soon . . ."

The mud came slowly at first, then faster. It was down the side of his legs now, oozing across the carpet in a thick sheet. Now it was round his feet, banking up where the carpet was bunched.

The mud banked up slowly round his legs, blocked by the carpet at his feet. Then it was up to his knees. Then up to his hips, and he felt panic. He clenched his teeth, trying to control it, the desperate fear of death by mud. Mud slowly rising up to her chin, to her mouth, to her nostrils. He scooped with his good hand, trying to sweep the mud away, trying to make waves to shift the blockage below. He moved his feet, trying to push against the bunched carpet.

The mud lay like a black swamp around him. He groped for her hand. There was no mud touching her yet: she was higher than he.

He did not want to frighten her. The only hope was to scoop the mud over the low crest in the broken floor to his right, away from her. With his bad hand. Sweep the back of his right hand through the mud and scoop it into the blackness beyond.

He felt his right hand. The flesh raw down to the knuckles, the fingernails half ripped off. He clenched his teeth tight and sank his hand into the mud. He screwed up his face and swept his hand furiously through the mud, over the broken sloping floor.

45

It was Tuesday noon, dark misty gray in the rain. The arc lights were blazing. Jack-the-Fire Evans had had six hours' sleep, but his body ached for more. He stood in his command post tent and snapped into the radio transmitter:

"C.F.O. Evans reporting, taking over from Mr. Wang. Army and Civil Aid Services personnel changing shifts also in next few minutes. We need the following items immediately:

"At least another one heavy-duty rock drill. Ask public works department. Ten numbers minuteman cylinders. Ten numbers three thousand pound B.A. cylinders. Ten or twelve numbers oxygen cylinders. And a dozen or so kerosene pressure lamps. And more blankets. And we've got to have better supplies of hot food than last night! Half of us were hungry and a hungry man can't work properly. Are you reading me, over."

"Roger, items requisitioned will be on their way. About the food, private caterers have been contracted for and have been delivering well this morning. Over."

"And send a large jar of instant coffee. Hold there!" His walkie-talkie radio was rasping to him. He listened, then said to headquarters, "Mr. Wang says we're going to need a coffin van soon. They've just made contact with a whole bunch of bodies on the ninth, must've been a typhoon party, and they're all very dead. They'll be decomposing soon, no sense burdening the ambulances, they've got enough to do. Out."

He picked up his walkie-talkie and said, "Evans to director fire services, good morning. What's the position with the army heavy-lift crane? I see it still isn't working, over."

From somewhere upmountain the voice came back:

"Good morning, Jack. They've been having trouble building a strong working base because of shifting mud. But Colonel Tompkins expects to have it functional in a few hours. Over."

"Well—hope must be fading fast for the rest of the survivors, they've been down there nearly twenty-four hours. How're the barricades, any more slips?"

"Barricades have been considerably strengthened. Only one minor slip from high up, but the barricades stopped it. Lookouts still being maintained. But a lot of water and mud is still getting through the wreckage. Over."

"Yes, so Mr. Wang complained. All right, sir, out."

He plodded out into the rain, eyes crinkled up, aching for more rest. The relief crews were getting to their positions, the old shifts coming out, sodden, covered in mud, exhausted. He saw Champion.

Bernard Champion was up to his shins in mud, head down, hands on his knees, just letting the rain hammer down on him. Jack walked up to him, dropped his hand on his shoulder. "Have you been here all the time?"

Champion turned his head up. Muddy, haggard, greasy. "No, had some rest, came back early . . ."

"You're finished, Bernie. Go home, you can't work like that."

Champion rasped, "I'm staying . . ."

"Bernie? There's not much hope, mate. It'll be a long time before we get to those middle-floor sections. There's simply no access."

"Then I'll make an access!" He shook his muddy gloved hands in Jack's hands. "With these hands!"

"You'll do as you're told. Or I'll have you sent home. *No unauthorized person goes into any tunnels!*" Then he turned and strode away downhill.

Champion glared furiously after him, chest heaving. Then he turned and plodded toward the wreckage.

Inside his sodden gloves his fingers were almost raw.

Twenty minutes later he found it, behind a great slab of flooring: a big jagged opening in the wreckage. He crouched down and looked. The opening disappeared into blackness over broken rubble. He pulled out his torch.

The yellow light shone in ten feet, then hit fallen concrete. But the tunnel curved here.

He looked around. The fire officer in charge had his back to him.

He dropped to his hands and knees, then to his stomach. He crawled and wriggled into the hole.

His elbows scraped painfully. He had only short sleeves on his police tunic. His knees tore. He shoved himself forward, cursing himself for not thinking about long sleeves and trousers, trying to take the rubble on the flats of his forearms. He filled his lungs and bellowed.

"*Jake! Vanessa!*"

His shout hit the concrete, deadened. He lay listening for an answer. The roar of rain and the rushing of water. His torch shone ahead, yellow, making black shadows. The concrete was two inches above his back. The broken ceiling sloped down on one side. On the other side was crushed bedroom furniture. Water was dripping everywhere, glinting in the torchlight. There was no answer.

He worked his way forward on his stomach, the light jerking ahead of him. The ceiling sloped upward, giving him more room. He could crawl. Ahead was a red carpet. A child's doll. He was out of the bedroom now. If he could find the front door he would know what floor he was in. He thought it was the seventh. He looked to his right, downhill.

There was no floor, only crashed ceiling. A hand stuck out. Female. He shone his torch on it, panting. He pulled off his sleeve and touched it. Cold. He lifted a finger. It was rigid.

"*McAdam! . . . Vanessa . . . !*"

Nothing. Just the rushing of water.

Now he was crawling on fallen wall. A corridor? The collapsed ceiling was just above his back again. Onto his stomach again. He saw a porcelain ornament, of the type stuck on doors. It read, *Wendy's Room.* He stopped.

"Wendy . . . !"

Nothing.

"Anybody here . . . ? Wendy!"

He looked for an opening to Wendy's room. He carefully shoved the rubble on his right. He pulled a piece; it came away. Another. Then another. Then here was a small opening, a space beyond. He shone his light in.

Yes, this used to be Wendy's room. Under the rubble he could see the golden hair of a big doll, a drawing of a donkey, some crayons, a corner of a patchwork quilt, the smashed legs of a bed.

He pulled away some more rubble. Put his head into the hole.

The room was squashed down to a height of eighteen inches, except in one corner. There the floor had fallen away, and there was a jagged black hole. Above the hole was another, into the ceiling. Water cascaded through the upper hole, disappeared into the lower. In the other corner the bed and dressing table had been crushed flat. More dolls, a slipper, broken glass.

"Wendy!"

Then he saw her. The golden hair was not a doll's, it was Wendy's. "Oh, Christ . . ." He stared at her, panting. He pulled away another chunk of rubble. He shoved his whole shoulder in; his hand touched her face.

He lay, trying to interpret what he was feeling. The eye. Cold. He felt down her little nose. He waited, trying to feel breath on his fingertip.

"Oh, little girl . . . I'm sorry."

He pulled himself out of the hole feverishly. He wriggled forward on his guts. Ahead was a big block of concrete, blocking his way, but he could see the shadow of a hole on one side. He shone his light in.

It used to be the living room. He could see crushed furniture, a smashed television. The front door must be somewhere in there. And beyond that the elevator foyer. Then the west wing, McAdam's. He began to tear rubble out of the hole.

He pushed through on his stomach. The ceiling was six inches above this. Rubble and glass on the floor. A carpet. The sofa and armchairs were crushed on the far side. He wriggled toward where the front door should have been. A dining-room table was smashed in front of him. He shone his light around it.

Beyond, the ceiling was crushed right down to the floor.

No way through there.

Then he saw the corner of the front door.

It was under the table. And the crossbeams of the table would just let him get his hand in. He wriggled into position, grunting, and stretched in, feeling for the number on the door. He swept away rubble, groped. Then he found it.

He pressed his cheek against the table, his arm stretched in. Carefully his fingertip traced the metal number.

Five . . .

5B.

He pulled out his hand, his heart hammering. So the sixth floor was one up. 6A was just a few yards above and on the other side of that collapsed wall.

He scrambled on his belly across the rubble toward the crushed sofa. He peered all around, flicking the torch. Absolutely no way out.

The only way was up through Wendy's room.

He turned around and scrambled back toward the hole he had come in by. He cracked his head on the ceiling but he did not feel it through his riot helmet. His elbows and knees were raw but he did not care. *Thank God for Wendy's room.*

He reached the hole. He got both hands to a chunk of rubble and jerked it. It came away in a cloud of dust. He stared at the crushed ceiling above him. It stayed still. He got another chunk in both hands, tugged. It came away.

He tugged out four more pieces and the low jagged hole was just big enough for him to crawl through.

He wrestled through the hole into Wendy's room. The ceiling scraped the top of his helmet. He pulled himself through the rubble, shoving with the sides of his boots. The ceiling scraped across his back, but he could just make it. Then he was at the hole in the corner.

He could not turn himself around and lower himself into the hole feet first, then climb upward. There was only one way in, and that was head first. He clenched his teeth and shoved his head and shoulders into the cascading water, down into the hole. Now he was looking upside down into the room below.

He gasped as he looked straight into the staring eyes of a dead man.

The head was six inches from his inverted eyes, face up, eyes open, bloody, streaked with the spray from the water.

Champion shoved himself further into the hole. His helmet

touched the floor. He shoved with his feet. Now his waist was over the edge of the hole; he bent his neck. Now he was bent in the shape of a U. He shoved again. He could not move.

Could not move.

His buttocks were jammed against the edge of the upper hole. His spine and neck could bend no more. The blood was rushing to his head. He tried to scrabble his feet to find some purchase and they just slipped. Panic swept through him. He groped upside down into the squashed room below for something to grab, to pull on. All he could grab was the corpse. He grabbed it by the shirt and pulled. He could not budge. The jagged edge of the hole was digging into his stomach. He heaved again with all his desperate strength and the shirt tore.

"Jesus Christ!"

He was gasping, whimpering now. The blood pounded in his head, water ran into his mouth and eyes and nostrils. He coughed and spluttered and kicked and wrenched wildly. And he tried to push himself back upward, shoving with his hands, and the jagged edge of the hole gouged into his flesh. All he knew was the horror of being stuck like this, unable to move one way or the other, and the water choking into his nose and mouth, the horror of dying like this upside down. He grabbed desperately at the corpse and got him by the chin and one armpit and he sank his fingers into the dead flesh and heaved with all his might over the jagged hole.

The corpse's head and arms moved stiffly under his frantic pulling, but its legs were jammed under concrete. Champion wrenched and wrenched again, his face about to burst with blood, spluttering, and he jerked another two inches with all his might, and fell into the hole.

Bernard Champion crashed into the hole, half on top of the corpse.

The message came through the rain from headquarters to the command post and from there to Jack's walkie-talkie.

"Urgent informative—reliable report received that Queen's

Court Towers apartment block above Hillside Road on the edge of the landslide area appears to be leaning over—"

Jack jerked round and glared uphill through the rain.

"Oh, shit!" Then he shouted furiously into his walkie-talkie: "Sound the alarm!"

The low-pitched siren began to wail. Jack was running uphill, plowing through the mud, rasping into his radio.

"Call P.W.D. building inspectors . . . tell Colonel Tompkins to meet me at Hillside Road—"

Rescue workers were scrambling through the mud away from the wreckage. Jack plowed through them, boots sucking in the mud, up to Hillside Road. His legs were trembling. He peered through the rain up at Queen's Tower.

"Jesus . . ."

The tall apartment house on the very edge of the landslide was definitely leaning over at a slight angle. He shouted into his radio.

"Evans to Command. Evacuate Queen's Court Towers. Send two men to each floor ordering people out—no use of elevators, stairs only. Cordon off the area. Also evacuate the apartment block immediately below it, and the one next to that."

Colonel Tompkins of the army engineers came hurrying through the rain.

"She's leaning, all right."

Jack said gruffly, "I want sentries, please. I'm cordoning off the whole area. What do you think of her chances of falling?"

"With this soil? Anything can happen. Elsewhere, on hard ground, I'd say she's fairly safe."

"Oh, shit!" He glared at the colonel as if it were all his fault. "If she falls, she won't come down on top of us. She'll hit those apartment blocks there."

"Depends on how she falls, Mr. Evans. If she falls on her side—"

"She won't fall on her side, for Chrissake! She's leaning more downhill than sideways."

"It also depends on how she breaks up. Part of her could certainly fall on your men on this side. And on the wreckage."

"Oh, Christ!" He shouted into his radio. "Where're those goddam building inspectors?"

Then he snapped at the colonel: "Well, *my* men are going back to work! Are yours?"

Bernard Champion half straightened himself in the hole. The

252

water cascaded onto his shoulder. He shone his light into the room above Wendy's. The sixth floor.

It was squashed flat.

Almost absolutely flat. Only rubble and smashed furniture held ceiling and floor apart. He cursed. His chest and stomach were red with blood. Then he reached up to the next floor. He put one foot on Wendy's floor and heaved himself up.

The seventh floor.

And *yes!*

The ceiling had collapsed in the middle: but on one side it was held up by a heavy desk and a filing cabinet. They were half crushed but they held the ceiling twenty inches off the floor. He shone his torch down the side of the desk. Then he worked his head and shoulders into the gap. He reached into the room grunting, looking for something to grab. The edge of the hole cut into his chest again.

The only thing he could reach was the filing cabinet.

He hooked his fingers round it. He gave it a tug. It held. Then he kicked his feet up from Wendy's ceiling, grunting, and heaved his stomach over the edge into the room. Now the cabinet was taking almost all his weight. He swung his knee up over the edge; it crashed against a spike of concrete. He cried out, then swung it up again.

He just got it over. He clung there, half in, half out, gasping at the pain in his knee, and his raw stomach. He heaved his other knee into the room, then the filing cabinet gave way.

It went in a screech of steel on concrete and the ceiling crashed down another inch, then stuck. Champion lay on his guts, terrified, in a shower of dust. Then it was still.

He lay gasping, eyes wild. The dust still falling.

Then it came again. It began as a long, creaking, tearing sound and Champion screwed up his eyes in terror and tried to make himself flat. The noise screeched deafeningly, and the ceiling crashed another inch and then stopped. Dust everywhere.

He opened his eyes, and he saw the desk crunching further.

Then it stopped.

He lay there, heart hammering. He looked at the desk in the torchlight. He did not know whether to scramble on or scramble backward. If the ceiling didn't come down now and kill him it could come down in two minutes or two hours. And he could never get back.

Then he clenched his teeth and scrambled wildly forward.

He pulled aside the rubble in the kitchen and peered through the hole. *Stairs!* He could see them plainly. That meant McAdam's gallery, 7A, was just over there on his left. He pulled out another piece of rubble feverishly.

"Excuse me, sir . . ."

He whirled around on his side. His torch shone into the ghostly face of a small, wide-eyed boy. Champion stared, heart pounding.

"Who're you, son?"

"Mike Stevens, sir. Are you a fireman?" The little face was gaunt and stained with dried tears.

Champion closed his eyes.

"No, I'm a policeman. Are you all right, Mike?"

"Yes, sir. Are they coming to get us out?"

"Yes. It won't be long now. Where do you live?"

"8B," Mike Stevens said.

"This isn't 8B, is it?"

"No, sir. I came down a hole when I heard you. 8B is upstairs."

"Where're your parents, Mike?"

"They were at work. There wasn't any school because of the rain."

"All alone?"

"Yes. It was the amah's day off."

"Have you found anybody else?"

"No. I heard some people talking, but they stopped."

"Are you hungry? Thirsty?"

"Not thirsty," Mike Stevens said. "There's plenty of water even though it's dirty. I'm hungry, all right."

"Here." He pulled off his glove and wrestled his hand into his pocket. "Boiled sweets. Good for energy."

"Thank you, sir. You can come up to my room if you like, sir, there's lots of room. I can almost stand up in one place."

Champion smiled, exhausted.

"Are you scared, Mike?"

"I was, sir, not so much any more, they must be here soon. I've got my dog, you see. And my torch."

"Where is he?"

"Up in my room, sir. I couldn't bring him down the hole. I called, didn't you hear?"

"No, I'm sorry. Listen, son, you've got to get out of here."

"Yes, sir," Mike Stevens said earnestly.

"Now, listen. I know a way. But there's somebody I want to look for first. You come with me."

"Yes, sir, thank you. Can I fetch Billy?"

"Yes, of course."

"If I lower him down the hole, you just take him."

Mike Stevens crawled upward across the kitchen with his flashlight. In the corner was a hole, as in Wendy's room. He disappeared up it like a monkey. Champion wriggled after him on his belly, grunting.

"You there, sir?"

"Yes."

"Here he comes."

The hindquarters of a young fox terrier appeared. Champion took it by the chest. He could feel its heart beating. "Good dog, Billy." He brought the dog down. It tried to lick his face. "Come on, Mike."

Mike appeared, feet first.

Champion said: "I'm looking for Mr. McAdam's flat, 6A. He also owns 7A. Do you know a way to get there?"

"No, sir."

"All right. Follow me."

The number on the smashed door was 7A. Champion pulled feverishly at the rubble again and bellowed into the hole: *"Jake. . . . ! Vanessa!"*

He lay, trying to listen above the muffled roar of the rain. All he could hear was water.

He grabbed more rubble with both hands and heaved. Then more.

"McAdam!"

Nothing. The hole was not yet big enough for his head.

"Mike? Can you stick your head in there, and your torch? And tell me what you see?"

Champion did not even feel the rubble on his raw flesh. Mike Stevens wriggled his head into the hole.

"A spiral staircase, sir. And mud."

"Mud . . . ? All right—come out!"

He gripped another chunk of rubble with both hands. He wrenched it out. Then another, then another. Then it was big enough.

Mud. The crashed floor of 7A was about two feet above the

255

floor of 6A, here, partially supported by the iron spiral staircase. There was a big hole there, down into McAdam's tomb. But the slanting floor of 6A was deep under mud.

"McAdam!"

Nothing. Champion scrambled down the hole around the spiral staircase, into the mud below. On to his hands and knees. The ceiling was above him, the floor caved upward in the middle.

"Jake! Vanessa!"

Nothing. Just the wild hammering of his heart. He got down onto his stomach in the mud and scrambled up toward where the dining area used to be. He could just get under the ceiling. He shone his torch desperately at where the kitchen used to be. He shone it the other way. Then he saw her golden hair in the mud.

"Vanessa!"

He started frantically toward her, clawing across the sloping floor.

47

She was completely still. The back of her head in mud, up to her ears, mud up to her chest. Her right arm was buried in mud. "Vanessa!"

He shook her shoulder, then he ripped his sodden glove off, felt her forehead. But his cold fingers could not register temperature. He looked desperately downward, trying to see how she was pinned—her hips disappeared into mud. Then a hand rose out of the mud right in front of him.

He jerked back. A man's big hand, dripping mud and blood, groping at him. He swung his light sideways. "Jake!"

The mud was right over McAdam's ears, mud lapping at the corners of his mouth. His head was twisted desperately upward, encrusted with blood, his mouth open, trying to speak.

"Jake!" He grabbed his hand. McAdam's eyes were desperate, his mouth tried to say "Vanessa . . ." Champion looked wildly around the hell hole, then he grabbed a flat chunk of concrete.

"Put this under your head—get it out of the mud . . ."

He burrowed his fingers under McAdam's head, lifted it. Then slid the chunk of concrete under.

"I'm going to try to drain the mud."

McAdam mouthed, "Can't hear . . ."

"What?"

His hand rose up out of the mud again, running red with blood, and he brought his muddy fingers to his left ear and began to try to poke mud out.

Champion writhed round on his stomach. "Vanessa. . . ?" He groped his muddy hand onto her face, then wrestled the torch onto her. He tried to lift her eyelid, then cursed. The mud on his fingers. He buried them into his mouth and sucked them clean. Spat. Then he groped back at her face, and lifted her eyelid.

Her eye stared blankly. But he could not see properly. He scrambled his fingertips to her nostrils. He held them there, holding his breath, trying to feel her breathing. He could feel nothing. He slid his hand frantically down to her left breast.

He lay there, his hand over her heart, holding his breath. Then he cried out, "She's alive!"

He grabbed McAdam's shoulder and shook it joyously and yelled, "She's alive!"

McAdam closed his eyes and his blood-caked mouth broke into an incredulous grin.

"Mike!" he shouted.

"Yes, sir?"

"Come in! We've got to get this mud drained!"

Champion writhed down the sloping floor into the mud on the other side of McAdam. At the bottom he could get to his hands and knees. He felt feverishly for what was blocking the mud. The bunched carpet. "Hold the torch, Mike!" He got a grip on the carpet and tried to heave it up. The weight of mud held it down. He heaved again fiercely. It sucked slowly away from the smashed corner of the floor. He held it with all his might with one trembling hand, and with the other he groped under, feeling for a hole.

None.

He whimpered and heaved the carpet back farther with all his strength. Then he stretched in and seized another two handfuls under the mud and heaved. And there was a big sucking noise and the mud began to pour out of a hole.

"Shine the torch down more . . ."

Arms trembling with the strain, watching the mud drain out in the torchlight, the carpet tearing at his bunched hands. Then his fingers could take no more, the carpet tore from his hands. He crouched there, arms aching.

Then he maneuvered his hand into his pocket for his knife.

He got down onto his stomach in the mud. It swamped over his back. He shoved himself forward. Then he groped in under the crashed ceiling, as far as he could reach. But he could not reach far enough. There was only one thing to do.

He took a big breath, screwed up his eyes and plunged his head under the mud. He groped furiously under the carpet, heaved it up off the hole with one hand, and with the other sank the knife into the fabric, and sawed.

He ripped the knife toward him, then he twisted his head sideways and got his mouth out of the mud and gasped in air, spat, then plunged his head back under and sawed again.

He sawed a gash sixty inches out of the carpet, then sawed off the long strip. Then he writhed backward, black with the muck.

He crouched on his hands and knees, gasping, letting the mud run off his face.

"Jake! It's all right. It's going."

He wriggled into the crushed wreckage of the kitchen. He found what he was looking for straightaway: a large empty beer bottle. Two, and there, lying under rubble, was a bottle of whisky. But no water!

"Mike, you know where there's water . . . ?"

"Yes, sir. Up in my apartment, lots. If you keep Billy."

"For Chrissake be careful."

Champion writhed back across the floor.

"Jake?" We're getting you water." He shone his torch on Vanessa. Her eyes were open. *"Vanessa! Are you in pain?"*

She turned her face to him, the mud on her neck and hair. Her lips were cracked and dry. She closed her eyes and shook her head and tried to smile.

She whispered, "Come to . . . pull us out of . . . the shit again?"

"It's all right, Vanessa! I've drained the mud. Water's coming. Then I'm going to fetch them to get you out. Everything's going to be all right!"

"Hogan . . . ?" she whispered.

"He's fine—look at him." He writhed backward out of the way and shone the torch on Hogan. He had his bloody head turned to her; he tried to smile.

"Do you want some whisky?" Champion panted.

She shook her head and whispered, "Water."

"It's coming . . ." He shone his torch down her body. Her legs were still under mud. So were McAdam's. The concrete ceiling was pressed down on her stomach. Why wasn't she in pain? The cold? Numb?

"Sir?" Michael Stevens said behind him.

"Good boy, Mike! Help Mr. McAdam . . ."

He grabbed the first bottle and wriggled closer to Vanessa, panting. "Vanessa? Open . . ." He brought the bottle shakily to her mouth. She opened her cracked lips, they groped for the bottle rim. He pushed it in gently and she sucked.

The water ran out the corner of her mouth, she sputtered, swallowed. Her muddy hand came up and took the bottle from Champion's. She sucked and sucked.

"Hold it in your mouth and swirl it round . . ."

She swirled it round her mouth, eyes closed, trying to get it to soak through the dry membrane, then she swallowed blissfully. McAdam held his bottle and drank, and swallowed and drank. Champion and Michael Stevens lay there on their stomachs, watching them.

"There're more bottles in the kitchen. Can you fill two more, Mike?"

"Yes, sir."

"And do you have a big ball of string?"

"Fishing line, sir. If I can find it."

"Good boy . . ." He grabbed the lad's skinny shoulder and shook it. "You're a good man, Mike!"

Michael Stevens blushed under his muddy pallor, then wriggled away manfully into the blackness.

McAdam finished his bottle. He lowered it, then smiled brokenly at the ceiling.

"Marvelous . . ."

"Do you want some whisky?"

"Yes . . ."

"Just take one mouthful. It'll go straight to your head."

"Vanessa first."

Champion turned to her. She was just finishing the water. "Vanessa—take some whisky."

She smiled through cracked lips. She whispered, "Think of everything . . . or are you . . . trying to get me drunk?"

She took the bottle shakily. She closed her eyes and took a sucking mouthful. She rolled it round her mouth, then tried to swallow and gagged, and the liquor snorted out of her nostrils and she coughed. She wiped her muddy hand across her mouth. Then she lay still, eyes closed, getting back her breath.

"Hey . . ." she whispered, mud on her mouth, "that's good."

"Some more."

She squinted in the torchlight at the bottle, brought it shakily to her muddy mouth. She took a big mouthful, eyes closed. She whispered, "Now Hogan . . ."

He gave the bottle to McAdam. He took a mouthful, while Vanessa watched him.

"Here, sir," Mike Stevens piped out of the blackness. He had two more bottles of water and also a reel of nylon fishing line.

"Beautiful, Mike!"

Champion put a bottle next to each of them. The mud was almost all drained out now. If he got his head down low he should be able to see what was holding them. He writhed forward down the muddy floor, until he was stopped by the beam that held them. He put his cheek flat and wrestled the torch into position. He peered down under the beam in the yellow torchlight.

At first he did not grasp what he was seeing. He saw the ceiling crushing her legs. Her legs were covered in mud. He could make out her knees. But there was another bend in her muddy flesh that should not be there. Another beam was lower than the rest of the ceiling, across her thigh. And her thigh was bent. And sticking out of her muddy flesh was a spike. He stared at it, not comprehending. He thought it must be a piece of wood sticking into her. Then he saw the red, realized it was blood; he saw the red-black of her thigh; the thing sticking out was bone.

He stared, horrified. His mind fumbling. But she feels no pain. Then the terrible fact dawned on him.

She feels no pain because she's paralyzed!

He stared, shocked; then he felt the anguish sweep over him. Then he screwed up his eyes and scrambled backward.

"I'm going now! To fetch them. We'll be back in no time!"

He grabbed Mike Stevens's fishing reel, peeled off a length of line and tied it round a piece of rubble feverishly.

"I'll leave you Mike's torch. The whisky's here."

"Sir, shall I stay to look after them?"

"No," McAdam rasped. "You go, Mike. Thanks."

Champion slithered round and scrambled away. The fishing reel spun in his hand, peeling off line. The tears were welling in his eyes. He did not hear her try to call, "Thanks, Bernie . . ."

Then she said, "Hogan? When we get out of here . . . I've got to stop my story about Champion being published . . ."

48

Queen's Court Towers and the apartment blocks below had all been evacuated. The whole area had been cordoned off.

The men were back at work in the rain and arc lights. The army engineers had finished erecting the heavy-duty crane. It was swung out over the middle of the wreckage and two soldiers were standing on top of the rubble, ready to hook up the first load. Then one of the lookouts posted on top of the apartment blocks saw the new landslide starting, and he shouted into his radio, and the siren moaned.

Bernard Champion and Michael Stevens heard the siren. They were just scrambling out of Wendy's room, the dog called Billy trotting quickly behind them.

"Quickly!"

He scrambled forward flat on his stomach, his forearms bloody. The fishing reel peeled off line. He came to the end of the crushed corridor. He stopped, desperately trying to remember which way he had come. Then he scrambled right. And there was the hole into the first room he had entered.

"Come on . . ."

He scrambled into it, hitting his head. He looked behind him for Mike, then went on, the torch jerking in front of him. Then there was a hole to the outside world ahead of him. The siren was still wailing, the hammering of the drills had stopped.

"Through!"

He squeezed aside and grabbed Mike by the scruff of the neck and dragged him toward the hole. Then Champion writhed through after him. And the rain hit him, and the siren roared in his ears.

The gray light was blinding bright. He clambered up, staggering, and looked through the rain for the danger and he could not see the landslide coming. He grabbed Mike Stevens by the wrist and ran him five paces across the steep muddy slope, slipping, sliding, and through the siren he heard the shouts, and then he dropped the fishing reel. He let go of Mike Stevens and shouted, "Run!"

And he doubled back for the reel, and as he picked it up he saw the new mudslide coming. It was seventy yards above him when he saw it. Coming big and terrible in the arc lights, a great mass of orange mud seething down the steep raw mountain, dragging its long tail behind. He saw it hit the second-last army barricade. And the stout wall of wood and steel buckled and the great head of mud flowed over it, and the barricade burst. And the mud came headlong on down the mountain toward Hillside Road, and Bernard Champion did not hear the people shouting at him, all he knew was that it was going to hit the wreckage of Dragon Court and kill Vanessa and McAdam and he stood there rooted, out raged, and then he waved his arms and bellowed into the rain. *"No, no! They're in there! No—"*

And the mudslide hit Hillside Road in a great roaring swoosh, and leaped over it just thirty yards up there, and Bernard Champion recovered his senses, and turned and ran.

He ran furiously across the muddy slope, downhill at an angle, and all the time he was yelling at the sky: *"No, you bastard! No—"*

And the mudslide hit the wreckage of Dragon Court so the earth shook, and mud flew in sheets and crashed down the steep slope after Champion. When he was two-thirds across, he fell flat on his face and for a moment he did not care—he would die bellowing his outrage to the sky. Then Jack-the-Fire got him. Jack charged through the mud, screaming, *"Get out!"*

He grabbed him by the collar and dragged him blindly, stumbling, slipping, out of the way.

Jake McAdam and Vanessa did not hear the siren. They only felt the tremble as the mudslide hit Hillside Road; then there was a slow grinding sound in the blackness, and he felt the concrete creak underneath him and he clutched for the torch and shouted, *"Vanessa—"*

He heard her cry out in the blackness, and then the whole black terrible world cracked.

Cracked and shifted, and the blackness gave way underneath them. He heard her scream and he crashed his forehead against concrete and his feet were going down and his head was coming up; then it came to a grinding, jolting stop.

For a long moment there was nothing but stunned silence.

Then the sound of her gasping.

"*Vanessa!* Vanessa!" He groped desperately for her, and his hand touched her knee.

"*Vanessa?*"

And he slid his hand up her leg, groping for her hand. And his fingers groped the sharp hump of flesh in her thigh, then the sharp point of her thighbone sticking out and the next instant his hand touched hers.

She screamed into the blackness and he was shouting, "*Vanessa! Vanessa!*" and he wanted to lunge out and grab her in his arms and clutch her close and bellow his anguish and absorb all the shock and terrible injury into himself. *Oh, God, let it be my body!* His hand scrabbled desperately for the torch and he was gasping, "Oh, my darling, I'm sorry—I'm sorry."

And her scream suddenly cut off in a swoon, and she was silent.

He cried out again "*Vanessa!*" and his hand found the torch and he flicked it on and saw her leg within arm's reach, and it was bent in the middle of her thigh, the sharp spike of bone was sticking out, muddy, glinting in the torchlight. And he filled his lungs so his neck swelled and he bellowed to God: "*Why don't you come down and help us?*"

But God did not.

She whispered in the blackness.

"Hogan? I'm all right now . . ."

He lay there, eyes tightly closed, squeezing her hand tight. He did not know whether she knew about the bone. And, oh, God, he did not want her to know.

"Hogan . . . ? It was just the . . . shock that made me scream. Not the pain . . ."

He started to speak and she whispered, "There's no pain, Hogan. There really isn't."

She breathed deep. She did not know whether he knew about the bone sticking out of her leg, and she desperately hoped he didn't. And there *was* no pain. And that was really why she screamed. Because she had realized that she was paralyzed. Because her back was broken.

She breathed deeply and her voice caught. "I only screamed . . . . in delayed shock . . . about the concrete crashing . . . But I'm fine now, darling."

He lay rigid, holding her hand tight, and the tears were running down his face.

"Sure," he whispered. "We'll be fine, Vanessa. They'll have us out soon . . ."

She whispered softly, "Hogan . . .? Now shut up, you lovely bastard, and listen to me . . . I feel like talking. . . . Where's that goddamn whisky? Don't use the torch, save it."

He groped for the bottle in the dark, found it. He did not want to use the torch either, he did not want her to see her leg. He unscrewed the top, fingers shaking, the tears running down his face. "Here . . ."

Her hand took it. She maneuvered it to her mouth. She took a big trembling mouthful.

"Have some, Hogan. Let's go out in style . . ."

He hissed fiercely, "We're *getting* out of this, Vanessa! Not *going* out."

She whispered, "Sure, Hogan. . . . I meant that. We're going to have a great life, darling. So let's drink to that."

Through his shock and his anguish he did not think she should drink—*people in shock with gaping wounds should not drink*—but he would have given her the world. He just wet his lips with the whisky, to save it all for her. He held the bottle out into the blackness. "Take it . . ."

He felt her hand grope for it. Then she said hoarsely, "God, that's good stuff, Hogan. . . . What every girl in a landslide shouldn't be without . . ." Then she said, "Hogan, this stuff is going straight to my head."

Oh, my lover. "That's all right, Vanessa . . ."

"Hogan? Isn't it a pig. . . ? Just when I had that bastard Choi over a barrel . . . and we were going out to lunch. . . ."

He lay there in the blackness, teeth clenched.

"Don't talk about it, Vanessa."

She cried softly. "I *want* to talk. This is my story which I worked so hard on! And I alone cracked it, found the chink in his armor. . . . It should have been a landslide victory for me . . . and instead he nails me. With *his* fucking landslide."

"Oh, my darling, I'm sorry! *Talk* about it!" And he cried out inside for her to be in a soft white hospital bed, to scoop her tight in his arms and hold her and take her anguish from her and love her and tell her that it didn't matter, that he would still love her.

She breathed deeply, then took another swallow of whisky.

"I suppose the only thing that matters . . . is that we got him. . . . but . . . it's a pity it isn't my scoop any more . . ."

"It *is* your scoop, Vanessa! We'll see to that! And that bastard Choi's going to jail for the rest of his life!"

He held her hand tight, the tears choking his throat. "Vanessa! We're getting out of here. We're alive . . . we've survived . . . and as soon as we're out of here we're going to fly away, darling! To Africa. To anywhere you like. And see the animals . . . we're going to drink lots of wine in the sun . . . and stay in the best damn hotels . . . and we're going to sail that junk around the world."

She lay in the darkness, her teeth clenched to stop herself sobbing out loud, and her fingernails dug into his arm and she whispered, "Yes, darling . . ."

But her heart cried out, *Oh, listen to me, you darling Hogan, it's not going to happen because there's no way in the whole wide world I'm going to live with you in a wheelchair!*

"And we'll make those beautiful nature movies, Vanessa. . . . And you'll write wonderful stories. . . ."

And she wanted to cry out, *They're going to cut this leg off, darling Hogan! We've got to face it! What I'm going to have here is a goddam stump!*

And she held his arm fiercely, clenched her teeth and her voice shook. "Oh, yes, darling . . ."

She lay in the blackness, her chest heaving, holding his hand tight, the tears running down her cheeks and into her ears. Then she took a juddering breath and said, "Let's have some light on the subject, Hogan. And I don't mean my luscious legs. I want to see your beautiful eyes . . ."

He groped for the torch. He pointed it up the slope so that when he switched it on she would not see her leg, and as he was about to switch it on she said, "Hang on, Hogan . . . a girl likes to look her best."

She tried to rub the mud off her tearful face. She passed her hand over her matted hair, and sucked her lips. "God, I bet I look a wreck . . . okay. Lights. Action."

He switched on the torch.

She was looking at him, her lovely eyes anguished, dried tears on her dirty cheeks, and her heart was breaking. She put her fingertips on his arm and trailed them gently, then her eyes filled with the most wonderful smile he had ever seen, loving, pitying, and she held out her arm to hold him tight, to pull him to her, and all she could do was hold out her arm to him; and he held her arm, and nothing in the whole terrible world mattered except that she was alive.

She whispered, "I love you, Hogan. Just remember that . . . always."

The tears were running down his face.

"I love you, Vanessa."

<hr>

49

He did not know how long she was unconscious, from the whisky and the weakness, the exhaustion. He remembered the torchlight getting dimmer; her body faintly glowing, swollen, crushed, and the blood running out of the dreadful hole in her thigh. *"Vanessa . . . Vanessa . . . !"* he whispered, but she could not hear. *Oh, God, just let her lie there, unconscious, just let her know nothing until they get us out of here.*

He tried to feel her pulse. But each time his stiff trembling fingers could feel nothing; not even any warmth, just cold flesh. And he panicked, staring at her face, trying to see if she was breathing, and he could see nothing in the dying light, and he cried out, "Vanessa!" and he lurched at her, shining the torch, and he saw her breathing. And then shuddering, watching her breathing, shallow, so shallow; and the great slab of concrete so close to her breast. *But, oh, God, God, why didn't you hold it off her legs!*

He roared, "Champion! Come back and help us!"

He shouted many times, but he did not know how long it was since the last time. And he prayed, his eyes tight closed, trying to concentrate, trying to pray constructively to the God he did not believe in. *Please, God, protect her. . . . Please, God, her leg is going to be all right. . . . Please, God, she is not paralyzed. Please, God, give her strength. Please, God, give me the strength to shout.*

Later in that long, terrible blackness the gangrene set in. And the delirium.

Her moans and her shouting and her laughing and her sobbing

266

and her talking. He did not know how long it lasted between silences: all he knew was the sick shine of her sweat in the dying torchlight, glinting silvery yellow on her contorted face.

Sometimes she passed right out; her arm outflung, her matted hair wet with sweat, mouth open, quivering, the infection spread-eagling down her leg: and he lay there, praying, *Please, God, make her stay asleep, please, God, keep her still.*

But God did not keep her still. At some time the flashlight began to fade right out, and he tried desperately to save it for her—for what? For some last awful emergency when she screamed out for him? In the last dying light he saw the gangrene spreading out round the big hole in her leg as she lay there. He hoarsely cried, "God, come down and help us!"

But God did not come down. Neither that long black night, nor the next long, terrible, black day. That next afternoon he could hear the drills, and he tried to shout, but he could only whisper. That afternoon her delirium got very bad. Sometimes he managed to get her hand, and sometimes she did know who it was, and she tried to speak but she could not murmur more than a few words, then she pulled her clenched hand away. The drills and bangs got louder in the blackness, and he wept tears of despair and joy, but his shouts were only dry, thirst-crabbed croaks. He did not remember the last few hours.

He only knew the sudden shaft of black night sky in the wonderful hammering and crashing, and then a Cockney voice shouting "*Here* they are—!" and then Champion's voice shouting from above.

"*Jake—it's all right now!*"

And he was laughing-crying: "My wife has a broken leg—"

And the blackness was flashing with blinding torchlight, and a Chinese face was shouting for a concrete-cutter saw, and someone behind the Cockney voice was shouting "Morphine!" And then her moaning went wonderfully silent, and he was crying tears of desperate happiness. Then a spout was being held to his lips and he was sucking, sputtering, choking, but he could not taste the water through the dry scabs in his mouth.

"Do you need morphine?"

And he remembered trying to say, "Only if you cut me."

Jack-the-Fire's voice was saying: "Get another saw, we can't winch this lot up in one go—"

Champion's voice said, "Where's that bloody doctor?"

He tried to shout. "Don't let them cut her leg off, Champion!"

And he felt the needle slide into his arm.

The rest was very confused. He had the feeling of not caring any more, of complete trust in the skill and goodwill of their rescuers, the joy that she was safe. She was safe, and they were digging them out of this place and taking them to a hospital where doctors would put the bone back into her leg and heal her up and she was lying deep in clean soft white sheets. The noise of power drills and saws was all around him in the flashing torchlights, and he just wanted to laugh and make jokes, except that it was all a great effort.

He said, "How is she?"

"She's fast asleep, sir; we've got her out."

And he wanted to take his hand and tell him he was a wonderful fellow. "Are you a soldier?"

"That's right, sir, medical corps. Just you relax, we're starting on that beam now from the other side—"

"I'll buy you a drink afterward, you and me."

"That's right, sir."

"My wife and I want to invite you all to dinner. And Jack-the-Fire. And Champion. The whole fucking lot of you!"

"Very good, sir."

"Jake-the-fucking-Fire, you lovely fellow, you, I'm taking you to dinner tonight—"

She was the first to go, but all he saw through the flashing shadows was a kind of metal stretcher and he shouted, "Good luck, Vanessa!" But she did not answer. Then somebody saying, "Your legs are free now, see if you can move them."

And somebody was getting a rope under his armpits, and he had a wonderful feeling of security and trust; everything was going to be all right, and she was running into the sparkling blue sea and she dived so her whole body was golden, taut and perfect, flashing in the sunshine, and he swam underneath her and she was gloriously satiny, shimmering, slippery, against him, and they broke surface laughing, gasping, kissing.

Part fourteen

At 3:21 A.M. that Thursday, Vanessa Storm Williams died in Queen Elizabeth Hospital, without having regained consciousness.

First there is just shocked disbelief; it does not register as something that has really happened. Then slowly, through the disbelief, while they are explaining it, and you are staring at them, and demanding answers, and they are answering, kindly, firmly, slowly through this awful disbelief there begins to seep the terrible realization. And a kind of sick, white ringing begins to well up in your ears, and though you do not believe it yet you also believe it, but you are trying desperately not to. *No, no, no, it hasn't happened.* . . . And suddenly, like a long, stretched-out piece of elastic being released, there is a snap, and you believe. It really is true, the whole awful truth—this has really happened, to her. *To her.*

And it came suddenly welling up his throat, from his heart and guts, the outcry, and the despair, and the outrage, and the pity, pity, pity, and the grief, grief, grief.

50

The rain came down. Many of the telephone lines were washed out, but he could hear his attorney very clearly. The man said, "I'll write you a full explanatory letter, of course, but, briefly, the facts are these: Her mother was a Miss Stormo, an immigrant from Italy, and her father is indeed Senator Williams. However, her parents never married. I have spoken to Senator Williams and he admitted his paternity, privately, but he would put nothing on paper. He says he's never had anything to do with his daughter, for everybody's sake, and he doesn't intend starting now. You can understand that it wouldn't do his political life any good. He makes no claim on the estate either.

"Miss Stormo, her mother, was in the theater. Vaudeville stuff. Music hall. Her stage name was The Tempest. She died when Vanessa was an infant, of drugs. She was a heroin addict.

"After her mother's death, the child was brought up by her aunt, the mother's sister, in Brooklyn. Now also deceased.

"There are no other known relatives. The Senator does not make any claim to the . . . er . . . body."

McAdam sat in the hospital matron's office, numb, the telephone at his ear.

"Well, I do!"

"I understand. Well, in that event, you only need some kind of burial order from the Hong Kong authorities to . . . er . . . go ahead."

Outside the matron's window the rain came down.

"What about the other matter?"

"Yes. I have approached an editor at the *South China Morning Post* and asked about the possibility of, uh, withdrawing Miss Williams's article about Mr. Champion."

"Did you tell him I was willing to pay?" McAdam interrupted harshly. "I've got a hundred thousand dollars—did you tell him I'll give him all of it?"

"I indicated to him that you were willing to reimburse him for any expenses incurred by dropping the article, but it's not possible."

He shouted, "Then bribe someone else! Don't tell me it can't be done. Never mind, I'll go there and do it myself. That's what she wanted. And that's what she's going to get."

The lawyer said, "I'm sorry, but the editor told me that Bernard Champion was arrested at the Dragon Court site just before you and Miss Williams were brought up. Another policeman saw him there and reported him. It will be on all the front pages tomorrow; no amount of money can stop it."

Oh, God, Bernard, he thought. *The Champ.* But he couldn't feel it.

He walked slowly back down the corridor toward the reception room. The Chinese nurse walked beside him, but he did not need her. They walked slowly down the corridor. Then outside onto a covered concrete area. The rain drummed on the iron roof. The nurse stopped ahead at the double doors and smiled nervously.

"Mortuary. Mr. McAdam, are you sure. . . ?"

McAdam said angrily, "Who else should do it? She's mine, isn't she?"

"You go first door on left, please," the nurse said.

McAdam walked into the chill building, then turned into the room on the left.

272

She was lying on a slab, covered in a white sheet. A Chinese attendant was standing at the sinks. The nurse went to the slab and put her hand on the sheet, then looked at McAdam nervously.

He nodded.

The nurse peeled back the sheet.

"Do you formally identify this body as Vanessa Storm Williams?"

"Yes."

The nurse replaced the sheet. "Will you sign now?"

"Later . . ." Then he said angrily, "Only the identification document. No postmortem permission. I'm not having anybody cutting her up!"

"Yes," the nurse said nervously. "Do you want the attendant to help you?"

"No. Alone. You go too, please."

They turned to go. He said without turning round, hoarsely, "And I want the undertaker to fetch her as soon as I've finished cleaning her. She's not going back into any more damn refrigerators. And no more plastic bags!"

"Yes," the nurse said. "Do you want me to cut off the plastic bag?"

"No, I'll do it."

The door closed behind him.

He stood a long trembling moment, staring at the sheet. His eyes were full of tears. Then he slowly peeled back the sheet.

He looked down at her.

"Hello," he whispered. "Hello, beauty . . . I've come to tidy you up. . . ."

He took a big quivering breath and the tears were running down his cheeks.

"And to tell you what I'm going to do . . . but most of all to make you beautiful, my beauty. . . ."

Afterward, he walked back up the concrete path under the drumming iron roof.

Jack Evans was waiting in the reception room, at the window. Beside him was the suitcase with the change of clothes he had bought for McAdam. He turned.

McAdam said, thickly, "Well?"

"He refused to make a statement. His lawyer spoke for him. That he is not an architect or builder, he simply accepted the advice of his surveyors, he didn't know it was not solid rock." He shook his head. "We've got nothing to pin on him."

McAdam stared at him, then said thickly, "I want to borrow a gun."

Jack-the-Fire's red-rimmed eyes were astonished.

"What for?"

He said, "To kill a man."

51

The rain hammered on the taxi roof. The windshield wipers went slosh-slosh.

He told the driver to stop at the corner. He paid him, got out painfully into the rain. He opened his umbrella. Then he walked grimly, carefully up the street. He tested his legs, bent the knees. They were all right. He stopped outside the gates of the big house. He pressed the bell.

He stood at the communication panel, waiting. The rain drummed on his umbrella, splashed his trouser legs. Then a Chinese male voice said, "*Wei?*"

"Good afternoon. I would like to see Sir Herman Choi, please. In connection with the Foundation for the Blind and Physically Handicapped."

The voice hesitated, then replied in English, "The office for the Blind is closed now, it is the lunch time. Can you please telephone this afternoon?"

"No, I leave this afternoon. I wish to make a donation, you see."

Hesitation. "One moment please, sir."

He waited. The rain drumming on his umbrella.

Then the voice came back.

"Come in, please, sir."

A buzzer sounded and the iron gate opened.

He walked up the path in the rain. The big front door opened. There stood a Chinese man in a dark suit, smiling.

"Sir Herman will see you now."

"Thank you." He furled his umbrella carefully.

He followed the Chinese down the marble corridor. The man opened a door. On it was written: *Foundation for the Blind and Physically Handicapped.* Inside was a reception room. They walked through it. Through double doors, into a general office. Desks and typewriters. Empty. Through more doors. Into a big room full of equipment for the physically handicapped. Empty. Charts on the wall. Then a big door. The man knocked, then entered.

Sir Herman Choi stood up from behind a desk, smiling, his right hand extended. McAdam held out his left hand.

"Excuse my appearance, I had an accident."

"Oh, I am sorry . . ."

"I'm sorry to disturb you, sir, but I wish to make a donation and I'm leaving town."

The Chinese man withdrew and closed the door. Sir Herman Choi beamed.

"The foundation is never too busy to receive money. Do sit down . . ."

Sir Herman Choi began to sit down in an armchair.

McAdam put his left hand inside his jacket pocket. He pulled out the gun.

"Put your hands on your head," he said.

Sir Herman Choi sat and stared, astonished, the smile half fixed on his face.

"This gun has a good silencer; it won't be heard. Hands on your head."

Sir Herman Choi put his hands slowly on top of his head. "Who are you?" he whispered.

McAdam kept the gun on him and walked backward to the door. He dropped the lock. He walked back into the center of the room.

Sir Herman Choi stared at him.

McAdam lowered the gun muzzle and fired. There was a flashing pop and the bullet smashed into Sir Herman Choi's right thigh. He gasped, and his hands clutched his leg. He stared, shocked, at the hole in his trousers, the blood welling out.

"That is for her broken body you caused. . . ."

Sir Herman Choi looked up at him, his face creased in shock and pain.

"What do you want?"

The gun popped again and the bullet smashed his other thigh. He cried, and his hands clutched at the wound. The blood welled out between his fingers.

"That is for her broken flesh." McAdam stepped up to him, grabbed the man's hair and yanked back his cringing head, and his bandaged hand rammed a handkerchief in the man's mouth.

"Spit it out and I'll put the gun in your mouth."

He stepped back. Sir Herman Choi looked up at him, eyes bulging, terrified, his mouth stuffed with handkerchief. His hands clutched his left thigh. McAdam pointed the gun at him. He whispered, shaking, "You are a dealer in death. In slow, degrading death. . . ."

Sir Herman Choi spat the gag out and gasped: "I'll give you . . . one million dollars . . . American dollars . . . two million."

He grabbed the man's hair and yanked back his head, and rammed the hot muzzle into the back of his mouth.

"Where's your heroin refinery?" He twisted the gun hard.

Sir Herman Choi's cheek bulged round the gun muzzle, his eyes wild, his lips distorted. His tongue worked and his lips closed, distorted round the steel.

"New . . . Territories . . ."

"Where in the New Territories?" He twisted the gun.

The lips and tongue worked.

"Sekong . . . Yung Kee . . . duck farm . . ."

"How far from Sekong?"

"Two . . . mile peg . . ."

"Who's your supplier in Bangkok?"

The bulging mouth twisted round the steel.

"Major . . . Pattikorn . . ."

"Of . . . ?"

The lips worked. "Police . . ."

McAdam twisted the gun hard.

"Who do you supply in San Francisco?"

The eyes bulged, the lips mouthed, distorted, saliva dribbling.

"Ernest . . . Chang . . ."

"Address?" He twisted the gun hard.

"China . . . Youth . . . Club . . ."

He jabbed the gun. "In London?"

"Tran . . . Tranquillity . . . Funeral . . . Home . . ."

McAdam pulled the gun out of the man's mouth and rammed the handkerchief back in deep with the gun muzzle. He stepped backward.

He leveled the gun at Sir Herman Choi's head. The man stared at him, horrified.

"And this is for killing her."

He took trembling aim, then squeezed the trigger fiercely and the bullet smashed through the middle of Sir Herman Choi's head.

He did not hesitate. He yanked out the magazine clip in the pistol's handle, and rammed in a new one. He swung the gun on the door, then walked back toward the telephone. He picked it up, trembling, and dialed. It was answered immediately. He kept his eyes and gun on the door. He said hoarsely, "Narcotics Bureau."

There was a click. He said, "Whoever you are . . . get this on tape . . . Herman Choi's heroin refinery is at Yung Kee duck farm, two-mile peg, Sekong Road . . ."

It took him less than thirty seconds to dictate it all. When he finished the officer asked, "Who is this?"

He said, "Jake McAdam. Ex-Hong Kong Police. I am also reporting the murder of Sir Herman Choi. By me. I'll be reporting to headquarters in about twenty minutes."

The astonished voice said: "Where are you? We'll send a car—"

"No," McAdam said. "I'd rather walk, thank you." He hung up.

He went shakily for the door. He turned back the lock; then stepped to one side. Then opened the door. The exhibition room was still empty. He walked through it toward the general office. He stood to one side. Then opened the door. He walked through the reception room, opened the door to the marble corridor.

He knew he was walking the same route Vanessa had taken the day she ran from her interview with Sir Herman Choi. It was deserted, but he was sure Choi's men were waiting behind each of those closed doors, waiting for an alarm or a commotion in the hall. He walked quickly, calmly, so as not to alert them. And Sir Herman, of course, would not be signaling them.

The Chinese man was coming down the passage. McAdam said, "Sir Herman wants you, please."

The man came, smiling. McAdam stepped aside to let him come through. He closed the reception room door behind him. Then he walked out of the Foundation for the Blind and Physically Handicapped.

Down the marble corridor. He carried the gun, dangling, just behind his left thigh. He saw his umbrella at the front door.

He picked it up. He opened the front door. Stepped out into the rain. Then he remembered the buzzer on the gate. He pressed the switch. The gate buzzed and opened.

He closed the front door. He walked down the path.

At the gate he slid the gun back inside his jacket.

He walked through the gate. Pulled it closed behind him.

He walked down the street in the hammering rain. He forgot to put up his umbrella. The rain drummed on his head, and the tears ran down his face, and his heart was breaking.